Praise for *My Cleaner*

'This beautifully observed, intelligent and moving novel is one of those rare things – a small, carefully wrapped surprise that gets better and better with the unravelling.'
The Scotsman

'Like Margaret Atwood, Maggie Gee has always been prepared to tackle contemporary ideas on a grand as well as a domestic scale ... Her prose is rich and gossipy; it mixes the highbrow with the vernacular ... *My Cleaner* is a moving, funny, engrossing book.'
The Observer

'*My Cleaner* is both simple and subtle. It is structured around an elegant juxtaposition of the inner lives of two opposites.'
TLS

'Gee satirises the liberal conscience of the chattering classes with uncomfortable perception in this hugely enjoyable novel ... her portrayal of Britain's new underclass of immigrant workers is presented with her trademark stinging clarity.'
Metro

'Must Read: we get the trademark Gee humour and also a thoughtful, moving read.'
New Nation

'Maggie Gee is a superb and pitiless analyser of middle-class angst. Elegant, humorous and surprising, this is a classy performance.'
The Times

'A masterful study in Africa/UK relations which manages to be supremely uncomfortable without being cynical, and clever without being calculating.'
Big Issue

'Maggie Gee gives all her characters, white and black, male and female, the dignity of knowing that they live according to the choices they have made.'
New Statesman

Books by Maggie Gee

Novels
Dying in Other Words
The Burning Book
Light Years
Grace
Where Are The Snows
Lost Children
The Ice People
The White Family
The Flood
My Cleaner

Short Stories
The Blue

Maggie Gee

MY DRIVER

TELEGRAM
London San Francisco Beirut

This edition published in 2009 by Telegram, London

ISBN: 978-1-84659-052-8

Copyright © Maggie Gee, 2009

A full CIP record for this book is available from the British Library.
A full CIP record for this book is available from the Library of Congress.

Manufactured in Lebanon

TELEGRAM
26 Westbourne Grove, London W2 5RH
825 Page Street, Suite 203, Berkeley, California 94710
Tabet Building, Mneimneh Street, Hamra, Beirut

www.telegrambooks.com

For my mother Aileen Mary Gee, née Church,
whose spirit and flight bag came with me to Uganda.

PART I

In-Flight Entertainment

1

The sun is rising on Uganda. Light streams across Africa as the rim of the earth turns slowly towards it. It gilds the mountains, it floods the plains.

In London, people are still asleep, though Vanessa Henman hasn't slept a wink. (This evening, she will be flying to Kampala, and of course, she will have to get to the airport. She's tried to contact her ex-husband, who is obviously the right person to drive her. But he has been mysteriously hard to get hold of, and recently Soraya, his new girlfriend, is less friendly. So naturally, her son will drive her. But still she is nervous. Africa!)

She looks at her watch: it's 5 AM. She tries to visualise how it will be. She imagines the sun, rising on Uganda. Noise, colour. A river of black faces. River not sea, there's no sea in Uganda. Which sits right on the equator, in the middle of Africa. What does she remember? Loud, honking taxis on Kampala's main street, white Toyota vans spilling fumes and people. But the details ... no, it's still out of focus.

In Bwindi, western Uganda, near Congo and Rwanda, countless columns of soldier ants pour through the jungle, moving fast and low, layers upon layers, running over each other's backs and onwards, glossy, unstoppable, rivers of treacle, some smaller, reddish, others larger and blacker. Anything in their path, they eat (except the gorillas, who sometimes eat the ants, scooping them into their mouths in handfuls, until the stings are beyond bearing). It's cool and damp here, up in the hills.

The apes are just waking in their nests, great trampled baskets of wet green tree-ferns. They live in cloud – white nets and shrouds. Webs of pale rain blow across like curtains, veiling Bwindi Impenetrable Forest. A large grey furry hand extends, slowly, and plucks some breakfast. Its owner has a name, Ruhondeza, given him by humans, but he only knows he is the chief, the silverback, that he has been chief for years and years, though the family is getting smaller. He is staring at a tiny baby gorilla, skinny, little spider-legs and a great quiff of hair, sleeping curled up against the dugs of his mother. Ruhondeza frowns; something very important. He is the chief, but is he the father?

Not far away, there are human soldiers, bearing a confusing variety of initials: the UPDF, the ADF, the PRA, the FDLR, the FNL, Laurent Nkunda's rebel army, and remnants of the LRA, the Lord's Resistance Army, driven down south from Sudan. Too many names, too hard to remember. Many of the soldiers do not know what they are called. Most of them long to give it up and come home. But have they done things for which they can never be forgiven? Who is to decide what can be pardoned? The peace talks at Juba have been quiet for a while, and in the long nights it is hard to be hopeful. This soldier wears only rags of uniform, dead men's trousers, a dented cap, though he is a sergeant in the LRA. The gentle rain soaks through his clothes. Is he a boy or a man? A short-range radio crackles into life and his cortisol levels jag and peak with the daylight. A new day, another day to kill or be killed, though the newspapers talk about pacts, amnesties.

In Kampala, the capital, an eleven-hour drive north-east, cloud streams up, grey and thick, but moving swiftly: soon it will be hot. A marabou stork – a *karoli* – struts magisterially on the pavement, tall as the humans, who don't appear to like him, his long hairy pink gizzard swinging in the light like a warm, greedy chain of office. He cocks his head, and looks wise and cynical. A tourist behind glass in a jeep is thrilled, and takes a photograph. Smartly-dressed people are walking to work, in immaculate shirts and liquorice-shiny shoes, though the pavements are broken, red and dusty. The traffic is thickening: the taxis start hooting. They hold fourteen people, assorted bags of millet and potatoes, and crucifixes meant to keep the drivers safe from other drivers. Men ride *boda-boda* bikes crowned with thick hooked stems of green bananas, or with wives, in brilliant pink or turquoise, perched side-saddle behind them. Everyone drives more or less in the middle of the road, which seems to offer the best chance of getting where you're going. But mostly, Kampala seems peaceful, and organised.

Mary Tendo's in Kampala, getting ready for a trip. She checks her glossy helmet of hair in the mirror and smiles at herself: red plump lips. She is not too slim, which is excellent, for she wants to look good to go to the village. It's her last week at work before the journey, and she has to make sure all the right checks have been done. The first hour of the day, between seven and eight, is always her favourite, with the Executive Housekeeper's Office to herself, her computer screen glowing blue and orderly. Time to get a grasp on what there is to be done on this particular morning at the Sheraton.

It's the whitest, straightest hotel in Kampala, and the most modern, until a few years ago. Now it still stands tall on its flowering green hill in Nakasero, where the rich people live, but it seems to be straining up on tip toe, anxious. The truth is the Sheraton suddenly has rivals – the boutique Emin Pasha, the enormous new Serena, whose rooms are rumoured to be best of all. The Sheraton staff, too, are slightly nervous; everyone must be on top of their game. Someone important is coming to Kampala.

But outside the banks, down on the teeming main road, the navy-clad, rifle-toting guards can risk feeling sleepy as the sun gets hotter. Their rifles droop towards the ground. No-one is going to challenge them. It's a safe city, with a disciplined army. President Museveni's on top of things. (He's been on top of things for rather too long. Rather too much on top of things. He is rumoured to be going for a fourth term of office, and the First Family is getting richer. But give him his due, he has disciplined the army, at least when they are close to home.)

A lot of building work is in progress. Round the Parliament building, and near the Serena, pavements are being mended, with pick-axes and new white paving-stones, ready for the next torrential rains, which will wash the red mud underneath away, and spread new red diasporas of earth across the whiteness.

Hotels are going up: more slowly, they're falling down again. A skyscraper that rose up five years ago, right at the centre of the city, on Kampala Road, made of shiny pink stone, pointing boldly at the future, is peeling in the tropical heat and rain; long shreds of pink skin wave from head to foot, blowing in the wind, flapping hard against its body, and under the torn scraps of rosy veneer are grey panels of what appears to be cardboard. It will have to be mended, like everything else.

Mary Tendo frowns and smiles as she peers at her screen. She refuses to wear her glasses at work. Glasses are ageing; she is strong, and young. Hotel occupancy's 67 per cent, at the moment, not bad in view of all the renovations being done. For CHOGM is approaching, pronounced '*chogamu*', though British people call it 'choggum': two months away, less than two months, the Commonwealth Heads of Government will be meeting in Kampala. And the Queen, the Queen will be coming to Uganda.

Though not to stay at the Sheraton. The Queen will be staying at the Serena, or so it is rumoured. Mary tuts, softly. That ugly, dirt-red, overpriced hotel. With its terrible history, which we will not speak about (though the Sheraton has its own history, which Mary Tendo is used to denying. People whisper that, under Idi Amin, in the bad old days of Big Daddy, they used to hear screams in the middle of the night. But it's all so long ago it must be forgotten, or else Uganda cannot move into the future. Ugandans have become good at forgetting; and many of them are forgiving, also.) Mary is sure that the Queen did not choose to go to the Serena instead of the Sheraton. *Ebimu bya kwesonyiwa.* Even a Queen can be badly advised.

But the Business Forum is also important, Mary tells herself. CHOGM Business Forum is coming to the Sheraton. And delegations from Commonwealth countries. These prestigious guests will be coming to the Sheraton, where Mary is Executive Housekeeper. It is a big job. She was recently promoted. She is still enjoying her new, larger office, with its glass door and strategically-placed mirror so that she can keep an eye on what's going on even when she has her back to the door. Through the glass, now, she sees her right arm has arrived, Pretty the Desk Clerk, who channels all the messages from the floor Supervisors, the Linen Supervisor, F & B, and Ken Fixit.

It's not quite a normal day, today. Not just because Mary's getting ready for her trip, but because of the memo from the Director of Training and Standards, who is one of the two people still above her (for she has risen, through her skill and hard work. Mary Tendo can work harder than anyone.)

She came to the Sheraton two years ago as the Linen Room Supervisor, a job she previously held at the Nile Imperial Hotel. From the Linen Room she was promoted to Assistant Housekeeper. Now she is Executive Housekeeper (she likes the neat clicks of the syllables, like a key turning in bright new locks). The hotel is a theatre: she sees it like that. She is the stage manager, one of the few who make sure back of house runs like clockwork. The guests only see the well-lit stage, their gleaming glasses and enormous beds, the ironed linen white as the snow in London which Mary so loved when she first saw it, the soft light in the Piano Bar, the line of gold-uniformed receptionists standing behind the long desk in the enormous foyer, smiling like statues. But Mary knows the truth is all sweat and muscles. Beneath the desk, the legs of the receptionists are aching, because they are never allowed to sit down. Under the surface, the stately Sheraton swan is paddling, paddling, furiously. At the back of house, behind a slender partition, the washing machines are roaring, the huge ironing machines are creaking round, the men are standing ironing the details by hand, the linen-room maids are doing stain removal: pre-wash stain removal, post-wash stain removal. At the front of house, when the guests aren't looking, the maids are dusting and polishing the bedrooms, hoovering and smoothing, spraying and wiping, then hastily filling in their Room Reports.

But none of this must happen in front of the guests. The essential illusion: here is ease, and calm. *Kiringa kizinga*: it's the Sheraton, and the Sheraton is an oasis. Today the Director of Training and Standards has decreed that the maids need a training session. It's an update, really, on the Sheraton Brand. Mary sees the need: it is too easy to forget. Even she sometimes forgets to smile at the guests, which is the first essential at the Sheraton. (Of course, many of the guests are fat and rude and lazy, and when they complain, it is unjustified, and their only motive is to get a rebate, so Mary Tendo would like to go and kick them on the buttocks, and she could, because her legs and feet are well-developed. Besides, they have no right to be richer than her, just because they are American or European. But instead, she smiles. She's professional.)

Getting hotter now. Mid-morning. Overhead, the thunderclouds are building up, great bellying, Victorian, story-book clouds. The rains are early this year, and heavy, though the real rainy season has not yet come. But now there's a different smell in the air. Not rain, burning. An acrid smell. And the air is thickening with smoke, on Kyaggwe Road, in Old Kampala. The Kisekka market traders have sold spare parts for motors here for years and years, but now the government, which likes progress, has leased their market to Rhino Investments, who people say have links with the First Family. Does the government care about the little people? Perhaps it thinks they belong to the past, and Uganda must move into the future.

But Uganda contains both the past and the future. People hike into the city, out of the past, from the distant villages, which fear they are forgotten. They are hoping to see the President.

Outside Parliament House, on Parliament Avenue, a patient group of women, dressed in their best clothes, in bright clean *gomesis*, with a few men, not young, wearing jackets in the heat, are waiting, oddly still, sitting on the grass by the side of the road or standing proudly in the heat by the wall. They are waiting to see the President. They come from Mbale, in the east of Uganda, and President Museveni has promised he will see them. They are bringing him documents on many subjects. Their roads are flooded; many homes are cut off, and people have drowned; the water's still rising. And then, there are many problems with rubbish. Once Mbale was the cleanest town in Uganda, but now there is no money to collect the rubbish, and rubbish plus water could mean disease.

But there is something more important, too. They have something to say about forgiveness. They know that the government's consulting its people about what should be done to the LRA, whether Kony and his generals should be tried in the courts, whether peace can happen without punishment. And the people of the east have their own view on this, because they remember what the government did, which the western media don't talk about, to the Itesot people, just north of them, how the people were loaded in a train wagon at Mukura, and then something else, which must not be spoken, to teach them manners, and the air smelled of burning.

Yet the people of Mbale do not want vengeance. They simply want everything to be remembered, and then everything can perhaps be forgotten. Because maybe Kony is not a devil, or no more a devil than the government devils, and maybe the only way to stop all the evil is to set it aside and begin again. Most have a soldier somewhere in their family.

Maybe all the devils are only human: when things have been remembered, could they be absolved? For then they could sort out the roads, and the rubbish, and all the problems that have been deferred. When you live so far away, people don't remember you, so they have travelled to see the President, but they won't make trouble. They have good manners. If you show good manners, you deserve good treatment. They came the day before, but they are still waiting. *Perhaps the President will see them today.* They notice how bitter is the air in the city. It must be the cars, pouring past in the heat. But there's something extra: something smoky, stinging, which makes them uneasy as they stand by the roadside. The people of Mbale miss the air of the country.

In fact, the traders of Kisekka Market, angry in the heat, are making things hotter by burning tyres, blocking the road from the city, and lighting bonfires in the narrow alleys, while others are running to lock up their stores.

But this is Uganda. You aren't allowed to riot. Protest must be made by peaceful means. Police Acting Director of Operations, Grace Turyagamanawe, will decide to normalise the situation and make things more peaceful by using tear-gas. Soon everything will be quiet again, though a smell of burning hangs in the air until, at 3 PM exactly, the dark clouds burst, and rain drives down in straight sheets of water, as heavy as lead, seemingly from every direction, from left and right and even almost horizontal, and in minutes yards and pavements lie inches deep in water, and a beggar stands spellbound, not trying to shelter, feet wound in dark rags like bandages that slowly blacken, while busy Kampalans, smartly dressed but coatless, walk swiftly through the deluge under small makeshift roofs of briefcases, folders, newspapers, which are staunch for a few seconds, then bend and crumple darkly. Only a few have coloured golf umbrellas.

The people of Mbale have no umbrellas. They huddle together, chattering softly like wet birds, their garments less bright, their faces less happy. They will not look smart to meet the President. But it's only a shower: this isn't the country, and by four-thirty, the sun is shining again, and they move apart, and stand there, steaming. They will still be standing there as night falls, though one of them, smiling, tells an anxious white tourist who noticed them yesterday and also that morning, who stops, rather shyly, to ask them how they are, 'Don't worry, *Mzee*, we will see the President. And when it is night, they will put us somewhere.'

Yet three days later, without seeing their president, the people of Mbale go back to their district, or as near as the bus can take them to their district which is cut off by the floods that have swallowed the roads. There's a Ministry of Disaster Preparedness and Refugees, after all. But a lower-ranking member of the government has met them to explain: the Ministry of Disaster Preparedness was unfortunately not prepared for disaster.

Quite often, the President does see his people. He believes in meeting the unhappy and disgruntled, and he invites the newspaper, *New Vision*, to take photographs of these occasions. He is warm and charming, brisk and acute, with a youthful manner, although he's in his sixties. He has a big smile and a cute baby nose. Those who like him call him 'M' or '*Mzee*' or another, clever nickname: M7, short for MuSEVENi! He is the father of the modern nation! After the other fathers – Obote, Amin – who slaughtered thousands of their children, the international community is keen on Museveni, if a little less keen than they were at the beginning. And Ugandans, also, are distinctly less keen, though he tells those he meets that he will fix their problems. After all, he is the President; he just needs to make a phone call. They go away feeling honoured: all will be well. Over the months that follow, the warm feeling goes away. Of course, he is too busy to help them all. He is busy making sure that Uganda moves forward. He is leading Uganda into the future.

Mary Tendo belongs to Uganda's future. She believes in it: she is making it happen. She has made the great move from the village to the town, from the unwritten past into the urban future. She is educated; she does not make errors. (If she makes an error, she straightaway corrects it.) She knows there are dangers in making errors, and dangers in going back to the village, even though she will only be away for ten days. There is a chance for her rivals to make trouble for her, as used to happen at the Nile Imperial, when Sarah Tindyebwa thought Mary too ambitious. Now many people might like to have her job, and the Assistant Housekeeper, Rachel, is very capable, and although young, perhaps too capable ... Mary must leave all the paperwork in order, but then, her paperwork is always in order. She knows she is clever and organised. She remembers, with a smile touched with both scorn and pity, the collapsing towers of paper in Vanessa Henman's study, in faraway North London, where Mary once lived.

Vanessa. The Henman. Who once loomed so large, but now Mary thinks of her as small, and old. Poor Vanessa did not know how to manage paper: Touch Document One-Time only, Deal With, File, or Forward to Disposal Channel (though it is true that there are always some things Pending). Instead Vanessa hid things and let things slide. Long ago, in London in the distant past, when Mary Tendo was working as Vanessa's cleaner, to pay her bills while she finished her MA, Mary tried to sort Vanessa's desk out, and throw most of the messy paper away. But Vanessa had shrieked, and started waving her hands, though later she apologised. Mary went back to London quite recently, when Vanessa begged her to, and this time things were different, because Mary, of course, was a mature woman, and already successful in Uganda, and she was no longer a cleaner or a nanny, but advising Vanessa in her hour of need, because life had grown sadder for Vanessa. Little Justin was adult now, and in bed with depression, and asking for Mary Tendo, not his own mother. Of course, Mary flew over and sorted everything out (once Vanessa had agreed to reward her properly) and by the time she left, Justin was married with a baby.

But the paper situation had become a disgrace! Piles loomed like mountains on every side of Vanessa's expensive laptop computer, crumbling piles of old paper like great dead termite hills. Vanessa's whole life seemed to have slipped into Pending. But it doesn't matter. It's Vanessa's problem. Mary has her own life to live in Uganda. She looks around her office. Everything's in order.

And yet she feels a slight unease about Vanessa, because Mary is borrowing Vanessa's ex-husband.

Mary Tendo has invited Trevor to help her to mend the well in her village, and she has asked Trevor not to let Vanessa know, because otherwise Vanessa might want to come with him, since Vanessa seems to think they are still married, though she also likes to tell the story of the divorce, which she demanded bravely, as a feminist. However, Trevor's still allowed to do jobs around the house, and he has the right to be blamed for things – their son's depression, the loss of small objects, the occasional failure of his attempts to mend things. If Vanessa were to come to Uganda, Mary knows there would be stress for the whole of Uganda. And so she has sworn Trevor to secrecy.

Trevor is a plumber, and a very good one, but when Mary rang him in London and invited him to come and mend the well, he just laughed and said, 'Mary, I am only a plumber. There are experts at this sort of thing, you know.'

'Yes, there are consultants, they are very expensive. But Trevor, I think you will help me for free. We talked about it when I was in London.'

'But Mary, that was years ago. You can't just ring up out of the blue –'

'You are a practical man. You like to be helpful.'

Trevor had whistled, quite loudly, and started laughing. 'Mary Tendo, you've got the cheek of the devil.'

'Trevor, I think you know I am a Christian.'

'Oops. Sorry. It's just an expression ... I do know something about wells, it's true. I did some work on boreholes when I was in the Territorial Army. Royal Engineers.'

'You were the Queen's engineer?'

'It's just a name, Mary. Sort of weekend volunteer. But maybe your village doesn't have a borehole.'

'Trevor, a well is a well,' Mary had informed him, with more confidence than she in fact possessed, but Trevor had to be made to agree. 'I knew you would be pleased to be reminded. I remember how you wanted to visit me here, and I remember how you liked that book by Winston Churchill, *My African Journey*.'

'Yes, I gave you my copy.'

'Thank you, Trevor.'

'But did you read it?'

'Yes, I did not like it. He was always talking about "The Black Man" and "The Asian", but the only ones with brains were "The Asian" and "The White Man". I think you know that Ugandans have brains.'

'Mary, you're cleverer than I am,' sighed Trevor. 'You're wrong about Winston Churchill, though. Wonderful writer, Winston Churchill –'

'So that is settled,' Mary cut in. 'Will you come to my village, as my guest, Trevor? Charles and I will drive and pick you from Entebbe.'

There was a long, rustling silence before Trevor said, 'Yes.'

So now Trevor is coming to Uganda. And so will the Queen, a little later. And Kampala is digging everything up, and replacing it, painted and patched and riveted, buffed and re-routed and disinfected.

(And others are coming, far away to the west, on their long, long pilgrimage back into Uganda. Soldiers are stumbling and falling through the trees, half-asleep on their feet, with a wave of stink from their stiffened uniform, blood, sweat, old dysentery. They no longer smell it, but nocturnal animals, just waking up as the red sun plummets, pause, stilled by fear, warm flanks quivering. Sniffing the air. The badness is coming. And in a nearby village, an old woman shivers, who once lost her daughter, and listens, frowns. Something is near. Hope, fear. Somewhere in the shadows, life or death walking. A soldier, so lame he must be ancient, a commander, pushes the scarecrow ahead of him painfully onwards, poking and prodding with a darkly stained stick. Looking up, he suddenly sees between leaves a small silver sickle, a thin new moon, very bright in the heavenly glow after sunset, which reminds him, reminds him, but he will not remember. Is it a message? It stares straight at him. He shudders, terrified God has seen him.)

The Rhino Pub, at the Sheraton, is closed this week for refurbishment, and so drinks are served outside, by the swimming pool, as the sun grows pink, and the shadows lengthen, and sleeping mosquitoes near still stretches of water start to twitch, minutely, with faint signals of hunger (though there is no malaria in Kampala: at least that is what people tell the tourists, and the tourists nod and smile but keep taking their pills, and spraying themselves nervously with DEET, and they are quite right, because of course it is a lie, there is malaria in many places in Kampala, in the slum districts where no tourists go, in Kamwokya, on the way to Bukoto, and around Nateete Market, and although the haunts of the rich are mostly free of the disease, mosquitoes sometimes make mistakes and cross borders, and find the blood of the wealthy equally delicious).

So that few are swimming in the turquoise pool at the Sheraton as the sun dips down, as the date-palms grow dramatic upon the pink sky, as the flood-lights come on and pick out the ridges on the tallest palm-tree in stark black and white, and the birds – white egrets, white and black crows – all darken to cut-out colourless bird-shapes that fall or whirl up and drop down again in resistless spirals of sleepiness to their evening roost in the leafy branches. The sky's almost empty as its red starts to fade, then deepens to faintly starred indigo. The last bird to go is a lone planing stork making one last pass above the poolside drinkers, listening, perhaps; there are always listeners; so in Uganda, people are both brave and cautious. The dark is total, now. The stars steady.

A new moon rises: something in the offing.

2

And two hours later, since England is further from the equator, the same sun is sliding down over London, roosting in the blackening skyscrapers. Early September: summer is over.

The airport. Heathrow, Terminal 4. In here, there is no weather, no rain, no sunlight.

A giant ant-hill poked with a stick. The ants run everywhere, surely without purpose. Tiny limbs hurrying, dragging great parcels of earth or food almost bigger than they are. Great white birds swoop down on them, one after another – but then more ants stream out of their bellies.

No trees, no grass, nothing. Come down closer and the ants become people, but still nothing grows. Everything here was made by machines. Metal and plastic, silicon and paper.

The humans, though, are very alive, giving off waves of sweat and terror, adrenalin, joy and sorrow, as they say goodbye, or greet other humans.

Here's Vanessa Henman. Ah, Vanessa ... Vanessa, accompanied by her driver, long-suffering Justin, who has driven all wrong, so Vanessa has told him.

How small she looks, how agitated. Like grass in the wind; dry grass; straw. A chemical yellow, half a lifetime too late for the blonde of childhood, and her teeth are too white. Her little pale face is tense with excitement, her red lips pursed to say goodbye to her son, who has wheeled her luggage trolley through to Fast Bag Drop, offloading her enormous blue case, a sort of wardrobe on wheels that feels freighted with stones.

She might be in her forties, or fifties, or sixties. Nights of not sleeping, getting ready for her journey, have left her older. She clutches at Justin. The point of her life, but has she been a bad mother? He's a big handsome animal, lazily clever, with lips that curve in a deep cupid's bow and natural blond curls Vanessa envies. 'Justin,' she says, 'kiss Abdul Trevor for me.' She's a good grandmother, if rather anxious, and her little grandson is not quite well. She cries for a moment, then lets Justin go, and begins to heft her over-large flight bag into the lonely maze of roped-off gangways, endlessly doubling back on themselves, down which all travellers must go. Like a determined snail, with her house on her back. Surely it won't fit in the overhead lockers?

Be obedient, Vanessa: follow the path. If you go off the path, who knows what may happen?

Vanessa's on her way to Kampala, Uganda. She's going to a British Council Conference, where everything is organised. She has several memos with all her arrangements. There are Conference Programmes of enormous size, in multiple versions, clogging up her computer, as speakers drop in, or venues drop out. The unifying theme is 'The Outsider'. Some of the titles are long or repellent, but she's used to the longwindedness of academics. 'Dis-covering the Outsider in Heart of Darkness: Marlow or the Cannibals?' 'Orature: Can it be Spoken?' 'Exile and the Dis-grace of Coetzee: Solitude, Slow Man and the Lonely Modernist.' On the other hand, some events are very, well, up tempo. There are dub poets, beat boxers, a rap poet. She has printed all the versions, indiscriminately, and stuffed all the paper in the lid of her suitcase. (Vanessa has a small problem with objects: paper, photographs, books, bills. She loses them, or accidentally stockpiles them. She brings the wrong ones, and they make her anxious. She strains to be organised, and fails. Then every few months, she goes on the war-path, desperate to re-impose order on life. Woe betide anyone who gets in the way.)

But later, she's off to see the gorillas. The rare mountain gorillas of western Uganda. Near DRC, the Democratic Republic of Congo, where few tourists go. She's not entirely sure it's such a good idea, now the reality is coming closer. Yet she had boasted to Justin and his wife, Zakira, 'Real gorillas. In the jungle. Not a zoo. I'm going to – *actually* – *spend time with them.*'

They hadn't looked as impressed as she'd expected. (Of course they were young and ignorant, especially Zakira, who could be snooty. 'Upper-class Moroccans,' as she said to her friend Fifi. 'No-one is as haughty as upper-class Moroccans, and my son has to go and marry one.' In fact, she is immensely proud of Zakira. Justin, having been useless for years, has suddenly married a rather remarkable woman, a Moroccan with an MBA, and they've got a baby, poor little Abdul Trevor, a sweet child despite his ridiculous name. And Justin's doing an evening course in journalism. How clever of him to find a wife with prospects, a wife who will certainly be rich one day, for an MBA is the royal road to money.)

'I'm going to spend time with them *on equal terms,*' Vanessa had insisted, getting pink in the face.

'She's going to wear a gorilla suit,' said Justin to Zakira, and they both burst out laughing.

Vanessa remembers this with pain. In fact Justin had got extremely silly and doubled up, breathless, crying with laughter and repeating, every so often, through his tears, 'Mum in a gorilla suit! Mum in a gorilla suit!'

Little Abdul Trevor had been more sensitive, although he was only three. Disturbed by laughter he did not understand, he had crept up beside his grandma and put his arm around her, staring at her earnestly. 'Is it funny, Ganma?' he asked.

'Not very, darling,' she had said, with dignity.

'Not be a grilla, Ganma,' he urged her.

'Er – no, I won't be a gorilla, I promise.'

As she hauls herself along, out of the comfort zone, growing smaller, now, in the enormous ant-hill, crawling deeper into the nervous land of checking and re-checking money, passport, ticket, glasses, she remembers the kindness of Abdul Trevor. The little boy loves her, and she is grateful. She knows she isn't an easy person.

But as soon as she thinks that, she justifies it; she has high standards, she cares about things.

Justin watches his mother toiling away, with her hump of possessions, photographs, documents. He has brought her this far and can go no further. How slight she looks. Almost fragile, though people don't tend to see her as fragile. She turns and waves a gallant, abortive little wave and then pushes on determinedly towards the checkpoint. By now she has traversed a hundred metres of gangway, though she's only six metres away from him. To go as the crow flies is forbidden. Just before Justin turns and leaves, he sees Vanessa talking to the passport official. Oh dear, what is his mother doing? Screwing up his eyes, he lip-reads, incredulous.

She's saying, 'An upgrade ... if you could do anything ... well-known writer ... British Council ...' A flood of words. The man looks puzzled. Oh God, now she's showing him her latest book, and he is scratching his head and looking at her closely. Probably wondering if she's sane enough to travel. She's asking an *immigration officer* for an upgrade. Now, tiring of her, the man waves her on. His mother disappears into Departures, forgetting to look round at him. Justin fears she will try for an upgrade again.

He picks his way back through the halls of displaced people, dodging the trail of enormous possessions to which fretting owners are paying obeisance, labelling, locking and unlocking, worrying. Now he thinks of his mother with sorrow and affection. It's always such a relief when she goes, which is sad for her, he does see that. Even for a moment, even after lunch, when she goes for a rest to quell acid indigestion. Rooms are calmer and easier without his mother in them, tidying, improving, asking questions. She is always buzzing with ideas and plans, most of them involving work for other people. She lives other lives as well as her own. In the end the only way he could escape her was by giving up completely: work, social life, getting up in the morning. Justin had gone to bed for six months. Perhaps she'd got the message. Only Mary Tendo could cheer him up. And then he had got back together with Zakira.

Good-looking young women glance up as Justin passes, the harsh light of the airport halo-ing his curls, but there's something a little unfinished about him, as if he doesn't quite know where he's going, and long before he's out of sight, they lose interest.

Justin is focused on his mother. Why is she always searching for something? As if life itself owes her an upgrade. To be fair, how far she has climbed already, through her own efforts, from the dump where she grew up, in a tiny Sussex village, with a farm labourer and a depressive! Grandma was in and out of loony bins, she'd recently told him. Poor Mum! And like him, she was an only child, so all the loony-ness hit her undiluted. Yet she's become a published novelist and a lecturer in creative writing. And she can't be as bad at writing novels as Justin fears (he can't bring himself to read them, in case he's in them), if the British Council's chosen her as a delegate to an international conference. He supposes his grandparents must have been proud. Vanessa was her mad mother's wunderkind. ('I was fearsomely bright. I was *two years* ahead!') And she'd tried to impose the same role on him.

So I was always at classes, Justin reflects, Junior Einstein Fun with

Numbers!!, Dolphin Swim League, Teen Trapeze ... No wonder I got tired. Whereas Mum is fucking tireless.

How would he have survived without Mary Tendo? Mary had never tried to improve him. Just played with him, cuddled him, and fed him normal food, things like chips and baked beans which his mother had forbidden. Mary. Where is she? He misses her. He knows she would adore Abdul Trevor.

He has come to an unfamiliar part of the short-stay car-park. Harassed people are unloading, with sharp cries of effort, their rucksacks and cases and cellos from car-boots, trying not to quarrel when they're just about to part. He peers short-sightedly around for his jeep, which he's thinking of swapping for a second-hand Smart Car. There's a certain social pressure, now, against jeeps. And Justin is certainly as green as the next man. Ah yes, he's spotted it. He switches off his phone, so his mother cannot ring him, and revs up his engine, which needs a service: clouds of grey smoke. He loves driving, now, though he isn't wholly confident. When he was depressed, he had to give up driving, and was driven everywhere, like a baby. Mary Tendo helped him to grow up again.

Hunched in Departures with a skinny decaff latte, stopping every so often to pat the rucksack pocket from which her passport and boarding card might be stolen, Vanessa is already texting her son. Goodbye Justin, lots of love, goodbye. Thanks for driving me, good boy. Hide a key for my cleaner pls under the dustbin? Take care darling, you are always my baby, kiss Abdul T for me, Mum.

An hour later, the passengers for Entebbe are in a queue for boarding. Vanessa, hardly able to stand upright with the weight of her flight bag dragging back her shoulders, is pleading with the British Airways steward, who is smiling automatically, consulting his list. 'I am representing the British Council, and I will be writing about Uganda. I will definitely mention British Airways in my article, if you could offer me an upgrade.' His face becomes frankly puzzled as she adds, pink-faced with the foretaste of failure, 'I asked the gentleman in Departures. This is my novel. I'm Vanessa Henman.' It's hard to hold the book, her flight bag, her boarding-card and her litre of water. Why can't they make things easy for her?

'I've checked the list. You're in World Traveller.'

'*Thank you.*' She smiles, ecstatic: she's pulled it off. She's been upgraded to World Traveller. And then she's suspicious. A sinking of the heart.

'Is that an upgrade?'

'I'm afraid not.'

People are listening. She trudges forward.

Vanessa, oh, Vanessa. Travel safely.

3

In a street of new bungalows in a suburb of Kampala, Mary Tendo and Charles and their daughter Theodora and the maid, Mercy, are settled for the evening. Mercy is just finishing the washing up. Then she will lie down beside the baby, Theodora, who is humming wordlessly to herself. Mary is staring at the slightly clunky laptop that looked modern when Charles gave it her, four years ago.

She has come in here because she cannot be bothered to watch the shenanigans of Big Brother Africa, where people sit half-naked all day by the jacuzzi, and nobody talks in complete sentences, though of course she would like a Ugandan like Maureen to win it, and certainly not two-timing Bertha from Zimbabwe. Charles has fallen asleep as he watches on the sofa. So she's come into the bedroom to write her *Life of Mary Tendo*, which she has been neglecting, now she is so busy, and many would say it was a waste of time. She's enjoying re-reading all she has written. As she reads, she frowns, or laughs, or looks sad.

When she was in UK, it was shown to an agent, and for a while everybody got very excited, including a big British publisher. But they found Mary Tendo was no pushover. She would not rewrite her life to make it more thrilling. And particularly, they wanted to know more about the times when she shared a bed with Justin. (Because he was depressed, and she could cheer him.) And they wanted her to put in many details, of things which she never confirmed had happened. And they said 'It's normal, everyone does it, in the modern world there's no distinction between fact and fiction. Modern readers are sophisticated, Mary. And if you beef it up, you will have big sales.' As she thinks about this, she becomes indignant. Her strong, ridged fingers buzz over the keys like hornets hurrying to feed their brood. Because sometimes she can only talk to her journal. But after one paragraph, she feels discontented. She chooses a new, more assertive typeface, and as she does so she becomes aware that actually, she is holding off sadness.

I was right to refuse to add the passages they wanted. I am a Ugandan. And I am a Christian. We are not like the British, we are not immoral (though not all the British are immoral. Vanessa Henman was not immoral; no-one would care to be immoral with her. Though I sometimes suspected her of sleeping with Trevor. Since they were once married, it would not have been immoral. But I must have been wrong. He is a sensible man.)

The English publishers asked for a picture of me. I think they would have liked me to look slightly indecent. The photographer they sent, who was American, and sweaty, and smiled too much, with red eyes like a fish, could not remember my name for five minutes, and said, 'Loosen up, Maria, it's the 21st century!' I preferred to retain my glasses and jacket. The photographer got cross and went away. And many small quarrels began with the publisher, because I did not like the promises in the contract, and the woman they called my editor was young and impertinent. She had crossed eyes and too few clothes. She also had a poor grasp of English, and was not happy when I tried to explain it. Her level of education was not high, though I was tactful and did not say so. Perhaps I hinted at it a little. Then, just because I had not signed the contract, they cancelled it in a letter from a lawyer that began 'Without prejudice'. Without prejudice! Obviously the publishers were prejudiced against me.

I do not regret that I did not get published, though I felt a little cross when Vanessa, who was jealous, said, 'I thought it wouldn't come to anything, Mary.' The UK publishers never offered her so much money. Perhaps because her novels did not tell a story, and had sentences which trailed on for ever. I suppose she would not have refused to take her clothes off. She often did situps in her pyjamas.

In fact, perhaps I do regret it, though it is not worth being sad about. Other things in life are more important, but Vanessa did not realise it.

And Mary re-reads what she has written, and thinks, I am not really happy with this typeface. For what I need to write, it is a little loud. She scrolls through the list: *Consolas, Constantia, Futura, Lucida, Perpetua* ... the best, the most serious is *Times New Roman*.

I feel strange when I think about going to the village. I have longed and planned to go back to Notoke, but now the day is almost upon me. Because of what? I must look in my heart.

Jamil, my son, my lovely boy. My son is an absence, always trying to grow bigger, but I dare not let it eat up my soul. Life is hard, and short, and we have to live it.

And my *kabite*, Charles, is also in my heart, but he never troubles me (except when he is lazy about doing the shopping and goes to Garden City and spends too much money, because he likes to drop into Aristoc bookshop, instead of buying cheaply, in the market). He is a good man, if a little skinny. And then there is our daughter, as he always reminds me. She has a beautiful name, Theodora. Perhaps I wanted her to be a boy, but she is my daughter and I will love her.

And my brother, my sisters, and aunties, and nieces and nephews are in my heart too, though they have grown distant. I sometimes sent them money when I was in London, though not every month, because London is expensive, and some of those girls are not well-behaved, though of course my sister gets cross and denies it, because a mother must defend her children, but I know they go too often to the beer-shop near Notoke, and what if people say they are prostitutes? Still I wish that, like her, I had many children.

Oh, I do not want to go home to the village with only one small daughter. Without my son, nga silina mutabani wange.

When I was in London, nearly twenty years ago, I thought with longing about Notoke. I lay awake listening to the beat of my heart. It was loud and lonely on my cold pillow. I thought about the sound of the women of my village pounding groundnuts in their wooden mortars, thud-ah, thud-ah like the blood in my body, which longed to be back in the place from which it came.

But the village will have changed, and so have I. Mary Tendo is what? Is she a woman from the village? Mary Tendo has become a woman of the world.

Yet I will never forget my childhood, the hours under the mango tree on Saturday after we children had swept the compound, and fetched water, and seen to the goats. We were never ill-mannered to our parents. We were happy so long as they did not beat us. We would tell each other stories. People liked mine best. And the English publishers liked them also, although they were arrogant, and wanted to 'improve' them.

Will there still be villages, in Uganda's future? Perhaps

they will all have electricity and running water (although this is hard for me to believe). The children will no longer be taking it in turns, at nightfall, to peer out from the branches of the jackfruit tree on the hill, as we did, towards the distant city lights like a net of stars. The villagers will have their own line of bright streetlights, and travel to the city in safe, airy buses, with uniformed drivers who know road safety. (They will have to sack all the old drivers, for no Ugandan bus driver can be trusted!)

I cannot believe these days will come. Our leaders let us down, and the foreign governments. They give us money, but later they steal from us. It is not so easy to reach the future. We seem to have been running towards it for years, and it always slips away beyond the horizon.

And my son is slipping away, like the future. I can no longer see him clearly, my first-born child, my most dear and beloved, the child of my heart, from my first love, Omar. The full curve of his mouth, his long curling lashes, his skin, which is darkest gold, not black like me. I am left with only photos, which I look at every night, so that Charles is sad for me, and strokes my hand, and brings me a cup of milky coffee. But Jamil cannot look like his photos any more, though they are all I have of him. He is five years older. If he survives. If my son survives, he is over 20. If my son lives, he has become a man. With a man's jaw, and a man's memories of the years he has lived away from home. Years of which I, Mary Tendo, know nothing.

And happiness is what? To see your son become a man. There are many who take this happiness for granted.

But Omar and I could not stay together, and I try not to blame him for leaving me. For he was a good man, and true to his religion, and he became more devout, with the years, and of course, as a Christian, I could not follow him. But I knew that every boy needs a father. And if I had known, I would have given anything, I would have sold my flat and my furniture, I would have forced Charles to sell his business, to pay for Jamil to fly safely home to Entebbe, but my son wanted to be independent, and not to bother either of his parents; and his father, of course, has a new Arab family, and perhaps his new wife is mean, or greedy, but I cannot blame Omar, for Jamil did not tell him, he just set off overland by bus, which might have brought him down through southern Sudan and the terrible northern lands of the Acholi, where there has been war for 20 years, and perhaps Museveni does not want to stop it, and for this, for this he will NEVER be forgiven, *tasobola kusonyiyibwa, I could never forgive the death of my son* –

But I must not think like this. Perhaps I have lost focus. I must be positive, and count my blessings.

My history is interesting: thank you, Jesus. I have travelled the world, with Omar, my husband, who worked for the Libyan Embassy, and my husband loved me, as I never forget, although later we quarrelled, and times grew hard, and our families were not there, and could not support us, and Omar changed, and I changed also. But because of Omar, I had my son.

I cannot say, I have my son.

I must not think about my son.

Because of Omar, I saw Leptis Magna, and we were young, and we walked, together, on the Roman stones of the road to Carthage. And we saw the forum, and the carved jars of wine, and we stood, hand in hand, in the white stone theatre, which curved like the moon, and was open to the sea, which stretched away for ever, like our future. But slowly it has dwindled, and turned into the past.

Most Ugandans have never been to Libya. And even the British have never been there. Vanessa was impressed, and a little jealous.

And now she has her son, and I do not. It is rare for the British to lose their children.

I don't mind the British. Usually I like them, although they are ignorant of history. I grew quite fond of them when I was in London. They are like spoiled children, but some have good hearts. And when they come to Uganda, they become like babies, afraid of everything, so we have to help them. They fear the heat, and the mosquitoes, and the water, and snakes in the country, and robbers in the city, and go everywhere by special taxi, and waste their money, which they have too much of.

I am only writing this because my heart is aching. It is hard not to think about Jamil today. I am no longer able to be completely hopeful, which is a weakness, but my strong heart falters

so now I must get up, and go to the kitchen where Mercy is sleeping with little Theodora, and scoop her from under the mosquito-net, and hug her beautiful fat small body, and bury my face on her sweet hot neck, to remind myself that I am not barren, that I still have a child, thanks God, thanks Jesus, and then, when she begins to wriggle and mutter, I slip her back in beside Mercy, and then I feel stronger and can write again

I am better with this baby when she is asleep, for then she reminds me of my son

but when she cries, she cries differently, and my heart hardens, which is not her fault

and also, I fear losing her, I lost one child I could lose another

If Jamil came down through the north, on his own, he could have been captured, he could have been killed. Because the Lords' Resistance Army replaces its soldiers with abducted children and young people. They make the children kill other children.

And yet I have become like a starving man who longs to gnaw shoes or string as food, because I would rather

I cannot write it, No, I will write it

Because I would rather Jamil was a killer, that my kind young son killed and tortured others, than that he is lost. Entirely lost. Perhaps my son is utterly lost. And now I will be lost, because I think these things.

Jesus forgive me for thinking these things

'Honey it's time to stop writing. You will hurt your eyes, and need stronger glasses. I am going to bring you a juice before bedtime.' It is Charles, with his shirt-tails outside his trousers.

But in fact Mary is no longer writing, she is staring at the screen, because the pain has become too great to write down.

'I will stop writing, though I am not tired.'

She will never rest until Jamil is found.

4

'You go.'

'You go.'

'Oh, you go, I'm dead.'

'OK, I'll go.'

Young parents' early morning conversations. They aren't really being selfish: too sleepy for that. Each body is speaking from primal need. Today, Zakira's is more pressing than Justin's, and so he rolls sideways off their futon, and blunders next door, into the blue-themed bedroom with its alphabets and numbers, its mobile of African animals, elephants, giraffes, hippopotamuses, its big single bed that makes his son look small, for he has not long left the comfort of a cot. Justin looks at his watch: 4.45 AM. 'My favourite time,' he mumbles to himself. Abdul Trevor has not been sleeping well. He has a cold, and he sometimes has nightmares.

Justin gazes down lovingly on his flushed son. 'Coffin,' says Abdy, reproachfully, and Justin decodes it as merely 'Coughing.' 'Sorry, old chap', he says, 'Daddy's here. Let's give you a drink of water, shall we?'

He feels his son's forehead. Very hot. Then he feels his own, which is even hotter. Either both or neither of them is dying. He knows he mustn't be an anxious father. But his own father, Trevor, was quite laid-back, and got it in the neck, for that reason, from his mother.

He inspects his son's bed. It is only September but he does seem to have rather a lot of blankets. Vanessa's always saying so, in any case. She thinks Zakira puts too many clothes on him. These views she conveys to him in strict confidence. 'Don't say a word to Zakira, of course. It's *cultural*,' she says, grandly. 'Moroccans naturally think England is freezing.' (Though actually England is getting quite hot. This year it has sometimes been hotter than Morocco.)

Sighing, tentative, Justin removes a blanket. It is soft and blue, with a giant cream bunny. If Zakira notices, he will blame Abdul Trevor, who is capable of kicking anything off. Justin leaves it in a deliberately crumpled heap on the floor. 'There you are, old chap. All better,' he croons.

Abdul Trevor wants to tell him about his dream, but he hasn't got the words. 'Ganma hairy,' he says, conversationally, hoping to make his father stay a bit longer.

'Yes, Grandma's gone away, but she'll be back,' agrees Justin, stroking a sweaty streak of hair from his son's forehead.

'Ganma a grilla,' Abdul Trevor explains, but Justin isn't getting it: too early in the morning.

'Grandma loves you. She sent you a kiss.' He plants one softly on Abdy's cheek. 'Night night, sleep tight.' He is tip-toeing away.

'Grilla was bad,' the child cries half-heartedly. But Daddy has gone, and Abdul Trevor sucks his thumb until he falls into a dream where his grandma is back to her usual self, and no longer crossly swinging black hairy arms from the top of his sky-blue, cloud-painted wardrobe.

5

Thirty-one thousand feet above the ground, Vanessa Henman is trying to sleep, though she can't get comfortable, in all her clothes. She has moved her watch to Uganda time, she is getting ready for life in Kampala, and in Kampala, it is 1.15 AM, so there are not many hours before she has to wake up again. They will be landing at 7.45, breakfast should arrive around 6.45, which would still be the middle of the night, in London, and all this maths is making her anxious. Besides, last night she did not sleep at all. Perhaps it is the Malarone, which always affects her, her little red pills which should keep her safe from cerebral malaria, though as she told her friend Fifi, 'There's no 100 per cent guarantee, you know. It *is* slightly risky, even with Malarone. And Malarone does have side effects.' She wanted Fifi to think her brave, because Fifi has certainly never been to Africa, but Fifi just remarked in a rather casual way, 'I knew somebody who used homoeopathy instead.'

'Did it work?'

'It worked for *weeks* –'

'Perhaps I should try it –'

'Until she got bitten, which was bad luck.'

Vanessa did go and ask her doctor about it, but he was a tad narrow-minded, and brisk. 'There's a name for people who protect themselves from malaria with homeopathy.'

'Oh, what is it? I'll put it in my story.' (For she's planning to write about her African trip. It is certainly time for her to publish again.)

'A corpse,' said the doctor, looking pleased with himself.

But still, Vanessa does not want to die, and she has four white boxes of pills in her luggage. She shifts, restless, in her narrow seat, and moves her wedding ring around her finger, the thin Irish band that Trevor bought her so long ago, when they were both poor, which she's wearing to Uganda because it might protect her. She is trying to forget what had happened upon boarding.

Thank God no-one she knew was there to watch. Her flight bag wouldn't fit in the overhead locker. She had hauled it up, she had heaved it sideways, she had pushed and pushed, but nothing happened. A man offered to help her, but she refused. She remembered her Pilates, and engaged her core muscles, and melted her shoulder blades down her back, then took a deep breath and shoved: no luck. Now the stewardess (*young*, she thought, and mean, too much make-up, with that terrible perky look they have) was watching her closely. 'If it won't go up, Madam, I'm afraid it will have to travel down in the hold.'

'Impossible. My laptop's in there. I am a novelist. It is essential.'

'We would ask you to unpack essential items, and then the bag can go down in the hold.' Her tone was bright, her smile adamant.

'No, I need this bag. I am sure it will fit.'

Now the helpful man (who was built like a weightlifter) got up and took the bag from her hand. 'Let me help you, Ma'am.' American. Vanessa cocked her head at the stewardess, triumphant. She was not too old to have male supporters.

But two minutes later, he had given up. 'I'm sorry, Ma'am, it's impossible.' Americans, of course, were cowards and weaklings. And so the case had come down again.

In the end Vanessa, watched by the entire cabin, had been forced to unpack the bag on the floor. The cabin staff remained forcefully pleasant; Vanessa struggled not to cry. The laptop was new, and not unimpressive, but she wished she had packed better underwear. In fact, those pants looked distinctly grey, and the light in the cabin was very harsh. She had blushed to remove, in full view of everyone (and they were all staring, or looking at their watches) her statutory see-through bag full of liquids – did she need more liquids than everyone else? She seemed to have litres and litres of the stuff. Toothpaste, cleanser, toning gel, moisturiser, contact lens fluid, sun cream and insecticide, ready for the dangerous Ugandan morning. And then all the other stuff she really needed. Her teeth, which she looked after extra carefully since she got them all sorted, five years ago, required interdens brushes, toothbrush, floss. And then there were her contact lens case and spectacles. And her pens and notebook and tissues, of course, and her *Guide to Uganda*, to refresh her memory. And her low-dose aspirin, for flying; and her high-dose aspirin, in case she got toothache; not to mention two blisters of Malarone, one spare, in case her luggage got delayed. Her sunglasses, in case tomorrow was sunny, and her umbrella, in case it rained. And of course the flight bag was so tightly packed that at first she couldn't drag anything out, and the passengers all gawped as she hauled and sweated, and the stewardess brought her a plastic bag and stood there, imperfectly concealing impatience. She thinks I'm old and stupid, Vanessa thought, wincing. But at last it was over, and she could sit down, unable to meet her fellow passengers' eyes.

Now her plastic bag of junk is wedged at her feet. She broods, if only they had given me my upgrade. I'm sure they should have given me an upgrade. The first man, in Departures, hadn't actually said 'No'. He had practically encouraged her to ask elsewhere. In Business and First they must have bigger lockers, and the bag would have fitted in perfectly.

Still she mustn't obsess. Vanessa knows her faults. It's not important. She tries to let go. She clenches her toes, then relaxes them. Her calf feels odd. Could it be a thrombosis? And she does not know what to do with her head, with her long fragile neck, rather too long for her body, and prone to arthritis if she doesn't take care. She does take care: she exercises. And tonight she has already done her exercises, discreetly of course, head- and shoulder-circling, though the bad-mannered child next door had stared, and his mother seemed to have no control over him. And now he is watching three different films, switching from one to another, on the in-flight entertainment, a contented smile upon his face, as if he has never seen a film before (it is possible, she thinks. He is African.) His mother does not tell him to go to sleep, and Vanessa is maddened by the sound effects, even though he has got the volume on low. There are incessant faint bursts of gunfire, or screaming. As if the world is nothing but war.

She was a post-war baby, born just after the end of World War Two, and sometimes she feels as if all her life she has miraculously kept just ahead of war. She knows she has been lucky, but how long can that last? On 11 September 2001, Vanessa held her breath, like everyone else, and waited for a world war to break out; she had worried about Justin, and, oddly, Trevor. But after ten frightening days, it had blown over. And then there were the bombs on the London Underground. Fortunately, she is claustrophobic.

But the shooting goes on in the seat beside her, rat-a-tat-a-tat, and the whoosh of explosions. There are wars, she knows, on the edges of Uganda. The war in the north is supposed to be over, the war between the LRA and the government, but she's read that the Juba peace talks aren't working. And then there are always wars in Congo, or DRC as the Ugandans like to call it, and some of the LRA have regrouped down there, on the border between DRC and Uganda. Which makes Vanessa nervous, because that's where she is going. Not yet, but after the end of her conference, on her long-awaited trip to see the gorillas. She fears that, at last, war might find her there.

A bigger explosion from the seat next door. Vanessa taps sharply at the child's thin arm, then reminds herself to smile, and points at his screen, so he looks at her, puzzled, as she mimes tiredness. Light seems to dawn. Bright-eyed, he leans across her, switches on her screen, and scrolls the arm control to Movies. Instantly gun-fire breaks out in front of her. He looks so satisfied with what he has achieved that for a moment he reminds her of Justin, and Vanessa remembers, with a small stab of guilt, how often she had hurt her son by insufficiently appreciating his achievements: or so he has recently started to tell her. Swallowing her dismay, she says, 'Ah, thank you,' grits her capped teeth and endures for a while, until she can decently turn it off again ...

But in fact she sleeps, and is carried, unresisting, released from fretting or struggling, high above the clouds which are heavy with rain, high above Sardinia, high above Sicily, high above Libya's lost Roman cities, and the wars go on, only inches from her face, just in front of her safely sleeping eyelids, as the air warms over North Africa, swooping down over Sudan now, coming closer to Entebbe, her little feet twitching, sometimes, like birds' feet, her thin mouth smiling, in a happy dream in which Mary Tendo will be waiting to meet her, and at last, this time, they will be like sisters.

'Tea or coffee, Madam?'

Hallo. It's morning.

6

'Cabin crew to positions for landing.'

Vanessa braces, and clutches her landing card, her passport, her Yellow Fever Certificate, and worries that the pilot's coming in too fast. Isn't Uganda rather high, she wonders? In which case, he might bump into it. The voice on the intercom was confident, perhaps over-confident, and certainly too young. They are bounding through the clouds now; there's turbulence. She finds she is sweating, and frankly, frightened, but she must remember not to try to fly the plane. Twenty-seven years ago, when they were just married, Trevor had told her that on the flight to Paris where they were going on their honeymoon. 'Relax, Nessie. Try to enjoy it. He's a trained pilot. Let him fly the plane.'

She dares a glance out of the window now and is relieved by the sight of toy trees and houses. If the engines failed now, she might still survive, and she's suddenly near enough to see sharp fronds on a palm tree, she's level with a roof, red ridged roof-tiles – and with two bumps, they have landed, and her heart leaps up as the engines throttle thunderously down the runway. She beams a triumphant smile at the boy, it is always such a relief to have made it, but he looks back blankly, eyes veiled with sleep. And suddenly Vanessa's full of energy, re-infused with hopefulness, the first on her feet as they roll to a halt – though the mean stewardess motions her down again.

She emerges into a warm pink morning. The air smells wonderful: of earth, of growth. The sky is low and misty, with a thinly veiled sun. It's a small airport, and they set off walking, a narrow stream of passengers, white people and Africans. Only one stream is open in Immigration, so everyone goes through 'Ugandan Residents'. It's as if Uganda's giving her a personal welcome.

The baggage hall, by contrast, is hell. Only one carousel is working, reluctantly, its armoured plates rubbing over each other like the broken shell of a dying armadillo. On one particular corner, all the cases get stuck, and baggage-handlers zestfully chuck them on the floor. This seems to be the baggage-handlers' main function, so a great bruised herd of unwanted cases is slowly surging across the room. Anxious passengers strain to keep an eye on both the herd and the tame line of cases traipsing in from outside.

Vanessa's flight bag arrives quite quickly. She strides forward to claim it, one of the elect. But the other case, the real, important one, with almost all her things, doesn't follow. At first Vanessa stays cheerful. She offers a harassed-looking woman beside her an old hand's smile: 'Well, this is Africa! T.I.A.!' (An expression she learned on a travellers' website, and has been dying for the chance to use.) But the woman says, '*Bitte? Verstehe nicht,*' and then darts forward, as Vanessa's heart sinks, to collect her own bag with a cry of belonging.

As the baggage hall empties of people, Vanessa learns how much she loves her suitcase. The familiar faces from her flight light up in turn as their luggage is reborn through the flap in the wall. How gladly they bundle them on to trolleys, how gaily they speed away out of sight. She's alone, destitute, in Africa. Why ever did she come? It was all a mistake.

Then the worst moment: the next plane arrives, new chattering strangers flock into the hall, and soon their luggage will be driving out hers. By now only one last lonely bundle from London is circling the carousel, wrapped in layers and layers of glittering plastic, so small it is ignored even by the baggage-handlers, who refrain from casting this one on to the floor. It makes her think suddenly of her grandson: so small and vulnerable, encased in all his layers.

And then the ugly flap lifts one more time – and everything changes, for there it is, the very last case to arrive from London: blue, battered, but her own. Vanessa runs round the carousel to meet it, and swings it, mighty midget-style, on to her trolley. My things, my things, my most beloved.

But the Sheraton bus, to her dismay, has gone. 'They knew I was coming,' she complains to the polite and passive woman in Sheraton uniform, whose dark eyes are lowered over her golden jacket. 'Dr Vanessa Henman. I was *confirmed*.'

'Ah, sorry,' the woman agrees, caressively (Vanessa remembers those Ugandan 'sorrys': how kind they sound, a descending bird-call). 'But the other guests, they sometimes do not like to wait. So would you like to pay for a special taxi? I can arrange it. Only 20 dollars.'

Vanessa's battle-light comes on. She is hot, and tired, and it isn't fair. 'No, I wouldn't,' she says, shortly. 'I was down for the bus.'

'So would you like to pay 15 dollars?' the woman inquires, cautiously. 'It is OK.'

'*I just want to get there*,' says Vanessa, '*soon*.'

But soon, very soon, she is regretting she said it. The young, eager driver of a special taxi arrives, smiling and out of breath, and she remembers, with relief, that a Ugandan 'special taxi' does not mean a specially expensive one, but merely a taxi for one person, as opposed to ordinary taxis, which hold lots of people, vegetables, chickens. Her driver's name is Isaac. He has bright, dark eyes, an American t-shirt, cut-off trousers. At first, Vanessa thinks he looks sweet.

Urgently instructed by the Sheraton woman in their own language, Isaac begins a headlong, hooting dash for Kampala, apparently taking the straightest line no matter what bends there are in the road. He claims she has interrupted his breakfast, which he had been about to eat at the airport. 'Ah, sorry,' Vanessa says, and realises she is accidentally mimicking the caring intonation of the Sheraton employee.

'Of course, I did not mind missing it, you must not be late for your appointment,' he says, with eager, reproachful virtue, and accelerates to show his keenness, jerking erratically through grinding gears. 'Luckily, I am a fast, safe driver. This is not my car, but I can drive it.'

Soon he 'wonders', as he drives at breakneck speed, whether she will buy him breakfast in Kampala? He smiles so sweetly, and she is so surprised, that she hears herself agreeing, and at once regrets it.

Before long she finds Isaac has one obsession. He does not like Museveni; Museveni's family, even less. He thinks Museveni's family is ruining Uganda. He is driven to heights of irony if anything remotely connected to politics comes up, and sometimes when there's no connection at all. At first she does not understand his scoffing asides about 'the First Family'.

'There seem to be fewer trees than before.'

'Yes, they are being cut down for firewood. The First Family must have money.'

'Is the new shopping centre finished, at Garden City?'

'Of course! First Family must shop somewhere.'

'I'm a little worried about mosquitoes,' she says, to change the subject, but also to explain why she is rubbing herself with cream from the shameful plastic bag of unguents.

'Madam, do not worry about the mosquitoes,' he says, turning to look into her eyes so an oncoming bus bearing the slogan GOD SAVES almost hits them, and Vanessa sees the frightened face of its driver. 'There is no malaria in Kampala.'

'People always told me that before,' says Vanessa. 'But all the Ugandans I met had had malaria. Have you had malaria?'

He shrugs. 'Of course. But the *bazungu* do not get it. And the rain will wash away the mosquitoes.'

'I thought mosquitoes liked water? I'm sure they do.'

But he looks sulky, and ignores her. Perhaps he knows his epidemiology is sketchy. Or else he wants to fob her off with nonsense. She grips the seatbelt hard with both hands as he honks oncoming traffic out of their path.

Bip-bip-bip-BEEEYUP! Pip-pip-pip-pip-B-A-A-A-R-P! It is a fanfare of arrival. A famous writer is in Kampala!

'Are you ready for CHOGM?' huge billboards inquire, or more defiantly, 'Uganda is ready for CHOGM'. By the side of the road, red earth, low shacks, rather fewer of them than she remembers, but a lot of brick building is going on. 'Is this building work for CHOGM?' she inquires.

'Everything is for First Family.'

She had forgotten how enchanting the children are. Small troops of them, single-file, leap neatly off the road and back again as they thunder past. 'I love your school uniforms, so smart,' she says.

'Of course you like them, they are British,' Isaac says. He seems less polite than when she first embarked, as if she's broken some pact by disagreeing with him, although the subject of dispute was only mosquitoes.

'Our children would refuse to wear them,' says Vanessa, stung by the idea that she is typically British. 'Actually I like Ugandan things.'

He seems to snicker to himself, and she feels insulted, but of course he is just young. She tells herself she must not take against him. He is not so much older than her son Justin.

She spots a big pile of what must be charcoal. So that's where some of the trees have gone. But some remain; lush date palms, pineapples, and are those ...? 'Are they *matooke*?' she asks, proud to deploy a local word.

'Obviously they are bananas,' he says, smiles sideways annoyingly, and just misses a lorry.

'It doesn't matter, *please* watch the road.'

But the nearer they come to Kampala, the less he can do anything but join the great clunky jam of white metal public taxis, and they slow to a heaving, parp-parp-ing halt. And now they are in the Kampala Vanessa remembers. The roadside is a seething mass of stalls and sellers, going back as far as the eye can see, with hand-painted signs whose cheerful ambition flares gallantly over tiny box-sized shops: WISE AFRICAN AIDS RESEARCH CENTRE; MAAMA SOPHIA GENERAL MERCHANDISE.

'I love all this. It's so *interesting*,' she says, good humour coming back. 'What is this district called?'

'It is Nateete Market,' the driver answers. 'The government has sold it, because of CHOGM. Soon we will have a modern market!'

'Is this a good thing?'

'Of course. Except the market traders do not think so, or the customers. Profits will go to the First Family.'

Now Vanessa's hips are starting to ache, and she's bored with the First Family, and the red dust is blowing in through the window, slipping grainily under her contact lenses. It *is* exciting, but she wants to sleep, or eat, or do anything except keep travelling.

It is a huge relief when the Sheraton guards raise the red-and-white-striped pole to let them in. They sweep down the drive through the Sheraton gardens, gold-jacketed men salute their arrival, the driver unloads Vanessa's cases, and they march through the arch of the metal detector, which blares shrilly, but the armed guard waves them through: she's a middle-aged white woman, she can't be a terrorist.

And Isaac? Oh, he's just her driver. They barely look at him. All the guests have one.

Vanessa is keen to pay him off: 15 dollars, as agreed, plus a tip of 4,000 Ugandan shillings, about 2 dollars, which is more than 10 per cent, and uses nearly all the currency she'd saved from her last trip to Uganda. But Isaac still lingers, as if expecting more. 'That should cover you for something to eat,' she urges. Isaac looks at the floor, and says, 'It is OK,' but his body language implies that it isn't. (Yet he's hardly going to eat at the Sheraton, is he, where breakfast would cost five times as much!) Her own mouth waters in anticipation. Golden fried potatoes, eggs, steak, smooth terraces of mango, watermelon, pineapple, glistening on enormous china dishes. Sheraton breakfasts are an event!

The back of his red t-shirt and Harlem-style cut-offs look suddenly poor as he crosses the bright foyer. Has she done right? But of course she has. She has been more than fair. She dismisses it.

The receptionists stand like gleaming statues in a gold-clad row behind the long desk. Poor things, thinks Vanessa, why can't they sit down?

On the other hand, why doesn't someone help her with her cases?

Now, at once. Is she invisible?

Somebody does. He is old, and smiles a lot. His eyes look damp, as if they are melting. She'd forgotten how black Ugandans are. Or is she unnaturally pale? In the mirrored lift, the contrast is startling. As they fly upwards, he smiles some more, and Vanessa begins to find it oppressive. 'So sorry I can't give you a tip,' she says, with emphasis, to be sure he understands. 'I have only large dollar notes.' 'Dollar notes,' he nods eagerly, but then his smile fades as her apologetic hand signals get through. 'It's OK,' he says. It's another disappointment. But with kindness, and good manners, he smiles at her again. Then he wheels the great case right into the room. 'Thank you,' she says, and changing her mind, she gives him her few remaining Ugandan shillings.

And the room? It's fine. An enormous bed (how long is it, she wonders, since I shared a bed? Will anyone, ever, share my bed again?) – an emperor-size bed, with snow-white linen. One whole wall of her room is window, with a view over the lush Sheraton gardens – rows of palms, pink and purple blossom – and behind them, skyscrapers selling insurance, traffic jams, smoke, half-built buildings, and the hills she remembers, Kampala's green hills – though there are definitely more new red roofs, marching out from the centre into low hazy cloud, stretching away into the distance.

Yes, she is here. In Africa. Vanessa can't wait to get acclimatised. Unlike most white people (she tells herself) she is not afraid to go out on foot. She will just lie down and relax for a second ... Then she will have breakfast, and go and meet the natives!

It's 9.15 AM. But when she wakes again, breakfast is over. It's nearly lunchtime.

(If Vanessa had in fact gone down at 9.15, she would have met a native, the Executive Housekeeper, who had just popped down for a word with Front Office. Mary Tendo would have been as amazed as Vanessa. And both women would have laughed and hugged, and Vanessa would have cried, though Mary Tendo wouldn't, and our story would have untangled in a flash. Instead, Vanessa slept like a baby, and Mary sang as she got back to her office and spotted an email from Trevor in her inbox.)

7

Vanessa has a whole free afternoon. The conference doesn't start till tomorrow. She drinks the two complimentary bottles of water she finds by her bedside down in one. Then she lets the shower run and run. Beautiful, African hot water, in the walk-in shower with its faux-stone facings. It's a sensual thing. Yes, she is sensual. She congratulates herself on still being sensual. Reluctantly, she turns off the tap.

Then it's time to look around Kampala. Of course she mustn't appear too wealthy, but nor must she be scruffy, for Ugandans, she remembers, are very smart people. She settles on multi-pocketed beige trousers, good for carrying a few Ugandan thousand-shilling notes, once she's changed some money down in the foyer. The trousers are meant for the trip to Bwindi, but she feels like getting in the African swing. She adds a crisp white shirt, a neat beige jacket and her safari boots, which she needs to break in, necessitating slightly hot woollen socks. OK, the label of the boots says 'Lake District', but Kampala and Cumbria have lakes in common.

She's halfway down the landing when she remembers her phone, and goes back for that. Ditto camera: sun cream: insect repellent: map. Two minutes later, she returns for her notebook, and remembers she lost her pen on the plane, which involves a ten-minute search for another. She's shooting down in the lift, they have reached

Ground Floor, the doors open, and without warning Mary Tendo strolls by at a leisurely pace with a message for her colleague Patrick in Reception – oh look, Vanessa, please look up!

But Vanessa, realising she hasn't got her sunhat, is peering at the button for '8th Floor', and gliding back up again, feeling foolish. And down again, to change her money. And up again, to stash the surplus in her safe. Eventually she is down for good.

Her first intention is to try and contact Mary, for Reception will have a more current number for the elusive Nile Imperial Hotel, but the line of golden statues are all bent to their work, dealing with a host of pale- or red-faced guests who are holding out their wafer-thin laptops towards them like supplicants at a long altar, complaining with agitated, dwindling politeness that the hotel internet is down *again*. She waits for a second, and then gives up. There will be time this evening, or tomorrow.

'Taxi?' the porters outside offer, but she repels them with a stern smile. She isn't a tourist, she's practically Ugandan. The cloud has lifted into a white story-book castle, and the sun beats down, glorious, implacable. Vanessa sometimes thinks of herself as cold-blooded, needing extra blankets and hot-water bottles, but now she thrills to the warm sun on her cheek, the moist rich smell of hot broad-leaved grass, hibiscus bushes, and blowing from the road, petrol, dust. So ... African! She strides past the armed guards in their navy uniforms and leaves the enclave of the Sheraton.

At once there is a choice between walking in the road and trying the bank of red mud beside it. It's crowded: a man tries to sell her an *Economist*; two boys offer taxis; here's her first beggar, but she shakes her head firmly and marches forward, trying to look as if she knows exactly where she's going, and she does remember this big roundabout, with people selling nuts and sweets and MTN phone cards, though she doesn't have a clue which road to take off it. She plumps for sharp left. Nile Avenue.

It's a dual carriage-way, at first, with a green swathe of grass and trees down the middle (and she suddenly remembers five years ago, her first trip to Kampala. On that same long green runway, the shock of discovering, early in the morning, a family from the country, the adults swathed in bright cloth, who had clearly slept there. They were stretching in the sunlight. Small hills of rag bundles. Two young children were naked. The dirty urban taxis swept past on either side of them. Vanessa, a white woman, had paused to look, and they stood staring at each other, framed, trapped and bemused by the twenty-first century.)

But Vanessa has been told that Kampala has changed. Five years is a lot in a developing country, and Kampala is getting ready for CHOGM.

And then she wonders, has she changed?

Surely she is humbler? She thinks she is. And yet, her career's gone from strength to strength. This time she's invited in a different capacity, not just as a teacher but as a writer, a Featured Writer on an International Programme (yes, she was asked a little late, but that just showed people were disorganised). Which proves her reputation is growing, the reputation of the two literary novels she wrote a while ago in the 1980s, which received wonderful reviews. The sales, of course, were not all that great, because the publisher was inefficient, but the critical raves were emblazoned on the paperback, and still sustain her when she's low: 'Henman's ambitions are great ... praiseworthy.' *The Times*. 'A brave attempt ... literary innovation ... to be encouraged.' *Independent on Sunday*. Vanessa knows them both by heart.

(She has forgotten the full text of *The Times*. 'Even though she does not always succeed, Henman's ambitions are great. Granted, the prose is overworked. But in the dismally dull landscape of today's fiction, her stylistic flights can seem almost praiseworthy.' While the *Independent on Sunday* called *My Pale Ark* 'A courageous attempt at poetic prose. Though the author of this ambitious second novel has no insight into her own characters, she makes a brave stab at literary innovation. Her efforts to escape her own limitations are, surely, to be encouraged.'

On the weekend these reviews appeared, Vanessa had rung her friend Fifi in tears. Fifi promised to read them and ring her back. 'Darling, I scoured the shops until I found them. I don't see what you're complaining about. For a start they both say how ambitious you are, and for a second, that photo is at least ten years old. It's very flattering, honestly.'

'Do you think so?' Vanessa was cautiously encouraged, though 'flattering' wasn't quite the right adjective – Fifi was not very good with words. 'Well, it's interesting to hear the view of a non-literary person, as it were.'

'I am a great reader,' Fifi had said, hurt. 'You never asked *me* what I thought of your novel.'

'OK, what did you think of my novel?'

There was a long silence. Fifi knew this was important. 'I think I agree with the reviewers.' Then Vanessa felt happy, and rang off, reassured.

Soon, in her mind, the book was a triumph.)

Five years ago, many things were different. Justin had never been depressed: he was happy and successful, just out of university. Five years ago she would never have believed that her son would go to bed for six months, would stop talking to her, and washing, and reading – in a house that was full of wonderful books! He had lost his job, which was not wholly his fault, then his love life went wrong, and he had just given up. Which Vanessa could not bear, of course, since determination was her strong suit, it had carried her out of that pathetic little village, had brought her to London, had made her a writer. Perhaps Justin takes after Trevor, who is perfectly content to remain a plumber. Vanessa knows she has been a good mother – no-one could care more, or try harder, than her – and yet for some reason, her son had failed her. (But she mustn't think like that. She herself isn't perfect. She has learned some hard truths about herself, through all this.) It hurt when Justin started asking for Mary. 'I just want Mary. Get me Mary.' But by that time he was naked and semi-incontinent, and Vanessa would have done anything. She had managed to track Mary down in Uganda, though nothing had been easy, far from it. A *great* deal of money had changed hands, and Mary eventually came back to London, quite a different person from the sweet young girl they had known before.

Yes, there had been a certain amount of tension. Occasionally she'd felt a little excluded, for Mary and Justin became very close. And Mary got on very well with Trevor, who despite the divorce, liked to hang around the house, tinkering and pottering as men do (and to be fair, Tigger was sometimes useful). Vanessa was mature enough not to be jealous. And with hindsight, Mary had been perfectly right, she could not really be expected still to do their cleaning. Indeed she had more or less taken charge. Everything had changed, their diet, their routine, until slowly, Justin got back on his feet. Mary was something of a power-house, and Vanessa had tried to appreciate that. As a feminist, she naturally approved of strong women, but two in one house wasn't always easy. Perhaps she was relieved when Mary went home, but the two of them had become firm friends, a friendship that will last to the end of their lives, she suddenly thinks, with a rush of emotion – *We'll always be grateful to one another.*

It was true they had got somewhat out of touch.

The problem was distance, and poor communication. If the British Council had invited her earlier, Vanessa would have been sure to contact Mary before she left the country, but as it was, though she had emailed Mary several times at the Nile Imperial Hotel, they had bounced back, and the phone number was wrong, giving a constant 'unobtainable'. Vanessa isn't worried; she is used to Uganda. She will track down Mary in person, instead, and it will all be a wonderful surprise. She will ask her to supper at the Sheraton; Vanessa imagines this with a warm glow. She doubts whether her friend has ever been there. She will find the Piano Bar quite impressive.

Yet doubt wriggles somewhere like a wire worm as she strides, lost in thought, on and on down Nile Avenue, not getting anywhere, dazzled by the sun, blinking it to blackness, the beginning of a headache. How much, really, does she know about this country, or even (she dismisses this thought) about Mary?

They are such good friends, but ...

What if I can't find her?

Uganda suddenly seems big and – dark around the edges, which shade into war zones, Sudan, Congo ... Why on earth is she planning to drive to Bwindi when she can't seem to find her way around Kampala?

8

Vanessa has been walking at quite a lick, not really noticing where she is going. The road has got rougher, and the traffic heavier, probably because this is Kampala's lunch-hour. She suddenly notices how hot she is. The sun beats down through the cotton of her hat. The dust gets under her contact lenses and dries the lining of her nose, which itches, there is sweat trickling under the neck of her jacket and her feet in thick socks feel like over-swaddled babies. The left heel is just beginning to rub. The light is fiercely bright, yet her sunglasses seem to make it harder to see. Perhaps there is sun cream on the lens.

Workmen loom in front of her, digging up the road. She can't veer left, where paving-stones are piled, and she daren't go right, into the traffic. She believes she is heading for Kampala Road, the main highway of the city, with banks and cafés, but this road seems to go on for ever, and no-one is walking here, not even Ugandans. And now the navy-clad workmen are shouting at her, but she doesn't understand what they are saying.

'Kampala Road?' she inquires, slowly and clearly, but they are shaking their heads, and pointing behind her. 'English!' one of them shouts, unhelpfully, and yet they don't appear to speak English. Now they are laughing, which she doesn't like. She is not against people having a laugh – her ex, Trevor, is a terrible tease, and he has explained it's a sign of affection – but nobody enjoys it when they can't get the joke. She stops, firmly, in the middle of the workmen, and pulls the map out of her trouser pocket. She points to the long streak of Kampala Road. 'Kampala Road. Nando's,' she says. To her delight she has remembered the name of a restaurant, though she can't be sure these workmen would eat there. It's a Ugandan place, not like English Nando's, but perhaps it isn't entirely authentic. 'English, Kampala,' the loudest one says, and once again, they laugh a lot. 'QUEEN!' he shouts, and they laugh even more. 'Queen is coming!' They don't look at the map. Some of them give the thumbs-up, and smile at her, though a young one looks down darkly, and mutters. The general atmosphere is slightly too lively, and she isn't there for their entertainment, though of course she loves Ugandan *joie de vivre*.

In the end she has to retrace her footsteps, and the heat beats down much harder than before. She finds she is tired – probably from flying. She gazes at her feet, so as not to trip up. There is suddenly a presence in front of her. And then she realises it isn't human. A stork has landed on the empty stretch of pavement. It is looking at her, from nine feet away. She stands motionless: they stare at each other, and then it begins to pace in her direction, grey and gangly, harshly protuberant.

It has a long, sharp beak, a dirty flesh colour, and a long wrinkled gizzard, like a stretched scrotum, and two long white stick legs, with little cartoon knees, neat bumps from which the legs swing forward with great delicacy, bringing down stretched claws upon the pavement like a stately woman walking in high heels, though in other respects it is fiercely masculine, wearing its hunched black wings like an academic gown, and its hanging gizzard like a mayoral chain. Its eyes are large and bright. It is coming towards her. As it does so, it shits, profusely, on the pavement. It is very large. Vanessa's paralysed. There aren't any other human beings around, and this stork seems to know it owns the road. 'Go away,' she says quietly, then more shrilly,

'Shoo!' It opens its great razors of beak, and laughs. But it pauses, too. They both stare at each other. It looks supremely intelligent. She veers into the road and walks gingerly around it, hoping it won't suddenly dart its neck out and spear her. A Japanese jeep tries not to kill her. Once she is ten feet past, she turns and stares back at it. The stork carries on, impervious, well-sprung. It seems to be saying, 'You don't belong here.'

'The storks are so weird!' she writes in her Sheraton postcard to Fifi, sitting in the window of Nando's at last, gulping down bottled water and the lukewarm buffet. 'That thing could have eaten Mimi for breakfast!' Too late she thinks, that wasn't tactful, for Mimi is Fifi's child substitute, an adored and pampered Siamese cat, neutered, of course, and becoming fat, though Fifi feeds it an organic diet. 'I am getting acclimatised, and seeing friends.' That isn't quite true, but soon she'll meet Mary. She and Fifi have written books about Pilates together, a successful series called *The Long Lean Line*, but Fifi does occasionally take her for granted. (It has never ceased to rankle with Vanessa that the books used Fifi for ALL the photographs, though she, Vanessa, was very little older, and could perfectly well have demonstrated some postures. It was a point she had expected Fifi to take up with the publisher, but Fifi just said, 'Well I *am* the Pilates teacher.' 'But I am the writer,' Vanessa had said. 'In general, books use photographs of the author.') In any case, they had got over that quarrel, and now Fifi thinks she is Vanessa's best friend, though Vanessa naturally has reservations ... Poor Fifi! She is hardly an intellectual. 'Love from Vanessa in up-town Kampala.' That ought to make Fifi slightly jealous.

The waiter is hovering beside her. Vanessa realises that she has demolished a huge plate of starchy potatoes and plantain, cassava, chicken and pink groundnut sauce. (How Mary would have approved of that! Her mission in London was to feed them fibre. The loo was constantly in use.) The bill is 18,000 Ugandan shillings. She offers him both her 10,000 shilling notes.

Wind blows through the window like a whirling dervish and nearly snatches the money away. Paper napkins start flying around the room. Outside the window, it's suddenly dark. She peers out and sees that the storybook clouds have bellied blackly up over the sun. The leisurely walk of the people on the pavement has turned to a trot: almost a run. There's a clap of thunder. Oh dear. Among all the kit she has brought with her, she did not manage to include her umbrella. She can't leave the restaurant until the storm is over. 'Bring me some tea,' she tells the waiter. The room lights up, livid: then another crash. The rain begins, slow and determined, and the waiter brings her tea with hot milk, and is not happy when she sends it back. 'Black tea, cold milk, English-style,' she says, slowly and with emphasis. Why can't they ever get tea right?

Mary Tendo is running down William Street with a stately, pounding rhythm. She is slightly annoyed; she does not like to run, and her shoes do not lend themselves to running, but her lunch break is only half an hour long, and she knows that in two minutes the skies will open, and she has to meet Charles at Owino Market. Because, very soon, Trevor will arrive, and she cannot put him in a room without curtains. He will be sleeping in the maid's room, which is a cosy side-part to the kitchen, and Mercy will sleep in the lean-to at the back. So Mary's friend Mirembe (who has a stall in the market) has been told to look out for some English curtains. 'I would like velvet, that soft warm stuff,' Mary Tendo has instructed, because Vanessa's house had red velvet curtains, so Trevor will feel at home with them. Mercy will remake them to fit the window, using Mary's sewing-machine.

Owino Market, below Kampala Road, near the taxi-park, where tourists are advised not to go. It's the largest market in Uganda, with the most people thronging to buy, hundreds of thousands of them every day, though the paths between the stalls are only two or three feet wide, and this lunch-time, mixed heaps of garbage are getting pounded by the rain, glistening fruit skins, fish-heads, bones, and the lanes are rapidly becoming near-impassable as buyers crowd to shelter under broken bits of roof, but Mary is made of sterner stuff, and presses on past them, uttering threats at a scoundrel trying to sell her a broken umbrella.

The umbrella man wonders, is she a demon? Flashes of lightning make her eyes gleam yellow and her hair almost electric, oily bright. Her limbs move like pistons, unstoppable. The rain gets heavier, and sheltering people are curious to see her press onwards, onwards down the dirty furrow. What is she looking for, peering out under the black imitation-leather Sheraton folder she is now using as a rain-hat?

'*Mama wange jangu wano ogule ebyabazungu. Anti bafa dda*! Hey, Mama. Buy very nice dead woman's dress!' Mary ignores the impudent woman. Being called 'Mama' hurts her heart. What good is a Mama without a son? Then the woman recognises Mary's uniform. 'Ey-ey, Sheraton! Millionaire-y!'

It is true, getting spotted and darkened by the rain are dead people's clothes, and unwanted clothes, and worn-out clothes, as well as very smart, nearly-new clothes with British charity shop price-tags still on them (Mary thinks, I will pick some gifts for the village). Here there are shoes in every condition, men's and women's, children's and babies', all of them shaped by the bones of distant feet, and now slicked and polished with rainwater; suit jackets without trousers, suit trousers without jackets, a thousand garments that have lost their owners, party dresses from long-finished parties. Most of it is western, not African. They have been cast off, perhaps by several owners, and shipped from richer countries in 40-foot containers, then fought over in Customs where the best has been stolen. The remnants are now scattered across tiny stalls not much bigger than an

English dressing-table. The African clothes are the most expensive, in larger, superior stalls of their own. 'Encore Fashions', 'De Luxe Shopping Mall'. Mary, however, thinks their prices a racket, and kisses her teeth at some brand-new *gomesis* which are selling for over 100,000 Ugandan shillings.

Charles, her *kabite*, is very generous (though sometimes he has made small mistakes with money). Last month he had offered to buy Mary a beautiful *gomesi* for a marriage introduction they were attending, but Mary is cynical about 'customary' marriage, which makes the young men spend far too much money, and does not see the point of traditional dress, and does not want Charles to get in trouble with his bank.

'Charles!' She has spotted him. His dear narrow shoulders, his handsome curved nose, his big healthy smile, with straight milk-white teeth. OK he is not quite so tall as she is, but he is smart, very smart, in his pin-stripe suit, with perfectly matched trousers and jacket. He is chatting politely to her friend Mirembe, pressed close to her under the corrugated roof, but his face lights up when he hears her voice, and he comes across at once and takes Mary's hand.

'Hallo, honey,' he says. 'Did you get wet? Mirembe has got very nice curtains for us.'

Mary looks judicious, and refrains from smiling, partly because Charles was talking to a woman, but also withholding the balm of her approval until she has seen the merchandise. Mirembe pushes it forwards, a pile of soft orange, the colour of sunlight at the end of the day. 'Ey,' says Mary, non-committal, but it is hard to stop herself smiling a little. She likes them better than Vanessa's red curtains. 'Very nice,' she says, 'but they are worn, here. And here. Look. They are a little old.'

'Very good curtains, extra quality.' Mirembe is used to Mary's bargaining. 'If you do not like them, I will keep them for myself. But your sweetheart will be sorry.' In less than two minutes, they agree a price, and both of the women feel they have won. The drumming of rain on the tin roof is getting less.

On her headlong dash back to William Street, Mary buys six second-hand men's shirts, four pairs of trousers, two pairs of men's shoes (one black, one brown), a selection of t-shirts, and a nearly-new grey nylon zipped jacket for her uncle, and piles them all neatly on top of the curtains, so Charles can carry it all to his car. The rain has stopped, but the street runs red water. Charles says goodbye to her and picks his way delicately down the crowded pavement, manoeuvring a pile almost as large as he is, anxious not to drop anything. Their shopping trip has been faster than expected, and Mary's not quite late for the hotel, so she watches him fondly till he's almost out of sight, and the sun comes out and lights up the fat bundle of orange velvet protruding on both sides of his slim striped back. He is a very sweet man, she thinks, good at fetching and carrying despite his small size. But somehow she must stop him being jealous of Trevor. Jealousy in a sweetheart is a very bad trait. She must also stop him talking to other women.

The man Charles is not to be jealous of, Trevor, is talking to his on-off Iranian girlfriend in London. She is off, really. They both know it. They have tried to love each other, given up. His reading, when she wants them to go out, annoys her: 'What is point, Trevor? Always reading books.'

Soraya's charming, fractured English no longer charms him. Nor her youth, which merely makes him feel old: besides, at 32, she's aware of time passing. She's accusing him of being 'unavailable', a word she picked up from an American TV talk show about Men Who Cannot Love. 'Unveilable?' he asks her, puzzled. 'You came here to get away from the veil.'

'You make always stupid joke, Trevor.'

'No, really – oh, I see! UNAVAILABLE.'

'You correct always my English, Trevor!' And with that she bursts into tears again, and says, between sobs, 'You never, never marry me, either. I am not joke. I am art teacher. *AN* art teacher. I am good at job – good at MY job. Do not correct. I come here four years ago and learn everything, English from start-up. And make myself something. But to you I am nothing.'

'Remember I've done this marrying lark before. I was hopeless at it, so Vanessa tells me. And how many times have you called me hopeless? I'm not rich enough. Nor young enough. Look, I'm boring, to you, But I like being boring. You need a nice, rich young genius. Someone like Damien Hirst, Soraya. And he could give you that skull full of jewels.'

Resignedly, she nods, and cries again. 'But is not genius, Damien Hirst. Only genius at making money. You are nice man, Trevor. Nice man. Sorry.'

He knows she needs British citizenship, but even when they were first together – he likes to please, but he can't go that far. 'You're a lovely girl, Soraya. Someone will marry you.'

'Yes. Is obvious.' He's hurt her pride. 'Now you must leave, Trevor, I am busy. Go please, now. I must prepare my class.'

So he leaves in a hurry, and forgets, in the bedroom, a postcard to Vanessa, in an envelope he has addressed, but not stamped, telling her that he is off to Uganda. Mary had instructed him to keep it a secret, so he's compromised by letting Vanessa know too late for her to ask to join him.

'SURPRISE!' is how the postcard begins. Justin, who is looking after the house, would have found it on the mat and let his mother know, only Trevor's ex-girlfriend will never post it, because she is too miffed to pay for the stamp. She nearly does it: Trevor nearly loved her: she nearly loved him; in the end, she doesn't. A door slams hard. Tears must fall. But for Trevor, as he packs for his trip to Kampala, another door opens, and after the storm, the air is fresh, washed bright by the rain, and the road stretches away into the past and the future.

All over Kampala, water is singing as it finds its way down the seven green hills. Vanessa has enjoyed her bird's eye view, from Nando's high windows, of the rainstorm, and the river of taxis, choked, stalled. So fortunate she didn't get caught in it. She feels this trip is going to be lucky. She wanders out into the street, nearly falling head first over the slender rope that divides Nando's forecourt from the world outside. The sun in her eyes is dazzling. A host of motorbike men descend on her. '*Boda-boda*?' 'Cheap, English!' 'How are you?' 'Taxi?' She walks determinedly away, but not before she's noticed that Kampalan men spend a lot of time picking and pulling at their noses, and shifting their genitals in the heat; all sticky body-parts need unsticking.

And suddenly, Vanessa is stumped. She can't remember how she came, and she can't remember how to get back. Was it Kimathi Avenue? Colville Road? She doesn't want to stand here, staring at her map, a target for every Ugandan robber (though of course, she reminds herself, with an effort, it's safer than London, she always says so). And though her eyes have always been particularly good, at least when she has her lenses in, she cannot deny that in recent months the small print has started to swim out of focus.

Find Kampala Road, she thinks, and I'll be fine. It's the biggest, busiest thoroughfare in Kampala, dividing the city roughly in two, with the rich above, and the poor below. I'll go back to Kampala Road, no problem. She heads back to the heart of the roaring and hooting; finds the main road; and sets off once again. The amazing concertina of taxis starts up, blaring and squeezing, going nowhere. Most have flamboyant personalised banners above the windscreens, to shield the drivers' eyes from the sun. 'LIVERPOOL', 'MAN UNITED'.

She is suddenly drenched up to her ankle as she plunges her boot into a pouring gutter. 'PRAY JESUS', a red metallic banner warns her. She doesn't quite recall this stretch of the road, which is veering left, and surely sloping downwards, and there are fewer banks and insurance buildings, the structures becoming smaller and humbler. And what is this massive parking lot? Something whirring and dark darts across her face, making her start as it tickles her skin: an enormous dragonfly: she stops, shaken, and a well-dressed young man is at her side.

'Hallo again, Madam. Good morning. You remember me? How are you today. Are you fine?'

She looks at him blankly. His smile is heartwarming, meltingly sincere, beamed straight at her. Of course, it must be an African writer. Perhaps she met him last time she was here, or he has recognised her from her book-jacket. 'I'm awfully sorry, I don't remember –'

His shirt is very white, his suit immaculate. 'I am your friend, John. We were together only yesterday. I wonder if you can help me?'

Vanessa's mood changes. Not an African writer. She doesn't know a Ugandan called John. Her bright pavilion crumbles away, recognition, fame, book-jacket photos. 'Yesterday? No, I only just arrived ... I wasn't here yesterday. I don't know you.'

His smile contracts, and with a little desperation he says, 'But Madam,' but she's hurried past him, and he only follows her a few paces, then falls away.

She is walking fast to leave the conman behind her, and she sees a roundabout ahead of her, and her heel is rubbing now, distinctly, sharply, and she hopes that there were no germs in the rainwater that drenched that boot, for the skin must be broken. And at that moment, with a lurch of her heart, she realises she's walking in the wrong direction, she's on Jinja Road now, heading out of the city, towards the slums and the charcoal smoke. She must have turned left down Kampala Road, when for the Sheraton, she should have turned right. Don't panic, she tells herself. You haven't gone far. But the sun beats down, and her foot is really hurting, and she finds, as she bends to loosen her boot, that she is a little dizzy, and sweating. It must be the malaria medication. She needs a drink of water. She wants to sit down.

It doesn't matter: get a private taxi back. But she hasn't got enough for a private taxi. Ah well, it won't kill her to catch a public one, which will only cost a few hundred shillings. She did it once or twice four years ago (though it was an ordeal. A man was coughing horribly – she did not want to catch TB in Kampala – and someone's scurfy chicken had pecked her ankle. Still this is Africa, and Vanessa is game, and besides, she is already imagining the arrival of the other British writers, and how she will tell them, 'Ah well, of course, I whip around the city by *matatu*. Though strictly speaking, only Kenyans call it that!')

She crosses the road, limping between onrushing vehicles, who honk furiously but veer to avoid her, and stops the first careering public taxi that rushes past in an uphill direction, with its conductor leaning out, touting for trade. 'Sheraton?' she asks, timidly, and he yanks her aboard, saying, 'Hallo, English.' A demure middle-aged woman in green traditional dress with a basket on her lap looks gravely at her and shifts across the seat, which yaws perilously from side to side, to let Vanessa sit next to her. The back seats of the van are full to bursting. No other white people, of course. At the next stop, three people push in beside Vanessa, who is now wedged solid, clutching her bag and constantly feeling, without success, for the reassuring shape of her mobile phone. Has she gone too far? Or not far enough? Her blistered foot has begun to throb. The dust blows in through the window, but she can't move to find her sunglasses.

They are turning off the main road, she realises, moving downhill, she knows not where. 'Please,' she says 'excuse me,' to her neighbour, who turns a kindly face upon her, 'Sheraton? Sheraton Hotel?'

The woman looks puzzled, and starts a lively conversation with the seat behind, who all stare at Vanessa. 'Sheraton-y' is the only word she understands. Then a young man in a jacket and tie says, 'You shall go to the taxi-park, then you can find another taxi in Sheraton direction.' General agreement, though Vanessa's middle-aged neighbour seems to shake her head.

Then Vanessa remembers. The taxi-park. Where tourists are told they must never go. Near the notorious Owino Market. Both of them haunts of conmen and robbers.

Mary's *kabite*, Charles, has locked all Mary's purchases in the boot of his beloved red saloon, and then he has a nice idea. How busy Mary is, and how tired she sometimes looks. And soon she is going away to her village, with this English Trevor, who he has not met. Mary has explained (and Charles completely trusts her, and not only because once, when he became a little jealous, Mary poured away his beer, and went to sleep with the maid) that this Trevor is quite old, and not particularly handsome, and is just a friend who can do something for the village. But all the same, Charles remembers Mary telling him she always liked Trevor, even when she was very young, and worked in England as a cleaner.

He has asked Mary about him, taking care to be subtle. 'And so Trevor is no longer married to Vanessa?'

'He has not been married to Vanessa for twenty years.'

'Ah, that is good.'

'Why is it good?'

'Because she will not miss him while he is in Uganda.'

'Actually I think perhaps she will miss him, because he does all the work in her house, even though he has a new, attractive girlfriend.'

'He has an attractive girlfriend, even though he is ugly?'

'I did not say that he is ugly. I only said that he is not very handsome. He is a nice man, and you need not be jealous.' And Mary had come over and rubbed Charles's neck, which she knows he likes, but sometimes forgets. 'But I never understood why he married Vanessa.'

'Perhaps you should have asked Vanessa to Uganda also.'

Then Mary became a little impatient, because she wanted to read her *Monitor* newspaper, which tells the truth, unlike *New Vision*. 'If she comes to Uganda, there will be nothing but problems. But Trevor is practical, and will mend the well. And you, dear, know nothing about Vanessa, because until now you have not met her, and if you had, you would not suggest it.'

For a while, Charles had let her read in silence. But she looked so pretty, sitting under the electric light-bulb, with a lovely sheen on her oily skin and the light bouncing off her curving bosoms, that he said, once again, in a casual tone, 'And yet, Mary, Vanessa is rich. Indeed I think she is richer than Trevor. It was Vanessa's house that we stayed in, in London, at Christmas, when she was away in her English village, and we had a nice bed, and a large television, and we had French champagne, even if it was old. And perhaps Vanessa could bring money for your village.'

'Vanessa would bring nothing but trouble for the village. And nothing but trouble for poor Trevor.' And then Mary had shut her mouth very firmly, in a way that Charles knew meant 'Discussion over'. And she had not talked to him until bedtime.

Which is why, today, Charles had offered, in his lunch break from Miracle Micro-Finance, to meet Mary at Owino Market and help with the curtains. But still he is not quite sure she is happy. And so he decides to go to Eat It! Bakery, and buy her her favourite ginger cake.

Vanessa swallows nervously: this is it. The taxi-park is a deep, noisy pit of metal. No-one can get in, no-one can get out. About a hundred identical dirty white Toyota vans are blocking the entrances and exits, and the drivers greet and insult each other at full volume through the open windows, and the fumes are thick and bitter, choking Vanessa, though none of the other passengers coughs and gasps. After hours of short, abortive, jolting manoeuvres, the taxi finally lurches to a halt, packed in side by side with its brother tin-cans. Vanessa's hands tremble slightly as she clutches her possessions and slides along the seat, ready to get out. But the woman beside her in the green *gomesi* takes her arm – Vanessa jumps, and then feels ashamed, because of course she doesn't distrust Ugandans – and says, in surprisingly good English, 'You can wait at my side. I am going further, in this taxi, after half an hour. I will tell you when the right taxi is coming. This area is not good for you.' She looks at her kindly, and then falls quiet, takes a Bible from her bag, and begins to read it. Vanessa settles back, grateful for the Bible. It's nice to have Christians about when you need them! Though of course she takes pride in being an agnostic.

As soon as most of the passengers have poured out of the van, half a dozen street sellers pile in in their place. They are mostly children, but there's one sullen young man. Vanessa is the whole focus of their selling. '*Muzungu, muzungu!*' they shrill at her. 'Soda, sweets, cigarette-y!' She tries fruitlessly to avoid their eyes, which are pleading, but she feels that the atmosphere in the taxi, with its remaining four or five passengers, is turning against her, as she sits mute and charmless, clutching her bag with its pathetic remaining shillings, failing to perform her rich woman's duty. No, she *must* buy something. Tentatively, she buys one boiled sweet, a hideous bright raspberry, and after a fearful scrabble in her pocket, hands over her last hundred-shilling coin, but the move is rewarded with a disapproving murmur, and she can't face the sweet, which she drops in her bag. Now the sullen youth presses too close to her, waving his packs of roasted nuts right under her nose. 'G-nuts packed by

Christian Family', it says. This time the Christian element is less welcome. He is saying something rude in his own language, and someone laughs harshly at the back of the taxi, and her legs are sticking to the plastic of the seat.

Vanessa cannot bear it. She is getting out. It feels as if someone follows her. Despite the stunning heat, she miserably buttons her jacket, which makes her feel safer, and clutches her bag underneath her armpit. Although she has no useful money, she is horribly aware of both her passport and a hundred-dollar traveller's cheque, at the bottom of the bag where she has concealed them, surely burning their way into public view. She walks as fast as she can manage (her left foot hurts every time she puts it down, but she struggles not to limp, not to look disabled) through a maze of hot metal and stinking petrol and drivers shouting their destination and ragged young men with hostile eyes. By pure blind luck she finds her way out, she is back on a crowded street again, and she knows she must make her way uphill, if she goes uphill she can't go too wrong, for the embassies, the Sheraton, the diplomats' houses, the rich, safe areas are all uphill –

And then she feels a thrust or pull at her bag, and at the same time, a man starts shouting.

The whole thing happened right before Charles's eyes. He came out of the bakery with his bag of cakes and almost walks into a white woman, quite pretty, he thinks, if rather small and shrivelled, with something almost familiar about her, but then, all *bazungu* look a little alike – and then he sees a hand dart lizard-like into her bag, a thin, young black arm against the pale leather. 'Ey!' Charles shouts. '*Omuube*! A thief! We have a thief!' As he tries to clutch the arm, which is surprisingly strong, whipping about in his grasp like an angry snake, a crowd clusters round them, shouting, indignant, and a green-clad matron grabs the thief's shoulders and starts calling harshly for the police, but the man (who is really just a scared-looking boy) wrenches himself clear, arms pummelling, and butts his way out of the yelling kerfuffle, trampling on feet and winding people, then runs zigzagging away towards Owino, leaving the air behind him thick with insults. The crowd is inflamed with real anger, for in a poor country, theft's as bad as murder.

'God put the thief in my path,' Charles tells Mary, 'and of course, I saved the woman, and chased the man away.' They are eating the cakes, in the sunset evening, which is when their front-room looks most attractive, with a pot of sweet, spicy, African tea. Mary's cat, who is expected to fend for herself, but loves to salvage cake from the floor, watches each mouthful, transfixed and gleaming. (Her belly is swelling. Are there kittens inside? Charles does not voice this thought to Mary. She does not like stress, after a busy day.) 'Is your tea fine, my love? I made sure to ask Mercy to have it ready when you came home.'

'It is delicious, Charles. You have been a hero. Tonight I will be very kind to you.' Charles neglects his plate so he can kiss Mary's cheek, and she pushes the cat away with her foot. Her *kabite* had resisted the coming of the pet, but Mary explained she cannot tolerate mice, and now he accepts it as part of his new family.

'Should I have stayed longer with the *muzungu*? She seemed to know nothing. She was from UK.'

'I won't encourage you to stay with any woman.' Mary looks teasing, and is patting her hair, and she has removed her uniform jacket so Charles can feast his eyes upon her curves.

'So you also are a little jealous, dear,' says Charles, and they swallow their sweet tea, and smile at each other, and enjoy the calm silky sound of blades snipping as Mercy starts cutting down Trevor's new curtains.

That evening, Vanessa sits in the Sheraton Piano Bar, drinking a Bell beer, which is wonderfully refreshing, her bandaged feet comfortably stretched out before her, sending an email to her son. 'Today your mother has had marvellous adventures and proved the essential goodness of Uganda's population! I had a stand-off with an African stork, about seven foot tall, which almost attacked me! Then I was caught in torrential rain! Later I was exploring a remote bit of Kampala, not a single white face for miles, of course, and a young man tried to snatch my bag, but a VERY smart Ugandan businessman in a pin-striped suit (rather handsome!), who I suppose must have been looking at me, saw what he was up to and shouted at the thief, and then a wonderful old Ugandan woman in green traditional dress (who I had befriended on the local bus) positively flung herself upon him, and the thief had to run for dear life! And afterwards the old woman insisted on walking me back to a safer part of town. I ask you, would that have happened in London?

'Now, sweets, how are you, and Zakira, and Abdul Trevor? Kissy kissy kissy to my little man! Don't forget, you must not SMOTHER him! Hugs and kisses from Mumsy/Gran.'

She presses 'Send', but nothing happens. She presses 'Save Draft', and gets the 'clock' icon. All round her, other huddled laptop owners are also jabbing buttons in frustration. The network's down; why has this happened to them? They have a right to good communications. It's the twenty-first century. The whole world is connected. Except it isn't. They stare blankly at their screens, which cast an ageing, ghastly blue light on their faces. Ghosts of human beings, drained by machines. Then the other lights go out, and the bar's plunged in darkness; the pianist, who has been giving his all, with excessive use of tremolo and loud pedal, skids to a halt with an arpeggio that horribly misses its final note; but the generator kicks in, the light blinks and steadies, and there's a soft explosion of shared relief and laughter before they return to the lonely cyberhighways where Vanessa's email has been lost for ever.

And out in the suburbs, where there are no generators, and everyone's used to daily power-cuts, Mary and Charles, in total darkness except for brief swoops of homing car headlights through the window, decide they will not light a candle because it is so nice to go to bed. So very nice to be together, close to each other in the warm kind night.

PART 2

Outsiders

9

In Mongbwalu, in eastern DRC, to the west of Uganda, the hills are beautiful and fertile. But thousands of men cannot see the hills. Their heads are bent over mud and sand, sieving and sieving for flakes of gold, rare and tiny on the tip of a finger, there, there, and a few stop and stare as one happy man holds his up to the light: something at last, after two days of sieving. Ten dollars' worth of gold to feed his family. You pay a dollar a day to sieve for gold, but in other mines, there is forced labour. In Bunia, close to the Ugandan border, a day away by car, three days on foot, there are hundreds of tiny shops buying gold: a calculator, a pair of scales. When a shopkeeper's collected a few thousand dollars' worth, he flies to Uganda and sells what he has to an Asian working in a suburb of Kampala, who swiftly spins the dish of gold flakes into a bar of gold the same size as the finger which the first man held up to the sun, to marvel at the bright fleck which will support his family. The gold will be exported by Ugandan firms to rich countries: Switzerland, South Africa. Some will make fairy-tale wedding rings for happy couples: some will make watches (for time is money, unless you are a miner sieving the mud): some will make ingots, to withstand inflation, for gold is safe when economies wobble. President Museveni has honoured these firms in his Presidential Export Awards. Uganda must not be a poor country! Uganda must move into the future.

But Mongbwalu has been fought over half-a-dozen times in the twenty-first century: ethnic Hema against ethnic Lendu, the RCD and the MLC against the UPC, Rwanda against Uganda against Kinshasa, the FNI against the UPC, in a constantly shifting pattern of alliance: but somehow, the gold always gets out. Throats have been cut, chests torn open, intestines dragged forth, Achilles tendons severed, babies macheted and thrown in latrines, but somehow, the miracle of gold keeps on coming, the miracle of money spreading round the globe, at each leg of the journey growing cleaner, brighter, until it is so dazzling that everyone falls silent.

Even nearer Uganda, there are more soldiers. This one is sick, now. Very sick. When the prisoner escaped from his prodding and stumbled forward three or four paces till he fell and died where the others' knives pierced him, they realised he was no use any more. They left him in the shade, but the sun has moved. He cannot see: the light is too bright. He is shivering, but his brain is boiling. A family of colobus monkeys look down at him from a hole in the canopy, and whisper to each other, agitated, anxious, black and white paws nervously flickering, flowing white tails waving like feathers, nostrils quivering, then bound away from the gag-making smells of minerals and men, gold and oil, blood and faeces.

Waking in Kampala. White, so white. The duvets and pillows are snowy, dazzling. It stretches away from her half-open eyes, a long slope of sunlight, young and hopeful. She does not remember, and then she remembers. She is Vanessa. She is in Uganda. The bed is wide: such a wide, white bed. The bed is luxurious. The bed is empty.

She is in the last third of her life on earth; this Vanessa only rarely remembers, and never in the morning, with the sun so bright.

When she first wakes up, she is beautiful. Her son has grown up, and anything could happen.

Today the other writers are due to arrive. Some of them, she admits, rather minor, but one or two of them quite worthy companions. She has a passing interest in Geoffrey Truman, who she has sometimes glimpsed in the distance at parties, and of course, his craggy features are quite well-known. He has sold a few more novels than Vanessa, true, but she surely has a certain cachet that comes from not compromising her art. He will be aware of her reputation; perhaps he has noticed her reviews. Yes, he is slightly younger than her, but luckily, she thinks, she looks young for her age.

She springs out of bed, slightly twisting her knee, and begins her 'Salute to the Sun' from yoga. As she comes up again from her deep bow, she catches her reflection in the sun-dazzled mirror, her neck very white, her blonde hair shaken out in a fluffy puffball by gravity, her athletic shoulders, which are still youthful, though possibly the very young are less bony (the mirror cuts her off at hip level, so she doesn't have to focus on her legs, which she knows are the teeniest bit skinny and bandy).

Naked, her lower half's a stripped wish-bone.

The thought pokes uncomfortably into her mind, but just as quickly, she shoves it away.

Bones, she tells herself, are elegant things. People always tell her she has good bones.

The other writers from the UK are less well-known. Deirdre Mullins, who is frankly second rate. Probably invited at the last minute. A northern man said to be a gifted poet. Graham Somebody. Quite literary. The name escapes her. An exiled Chinese playwright she's never heard of. Then there are the black ones. Fair enough, this is Africa. Including a 'rap poet' called Banga. But can you, really, call rap writing?

Quite soon Vanessa, by now dressed and showered, a little dizzy from her anti-malarials or possibly from quarts of strong coffee at breakfast, is standing in the lobby feeling slightly apprehensive as she watches the other writers check in. Of course some of them have come on the same plane, but they seem to know each other well already. It suddenly reminds her of starting school; the others paired off, herself still lonely.

At the low table nearest the reception desk, a dreadlocked figure is holding court, sprawled along the dark leather sofa with his luggage, little gold glasses, a rainbow-knit scarf tied loosely round his neck. There's an open bottle of whisky in front of him. He's laughing loudly and talking fast. Vanessa can't help feeling intimidated, but she reminds herself she too is a writer, she is here by invitation of the British Council, she is probably the senior writer here –

Not that she is older. Just – *senior*.

Right, she will go and introduce herself to Banga, who is talking to a quite straight-looking man, fair-haired and fattish, in a dark suit and tie. Perhaps his manager?

A few seconds later, she is mystifying the young man with the whisky (a musicologist from Kenya, Dr Alex Saitoti, who will be giving a paper on 'Poetics and Jazz: from the Inside Out') by hailing him as 'Banga!', while seizing his hand. 'I'm Vanessa Henman, your fellow writer.' He doesn't look as pleased as she expected him to. It's almost as if he is shaking her off, but she says, even louder, 'VANESSA', with her biggest smile, baring her new white teeth (not as new as they were: bought with her earnings from *The Long Lean Line*).

'Vanessa? You must be Vanessa Henman. I'm Peter Pargeter. So good to meet you.' The man in the suit next to the dreadlocked African swiftly takes charge of her unwanted hand, and the situation, with the easy grace that tells her, yes – 'I'm from the British Council. Director, Uganda. Welcome to Kampala.' His hand is soft, and furred with blond hair.

Vanessa warms to Peter Pargeter's deferential manner, and turns her attention away from Banga, who's obviously ignoring her because she is white, and pretending he hasn't even heard of her. Peter Pargeter must know her work fairly well, so she starts straightaway to discuss the coming evening, when there's a Welcome Dinner and Ceremony.

'I'm wondering how long a reading you'd like this evening. I mean I'd like to keep something in reserve, as it were, for my event on Thursday, if that's OK.'

'This evening?' he says, looking puzzled. 'This evening? Oh, I see. No, that's really very very kind, but this evening we're having a reading from Veronique Tadjo. Wonderful writer as I'm sure you know. From Cote d'Ivoire. A star.'

'Ah,' says Vanessa. 'Yes. I see.'

(*I* am a star, she thinks. *I* could shine.)

'In fact she's over there,' says Peter Pargeter. 'Just arrived. I must go and have a word. If you like, I'll introduce you –' He gestures vaguely at a striking woman with fine features and tumbled black curls, standing at the Reception Desk at the hub of a laughing, lively crowd.

'No need,' Vanessa breaks in, scenting advantage. 'She's with Bernardine Evaristo, who I know very well. Bernardine!' she cries, giving Banga up and racing Peter across to the group, where she rises on tiptoe like a ballerina to kiss her slightly startled black acquaintance. 'How lovely to see you, Bernardine!'

'I know I know you, but I've forgotten –'

'Vanessa Henman,' says Vanessa, mortified. '*Vanessa*! We read together in Ipswich.'

'Oh yes ...' But Bernardine still looks vague, or jet-lagged. Still she's smiling at Vanessa pleasantly enough. 'Do you know Veronique Tadjo? Veronique, this is – Valerie Henman.'

'Vanessa,' Vanessa corrects her, sharply, but she beams on

Veronique, and pumps her hand. 'I am really looking forward to your reading.'

'Do you work for the Council?' Veronique enthuses. 'Thank you so much for inviting me.' Before Vanessa can disabuse her, Peter Pargeter has arrived, and embraces Veronique, who turns the full force of her attention on him. Vanessa is left with Bernardine.

'So how are you?' she asks her, a little less warmly.

'Oh well, well. Got two new books coming out. How about you, what are you working on? You're a poet, aren't you?'

'Novelist,' says Vanessa, miserable. She dreads being asked what she's working on, for she's been stuck on a novel for over a decade, and though it is a very major piece of work (she is sure it will be fairly major), other people's publication rates are so excessive, they are churning out stuff almost every year, probably because their standards are lower. Which makes her look lazy, or ... less creative. Yet no-one could be more creative than she.

She changes the subject with a sudden lurch. 'I love Kampala,' she tells Bernardine. 'If you like, we could go for a walk, this afternoon. I could give you a little guided tour.' At least she can call on her knowledge of Uganda.

'Actually Veronique's got friends in Kampala,' Bernardine says. 'The two of us are meeting them for lunch, sorry. Maybe we could have a walk another day.' Perhaps she sees the wistfulness in Vanessa's face, for she adds, at the last moment, 'You could join us.'

And the hours that follow are pure delight. What fun it is, sitting out in the hot sun on the green lawn outside Ekitoobero, all the writers together – all the African ones, who were the ones that really counted, and her, a veritable honorary Ugandan – long Bell beers bright as salt in their hands, blue sky and big white clouds overhead, toucans clattering in the eucalyptus, white jackets of the waiters echoing the clouds. Vanessa one of the writers! Accepted!

Alongside Veronique Tadjo and Taban Lo Liyong, two of the best-known writers on the continent! It is all as she had imagined it would be. They drink to each other: they laugh: they feel free. They toast all artists, outsiders, exiles – Joyce, Beckett, Wole Soyinka, Ngugi W'a Thiongo, Bessie Head – despised by governments, but loved by each other, 'and by the people', someone adds, 'so in that sense, we aren't marginal.' Though Taban has reservations about Ngugi, and someone else can't stand *Ulysses*, in that circle of sunlight on chinking glasses, it all becomes worth it to Vanessa, her marginal life as a literary novelist, her writer's block, her commercial struggle. It's glorious, in with the other outsiders.

There's a slightly awkward moment at the end when one of the Kampalans, a delightful young woman with very short hair and a lot to say, turns to Vanessa and remarks, 'I have not brought my money. Is it OK? I think the British Council is paying.'

'Really?' says Vanessa. 'Good. No-one told me.'

There's a puzzled pause, and a tiny frown. 'Veronique sayed that you work for the Council.'

'Oh no, no!' Vanessa laughs, 'Not at all. I am just a penniless writer, like you!'

And then the young woman looks rather hurt, and says, 'No, I am not penniless. It is only that I did not pick my handbag from the house.'

In the end they all split the bill between them. So what if Vanessa pays slightly more? When she works it out in English money, it costs less than a couple of lattes in London. Perhaps the beer has made her more relaxed, for she never, never drinks at lunch-time.

Indeed she is feeling so effervescent that after all the writers troop, shrieking and laughing (and her as loud as anyone! Vanessa knows how to have a good time), back in the heat along the rough red road to the Sheraton, she takes herself out again to Kampala Road (the others are all too tired to go with her), spots a little Indian clothes shop, and (encouraged by a small crowd of onlookers as she hauls herself into and out of dresses, only partly screened by a torn curtain) buys a very pretty, youthful, top, all handkerchief points and patchwork flowers and a rather daring plunge at the front.

She means to wear it to the Welcome Ceremony, where it should look nice in the photographs. It's not the kind of thing she usually wears, but then, she isn't usually in Uganda, and off-duty, after all these years, from her son, and for once representing herself as a writer, the part of herself she loves the most. 'Vanessa Henman, Novelist'. (Not what she sees on notice-boards and memos at her university: 'Course Leader, Vanessa Henman', or 'Dr V. Henman, Senior Lecturer'. Impossible now to remember how she once waited and longed for that 'Senior'. As she treks through her decades, she is irritated that they haven't yet made her a Reader, or Professor. But today she is not going to brood on these things, when she is so far away, and so happy! Today all annoyances seem petty.)

The mirror in the lift as she swoops down to dinner from the 20th floor of the Sheraton is not as encouraging as she hoped, but she smiles back at herself, undaunted. Fluorescent light is always grim ... her hair is certainly not thinning, and her teeth are obviously a strong point, and so they should be, given what she'd spent on them, but this evening they look too big for her face, as if she is growing smaller, more bony, which makes the young, flowery top look ... *stop*. She suppresses the fear that she looks ... *grotesque*.

Vanessa has noted the distortions of fluorescent as she's grown older, and now she discounts it, straight away. She knows she's attractive, she isn't one of those whining women, like Fifi, her friend, always doubting herself and hating herself, then trying to meditate herself happy. (Yet daylight, these days, has the same effect. Indeed light, in general, is becoming a problem.)

And then she thinks: *global warming*. There's probably just more light about. It is not a thought to pursue in detail, because, in broad outline, it makes her feel better.

Deciding the fault is in her stars, Vanessa shakes out her hair, and shimmies forward, all hope, all happiness, as the doors open, into her wonderful African evening. It's my Indian summer, she tells herself. If that makes any sense in Uganda.

10

Mary Tendo has just arrived home from work. The traffic was, if possible, worse than usual, and the taxi more crowded, and dirtier. She is a mature woman, with an excellent job. She is not a schoolgirl, or a peasant! And yet, she must travel by public taxi, like any maid or garden *shamba*.

'I need a car, Charles,' she says, determinedly. 'Why should I travel in these dirty taxis? There were fifteen people, or maybe twenty, all sneezing, and one doing something worse.'

'My love, I will drive you whenever I can,' says Charles, who is home from the office early. 'You are right, you are the Sheraton Housekeeper, you should not have to go by taxi. In fact, they should send a car for you! Or maybe ....' He looks down, cunningly, for he wants to please Mary Tendo even more than usual, he definitely hopes she will be kind to him again before this Trevor arrives to spoil things, lying in the house awake at night and listening for noises, making her shy. 'Maybe they could give you a car to use. A company car. It is normal in America. *Nga Mu America kiri normal. Teli kubusabusa*!'

Charles has one advantage over Mary; he has been to America, she has not. He attended business school for a year, not quite such a good one as she imagines, but he likes to refer to American knowledge, not all of it entirely well-founded.

Now she rewards him with a gratified smile that is guarded by a hint of suspicion. 'And yet, they have not offered me one. They do not know how well I drive.' She looks at him, smooth round eyebrows lifted, waiting for confirmation.

'Ah yes, you are a very fine driver!' They nod and smile at each other, complacent. But then a little devil awakes in Charles, because, even with the most loving lovers, there must be small wars, and competitions. 'Although there was the slight problem with my car ...' She had crashed his car, disastrously, last year, crumpling the bonnet and smashing the windscreen. She paid the repair bills without complaining, but the car is not quite the car it was.

'The problem with your car was because of many factors.'

'Yes. But you crashed into the back of the car in front of you, just before the roundabout on Jinja Road. It crashed because of what?' Now Charles is laughing, patting his thighs in their smart black business trousers and looking at Mary teasingly. 'It crashed because you could not see it, Mary. It crashed because you did not wear your glasses.'

'No, Charles!' Mary Tendo looks especially forbidding, and her nostrils flare slightly, in a way that makes him nervous. 'The car in front was very badly maintained. You remember, the door was made of cardboard.'

'There was only one door left, after you crashed into it.'

This time she ignores the provocation. 'I am almost certain the brakes were defective. It braked too quickly. It may have been backing ...' But as she makes this claim, Charles snorts with laughter, his shoulders heave, and he looks straight at her, so she cannot keep it up; he is her *kabite*, and her mask of indignation cracks into smiles.

'Mary Tendo, you should be in State House! *Nawe oli nga Muzeveni atakola nsobi*. Like Mr Museveni, you never make errors.'

Mary Tendo goes over and sits on Charles's knee. She enjoys his teasing, up to a point. At work people fear her, but not at home. She is glad that Charles can be frank with her (although she will not let him go too far). 'No, it is true, I did not wear my glasses. When I wear my glasses, I have eyes like an eagle. And so, perhaps I did not see the vehicle was backing –'

'Mary Tendo!' It is an effort to laugh, with Mary perched so firmly upon his knee. She is slightly taller and heavier than him. Of course he is not afraid of her.

'Yes, Charles, the vehicle was backing.' And now she is stroking him, and holding his hot head between her big hands, and he is too busy to keep contradicting. There is a short interval of sweet, warm kissing, before she breaks off, and looks deep into his eyes.

'And so, my darling, as you were saying, I am a good driver, and I should have a car.'

'Yes, yes, Mary, but must we discuss this now?' Charles is eager to go on with what they are doing. The maid has taken Dora to buy some groundnuts.

'No, Charles, we need not discuss this now. Although if I think I will never get a car, I will become less happy, dear.' And she stops kissing him, and sits upright, so her full weight falls on Charles's left thigh, which makes him yelp, suddenly, in pain. 'Ah, sorry. Because maybe the Sheraton will never buy me one.'

'That is true. One must not count one's chickens.'

'You remember my friend Jackee, from Church.'

'Of course.' Charles shifts, in agony. How come that Mary sometimes feels so light, yet today she is so painfully heavy?

'Did you know that Jackee's husband has bought her a car?'

'No, I did not know. Mary, I want to kiss you.'

'So husbands should do what?'

'I do not understand.'

'Charles, I think you are a very clever man.' Mary Tendo makes as if to get off his lap. The effort increases the stress on his thigh bone, yet Charles still tries to pull her back towards him.

'That is nice of you, Mary. You are clever, also. I was wondering ...'

'Yes?'

'Perhaps ... perhaps I could buy you a car for your birthday.'

'Charles, that is wonderful! Yes, I agree.'

'Then that is settled,' Charles says, a little hastily, and starts caressing Mary's stupendous breasts. 'A car will be yours. Do not worry, Mary. And now, I think we need a little lie down – '

But the door bangs, suddenly, making them freeze, and then they both hear the voice of the maid, rather shrill and grating, and slightly out of breath from the long walk home, carrying the heavy child in her arms as well as two plastic packs of groundnuts. 'Aunty, are you there? We are back. I must show you the curtains for the *muzungu*.'

'Ah. Trevor's curtains. I am sorry, Charles. I must go and see what the maid has done,' sighs Mary Tendo, and slips from his lap. Yet as she goes into the kitchen, she is smiling.

Charles sits for a moment, not smiling, reflecting. He rubs his sore thigh, and sighs in the heat, in the sitting-room that has got so much smaller since Mary Tendo moved in with him, and gave up the white flat where he could visit her, where she was never busy with the maid or the baby. He looks back on those days as paradise. No cat-hairs on the sofa, no baby crying, hours when he could watch TV or read the paper. Yet he had begged Mary to marry him, after she went to UK and discovered she was pregnant.

Does she still love him? He is not sure. She works too hard at the Sheraton. And sometimes she comes home and works hard all evening, and too often she makes him and Mercy work hard, also. She often asks questions, such as 'Charles, I was wondering. Have you sorted out the problem with the man in Jinja who says you owe him money?' She will not let him rest until the letter is written (she does not understand the role of borrowing in business). No, he is not sure that Mary loves him. And a man has needs. A man must have love.

Then her strong, low voice calls through from the kitchen. 'My darling, perhaps you would like your beer?'

And at once his heart lightens. Of course she loves him. 'Yes, Mary Tendo. I will have my beer.' And he reaches for the radio, and loosens his collar, and puts his feet up on the window sill, though when he hears her coming, he will take them down, or she will say, with her nostrils flaring, 'Charles, my *kabite*, what are you doing?' A man should not always have to answer questions.

'I'm off to build a well, as a matter of fact,' says Trevor, at Heathrow, to the steward who is trying to sort out his online check-in. He's a kindly man not much younger than Trevor, who shares Trevor's disdain for the virtual.

'No trace of it, Sir, I'm really sorry.' He stares with disbelief at the screen. 'Computer system was down this morning.'

'I thought the idea was to save us from queueing?'

'In theory, yes. It's a lot of nonsense. Not that I am supposed to say so. Did you say you were going to build a well? The Chinese are doing a lot out there. I'm glad some British companies still get a look-in.'

'I'm not doing it, really, as a job,' says Trevor. 'I've got a friend out there, from a village in the sticks. I'm doing it, like, as a volunteer.'

'Good for you Sir,' says the man. 'Sorry to be messing you about.' Something seems to strike him, as they stand there in limbo, two human beings in the maw of a machine. Now he's bending over his screen, eyes narrowed, then looking up at Trevor, making some calculation, lightly tapping his keyboard. Now his brow is no longer furrowed.

'OK, that's done. I think you'll be all right. Have a very good flight,' he says to Trevor. The smile seems genuinely warm. Trevor moves on, happy to get rid of his case with its rapidly thrown-in clothes and presents, but his tools, the precious tools of his trade, what he always thinks of as his right arm, are hard for him to entrust to the conveyor belt. He turns back, briefly, to watch them glide away. Then he tells himself: *Still, they're only things*, and he carries on walking, light, sturdy, happy as he wanders through the riches of the airport, pleasantly off-duty, just for the moment, yet not at a loose end, for he's a man with a mission. Off to Uganda: a first for him.

And then, there's the relief of escaping women. The thing with Soraya had become a burden. And no Vanessa to fuss over him! He can imagine what she would have been like, if she'd known: she'd have made endless lists of things he ought to be taking. As it is he's chucked stuff into his case at random. And he bets he'll be none the worse for it. Still, dear old Ness. He hopes she is well. And at least when she nagged me I felt she loved me. He dismisses this thought. Great to be free.

It is good to have a wife when she cares for you. Charles smiles as he watches Mary walking away, her fine strong hips and curving waist, and feels the cold curve of the glass in his hand. 'Thank you, Mary. You are the perfect woman.' Ah, to drink deep, for the day's work is done, even if he has a few problems outstanding.

Charles's mood improves further when the radio comes on, because too often there is no power, and recently there was no power for three days, and they had to boil water for washing, et cetera. But this evening, he can find BBC World Service! It is not quite as good as it used to be, but it is still the best station for news in the world. And if he can sit, in his house in Kampala, the house he has been paying for for nearly seven years, the house which will soon be more his than the mortgage company's (so long as, God willing, he can keep up the payments, which, with the new arrangement, should be possible; he has not told Mary about the new arrangement, she is a good woman, but not always understanding) – if he can sit here, in his house in Kampala, and there are no soldiers in the street outside, and no immediate threat of war (for the whole of his childhood was shadowed by war), with his beautiful wife and baby next door, with a beer in his hand from his own refrigerator, and listen to the news, like a man of the world, who is in touch with London, and Paris, and Beijing, then his life must be good: life is good.

For a minute or two he drifts in and out of focus, letting the icy sweet-saltiness slip deliciously through his teeth to his tonsils and down his throat to the hot tightness of his stomach which savours the glorious shock of coolness. Cool, cool, shady and cool. He becomes his body; he stretches; relaxes. All the money worries fade, and he lives his moment.

Then the voice of the newsreader starts to pierce, in meaningless fragments at first, his bliss.

'Border incidents ... recent weeks ... Kinshasa ... denials ... DRC.' It is those idiots in Democratic Republic of Congo again, he thinks, and feels happy to be Ugandan, not Congolese, for the Congo is hell: everyone knows it. There everyone is fighting, every country in the world, and Uganda was fighting there for years and years. Uganda became richer, during the war, and DRC poorer, and more bloody. Charles knows that money makes the world go round, for he needs money every day in business; and when there is no money, life breaks down (as he has found for himself, when his life went wrong) – and yet everyone says, unless they are in the army, that Uganda was stealing gold and diamonds. And everyone knows that Ugandans are still there, though now what they are doing is investing, or peace-keeping, or stopping atrocities, et cetera. But still people whisper it is all about money.

Charles takes a deep draught of his perfectly cold beer, and argues with himself, as he half-listens to the voices. On the other hand, all the rich countries are enriching themselves by robbing Congo, although they are hiding behind private companies. And all of them are trying to steal what is hidden: gold, oil, diamonds, and that strange new substance that is so important for mobile phones, *coltan*. This thought makes Charles get a little fired up, and he drinks again, deeply, to cool himself, and remembers he is waiting for a message from work, from a man who he hopes will invest in a scheme, so he flicks on his phone, but it is blank: nothing, so he puts it away, with a short, deep frown that makes a river-bed furrow between his eyebrows, and blinks, once, twice, then returns to his reflections.

And so, if all the rich countries are there in the Congo, why should the Ugandans not take a share? Why should only the rich countries get richer? He nods to himself, and sits up straighter. There may be investment opportunities, and he, Charles, knows many investors. It is only right that Uganda should be there, though in general, he does not trust Museveni.

'Mary! I will have another cold beer.' Conviction makes him sound peremptory.

Mary Tendo is not pleased with the form of this request, but she thinks of her car, and comes through, smiling, with a beer and some groundnuts. 'Another beer, my love. So are you now fine?'

Thus cued to respond, Charles says, 'Thank you, my love. I am fine.'

'What is happening in the world?'

'I am listening,' says Charles, with a stern little frown to deter conversation, not his river-bed frown, a social frown that says he is master in his own armchair, in his own moment, with his own beer. This is men's business. No woman understands about the news, how men must listen, to keep a grasp on events. Women frequently talk right through important announcements.

'And so what have you heard?' She is insistent.

'Oh there is a problem with DRC, as usual. A border incident, in the west. Some people have been killed on Lake Albert. And now there are arguments between Kabila and Museveni.'

'They are both devils.'

'Shhh, you must not say so. And besides, I must listen, Mary.'

And she thinks about her car, and smiles at him forgivingly, then goes back into the kitchen, where the rich orange velvet curtains are spread across the table, and the beef stew is bubbling on the cooker, and the baby – who is no longer really a baby, being three years old, though for some reason, not yet talking – is sitting on the floor, watching something, rapt.

'*Kiki* Dora?' asks the maid, who talks to the child although she never answers, whereas Mary Tendo does not seem to try (Jamil started talking at eleven months old, and his mother still remembers the joy of that, his lisping, singing bubbles of speech.)

Mary peers downwards. Two beetles, fighting. With a sharp exclamation, Mary kills them both. Theodora gasps, and runs to Mercy.

Now Mary's attention has returned to the curtains. 'Did you measure them carefully?' she asks the maid.

'Yes, Aunty. I held them by the windows. I marked the shape of the windows on the curtains. And then I cut, very carefully.'

'So the curtains are the same size as the windows ...' And Mary tuts, sharply, grabs hold of the velvet, takes them to the window and tuts again. 'You stupid girl, have you never seen curtains?'

The maid stares at her, frightened, with big round eyes. '*Nedda*, Aunty,' she says, deferentially. 'In my house we did not have curtains. Only we had something to hide my father's mattress.'

'You have made them too short, so the light will rush in. The curtain must be longer than the windows. And so my friend Trevor will wake up too early. *And you have spoiled this expensive velvet.*'

'I could sew it back again,' the maid says, desperate. 'I did not throw any of the trimmings away.'

'And this would look like what? This would look like rubbish!' shouts Mary, exasperated past endurance, and then her small daughter begins to wail. 'And besides, you have been giving too much food to the cat. She is getting fat, and food is expensive!'

This is not true, but Mercy dare not deny it. In fact, she does not like the cat. 'I am sorry, Aunty. I wanted to please you.' She picks up the child, and strokes her hair, and at once the little girl stops crying. Mary thinks, at least she is good with her.

'You told me you could sew,' says Mary, more reasonably. 'Your father said you could cook, and sew. It is true that he did not mention curtains.'

'Sorry, sorry. Please do not tell my father.'

Mary sees a small tear creep down the girl's face, and at the same time, the small chubby hand of her daughter reaches up, gently, and rubs it away.

'I will not tell your father.'

'Oh thank you, thank you.' And yet this remission makes more tears flow. 'Aunty, please take the money for the curtains from my wages.'

'They are not wages,' says Mary, annoyed. 'You are "in the family", as they say in Europe. Arn Fameey. It is French,' she explains. 'We supply you with everything. It is spending money.'

'Please take from the spending money,' begs the maid. 'I am ignorant, Aunty. I have never been to secondary school. I do not know about French, or curtains.'

Then Mary, whose self-esteem has been boosted by a demonstration of her worldly knowledge, bursts out laughing, and stands, arms akimbo. 'I will not take away your spending money!'

She looks at the pair of them, and shakes her fist. 'No more crying,' she says 'from either of you. And we shall not talk any more about the curtains. It is only sunlight. Trevor will survive it.'

And then all three of them are laughing, and Charles, who has been keeping his head down as he picked up waves of discord from the room next door, comes cautiously through, and, with his head on one side, and a look he has perfected, both charming and wheedling, says, 'I think we will be eating supper soon? My beer has made me a little hungry.' In minutes, the gleaming green banana leaves are being unwrapped to show golden *matooke*, and the chunks of beef-bone, heavy with meat, are being ladled on to the clean white plates that were part of what Mary brought to the household, and so what if they came from the Nile Imperial, and still bear the hotel's illustrious initials, with its tacit reference to a long-ago empire?

They eat. They are happy. And then they sleep, though Mary lies awake, just for a while, after making love to Charles, who is snoring gently, totally content, and thinks about Trevor, and the trip to the village, and then a little shadow comes creeping towards her, the shadow of the absence that never goes away.

11

Geoffrey Truman is the first disappointment, although Vanessa will warm to him later. His jacket photos must have been taken a decade ago. She spots him in the lobby, on the way to the reception, and recognises him with a sinking heart: the heavy eyebrows, which are boot-polish black; an amused, even cynical, twist to his mouth. But he is smaller, rounder-shouldered, greyer, balder in every way than she had imagined. Certainly not a romantic prospect. His face is red, and he is clutching a glass.

'Geoffrey Truman? Vanessa Henman,' she says, going up to him, little white hand extended, showing off her rings, with her kindest smile, for he must be aware, poor chap, that his readers will compare him unkindly to his photos. But he looks at her blankly, as if she isn't there.

'Vanessa,' she repeats. He is probably drunk. 'The International Writers' Conference.'

'Oh, right,' he says. 'Are you the organiser? Cos there's no bloody bath-plug in my bath –'

'No –'

'I've asked in reception, and they don't know owt. And I can tell you, I've sweated like a pig in this heat.'

Very true, she realises, and steps back slightly; he has certainly sweated, and not changed his shirt. 'I'm a writer, like you,' she says, repressively. 'Vanessa Henman, novelist.'

'Never 'eard of you. Never mind!' he says. 'Would you like a drink? I'll stand yer one.'

'I'll wait,' says Vanessa. He is old, and ugly, and the literary pages wouldn't touch him with a bargepole, which is probably why he is getting tanked up, because sales, she reflects, aren't everything: he must feel nervous coming into this company, herself and Bernardine and Veronique Tadjo, and even poor Deirdre gets reviews. And with that comforting reflection, the sting disappears of that terrible 'Never heard of you'.

So, pitying him, she is saved from hurt, and can sail onwards like a butterfly in her thin, inappropriately youthful kaftan, fragile but afloat on a warm breeze of hope, the September hopefulness that comes before winter. It drives her on; it buoys her up. She escaped from her village, escaped from her parents, she got to Cambridge, she will make it as a writer. So what if the cold shores of fifty and sixty are somewhere in the mists of the middle distance? Vanessa will make it; she will; she must.

How she loves her lapel badge, though it looks a little odd perched precariously on the tiny straps of her new top. 'Dr Vanessa Henman: Novelist, UK'. No-one, surely, could argue with *that*.

By contrast, the place-names on the tables in the big hall are very badly written, which is silly when some of the writers are mature, like Vanessa herself, with her slight problems of focus. She finally finds her placement on the table near the microphone, right next to the Director, Peter Pargeter, which is gratifying, and her heart lifts with pleasure, but all she clearly makes out is the 'V', and the 'Henman', frankly, is just a hopeless squiggle.

She sinks down with a sigh of relief next to Peter. 'Did someone Ugandan write these place-names?' she asks, with a forgiving, faintly conspiratorial smile. He seems oddly surprised to see her there, but then she realises, he's just nervous. It's her reputation as an intellectual, and perhaps that 'Dr' intimidates some. She widens her smile, tries to dazzle him. But he still splutters, rather hopelessly.

'Er ... no. Oh, I see. I'm sorry ... In fact, Veronique – that is to say, Vanessa, that Veronique – but look, never mind – no, stay, stay, it'll be OK. She seems quite happy where she is.' And puzzlingly, he's indicating Veronique Tadjo, who is sitting at a table of other Africans. 'She has a lot of friends,' he finishes.

Vanessa would not want a comparison to be made. She had too many friendless years at high school. 'Oh yes, we had a wonderful lunch together. We joined them, my friend Bernardine and I. I also have friends in Kampala, as it happens. A Ugandan writer called Mary Tendo, who I made great efforts to get published. She has been to stay with me in London.'

'I'm afraid I haven't heard of her. Pity. As you know, I only recently replaced Richard Weyers. We might have invited her to join the programme. Our local links aren't always perfect. Perhaps it's not too late, Vanessa.'

That isn't what Vanessa wants at all. If Mary were invited, she would be, frankly, insufferable. Fond though Vanessa is of Mary. She would get the idea she was – on the same level.

'Oh, I don't think Mary is quite ready for that. She is, in some ways, unsophisticated. She still works at the Nile Imperial Hotel.' Vanessa realises too late this will make Peter Pargeter think her African contacts are rather low level. She swiftly tries to turn this remark to her advantage. 'Not that that in any way lessens our friendship. One cannot afford to be a snob, as a writer.'

'No indeed,' says Peter Pargeter, but Vanessa sees his attention is elsewhere; there's a man tinkering with the microphone. 'Ah. Very good. I'll have to leave you for a minute. I think we're nearly ready to begin.'

Peter Pargeter's speech is full of jargon. She thinks, 'He likes the sound of his own voice. My father would have called him "pleased with himself". Then there is dancing, not the traditional Ugandan dancing she has seen before, which is really most impressive, including strong-thighed leaps and kicks in the air and vigorous wrigglings and thrustings of the hips like the ones Mary had deployed so freely at a Sussex village dance on her visit to England (when Vanessa had, admittedly, been rather embarrassed, because there is a time and a place for these things, and the men had all stared, which made the other women tetchy, and Mary had looked like a bit of a show-off) – and yet, in context, with the blue grass skirts, it would surely be a better advert for Uganda than the anaemic pair of modern dancers who wind and unwind themselves in coloured sashes, not quite reflecting each other's movements and at one point plainly getting tangled up, while a third dancer squats like a sack of potatoes in a corner, playing the unrewarding role of the Outsider, as Peter Pargeter helpfully explains to Vanessa in a stage whisper. 'Rather fine, don't you think?' Then the sack of potatoes suddenly jumps up and unravels the sashes, and they all join hands. Everyone claps.

And then there is Veronique Tadjo's speech. Vanessa is not jealous, fortunately. She has never been jealous of other writers. And yet it is an effort for her to listen, partly because she is asking herself questions, such as: 'How much younger than me does Veronique look? Is she a good reader? Is she better than me? Is she really the best writer in this room?' Perhaps the point is, she is African. But Vanessa claps at the end, like all the rest, and says to Peter Pargeter, 'That was very nice.'

'She's a star,' he agrees, still clapping loudly and smiling. 'Jolly lucky to get a name like her.'

But am I a name, wonders Vanessa?

'Trevor Patchett,' says Trevor to the smiling woman who is ticking off names at Gate 27.

'Ah yes. I see you've got an upgrade,' she says. 'You'll be flying Business Class this evening.'

'Are you sure?' asks Trevor. 'Trevor *Patchett*?'

'Yes, sir.'

'Bloody hell, that's great,' says Trevor. 'I've never flown Business Class in my life!'

She looks at him briefly, his astonished face, his rumpled red t-shirt and untidy hair, his flight bag, a plastic carrier from which a crumpled *Private Eye* pokes out, and quickly looks down at her list again. 'You are Trevor Patchett ... No, that's correct.' And her smile steadies.

He's got an upgrade! Yes, he's ahead! He can't help thinking how he'd love to tell Vanessa. His mobile's in his pocket. He hasn't talked to his ex-wife for weeks, because of this stupid secrecy business, which he'd never liked, but Mary insisted. If he'd called Vanessa it would have slipped out.

He misses Vanessa when they're not in contact. He is used to her. He is *fond* of her. And maybe that, in a way, was at the bottom of how things turned out in the end with Soraya. A lovely girl! Everyone said so. Everyone said how lucky he was. Mates of his own age were green with jealousy. And she was a lot more than just a pretty face: she was clever, she could paint, she was sweet-natured, though in four years she'd made no progress with English, while her Iranian mates spoke English like duchesses. Without language you could share few jokes, and Trevor has always been a bit of a joker.

His friends had assumed it was all about sex, probably because of the age difference. He thinks, most blokes are unimaginative. There'd been a lot of nudging, and thumbs-ups, and inquiries about whether he was getting exhausted. In fact the truth was, from that point of view, Nessie was – well, they'd been very lucky. It was perfect, really. And over the years, even after the divorce, he still fancied her like mad. He didn't know what it was about her.

Vanessa, Vanessa. Impossible, yes, but the mother of his son. He would never forget her.

And the thing with Soraya seemed flat alongside it. It wasn't going anywhere. Which wasn't fair. She'd told him before he knew it himself: 'You never really love me, Trevor.'

Not in the way I loved Vanessa.

He wishes, now, that he could tease his ex-wife. He could really wind her up, with this upgrade. But if the postcard he left at Soraya's didn't get there, and he just rings up out of the blue from Heathrow and tells her he's on the way to Uganda, she'll go mental. Women don't like surprises.

Yet what is the point of going practically first class if he can't show off about it to Vanessa?

She'd be mad with envy. He chuckles to himself. And yet she would also be pleased for him. Give her her due, she would be pleased for him.

Will he or won't he? Ten minutes to boarding.

All around Trevor, passengers are restlessly foraging and fossicking among their possessions, more fearful than ever that something has been stolen. Many of them are lightly encircling bags and newspapers and snacks and bottles with elbows or thighs, making informal stockades in which they contain the anxiety of flight. It's still slightly strange for small land-based mammals to be shot through the air, thirty thousand feet up, with a thin skin of metal and two fallible engines between them and death, at five hundred miles per hour, which is seven times faster than they drive on motorways. But they have to look calm, for everyone's sake; you can't have constant hysteria at airports.

Most aim a last phone call at their earthbound loved ones, an urgency suddenly puckering their minds because they know they are about to enter the silent zone between sky and land, the strange cold airlock where communication ceases, when it will be too late to change their plans, when the prospect of soaring becomes ineluctable, when massive doors will swing shut on London, on the ordinary, on their safe little lives. Last words, thinks a pessimist, then cancels the thought.

Transition time. Beginnings and endings. Always say goodbye nicely, in case, in case ...

Of course, Trevor thinks, that's what I should do. I should talk to Justin, and the little feller too. But I can't do anything to hurt Vanessa.

12

At the end of the evening, looking back, Vanessa's not sure when the argument began. The food is 'international', and not quite what she is used to, richer, oilier, and yet she is hungry. She's drunk deep of the wine, she has eaten every dish, so why does she still feel – dissatisfied, unsated? As if she can never quite get enough?

She has studiously been avoiding the eyes of Geoffrey Truman, who is seated on Peter Pargeter's left, but although she herself is deep in conversation with a nice enough epic poet from Mauritius (a teeny little man with bottle-glass spectacles who's keen to come and stay with her in London), the sound of male voices drifts across, then rises.

'What we're trying to do isn't Thatcherism, Geoffrey,' Peter Pargeter is saying, and he's laughing, but you can hear he's annoyed. 'That's an out-of-date model, if you don't mind me saying so –'

'I do bloody mind,' mutters Geoffrey Truman, 'but I don't suppose that'll stop yer, will it?'

'– The point is, we all have to move on. The Council cannot get stuck in the past. I believe there are partners across Africa who will be eager to, um, partner with us.'

'That's not bloody English,' Truman continues. 'Is there any more wine?' He calls out, more generally, until a Sheraton waiter comes over.

'No need to get hung up on libraries,' says Pargeter, affecting breezy charm. 'We have other focuses. Like leadership. We are running a very successful series of seminars on leadership, here at the Sheraton. It's all part of the exciting new offer.'

'Why do you need an exciting new office?' bellows Geoffrey, who Vanessa realises is deaf. 'And what's all this about leadership? Bloody bollocks,' he adds, 'that's what it is. You're supposed to do culture, not leadership. Africa's got enough bloody leaders. Books, that's what they want. Believe you me. I've got a girlfriend out here. I come over and see her. Without boasting, I'm putting two of her kids through school. That's why I said "Yes" to this jamboree. I thought "Why not let the Council stand me a flight?" I pay my taxes like the next man. Maybe a bit less, I've got a good accountant. That's what the British Council is, taxpayers' money!' He seems to be aware he is being too frank, for his next statement is more muted. 'I mean, it's not just a bit of "how's your father". I've been in a relationship with Sanyu for years.'

'Relationships,' Peter Pargeter seizes on this. 'I couldn't agree more. Now that *is* our business. The Council has to make relationships. It's the quality of our relationships that matters.'

'So why are you closing the bloody libraries? You've got people coming in to read the newspapers, and use the computers, and go online. You're really going to cock up that relationship.'

'It's the old model!' Peter Pargeter rises above him. He's argued with too many people like Geoffrey. 'You can't get hung up on the old model. In fact, our libraries serve a very small readership. Our new projects will have throughput in the millions. We do have a vision, a real vision for the future. The library isn't closing, Geoffrey. Far from it. Yes, it won't exist in a physical space, but it will be accessible to everyone, online. Customers all over Uganda will be able to input and order titles. Then we'll courier material all over the country.' It was gleaming and whirring, his new model. 'We've already put the courier business out to tender.'

'Internet don't work here, 'aven't yer noticed?' Geoffrey remarks, scornfully. 'And 'ow will folk know what titles to ask for? You're throwing the past out the winder, aren't yer?' He sounds more northern as he grows more drunk.

'In the past, the Council's been too risk-averse,' says Peter. 'I won't be making that mistake.'

Vanessa vainly tries to join in, but they are too busy clashing antlers. She has a very clear view of Peter Pargeter's ear, because his head is turned so firmly to the left, but its fleshy pink well is blocked with pale wiry hair. On the other side of her, the bottle-glassed midget is waving his card, assiduously, and Vanessa is getting a stiff neck, ignoring him, but she wants to join in this important debate. As an International Delegate, she needs to contribute.

'What about novels?' she says, suddenly loud as both the men fall silent at once. 'Are they the old model? And writing?'

'We don't want to get hung up on text,' says Peter Pargeter. 'Look at it organically. We are partnering in so many new projects. It's a very exciting time, in Uganda.' He suddenly remembers her mention of Mary as a local writer, and feels uneasy. Perhaps he has spoken a little freely. 'If you don't mind, Vanessa, perhaps you wouldn't mention our plans for the library to any of our local writers just yet. First I want to get all my ducks in a row. But I'm very pleased with our latest initiative, which we are trialling now in Nairobi. We're going to be running graffiti workshops here. We think the takeup will be impressive.' He sits back, delighted by his own daring. These silly old fogies will have to learn.

'Graffiti workshops in Kampala?' Now Geoffrey Truman is roaring with laughter. 'They'll all get bloody sent to jail, you fool. Whose idiotic bloody idea was *that*?'

Vanessa watches Pargeter's large pink ear redden, flooding slowly with blood, yet he is still smiling, a professional smile, clench-toothed, diplomatic. He has got a mission statement: he will stick to it. *Relationships, Organic, Leadership, Future*. It is his mantra. He *is* the future. 'Ah, excuse me, Geoffrey. I must just go across and have a word with my colleague Heather.'

After he has gone, like Superman, disappearing in a cloud of faintly acetone man-scent, Geoffrey Truman peers vaguely in Vanessa's direction in something that seems like companionship.

'Bloody dinosaurs, aren't we, you and me,' he says. 'I could eat that little mammal for breakfast, though.'

Vanessa doesn't want to be a dinosaur, though she likes the idea of Peter Pargeter as a tree-rat. 'My work is rather modern,' she says, then hears herself, disconcertingly; there is a note of hollow grandeur. Graffiti workshops. Is this the future? Shouldn't the young be doing that on their own? It's like policemen teaching schoolkids to burgle.

'He'll be gone in two years,' says Geoffrey Truman. 'Mark my words. Ambitious little shit. Then it'll be All Change. Some other bugger, with some other big idea. And the decent people, the ones like that 'eather who loves books and reading – and believe you me, there are plenty of decent ones in the Council, poor bastards, you've met 'em, so've I – they won't get a look-in when the jobs are given out. And poor old Kampala will have lost its library.'

After supper, it is rather a relief to Vanessa to join the women having drinks in the garden. Somehow, the white women have ended up together, and though in general Vanessa prefers the Africans, it can be a relief, for a while, to be with one's own. And with women, after all that testosterone! She makes the others laugh by describing the row.

'Oh men, they're just *different*,' says Deirdre Mullins. 'That's what all the wars are about, round here. If these African countries ever had a woman in charge ...'

'Well Thatcher was hardly a pacifist,' says Vanessa. '*She* went to war against the Falklands.' Suddenly she isn't quite so down on testosterone.

'At least that was a sensible war, that we won.'

'In retrospect, wars you win look sensible.'

'Well, African wars just go on and on.' That was Heather Hughes, the British Council literature officer responsible for the conference. 'Have you read about the LRA? They're terrifying. In the north of Uganda. It's supposed to be over, but they are still abducting people. And some of them have fled into DRC. Along the border between DRC and Uganda.'

'Things do seem to be, you know, *different* here,' says Deirdre. 'I don't want to think it, but it's true. I mean cutting off, you know, lips and noses ...' She has been to Africa once before, 'on safari' with a friend, 'you know, budget safari'. 'We were staying in a *banda* on the Ssese Islands, just the two of us, and in the middle of the night, some-one banged on our door ... We nearly died. We were terrified.'

'I'm thinking of going to Bwindi,' says Vanessa. 'To see the gorillas. I always wanted to. But it is rather near the border with DRC.'

'I wouldn't go anywhere near Congo,' says Deirdre, though no-one else seems to have heard what she said, which is a pity, since Vanessa hoped to make an impression.

Deirdre has spiritedly resumed her story. 'I had this teeny-weeny nightdress on, and my friend Polly was sleeping naked, and this huge black man –' She stops her story as a tall Ugandan waiter brings her another beer on a tin tray. 'Enjoy your beer, dear,' he says, but they cannot see his face, outlined against the palm trees and the blue starry night, and he walks away, silently, back to the hotel, to the bawling white men in the crowded bar.

'What was I saying ... Oh yes. In fact, he was just bringing a phone message ... But of course, we were, you know, absolutely terrified. By the way, what do we do about, you know, tipping?' Deirdre hasn't tipped him, and now she feels guilty, only partly in case the others have noticed.

'Well, what you'd do at home, I guess,' says someone.

'But I mean, we're *staying* here. We can't tip on everything.'

They sit and agree that they can't tip on everything, and then Deirdre Mullins retells her story, and the white women sit and talk of rape and murder, growing louder and more graphic as the night goes on, and the crickets trill thrillingly, increasing their excitement, until at some point the delicate equation between alcohol and food and blood sugar slips into deficit, the night gets cooler, and the sober black waiters in smart Sheraton jackets who have ferried out beers come and take away their glasses, and address the women customers with lowered eyes and voices, and a little later on, alone in their rooms, as the women check their screens and find the internet is down, which makes them feel lonelier, and more disconnected, as they squint behind their curtains in case a tiny rustle might be the dry wings of a stray mosquito, little pangs of real fear, little headaches begin. They double-lock their doors and lie awake, hearts pounding.

But Vanessa feels quite safe, and not sick any more. Tomorrow the conference proper will begin: sessions on many things she finds interesting, and she will track down Mary at the Nile Imperial. And then there's Bwindi glowing green in the near future, something rare and special, her very own adventure.

As she listened to Deirdre and Heather and the others, she has started to think that age is an advantage. She does know things, and she likes men, really: she had warmed to Geoffrey Truman, despite his rudeness, and she likes Ugandans: she doesn't fear them. She thinks, I have never really been racist. Or I would never have employed a Ugandan cleaner. Knowing Mary was certainly an advantage, for Justin ... If only he and Zakira had someone like Mary, someone calm and experienced, to help with Abdul Trevor.

Vanessa wouldn't dare criticise Zakira, but she's very busy, so it all falls on Justin. He doesn't always answer his mother's texts. About one in five, she thinks, drifting, drifting ... But at least the vital bit of information has arrived: 'Abdy is fine. Temp down. Do not worry!' It's a worry, though, that they haven't got a nanny. Though Trevor became almost too fond of Mary ... Trevor, Trevor ... so far away.

13

'I can hardly believe I'm in Uganda,' says Trevor. 'It's great, Mary, honestly.'

They are bowling along the road from Entebbe; they've left behind the lake, they are hurrying through forest that has recently been cleared, leaving pearl-pale stumps, and new buildings are rising, and workmen are singing, and others are walking to work along the road. Huge billboards ask questions: 'ARE YOU READY FOR CHOGM?'

'So it's a very big deal, this CHOGM?' he asks, as they drive past the umpteenth billboard. 'What does it stand for again? Commonwealth Heads of what?'

Mary tuts scornfully. 'No, it is nothing. Commonwealth Heads of Government. The Queen will come. For half a day, maybe. And they tell us to get ready.' She speeds up, crossly, then brakes deftly as a bicycle wobbles in front of her. He notices she is wearing her glasses. With her glasses on, she is a very good driver. In London, once, she had picked him up in Vanessa's car when his van was in the garage, and she'd had to drive with her nose on the windscreen, peering short-sightedly at the road.

'Nice car, by the way. You must be doing well.' Not that he himself would drive it. It's a red Toyota, circa 1998.

'It is Charles's car. Soon he will buy one for me. If you talk to

Charles, he will say something different about CHOGM. Charles is delighted the Queen is coming, I do not know why, she will do nothing for him. But many Ugandans think like Charles.'

'Good woman, in my view,' says Trevor, cautiously. 'Better than a president. But then, you Ugandans have presidents.'

'They are useless,' says Mary. 'They have all been useless. And Museveni will come and meet the Queen, and he will wear his bush-hat, which is supposed to remind us that he was in the bush with the NRA, and was a soldier, and a hero. But we do not believe that he was a hero, because it was his brother who did all the fighting, and even then, he got children to fight for him.'

'Right,' says Trevor. 'I see. I'll have to read up on Ugandan history. I had the impression things were better now. You know, more peaceful than under Idi.'

He looks across at her; he wants to get things right, but her nostrils are flaring in a scornful way, and her eyes behind her small gold glasses have narrowed.

'That is like saying a day in the Sahara is cooler than the middle of Virunga volcano. And we must stop talking about Idi Amin, because he is the only thing you *bazungu* know about Uganda, and he does not help us. First because he was a lunatic, though funny, and second because everyone says, like you, ah everything is good now, because he has gone.'

She is talking rather fast, and quite loudly, and Trevor remembers that Mary has a temper. Plus, she's glaring at him, and not looking at the road, and although it's very straight, it is not without its hazards, since the oncoming traffic is fast and heavy.

'I don't mean to annoy you, Mary, old thing. You've got to remember, it's my first time in Uganda.'

'Yes, it is your first time in Uganda, Trevor. I remember that. So I must give you information. You told me many things, when I was in London. And I was grateful. But now things are different.'

But she suddenly smiles at him, forgivingly, and looks back at the road just in time to miss a truck that says ON THE WAY TO HEAVEN on its windscreen.

'Are you tired, Trevor? If you are not tired, we will go to lunch at Lake Victoria. It is not far. And you will learn something about water in Uganda. And then, tomorrow, we will go to my village. I hope you have got your implements with you.'

'My tools? What do you think's in the leather bag?' He cranes round his neck for a moment's reassurance. Battered and stained, his whole life is in there. It sits on the seat, heavy, solid. 'At your service, Madame. Trevor Patchett Plumbing.'

'Though of course, Trevor, you will not be charging callout.'

It is very hard to read Mary Tendo's expression. Trevor settles, with a small sigh, back into his seat, in which he can detect one spring is broken. Now they're on a section of road that's not mended. Why does he always seem to deal with difficult women? Bumpy ride, he thinks. Hang on to your hat.

Vanessa's in Reception at the Sheraton, trying not to get cross with the receptionists. Two or three of them have gathered protectively around Rachel, the girl to whom Vanessa addressed her query.

'It can't *not be there*, my friend works there. Look, *Nile Imperial*. N-I-L-E, I-M-P ...'

The little gaggle of girls in their golden jackets exchange looks with Rachel nervously. They have all been taught not to contradict, but then how are they to deal with deluded *bazungu*, these strange, blind people who know they are right?

'Yes, Madam. I know the Nile Imperial –'

But Vanessa interrupts. She is in a hurry! She will miss the mini-bus to the first session! They are dragging their feet deliberately!

'It's *terribly* near. I mean, I could walk there, but obviously it's easier if I phone first. I am *just asking you to connect me*. To *phone*, you know, to the right number.' And she mimes phoning, elaborately.

Now none of them will meet her eyes, and they are calling over an older man, to whom they speak rapidly, in their own language. Vanessa can't believe how slow they all are. Outside she can hear some vehicle hooting.

'Good morning, Madam. I would like to ask, is it possible your friend is at the Serena?' His smile is professional, intentionally soothing.

'I have told them eight times, it's the Nile Imperial!'

'Madam, there is no more Nile Imperial. It has been demolished, two years ago. It has been replaced with the Serena Hotel.'

Vanessa is silenced. 'Demolished. Oh.' A stone of disappointment. 'Why couldn't they explain? Nobody told me.'

And with that, leaden-hearted, she turns away, leaving a cooing chorus from the women in reception, who are genuinely sad they cannot help her. 'Ah, sorry, Madam. Ah, sorry.'

But what she really feels is hurt about Mary. She had thought they were friends. *Why didn't she tell me*? And how can she possibly search for her, in this suddenly large and unknown city? She could be anywhere. She could have gone away.

Is it possible Mary never liked me?

She gets into the minibus, with the others, but looks out of the window as they chatter. At first she stares at every woman they pass, all those smartly dressed women, walking steadily onwards down their own paths, smiling, impervious, the morning sunlight blanking out their features and making all of them, potentially, Mary.

Were we ever close? *Did we share my son*? – Of course a carer was very different from a mother, but Mary had certainly done a lot for Justin, both when he was little and as a young man, when the strange shadow came over him. I thought, in a way, we loved him together.

– I wasn't always good at loving him.

She rejects this thought in a split second.

But Mary – poor Mary had lost her own son. Their driver suddenly hoots, in a long deafening wail, as a lorry teeming with dusty workmen cuts in front of them onto a roundabout. No, they're not workmen. She looks again. Khaki battle-fatigues. Oh, they're soldiers.

'Soldiers,' says Bernardine.

'They make me nervous,' says Deirdre Mullins; but they all feel a chill.

Vanessa tries to focus on Mary's son. His name was Jamil. She called him Jamie. I didn't encourage him to play with Justin. I felt she would be getting away with it, somehow, being paid by me to look after Justin and caring for her own child on the side. Perhaps I was jealous, since I was too busy to spend whole days with my own child. And then obviously, when Jamil was ill, it was unreasonable of her to want to bring him with her. I couldn't let Justin be infected. Even when he was well, I had concerns about language. The child's father spoke Arabic, Mary Luganda. Her English is more than adequate, but I thought Jamil might be less forward than Justin. A second child would have held Justin up, a second child less gifted at language.

But then of course Jamil disappeared. Which was a tragedy. Somewhere in Libya. Or on the way back. Mary hardly ever spoke of it. If she had confided, I might have been able to comfort her. I would have tried. She didn't trust me.

In any case, Mary had been very lucky. When Vanessa last saw her, she had been pregnant.

(They look so strong, all the women on the pavement, with books on their heads, or baskets, or fruit, so glossy and unstoppable that Vanessa feels jealous; Mary doesn't need her; she's gone on into her future, powerful and fertile, ignoring her.)

And yet a small tear creeps down Vanessa's cheek, which she dashes away quickly before anyone sees. 'I think I'll close the window, the air is so dusty,' she says, and it glides like a veil over the day, and she polishes the instant of grief away, but she is thinking of the package at the bottom of her case, nicely wrapped in silver paper with a pattern of balloons. It's a carefully chosen present for Mary's baby. Not a baby any more: Theodora must be three. Not so very much younger than her own Abdul Trevor.

'Those storks are amazing,' says Bernardine, and Vanessa half-registers them, lined up like sentries, along the high roof of the Parliament Building, listening, perhaps, to the speeches inside.

The little book, for Mary's Ugandan baby, cannot be recycled for Abdul Trevor, because Vanessa has already given him a copy. It is Hans Andersen's *Fairy Tales*. There is a picture of two tall storks on the cover, looking out on the world with intelligent eyes.

'I think I like animals better than humans,' says Vanessa, suddenly, with conviction, which just for an instant, silences the minibus.

'Odd woman,' hisses Deirdre Mullins to Bernardine, as they get out and troop across the car park to the social club where this session will be.

'Oh I quite like her,' says Bernardine.

14

Trevor has the warm, sticky child in his lap, and is feeding her another piece of banana. The maid is watching him, amazed, between her fingers. *Omuzungu munyumba yaffe*! *Ate ali ngomulalu*! A *muzungu* in the house! And he is crazy! Theodora will put food all over his clothes. But she's looking with new respect at Mary, who can order a *muzungu* about with such ease.

'You can pick her, Trevor, she will not bite you,' Mary said, almost as soon as Trevor arrived, and though the maid thought Trevor looked faintly grumpy (but all *bazungu* look faintly grumpy), he had put down his cases, and picked up the child.

And now Theodora's face becomes congested and she makes a curious straining noise that Mercy has come to know only too well, and she looks at Mary, and makes to rush forward, but Mary casts her a repressive glance, so the child is still squarely planted on Trevor when a warm, sweet, sickly smell fills the room.

'Ah Trevor, sorry, welcome to Uganda,' says Mary merrily. 'Help him, Mercy.'

Trevor is glazed with tiredness, and everything feels dreamlike. He would happily drop out of Mary's trip to the lake, but she looks at him sternly, her head on one side and a particular teasing, assessing air that he knows of old when she worked for Ness, and says, 'Trevor.

I know you are not old, or tired. I think you are ready now to drive to Lake Victoria?' And somehow, he hears himself saying 'Yes.'

But he knows he is not quite the full ticket. As they bucket along through the centre of Kampala, with Mary braking sharply as she throws out information at him in intensive bursts that feel like morse, he tries to focus, and he fails.

'And so this is Parliament Building, Trevor. Built to mark independence, in 1962. After which we were governed by the murderer Obote, because he had done a deal with the British, which is also the case with the murderer Mugabe, who also did a deal with the British in Zimbabwe, although now they pretend that he is an example of how Africans cannot rule their own countries ...'

He finds it impossible to concentrate. 'Those are bloody big storks,' he interrupts her. They perch along the top of the enormous modern gateway that's meant to mark the start of Ugandan democracy. In a minibus that's battling with Mary for the road, he sees that the passengers are also staring. The windows are dirty, but he gets a little jolt as he spots a thin blonde with pale hair, neck straining. She reminds him, sharply, of Vanessa, but sadder. Of how Vanessa might look when she's older. He is just about to point her out to Mary when the traffic moves, and Mary guns the engine and pulls past the minibus, still talking.

'That woman was a bit like Vanessa, Mary,' he says, but the moment has slipped into the past.

'Trevor, I hope you are listening.'

'To be honest, Mary – I'm trying, but I was on a plane all night, last night, I grant you in a bloody great comfortable seat and being waited on hand and foot, but I'm not in the best state to learn Ugandan history.'

Mary drives on in silence. He scans her profile; she has a thoughtful look that he knows might mean trouble. Quite soon, as they draw up at some big metal gates and a security guard comes strolling towards them, she turns towards him with an enigmatic smile. She's a beautiful woman: mischievous, intelligent. He takes in her pink gums, her strong white teeth, her brown amused eyes with their slight look of mystery, her oiled black hair in serried coils like the sea. Her shoulders are broad: her arms are well-muscled. In a fight, she'd knock the socks off Soraya or Vanessa. He tries not to think about women fighting. Naked women rolling in a sea of mud. He would have to go in and rescue Vanessa ... He finds he is dozing, on the hot plastic seat, as Mary gets out briskly and slams the car door.

She's suddenly grinning in through his window.

'So, Trevor, I see that you heard nothing at all. This is not Ugandan history: it is *British* history.'

The guard, who is waving his rifle as casually as a boy with a switch for cattle, comes over and tries to collect a fee, which Mary refuses indignantly. 'Where are the receipts?' she asks him, frowning. 'Show me your receipts, and I will give you a fee.' ('He is a crook,' she explains, aside, to Trevor. 'He is a crook, and he thinks I must be rich, because I have a car and a *muzungu* boyfriend, though of course, Trevor, we both know you are not my boyfriend.')

And he finds himself wondering, in the daze of heat as they walk into a wide expanse of green grass, and some big dark trees, and scattered, empty tables, and beyond it, beauty – a wide flowering lake, stretching out as far as the horizon, as blue as the sky except for islands of flowers, white blooms like stars on great rafts of fresh leaves – he finds himself wondering, as the dream continues, and Mary walks ahead of him, her powerful hips swaying, round surging mounds in the unreal sunlight, and a stream of words blow back at him like music, though he can't catch any of the individual notes – *What would it be like to be Mary's boyfriend*? He tells himself sternly not to be a fool, but for the last six weeks, with things breaking down, Trevor has not had sex with Soraya. Naturally his thoughts might be, well, untoward.

In his next coherent memory, he is sitting at a wooden table, on a wooden seat that is hard on his bones, with Mary opposite, the lake behind her, like a vast silver frame in which she glows darkly, and she is still addressing him about crime.

'And so, Trevor, this is Ggaba Beach Resort. It is just along the lake from Ggaba fishing village. It is a nice place. But unfortunately, as I told you, it is guarded by criminals, like those who are everywhere in London. I fear that we also have them in Uganda.'

Now Mary is ordering, from a child who is surely too young to be working here. Two enormous, dark red fish are delivered, all eyes and spines and heads and bones, and two plates of chips, while Mary harangues him and he's lulled by the sound of the waves and the leaves, the distant sound of some children laughing, and faint cars, like the sea, on the road to Entebbe. Did he really only arrive this morning? Mary's moved from history to biology. Meanwhile, in the background, the silver is darkening: the lake-light is streaked with gun-metal. And the sun: the sun is flickering.

'And so, your impressions of the lake are good.' He has said something praising to fob her off, so he can concentrate fully on the pleasure of the chips, which neither Soraya nor Vanessa ever cooked, because they were always putting him on diets. 'Ha! That is what I expected you to say. So now, Trevor, I have many things to tell you ...'

And she does; as he eats and shifts and dozes, as the branches of the tree above them start to stir, as the heat increases and the sky blackens, and across the paradisal floating tapestry of flowers ('It is water hyacinth, Trevor. It's a weed'), which is still crystal-bright in the afternoon sun, an astonishing purplish blue storm comes bellying, so very slowly growing, thickening, quickening, now eating the horizon, and the breeze tastes different, it is cooling as he listens, listens without hearing, as he watches her dark cushiony lips moving, and the air on his own lips freshens with rain, and Mary goes on talking and talking. She has waited for this chance for a very long time. It is her turn, at last, to explain her country.

And Trevor sits mute, in the meniscus of the moment, protected by jet-lag from this onslaught of fact. He is very happy; he is here; he is well. *So this is Kampala. This is Uganda. I'm nearly 60, and I've come to Africa. Well done, old son*, he says to himself.

'And so they are stealing the water of the lake. Museveni, you see, is not patriotic. He is building a new dam to make electricity, and yet it will not be for the people of Kampala, he will sell the power to whoever can pay. And believe me, at State House the lights never go out. But the rest of us often do not have hot water, though the level of the lake is always going down. So they have to build new jets, in Ggaba fishing village.'

'*Jets*? They build jets? That can't be right ... I thought you imported planes from America? ... Oh *jetties*, I see. Yes, you mean jetties.'

'They build new jetties, as I said, Trevor.' She stops and looks at him very sternly. At times she reminds him of Vanessa. 'And still the catches are going down. And because of the Nile Perch, which you have just been eating – are you awake, Trevor? I hope you are – did you enjoy the fish you ordered?'

'Very nice, Mary,' says Trevor, docilely. It seems uncontroversial, liking the fish, but no, the glint in Mary's eyes sharpens.

'Because of this fish, which you like so much, which is not Ugandan, but has been imported to please the tourists, and to send to London, and other rich countries, and which eats all the food in this Ugandan lake, there is nothing left for Ugandan speeches.'

This astonishing *non sequitur* wakes Trevor up, together with a faint pattering somewhere, a sound like a thousand ball-bearings falling, silvery, firm, a vast machine coming closer and closer, bearing down on them like the end of time. And something is draining away the light.

'Ugandan speeches? Nothing left, how so? I mean, Mary, you're not exactly silent …'

But Mary rushes onward at her audience. '*Ngege*, and so on, which the village people ate.'

'Oh *species*, Mary, Ugandan species …'

But all further speech ceases as, with a sound like thunder, the storm sweeps over them, rattling the plates, deafening them both as they run blind for cover.

By the end of the day, Vanessa's exhausted. She has listened to speeches, both dull and impassioned, about 'Dis-covering the Outsider in *Heart of Darkness*;' 'African Publishing: a Contradiction?' ('When will we African publishers come in from the cold? Your British bookshops do not welcome us, and yet Heinemann has closed its African list …'). She has nodded, to show enthusiasm, until the dry vertebrae of her long neck ache and click with empathy. She has scribbled furious notes on them all. She has asked questions to encourage the speakers. She has made little statements in support. She does her best to be a good International Delegate, partly so the British Council will ask her again, but partly because she is still indignant about Peter Pargeter's vision of the future.

It's not just that he saw her as old-fashioned, last night, her and Geoffrey Truman and all the British team. It is that so many writers are assembled here, eager Africans from all over the continent, all of them in love with books and writing, all aware that the colleges or schools where they teach are tragically short of books, pens, notebooks, all hoping something good will come from this confer-ence (it's Heather, she sees, who is the force behind it), all longing for contacts, a leg-up, an audience, the opening of a door into some magical universal library where luckier, richer writers come and go at will – they are all here, intelligent, hungry, but Peter Pargeter sees them as 'the old model'. They won't get books, they'll get graffiti workshops. He's already looking over their shoulders at teeming millions of younger customers.

There's a lunch-time session of rap and beat box which Vanessa rather enjoys, in fact (the real Banga is quite sweet and cuddly, and forty-two if he is a day, while the beat box rhythm has her clapping along) – and Peter is there, on his feet near the stage, making sure he is included in all the photographs, loosening his tie to get down with the beat, though at the end, as the cameras flash, he laughs so stagily, one arm round Banga, that an opportunistic bluebottle flies straight down his throat, and he stumbles from the room, grinning, waving, choking. 'Ah, sorry,' says a kindly poet from Makerere.

In the afternoon, the rain pours down, and they all get soaked between the bus and the hotel where the last two papers are scheduled to be held. Both of these, as it turns out, are by British academics. In the crammed ballroom at the Sheraton, Vanessa finds herself dozing off. The first paper's on 'The Lonely Modernist', by a man who draws a brave arc of exclusion from Woolf, Joyce, Faulkner to Sebald and Coetzee. Vanessa is expecting to like this one. But she finds herself thinking, are they really outsiders? They have all managed to be rather successful. There are other writers the man could have mentioned. Herself, for example. But people are myopic. It doesn't matter, her star is rising (though as always, when she's with other writers, a small worm of doubt wriggles up into the light. Perhaps she should have, well, written more books. Then the fact of her exclusion would be indisputable ... With a huge psychic effort, she squashes down the worm, and imagines her future in two stages. First, she will be recognised as an outsider. Then, she will be brought in from the cold in triumph – no-one wants to be an outsider for ever.)

The second paper's on – but what is it on? It is almost impossible to be sure. The title is 'Positioning the Outsider: a Semiotic Reading of Acts of Exclusion,' and the author is a young, fierce-looking woman, though she wears a kaftan with a dizzy plunge, revealing two round, jaunty breasts all set to break out and make a dash at the audience. 'Who is the Outsider?' she asks, rhetorically. Vanessa is galvanised by the question, which seems to slide straight into her soul: *I'm here*, she thinks: *why can't they see me*? All round her, the audience is sitting up, encouraged, but the second sentence makes them slump again.

'One is tempted,' the lecturer continues, 'when contextualising the *oeuvre* of the postcolonial writer *per se*, to neglect the fundamental importance of positionality in any historiographical act. In considering one's object, which is also one's subject, one must not beg the question of what, in this discourse, postcoloniality really might be.' Then she looks at the audience over her glasses, challenging them to disagree. In fact, as she continues in the same contorted style, throwing up great long earthworks of defensive abstraction before revealing the smallest glimpse of her message, eighty-five per cent of them are stunned into sleep, once the first fascination with her breasts is over. In the middle of the lecture, someone slams the door loudly, and Vanessa wakes up with a start, thinking 'Someone has summoned the courage to leave.' She turns her head to see, but is just too late.

(In fact it was Mary: Mary Tendo, standing quietly at the back, dark in the glare of fluorescent light. Having driven back from the fishing village, she has left Trevor sleeping in the red saloon outside, and come in to the Sheraton to see if she has any last messages. Remembering, in passing, the Writers' Conference, she's popped in briefly, curious. The room is full, and very stuffy. She stands at the back trying to pick up the thread. But there is no thread: just a series of knots, getting larger and larger, woollier and woollier, tying up the poor speaker in worse and worse nonsense. Besides, the woman looks like a prostitute. Yet the International Writers all sit there docilely, probably thinking her a genius ... Mary cannot see that most of them are sleeping. She's glad that it's rubbish, since she wasn't invited.)

15

The boy does not know who he is any more. He has no idea where or when. He lies on the ground, sodden, head spinning.

Once he was a child. He had two parents. He loved them both. He lived in a city.

There was milk and cake. His bed was warm. He had colds and coughs, but never this sickness. His mother was working from morning till night, but whenever she could, she brushed his hair, and cut his nails, and made him wash, and talked to him as she cooked the food. She taught him rhymes. She read to him. But she always hurried, and had to leave. His father was home, behind a closed door.

If I cried, he would come out and look at me. His face was puzzled, but he did not hate me. He was looking for something – was I like him?

All that time has become like a dream.

I thought that they would always be there. Then my mother started to shout at my father

everything changed   he took me away

But now I am entirely alone. I can never go back. They could never forgive me. I made wrong choices. I went the wrong way

yes I am Cain, in the Bible story   every man's hand is against me, for ever
if thy right hand offend thee, cut it off   If thy right eye offend thee, cut it out
we cut off ears, and lips, and noses   and worse things too   I can never be forgiven   I should be cut into tiny pieces   then scattered like dust where no-one will find me
My life ended, and I lived in hell
it hangs round my neck it has leather wings
I poke it forward but it's gripping, flailing

Above him, the sun moves briefly behind the thick leaves of a Cassipourea tree, and for ten minutes, his mind steadies.

There are ten commandments. He has broken them all. They start to seem useless, like rusted iron. They clank behind him, they groan in the night, the sound of torturing instruments. He has used those too. He has done it all. He is damned for ever. He can never go home. And the sun moves round, the sun moves on.

God's eye is in the tomb with me

16

Vanessa's sitting, just after sunset, surrounded by the other writers and a smattering of giant schoolchildren, through an 'Evening of International Writing' at the dark, dank National Theatre, which squats, hot and airless, like a square, chocolate brown excretum from the '60s, slap, plop in the centre of Kampala. Though at first she was astonished not to be on the programme, she soon realises these are mostly second-raters.

This was more or less what Peter Pargeter hinted when she found him to ask about the omission. (And Tadjo, for example: Tadjo's name is not there.) 'Oh, you're reading tomorrow, in a more intimate context. We felt that would show your gifts to advantage.' He looked uneasy, and then added, with a little flourish, 'And obviously, someone of your experience will have had many chances to read in bigger venues. Which is not true of all the Africans here.'

But Deirdre Mullins was quite full of herself when they met in the foyer before the event. 'You aren't reading? Oh, what a shame ... I expect we'll be hearing from you tomorrow, then.'

Vanessa looks at her hard. *Is she patronising me*? 'Yes, I will be reading with a different group of writers, who I believe include Veronique Tadjo.'

'Oh no, she's gone home, haven't you heard?' babbles Deirdre, her large plain face glistening with sweat and eagerness.

'You had better go and practise your reading,' says Vanessa. 'I think there are a lot of first-timers, this evening.'

And so it has proved, or if it wasn't their first time, they had learned nothing, and should soon give up. Yet some of them go on for ever, as does Geoffrey Truman, who has clearly had a few. How the heart sinks when the performer begins by saying, semi-audibly or shouting loudly, 'I am going to read from four of my books'. *One will be sufficient, surely*, she thinks.

But a few of them are a revelation. It is galling, yet good for her, Vanessa decides, to find that Deirdre Mullins has talent. When she finishes, Vanessa has tears in her eyes. And one or two others set the stage alight, and remind them all that what they do has a point.

Later she lies contented in her vast white bed, looking forward to her own reading tomorrow. She knows, for some of them, she's quite a dark horse, since the African writers are franker than British ones, unless you include Geoffrey Truman ('Vanessa Henman? No, I have not read you.') A white horse, maybe. A pale horse ... A pale horse running over endless white sheets ...

And her hot little feet start to twitch against the mattress.

But then something wakes her: for it's death, is it not? She is falling, soundlessly, and then she's awake. Something about Death on a pale horse. Vanessa still feels young. She's not ready to die. She's not going to die for ages and ages, till she's written her not-yet-written books, and is famous ...

But do I look old, to all these young people?

What worked this evening? The simplest things. Little bits of story that seemed – true. Details. When someone else's life came before you, bright and naked, saying, 'Look, I'm like you.' Even when it was Deirdre Mullins, because the point was, the point was ... She is drifting, but recalls herself, because it is important.

The point was, Deirdre Mullins only *looks like* Deirdre Mullins, and sounds like her, someone silly and boring, but really, it's just a façade we wear, our looks, our habits, the things we say. Something temporary, a crude tent for protection. But inside the tent, there is something living. And even that poor woman in the ill-judged kaftan, who talked such rubbish about 'positionality'. Her body was trying to make contact with us.

So Vanessa changes her mind about her reading. She'd intended to read from her novel in progress, the novel that stalled so long ago, a passage about the self-conscious writer, the doubts and self-protectiveness that cripple you. And suddenly that seems trivial, irrelevant. Real writers try to make life real for others.

She decides, I'll read a passage about my father. My father and the chickens. About my childhood. From my abandoned autobiography. And if people like it, I will be encouraged.

Because she does need encouragement. The last few years have been tricky. Of course she is happy that Justin is married, but naturally there has been – more of a distance. And Trevor himself ... Dear old Tigger. Fair enough, he has this other woman – though he once lost his temper when she called Soraya that; 'She is not the other woman, I am living with her! It is thirty-odd years since you threw me out!' – but why does he have to fixate on Soraya? After all, it was not as though he'd married her. (*No, whereas he had married Vanessa.*) Yet he made strange complaints about 'giving them a chance'. He no longer seemed to want their special times together, which had gone on, quite unchanged by their divorce, for decades. Quite suddenly he 'mustn't be unfair to Soraya!' He is so old-fashioned! *Yet how she has missed them.*

No Tigger and no Justin. The house has felt empty. There was a brief fling with a mature student, but too much to explain, too much to unlearn, and she realised how long it would take to train him. Whereas Trevor, well, he was already trained. ('I am not a dog,' he had told her, once. 'Though you can be a bit of a bitch, Vanessa.' And when she was outraged, he only laughed. 'Don't talk about having to train me, then.')

It was almost as if he didn't care any more. As if he didn't care about Vanessa. Yes, she is always busy with her teaching, but teaching writing doesn't feed the soul. And perhaps the house has felt a little empty, with Justin so busy, and Trevor away.

Of course there is little Abdul Trevor. Her grandchild, when she sees him, is a total joy. ('They're the meaning of life,' she'd once said to Fifi, which was ill-advised, since Fifi has no children. Yet Vanessa does believe it, in a way. Fifi has her cat, Vanessa has Justin, and Fifi's always seen the two things as the same, but she has no equivalent for Abdul Trevor. And it's through little Abdy that life goes on.) The way he pretends to read a book to her, with great expression, but upside down, the little gifts he thrusts into her hand – a spoonful of rice he doesn't want to finish, a squashed leaf he has kept in his pocket. And once he drew her: an enormous sun, or it might have been a collapsing balloon, with lots of straggly rays coming out, or perhaps they were legs, and she was a spider. 'It's lovely, darling. I will keep it for ever.' She feels faint at the thought of Abdy ill or unhappy. If he is all right, the world is all right. If he is not, it cannot be borne. Like the time when he caught an infection from the pool, and his temperature shot up to 103 ... Abdul Trevor must live for ever. And her thoughts circle back to Mary Tendo, and her little girl, who must be Abdy's age.

But it's too painful to think about Mary: the demolished hotel: the gift still in her suitcase, in its pretty paper, with its pictures of storks, for the child whose features she will never see.

With an effort, she drags her thoughts away. She must just do her best, with the work, and with people. She gets things wrong, she can't deny it, but she tries, she tries, she makes an effort.

And falling asleep, powerless to edit, agnostic Vanessa half-smiles, half-snuffles as her thoughts slip away into green valleys among flocks of drowsy, browsing sheep ... *I hope Someone Up There notices. I hope I'll get a bit of credit.*

PART 3

The Fountain of Life

17

The President has not slept well. There is the problem of the incident on Lake Albert, whose waters are shared between Uganda and Congo. Ugandan soldiers have been killed, so though Kabila assures him it's a misunderstanding, there must be apologies and reparations, and punishment if they are not forthcoming.

There is oil under Lake Albert, oil all along the rich, hidden border regions of Congo and Uganda. There is oil and gold and diamonds, no-one knows how much. Peasants pan for gold in Bwindi Impenetrable Forest; just a very little, a little at a time, in the dappled shadows, when no-one is looking. But foreigners are interested in the gold: for medicine, for technology, for fairy-tale wedding-rings, for ingots, the safe place to keep your money. Foreigners are interested in the oil. Foreigners are interested in the diamonds. And the oil price is going up. It is well over 100 dollars a barrel. Uganda is sitting on lakes of money, compared to which the revenue from tourism is peanuts. *Peanuts for monkeys and gorillas.*

So Museveni tosses, restless, in his enormous bed. Uganda must get hold of it before the foreigners! *Uganda etekwa okweyongerayo mu maaso nate nesubi*! They have to move forward, they have to think boldly, move boldly forward or they will slip behind. They will fall behind DRC to the west, and the savagery there might spill across the border, and the LRA, some of whom are hiding in Congo, might come back in triumph to murder them all, and abduct their children, as they did before, and turn the Ten Commandments into rape and murder. Uganda will fall behind Kenya and Tanzania in the east, and Museveni will not be asked to lead the new East Africa, which, as a great statesman and war hero, he deserves more than any other leader.

Compared to him, they are all midgets. Yet all he gets is criticism.

And then there are those, the NGOs and all those troublesome women who send emails and petitions, who want to stop Ugandans from developing their forests. Who say that the government should not be allowed to put banana plantations in Mabira Forest! He thinks, the *bazungu* do not want us to develop. They want us to remain at their feet, like children. They want us to retain our monkeys and our forests so we stay for ever at a lower level of development. But he is forward-looking. He will not do it. He will lead Uganda into the future. Perhaps, in the short term, this will mean war.

Another new day: hard times, for a leader.

Mary Tendo and Trevor are on the road! Mary is shouting at Mercy, who is in the back seat. '*Tomanyi kulabilira mwana oyo* ...!' It goes on so long, and at such high volume, that Trevor, whose ears hurt, finally asks, 'Everything all right, Mary?'

Mary turns and flashes him a smile and says, in a quite normal voice, in English, 'I am telling the maid to wipe Theodora's face. She leaves her like that, covered in breakfast,' before continuing to shout like a banshee.

They're en route, in theory, to Mary's village, two hours north-west of Kampala. But at 10 AM, they are still bogged down in a stop-start tour of the city's shops. Mary Tendo has bargained for epic quantities of household goods, for rice and potatoes, for sugar and tea, for salt and soap, for cooking oil and paraffin. At last she has settled on a rough-and-ready store where the answers she's got seem to satisfy her. Now the shopkeeper is sorting out boxes and bags, and scribbling figures on a scrap of torn paper.

'Mary, I need a newspaper.' Trevor has never been the type to like shopping. Besides, a man has to keep up with the news. He thought he saw a headline about trouble in Congo. Which is right next door. Trevor needs to know.

'Trevor, I will need you here in a minute.'

But his wish to have something he can call his own, that will tie him back to the habits he likes, to a rectangle of world where Mary isn't talking, makes him shrug her off. 'Back soon,' he says.

And on Kampala Road, the great thoroughfare that plunges through the chest and the bowels of Kampala, past the towering banks and the red-roofed *posta* where refugees go to pick up their parcels, past the bare wires and joists of half-built hotels and the pleasant coffee-smells of Steers' and Nando's, past the white metal chrysalises of briefly-parked taxis and the workmen urgently repairing the pavements – on a section of pavement that's not yet been repaired or cleared of its multi-coloured lichen of sellers, spread out on the concrete, legs flat in the heat, offering matches and lighters and sugared nuts, and chewing gum, biros, pencils, wallets – he finds, where he remembered seeing her, a thin, pretty woman selling newspapers, and most of them, he sees, intrigued, are old, single copies of magazines and weekly papers, some of them American or British, a *Time* magazine dating back to August, an *Economist* forecasting a hot, dry spring, although it is already autumn – but she also has a small pile of today's *New Vision*.

He pays, uncomfortably lordly from above, but as soon as he clutches the thin paper, he feels better, a man with the world between his hands, and everything, therefore, back in order, though the news is once again about the Congo. MUSEVENI TO SORT DRC. Which means, he presumes, sabre-rattling.

He ambles back down the sunny street, which is certainly an improvement on London. Yesterday everything had felt unreal, with the nine-hour flight and then the trip to the lake, and in the evening, in order to be polite, he had sat up talking to Charles and Mary (in fact Mary was doing most of the talking) until he actually fell asleep, his head sinking slowly on to the table, and Charles had escorted him to bed, although Mary seemed a little disapproving, as though he was failing in his essential task, which was to learn everything there was to know about Uganda. In particular, where Britain went wrong. He is used to Mary: he's fond of her. He doesn't mind listening while she talks, though he would like a bit of a rest now and then. But he doesn't suffer from the Guilt of Empire. If that's what she wants, she has got the wrong bloke.

When he spots the car, Mary is back inside, and the boot is bulged open by the stuff she has bought. But he hears Mary's ringing voice through the glass, and in a second, poor Mercy gets out, with a long trailing piece of dirty cloth, and proceeds to use it as makeshift string, tying the lid of the boot roughly to the bumper.

As she works, doggedly, eyes down, the instructions continue from the body of the car. 'Be careful that you do not damage the handle. Be careful that you do not damage the bumper. I have promised Charles we will cherish his car. You are doing what? Are you cherishing?'

When he's almost there, he hears the maid whispering something ferocious under her breath as she struggles to pull the metal maw together, but Mary Tendo continues, regardless. 'Have you finished yet? Have you broken it?'

'Let me give you a hand,' he says to the girl, and she yields to him, grateful, with a sweet, liquid smile. 'Put a sock in it, Mary, I've sorted it.'

'Sock?' Mary is calling from the car, suspicious. 'Have you washed the sock? It is for what? Is it to protect this valuable car?'

Now the maid returns to her seat in the back, where the exquisitely dressed daughter is sitting on her lap, in a pink shiny party dress, that looks too hot, and little sandals made of pale pink jello. Clearly they don't go in for child-seats, in Uganda. The rest of the back seat is piled with sacks of rice. Trevor gets into the front, beside Mary, who averts her face, with a disapproving air, and makes a great show of looking in her purse.

He decides to ignore it. Women are a mystery. In fact, most of them are clean round the bend. He wants them on the road, so he can read his paper. 'Are we ready for the off?' he asks Mary.

'Yes, we are ready.' But she goes on searching, probing her purse for invisible money. 'We need other things, also, but it is better if you buy them outside Kampala.'

Did she say '*you*'? He will not ask. But the business with the purse is hard to ignore. And the frown, pleating her usually serene eyebrows. 'What's the matter, Mary? Did you get a good bargain?'

'I always get a good bargain, Trevor. Except of course it was all very expensive. It is expensive with extra guests.'

He waits. Clearly there is more to come. A stork parades past them, small head aslant, its eyes sharp and amused, as if it is listening.

'And so the guests must be entertained ...'

'Yes. I think I see what you are saying, Mary.'

But Trevor is getting fed up with this. He is still slightly jet-lagged. He wants to read his paper. 'Well. Let's get going, in case it rains. Charles said to me the rainy season's coming early'.

'Charles? He knows nothing about the weather. He pretends he can feel the rain in his bones, but Uganda does not have a rainy season.'

Trevor won't encourage her to criticise Charles. Men, he thinks, have to stick together. 'Now I am going to read *New Vision* ... find out about this hoo-ha in the Congo.'

She is starting the car, but the lectures are not over. 'To Ugandans,

DRC is not ha ha. It can turn out to make very bad trouble, about gold, and oil, and we will have another war, and we have enough wars going on already.'

'I didn't say that. You misunderstood me –'

'And because you had to buy your paper, because you think it is good to read about war, you went away without paying for the shopping, but it is OK, you can pay me later. I know Vanessa often tried to pay me later. I think it is an English habit. I think you had to pay for the empire, later.'

Right. That's enough. Trevor has had it. He likes women, he's a gentle soul, but Mary has managed to get his goat. His goat is got. He won't take it lying down. And as she drives aggressively out of Kampala, klaxoning the horn on principle, whizzing through tiny gaps in the gridlock, Trevor gives Mary a history lesson, too, and for the maid in the back, who speaks hardly any English, but is strong on non-verbal intelligence – who cowers before Mary as before her God, since Mary has replaced her mother and father – Trevor Patchett begins to emerge as a hero.

'OK, Mary, it's my turn now. So maybe the village will have to entertain us. But I will be building them a well, don't forget. And so I dare say they'll be pleased to see us. But if you need money for the food, just ask.'

Trevor's a calm sort of bloke, but he isn't a mug, and he's not going to let Mary piss him around. He's stumped up 400 pounds just to get here, yes, partly because he felt like an adventure, but mostly because he is fond of Mary, and he's throwing in tools and labour for free, and he's short of sleep, and he can't read his paper because ever since he got it, she's been bending his ear, like a giant Queen Bee trying to nest in his earhole, being busy and buzzing and bossing him about and wiggling her bottom as she does it, all woman, and huffing her bosom right in front of him, and maybe that might be part of it ... But he brushes it aside. She's just annoying. Mary wasn't as bad as this in England. 'Now if you don't mind, I'm going to read my paper.' He hasn't really finished: he is building up steam, he has a few things to say about the empire, but he's blowed if he's going to be put off his read.

Mary drives in silence for a mile or two. She is thinking hard behind her glasses. Every now and then, she shoots a little glance at Trevor, under lowered lids, and her mouth is soft. 'I think we will stop to make a purchase,' she says, and swerves decisively across the traffic.

She leaves Trevor in the car with Mercy and Theodora and walks into the shop by the petrol pumps. A few minutes later she returns, not smiling, with a clanking plastic bag, from which she takes three cans of Fanta, two of which she shoots forcefully back over her shoulder at Mercy and the little girl in the back. There are cries of pleasure and surprise. 'Are you happy, Mercy?' she asks in English, as if she wants Trevor to know the maid is happy. 'I think you are fine now, with your Fanta.'

'*Eeee aunty tweyanziza.*' A coo of assent, and a slurping noise.

'And for you I have also bought a Fanta,' she says to Trevor, handing it over, 'and something else I think you like even better.'

It's twenty cigarettes. She is really trying hard. 'Well, that's kind of you, Mary,' he says, mollified. 'But tell you the truth, I've given them up. Didn't I mention it, on the phone?'

'I see! Vanessa has made you give them up.' He spots the glint behind her glasses. (Now he thinks about it, he's sure he told her.)

'It's not Vanessa,' he protests. 'I don't have to be told what to do, like a child ... I suppose it might have been Soraya, though, partly. Anyway, I'd better not start again.'

(In fact it was a newspaper article Soraya had left out on the breakfast table where Trevor couldn't miss it, about the connection between smoking and erections, because when he stopped shagging her, she went a bit crazy. In fact, she had gone clean round the bend.

Apparently, smoking decreased blood-flow, and therefore was a bit of a downer, as it were. But although the article definitely put him off smoking, because he reckoned he needed all the blood he could get, Trevor knew why he had gone off shagging Soraya, and it was nothing to do with smoking or not smoking. It was about warmth, and tenderness. When they started to run out, the sex did too. He had always been like that: sex and love were connected. Though they said it was only true of women. But men had feelings. He did, anyway.)

'Perhaps I will give the cigarettes to the village,' says Mary. 'Of course I could also smoke some myself, though as you know, Trevor, I rarely smoke.'

That was rich, thought Trevor, smiling at his paper. When Mary worked for Nessie, she was always smoking, and always having to pretend she didn't.

'You are smiling, Trevor,' says Mary. 'Perhaps you think that Ugandans are smokers. I know the Henman had the same delusion.' They are butting their way out of the suburbs, now, passing a market selling blowing dresses, the hangers attached to the spokes of big umbrellas, dancing in the wind like riotous skeletons.

'Did I say anything about Ugandans smoking? But come on, Mary, you did like a toke. You and me used to creep off and smoke in the garden. Or in the kitchen if Ness wasn't there.'

'Trevor, I will now explain about smoking. Your British tobacco firms are here in Uganda. They pay the farmers a dollar a day. And they make them cut down trees to cure the tobacco leaves, including the valuable shea butter tree, which is valuable because it makes shea butter. It is an English habit, smoking, that comes from the empire –'

She is in the clear now, on a good, straight road, her voice rising steadily and gaining in power as she zooms beneath a banner of blue bright air towards the hills and fields of her childhood, which she has not revisited for over two decades, and although she sounds loud and confident, the truth is, underneath, she is a little nervous; but how's Trevor to know this? He is a man. What he hears is a lecture, and he feels got at.

'I don't have a clue if smoking is Ugandan. Maybe you didn't smoke before you came to England –'

'Trevor, I never smoked before I came to UK, where I was forced to be a cleaner, once my grant ran out, and did *kyeyo* for dirty English people. In Uganda, only old and poor women smoke, in those parts of the country where these women grow tobacco. To make money, as I said, for the English tobacco companies, as they have been doing ever since the empire.'

'Can't see what the empire's got to do with this.' Trevor has never thought much about the politics of smoking. He isn't too keen on doing it now. 'How do you know these companies are British, Mary?'

'Because the biggest one is called British American Tobacco. I think you will agree that is British, Trevor. Yes, the British manufacturers are killing Ugandans.' And she sounds a long, triumphant blast on her horn as she forces a bicyclist off the road, an old man in shorts with skinny, wrinkled black legs who Trevor sees, with amazement, is balancing a light wood bedstead across his handle-bars, and the man veers wildly away over the verge in the blast of Mary's slipstream. He is not too old to shake his fist after them: at which the bedstead finally topples, and the thin shape dives after it, in slow, gape-jawed motion, and the maid in the back has a loud fit of giggles, and Mary tells her off in a brief burst of Luganda.

'Mary Tendo, *you* are killing Ugandans,' says Trevor, after a judicious pause.

18

It's just after 8.45 AM in England. 'Say bye bye to Mummy,' says Justin.

'Not say goodbye,' says Abdul Trevor, firmly.

'Mummy will be sad,' says Justin, conversationally.

Abdul Trevor looks hard at the ground.

'You want to go to Toddlers?' Justin asks. 'Cos you missed a go, while you were ill. And now you're a big strong boy again.'

Abdul Trevor looks unimpressed. Sometimes he is very like Justin's father.

'Bye bye Abdul Trevor, see you soon,' coos Zakira, and tries to kiss him, but he turns his head away. 'By the way, Justin, do be careful about the eggs. I think his skin is reacting again, poor little chap. Only if you get some from the organic shop.'

'Hmm. OK. If we get time.' Justin wonders if Zakira's wholly sound on nutrition. Her ideas involve a lot of extra work for him. She has strong convictions, stronger than his, about everything to do with Abdy: vaccinations (no, especially MMR, which the middle-class mothers discuss with passion, because it might protect against mumps and measles, but it's also been a suspect for autism!), nit shampoo (sometimes, when the social stigma becomes too great, as lice smoothly circulate the middle-class children, enjoying their clean shiny hair and sweet blood), organic food (*always*: Abdy's sensitive; his light amber skin tends to marks and rashes).

Abdul Trevor looks up, slowly, through long black lashes, to see what his parents will try next. They are looking at him uncertainly. So he tries a yell: long, exploratory, ear-shattering, and then takes a deep breath. Nothing happens, still, so he tries another, and within seconds he is screaming his head off, and, quite soon, he couldn't stop even if he wanted to, his whole being convulsed with crying, so preparations for his outing stall.

'I thought it was terrible twos, not threes.' Justin tries to stay calm, but his stomach curdles. It reminds him of something; himself, probably.

'Mummy's got to go out too,' he tells his son. 'Say "Have a nice day, Mummy," Abdy.'

Abdul Trevor goes on howling.

'At least he's not ill any more,' says Zakira. 'It's a miracle, isn't it. They're up and down so quickly. Couldn't you just, you know – yes, I think you'd better. Darling, you will have to take control of things. You're his father.'

She is smoothing her hair in the mirror, frowning at a lash which might be under her lens, worrying if she has her Oyster Card. It's OK for him, he doesn't go to an office.

'Well, you're his mother,' Justin says. 'Must I be the baddy? I suppose I must. In my family, Mum took control of all this.'

'Well, as you know, I was raised by nannies. It's obvious we are hopeless parents.'

'Oh don't say that,' says Justin, wounded. 'I really want to be a good dad. Are you saying I'm hopeless?'

'Of course not, darling.' And although she's in a rush, she is half-way out the door, she stops and kisses him. She knows he needs it. Justin too easily thinks he's hopeless. 'Bye bye, Abdy darling.' And Zakira is gone.

Finding himself no longer the centre of attention, Abdul Trevor, meanwhile, has stopped crying.

'Come on, Daddy. Going,' says Abdul Trevor, bossily. He has found his coat, and gives it to Justin. 'Daddy help,' he instructs him, and Justin kisses the precious top of his son's head, which always feels hot, with its silky hair, as he helps each small arm into its smooth tunnel: and then both arms suddenly give him a hug.

Justin is filled with happiness. 'Let's go, guys,' he says. And the show's on the road.

19

'It's a beautiful country,' Trevor remarks. 'Old Winston Churchill did not exaggerate.' His spirits are lifted to find everything so bright, whereas he had imagined something dark and jungly. Instead, the green land stretches away to low hills on the horizon, with flowering deciduous trees along the roadside, big red tulip flowers blazing against glossy green leaves and the white clouds towering up towards the sun, or spectacular pyramids of yellow blossom that Mary Tendo insists are 'common. It is not even Ugandan, it is just cassia.'

'The gardeners of London would love that tree.'

'We are used to it. We do not like it.'

It is the food trees which Mary points out: the mangoes and papayas, the yams and avocados, and everywhere low-growing banana trees, their strong palm-like leaves neatly serrated.

'It's fantastic, Mary. You wouldn't have to work. I mean, breakfast must just fall at your feet, out here.' And indeed he does seem to see people not working: they are standing by the side of the road, in the heat, some with big hats, some with bags or buckets to shade them from the enormous sky.

Mary snorts. 'You think Ugandans do not work? In fact they are working in the field all day. The people you see are waiting for lifts, because their journey is too far to walk. And it is true Uganda has many fruit trees, but firstly, the fruit trees are usually on somebody's land, and secondly, you cannot only eat fruit. Or you will spend your time in the pit latrine.'

'I see.'

'I think you got these ideas from Winston Churchill, in his famous book, *My Ugandan Journey*. And he thought the black man did not like to work. It was what they believed during the empire.'

More than ever, he regrets lending Mary the book. 'Well, I have got a lot of time for old Winston, but I don't take everything he said as gospel.' He is trying to be conciliatory, but he can't quite resist going on, after a pause. 'Though he did have a point about the Asians, didn't he? That because, well, you Africans are more laid-back, the Asians might take over if the white man pulled out. Old Idi thought the Asians were too good at business. And that was why he chucked them out, in the '70s –'

'And this is the ideology of empire!' snaps Mary. 'And this is why the British built three different toilets. One for the Africans, which, of course, was disgusting. And one for the Indians, who they called "Coloured". And one for you *bazungu*, our colonial masters.' She almost spits those three words out.

'I am not your colonial master, Mary,' says Trevor, annoyed. 'You worked for Vanessa, remember, not me. I never gave a bugger about the cleaning –'

'I am talking about the days of the empire. Fortunately, Trevor, you no longer rule us.'

'Look, Mary, I don't bloody want to rule you. Did I do much ruling in Vanessa's house? Remember, she ordered us both about!' And yet he finds he has begun to shout. Is Mary's whole intention to aggravate? In the back, the little girl begins to cry, quietly, but Mary, as usual, ignores the sound.

'As I said, Trevor, I am talking about history.' Her voice is softer, but she still sounds self-righteous.

'If you think I'm, you know, laden with guilt. If you think I came out to atone for the empire. You couldn't be more wrong, my friend –'

'I am your friend, Trevor,' says Mary, swiftly. 'But you should not praise Idi Amin, and Winston Churchill –'

'I feel glad to be here, I've come out to help. And as for the empire – look, we're in the same boat. My ancestors weren't generals and lords and ladies. They were private soldiers and cooks and midwives. One of my great-grandpas, the best set-up of them all, I should think, was actually a blacksmith, out in Essex –'

Mary Tendo nearly crashes into a lorry as she swivels, unbelieving, and stares narrowly at Trevor's pale blue eyes and pink skin. 'Your grandfather was black? I am surprised.' She starts humming, self-protectively. He sees she is no longer listening, but her shoulders, which were raised towards her ears in temper, have collapsed, as if pole-axed, and her mouth is uncertain.

'No, a *blacksmith*, Mary, he looked after horses. And then when he got old, they threw him out of the house, and he ended up in a hellhole called the poorhouse. According to the records, which I've looked at. You're not the only one who's interested in history. Point is – the same people who were grinding you lot down out here, were grinding my lot down, in England, Mary.'

But she won't be argued down by a *muzungu*, at least not when the subject is her own country. 'I am sorry about your black grand-father who was treated badly by the English. And yet, Trevor –' she begins, with renewed vigour ...

And then all conversation stops as, with horns blaring and a rumble like thunder, two long open lorries roar past Charles's car, both loaded to the brim with khaki-clad soldiers, standing up and swaying, shoulder to shoulder, lean and muscular, nervous and strong, and their hungry dark eyes stare in through the windows at Mary Tendo and the maid with the baby and the sturdy old white man slumped in the front, and for once Mary Tendo yields, brakes.

'Not keen on the army, then?' asks Trevor.

'The soldiers do not concern me,' says Mary. 'But the lorries are always causing accidents. In fact we call them I.F.A, Imported for Accidents. I do not want an accident in Charles's fine car.'

'What worries me is, where are they off to?' says Trevor, remembering the headlines in the paper.

Both the driver and her passengers feel smaller, lighter. They are on the same road as the beasts of war, and they sit in silence through the minutes it takes for the lorries to be lost over the horizon, diminishing to hornets boring into the far hillsides, their darkness disappearing in a haze of dust, blurring westward, always westward, fast and low towards Congo.

Justin sometimes feels odd, coming out of the house: the light's very bright: people, traffic. He leads a quiet life, with his son. But Yoga for Toddlers is a favourite outing. As he walks through the door, tugged forward by Abdy, who is yelling, wild with joy, the name of his best friend, he breathes a small sigh of pleasure and relief. Of course, he enjoys their life at home; the certainty that he can give care. For the first time in his life, he feels like an adult. And yet, it can be lonely, in there on his own. What he likes about classes is meeting other fathers.

Davey Lucas is one of them. He's almost two decades older than Justin, but his son, Dubois, is the same age as Abdy, born at Christmas, like him, and the two boys are best mates. Davey has done it all before; he's got a seven-year-old, Harry, named for Davey's stepfather, Harold Segall, while Dubois is named for his wife's father. He likes sharing fatherhood tips with Justin.

'So do you mind me asking why you left having kids so late?' Justin had asked Davey, soon after they met.

'Do I look so old?' said Davey, grinning. In fact, though in his mid-forties, Davey still seems vaguely youthful, in that old-young way typical of city-dwellers, with good hair, and teeth, and 'urban youth' clothes.

'No –'

'It's OK, you're right. See, Delorice and I were both just so busy. No-one would remember this, but I was famous, for a bit, I was on this crap programme called the Starlite Show – I know no-one young ever watches TV –'

'No, I used to watch TV all the time,' says Justin. 'Matter of fact I still do, when I can. The Starlite Show! Of course I remember! You're "TV's Mr Astronomy". Cool.'

'Are you being ironic?' Davey asks, cautious.

'Well, saying "cool" is always, you know, faintly ironic. But not in this case. What a fantastic job! You got to look through all those telescopes.' (Justin's trying to remember. Hadn't something gone wrong?)

'Well, it all went pear-shaped – long story. Life sort of came to a T-junction. Now I've got my own company, we make stuff for the Beeb, and for Four, when they want us to. I've stopped presenting stuff. Too long in the tooth. They want babies, like you.'

'I would love to work in TV,' says Justin, then (since living with his mother has made him hypersensitive) reads the ambivalent response in Davey, who has heard a hundred people say the same thing, and goes back to praising the Starlite Show. 'Really, you were one of my heroes.' From then on, the two men had liked each other, and fortunately, the two boys palled up. Maybe partly because they were both mixed race, though in the group of fifteen, half a dozen are mixed race.

(This is London, after all; city of plaiting and twining, throwing new ropes of life, in the instant of conception, across thousands of miles of the surface of the planet, across mountains and oceans that were once uncrossable, threading the blue air to their amazing destinations. Zakira is Moroccan, but born in England: Delorice is

British, but her parents were Jamaicans and her distant ancestors were stolen from Ghana, on the other side of the same continent to which Zakira's mother has mournfully returned, missing her birth family, warmth, love. They have the world in common – Africa, Europe – these two little boys who know nothing about it.)

Now they chase each other, shrieking with excitement, round the room. Then they try to drive Dubois's new red electric open-topped Volvo, a scaled-down version of the real thing, into the future, with Abdul Trevor's arm thrown round Dubois's shoulder, but they can't both sit down, so they try to stand up, and both of them fall out, eight bendy golden limbs intertwining on the floor, and both of them draw in their breath to cry, but a light touch from Davey stops Justin rushing forward, so instead of howling, the two boys look at each other, surprised by the adventure, and giggle – then get up again, grinning, and start hugging and jostling, forgetting the car, which drives on, gleaming, until it hits two little blonde pony-tailed girls who are peering inside their leotards. A mother bustles up and looks reproachfully at Davey. 'Did you see what happened? That could have been nasty. They did ask us, guys, to leave larger toys at home.' (But one glance around the room shows a lot of large toys: cars, motorbikes, dolls' prams, bicycles, a dolls' kitchen with refrigerator, and one poor little toddler with cool-geek spectacles is stabbing vaguely at a kiddy computer.)

'Sorry, Ruth, we won't do it again.' But once she turns her back, Justin and Davey chortle. She's a big-armed, bean-eating, strict type of mother, not the kind the two men know how to charm.

'Children? Good morning. Let's get mats! Time to start.' The calm voice of the (very pretty) teacher. Once the mothers have seen her, they joke that she's the reason why the fathers are keen to bring the kids to yoga. She's a bit of a legend, Ella Waddingham. 'And she got a first in physics, apparently,' the fathers whisper to each other, awed, and fall over each other to help with the mats, as if the physics is why they admire her.

The class is mostly girls, but there are three or four boys. The girls seem older, more docile, more graceful.

'Odd thing, they communicate by talking, girls. Not like our lot, who do it by fighting,' says Davey. 'I quite regret not having a girl.'

The two blokes are inspecting the inside of Dubois's car. 'It's absolutely brilliant,' says Justin, impressed, though he's also thinking, 'We couldn't afford it,' and 'Isn't it a teensy bit over the top?'

'Wish they'd had stuff like this when I was a boy,' says Davey, proud he can give his son everything.

But Ruth is back, and she's listening. 'When you were a boy, David, the planet had a future. I just wonder what messages we're giving our children. I mean obviously cars do constitute a problem. Adam and I *try* to be careful. And it doesn't mean, you know, depriving them. Paloma just *loves* her little bike –' She breaks off mid-lecture, spotting that Paloma has given up her clumsy attempts at yoga and is creeping up behind her graceful, innocent friend with a plastic hammer raised to strike. 'Paloma! Don't retaliate!' She is slightly flushed when she turns back to Davey. Paloma too often 'retaliates', and other parents aren't always fooled.

'You're right, Ruth, you're right,' Davey says, placatory. 'Sorry, sorry. Boys and their toys. By the way, I love Paloma's leotard. Obviously in a non-perverted way.' Ruth buzzes away, frowning, to remove the hammer. 'I can't resist winding Ruth up,' he says.

'Wonder what it's like having a girl?' says Justin. 'I sometimes think it'd be fun to have lots of children. But Zakira is so busy. I don't think she'd be keen. And after all, she's the one who brings in the money.'

'Time doesn't stand still though,' says Davey. 'Take it from me, you get old before you know it.'

Ella is demonstrating a back bend, young and graceful as a

waterfall. One day, she will have children of her own. Till then, all dads and kids may adore her. To the men, she looks like the freedom they've lost.

'Well, you know, Zakira's in the City. They just make so much money. Golden handcuffs and all that. Too good to give up. But she hates leaving Abdy.'

Davey looks at him consideringly. Handsome boy. Nice smile. But perhaps something slightly unfinished, somewhere ... 'You could maybe get a part-time job,' he says, cautiously. 'Then your missis might be keener to take time off. It's really why I set up the company. Get in some squids, so I could ease up. I knew Delorice wouldn't stay home. It's a snake pit, publishing. She's good at her job. And I didn't want to miss out on all this, either –' indicating the thrashing limbs and laughing faces of the fifteen young lives unfurling in the room; Ella's laughing too, she's a stream of sunshine ... Their own wives no longer look quite like that. Yet both of them adore their wives.

'Yeah, most of the time it's good,' said Justin. 'I wrote PR copy. I wasn't half bad. But this, what we do, this is a job.'

'Telling me,' says Davey. 'I'm knackered every day. But I go to bed happy. Well happy-*ish*.'

And they smile at each other, a complicated smile that says no-one's ever completely happy. Davey's been in therapy for five years now, and Justin, of course, had his total breakdown, and in some ways, has not been quite the same since, though he does enjoy the journalism course. They sit in safety, among laughing children, in their rich country, in good, clean clothes, they are healthy, educated, with money in their pockets, and yet they are not quite sure they are happy. 'It's rough when they're ill,' says Justin, solemnly, and then gets distracted by the sudden brilliance of Abdul Trevor's yoga. 'Oh well done, Abdy, what a super Tree! Oh no. Oh Sorry, Ruth. Say sorry to Paloma. No, Abdy, let go of Paloma's pony-tail. I don't care, that's not how you keep your balance!'

'By the way,' says Davey, 'I'm quite surprised so many have turned up today. I heard there was meningitis about. Or was it measles ...? No, meningitis. You know, moan moan in the latte queue. I don't believe a word of it, myself.' (There is an upmarket café, near the Montessori nursery, where all the yummy mummies meet to talk mummy-talk and get a blood sugar spike after dropping off their heirs. The two men are regulars, and generally beamed upon, as rare high-functioning and nice-looking fathers.)

'Meningitis? Nah, it's flu,' said Justin. 'Two-day flu. Little Abdy just had it. Temperature, coughing, kept on waking up. He bounced right back up again. Look at him now! Mind you, that rash is back. Zakira reckons our eggs weren't free range, whatever the local shop puts on the box. Makes you feel helpless, when they're ill.'

'Flu. There you are. The rumour mill.'

They smile at each other: the hysteria of women. It's good for the kids, to have blokes around.

(Yet the men need praise, and validation, and the women are too tired from work to give it. When the shrewd therapist asked Davey the question, 'Perhaps you have issues around self-worth?' he did, as expected, sign up for more sessions.)

'So you were a copywriter,' says Davey, thoughtfully. 'And now you're doing a journalism course. Does it include TV? I was just wondering ... Let's fix up a playdate for the boys, maybe tomorrow. You and me could have a little chat.'

20

Around lunch-time, what Trevor feels should be his lunch-time, for his normal working day is punctuated by snacks, by digestive biscuits and his flask of tea, there's a trading post by the side of the road, a single-storey concrete building hung with plastic mops and buckets and rugs and thin striped mattresses and Coca-Cola signs. He's missed his caffeine, now he needs his tucker. But he won't say so: Trevor is a stoic.

'We are nearly at the village,' Mary says.

Partly because he's feeling peckish, Trevor goes in with Mary and pays for the shopping. Groundnuts, white bread, flour, a big kettle she spots and looks at admiringly. He insists on buying it, which makes her smile a little. 'You are a good man, Trevor,' she says, grudgingly. Then they suddenly share a real, warm smile. They are over the quarrel. Possibly it was just something to get out of the way, so that he and she could be friends again. It's a bit like South Africa, he thinks. The whatchamacallit, Truth and Reconciliation business. Things had to be dragged right out into the open. He is in Uganda, and on her ground. She has to let him know this is not like London – though that doesn't mean he is going to like it.

Round the side of the building is an open stall where a man in a bloodied white jacket with rolled-up sleeves is selling meat in the flickering sunlight, as cloud begins to stream up over the sun. Dark individual hunks of flesh swing from the roof of the stall on string. The butcher has a giant machete, with which he hacks off great bony lumps of beef to Mary's instructions, splitting the spinal chord with a practised 'thuck'. To Trevor, the meat looks almost black in the daylight, and it has an iridescent retinue of fat flies, though a thin child with a whisk is employed to disperse them. Mary indicates 'More': the blows keep on coming, the muscular arm hacks the beast to pieces: there are splinters of bone, and brighter blood spattering. She's buying so much, almost a quarter of a cow. Trevor wonders if they have a fridge, in the village. The meat is wrapped in leaves, a glistening sticky bundle. 'The village will be happy,' Mary says to Trevor. 'Thank you, Trevor.' So he pays again.

Whenever, later, in faraway London, Trevor tries to describe his arrival in Mary's village, he is never sure that he is believed. And he also wonders: did it really happen like that? He thinks it did. Yes, he is sure. The kneeling women. The children flocking. The way they stared at him between their fingers.

After the trading post, they lurch on to the track that veers off at ninety degrees from the main road to Kampala, and are soon rocking like a ship on the sea, swaying helplessly from side to side as the track rears up and dips down underneath them, its ruts deepened to potholes by long-ago rain. Behind him he hears the maid laughing as she's thrown about as if riding a donkey, a happy memory from her lost village childhood, and soon Theodora starts laughing too, and he realises: *that child never talks. Not like little Abdy, babbling away.*

This road is a joke. Trevor thinks about the weather. If this is the only way in and out, they could easily get cut off, in the village. The rains, everyone says, can last for weeks (and last night Charles was so sure the rains were coming. 'It can rain any day,' he had said, laughing with the huge good temper life seems to have inspired in him. Did he have any worries? Trevor doesn't think so. How pleasant it must be to be Ugandan! The pace of life is so different to London – though it can't be a cinch, living with Mary ...)

They are slowing to a halt outside a bleak concrete house. Mary says, 'I think this is my brother's house, because I know he built it near the path that leads to the mango tree where we children told stories. My brother's wife is expecting us.'

And, hearing the engine, people come from the house. A thin man, not young, in pale shirt and dark trousers, then children, running, in ragged clothes, jumping and laughing, then suddenly shy, one or two of them hanging back and staring. 'My brother Jacob,' says Mary softly, turning off the engine, 'but he has grown old.' It is nearly a whisper. Trevor sees that her lips are moving in silence and is touched to realise Mary is praying. But it's only a second: with a powerful movement, she's out of the car and hugging her brother.

Jacob comes across and pumps Trevor's hand. 'Welcome,' he says. His eyes are bloodshot, and milky, but his smile is wide, showing strong white teeth. 'You have come to help us in the village. Thank you.'

Two other men come and shake Trevor's hand. 'My neighbour. And this is my uncle, the village councillor.'

'An important man,' says Trevor, politely, and is rewarded with a laugh of pleasure.

'You are very welcome to the village,' says the man. Then he embraces Mary Tendo, and they have a short conversation in Luganda from which Mary emerges looking displeased, but there isn't time to think about that, because now the women come from the house. Jacob introduces a queenly figure, taller than Mary, nearly taller than Trevor, in a wide-sashed dark red printed dress down to her ankles, with big puffed sleeves, and a square neckline that shows off her elegant neck and high cheekbones, but just as he is thinking, 'She looks like a duchess,' and wishing he weren't wearing a sweaty t-shirt, she sinks to her knees in front of him, in a fluid motion, bowing and smiling, clasping her hands together in what looks like prayer. 'My wife,' says Jacob, looking proud.

'No need for that,' says Trevor, touched but alarmed, and takes her by the hands, and pulls her up again, which causes a wave of surprised laughter. And then two golden adult daughters come from the house, and again they sink down, like trees bending in the wind, and come up again, gracefully unbroken, and he thinks, 'I could get used to this,' but he catches Mary Tendo looking across at him with an ironic expression, and as they follow the family into the house, she hisses in his ear, 'Do not be mistaken, Trevor, I will never do that to you.'

'I know that, Mary. It's OK.'

'It is not OK. But they are village people. My uncle said I had come back too late. He does not understand, life is hard in the city, and hard in UK, and I tried to send money, and I am very sad that my parents are dead, but I have been sad about it for a decade, and I paid for their drugs, in hospital, and it-hurts-my-heart-that-I-could-not-come-sooner.' This she rattles off rapidly, *sotto voce*, and Trevor pats her on the arm as she stares at the ground, and in a second, she's herself again. Then a sister arrives, a cross-looking sister, and squints at Mary, and smiles at Trevor, but another sister, she explains, is away, and Mary translates: 'Trevor, you will stay in the house of my sister, not this sister but the sensible sister' (her sister looks at her suspiciously) 'who has taken her daughters to boarding school, so you will only meet this other sister, and her silly daughters, who are worse than their mother. This is Martha.'

'How do you do,' says Trevor.

'Do not bother, Trevor, she does not speak English.'

And then Jacob's younger children are introduced, and their clothes are smarter than the clothes of their friends, and they stare at Mary for a long time, as if they have heard a lot about her, and five minutes later they reappear, having shucked off their smart outfits and got back into their shorts. There is much exclaiming over Theodora, and Jacob picks her up, and the daughter wails, and Mary removes her from her brother, irritably, and says, 'She is not used to the village yet,' and puts her back in the arms of the maid, who nobody at all has greeted. But some part of every child understands the country, and soon the little girl, despite Mary's protests, which become increasingly half-hearted, has shed her cardigan, her socks, her pretty dress, that fairy-tale cloud of pale pink nylon, and is running round half-naked in a conga of children, a joyous, noisy, animal procession, and all the adults are smiling at her. The maid, meanwhile, whose face has set like stone, is to be seen through the window with a giant pestle, thumping it, thud-ah, in a crude wooden mortar. Trevor asks if she's all right, for she's only a girl, could he help, could she use a bit of muscle? – but Mary tells him she's just grinding groundnuts. 'No, she enjoys it. Do not bother yourself, Trevor. We will have our food today with groundnut sauce.'

Mary has other plans for him. 'You will go and get the things from the car, now, Trevor.' He does her bidding, helped by several boys who are much stronger than their fragile limbs suggest.

The rice, the flour, the soap, the oil, all the big packs of foodstuffs are received without comment, as if they were expected, and almost insufficient, but some cans of Coca-Cola, three plastic footballs and two packs of biros are exclaimed over. The clothes are certainly the star of the show: Jacob takes some shoes, and tries them on, appreciatively, slowly, watched by his family, and the uncle is delighted with his grey zipped jacket. He zips it up: he zips it down. Then Mary shows the meat, and everyone laughs, and the women of Jacob's family take it and disappear behind a thin red curtain that divides the kitchen from the living space.

'You have done well,' says Mary Tendo to Jacob. 'This house is larger than our parents' house.'

'Our parents' house was large,' Jacob comments.

'That is what I say. You have done well.'

Trevor looks around him, but notices absence, despite the wealth of smiling faces, the children peering in through the windows. Yet Mary Tendo thinks they have done well. No carpets: just a stained concrete floor. No curtains. The sofa is a skeleton, brown upholstery worn through to the wooden bones. There is a table, and a tablecloth, but only two chairs for all these people. No pictures on the walls. No papers or books. Another neighbour has arrived to join them, and they stand, awkwardly, looking at Trevor.

But in a second, Mary's brother is showing him a book, a battered paperback, a textbook, which he keeps in a place of honour by the sofa. 'Macmillan Schools English,' he says, smiling. 'We are all learning it. My children study. I am a teacher at one of the schools.'

'There is more than one school?'

'There are two schools. But there are many, many children.'

Trevor looks at the shabby, dated textbook, and doesn't know what to say about it. 'Are your children clever?' he asks Jacob, adding hastily, 'I wasn't, myself.' The older daughter brings him a Coca-Cola, which he doesn't really like, but accepts, gracefully.

'They are average,' says the father. 'They do not try hard enough.'

'That's what my father used to say,' says Trevor. 'But it didn't stop me being good at my job.' The daughter smiles at him, gratefully, and disappears again behind the curtain.

'You are a builder of wells,' Jacob says, respectfully.

'Not exactly,' says Trevor, before Mary can stop him, but she comes in swiftly, 'Yes, he is. He is an expert on every aspect.'

'Well, not *every* aspect, Mary – that's going it a bit.'

'You should not be modest. Or else' (and she is looking at him meaningfully) 'I would not have brought you to the village, Trevor. Before, Trevor was the Queen's Engineer,' she explains to the villagers, whose smiles have briefly stalled. 'Royal Engineers,' Trevor protests, 'I was only in the Territorials,' but Mary ignores him and presses on. 'In London, rich people all want Trevor to work for them.'

'So there are wells in London?' Jacob asks Trevor.

Trevor feels the pressure of expectation, and of Mary, watching him narrowly. At last, he is visited by inspiration. 'Yes, well, there are fountains, which is almost the same thing. I do do them,' he says, quite truthfully. He'd fixed up a fountain for Vanessa's frog pond.

'It is true,' says the uncle, with some excitement. 'My daughter is in London, as you all know. You remember the postcard she sent to the school, because her brother was afraid of lions? There was a photograph of fountains, and stone lions, and she said this was a very famous square, in London –'

'Trafalgar Square!' Mary interrupts, triumphant. 'Yes, Trevor built the fountains in Trafalgar Square. Is it true, Trevor?'

'If you say so, Mary.'

The uncle nods, deeply impressed.

Having gloriously soared over this bar, Trevor is taken by the men on a tour of the village while the women cook in the room at the back. Two boys go with the men, carrying giant yellow jerry-cans.

'For fuel?' he asks.

'No, for water.'

'I will come with you, of course,' says Mary Tendo, and the men, for a moment, look at each other. But they daren't say no: she is not a normal woman. She went to the city and came back rich.

The tour soon feels quite long, to Trevor. The sun has gone for good: there is sullen heat, and he soon finds his t-shirt is drenched in sweat. It is open, rolling, scrubland, with patchy cultivation. He inquires: that's coffee, that's cassava, those are little green spikes of ginger, and he recognises scrawny tassels of maize.

But most of the land is unused. It makes it look attractive, to the casual stroller: skinny goats browse, under the care of watchful, half-naked children; a few chickens run squawking and pecking on the grass. Perhaps they are resting the soil, thinks Trevor.

They are certainly not resting their legs. The boys set off across the fields with their cans. 'How long do they have to go to get water?'

'It is not far. Perhaps two, three miles.'

They stop at the Protestant school where Jacob teaches. It is a one-storey building, a series of low brick-built huts, like the Nissen huts Trevor remembers from the war, which lingered as classrooms and homes through the sixties. 'The school I went to looked a bit like this,' he says, but he sees that they do not really believe him.

'The school needs many things,' says Jacob.

Trevor sees, painted on one exterior wall, a faintly familiar shape, in bright colours, a big bulging triangle next to a circle. Jacob is pointing to it and smiling.

'I think you will recognise this,' he says.

Trevor screws up his eyes. He can't see it. And then he does. It's a map of Great Britain, but the ragged head of Scotland has been sharpened to a point, and Ireland is a vague, squashed circle.

'UK!' says Jacob, triumphantly. 'Very important.'

Trevor feels surprised. Is it really still important out here? Maybe more will be expected of him, then. As he gets closer, he notices how the edges of the bricks have washed away. They look as though they have been eaten by insects, the straight lines turned to frail lace.

'It is the rain,' says Jacob, as Trevor indicates the brick. 'It washes everything away.'

And the windows: when he looks again, there is no glass in them. They are just holes, like eyeless sockets. Maybe glass is expensive, in Uganda. He starts to see that Charles and Mary's house in Kampala was well appointed by Ugandan standards. No windows! It is a bit of a shock.

A female head teacher appears to greet them. She is youngish, in a blouse and fitted jacket; she must be boiling in this heat. 'She is not from here,' hisses Jacob as they leave her. 'We do not think that she will stay. We cannot pay her enough money.'

'Not enough?' asks Mary, furious. 'She should be happy to be a head teacher at her age. And she has enough money to straighten her hair.'

Jacob shows Trevor and Mary around, and in every dark classroom, children rise to their feet en masse and stare expectantly at them. There seem to be hundreds and hundreds of children.

'Good afternoon, children.'

'Good afternoon, Master.'

Otherwise they do not seem to speak much English, yet Mary assures him all exams are in English, the exams they must pass to go into their future. The children look both strange and curiously familiar, and Trevor realises their uniforms are modelled on English ones of the '50s, tunics like his elder sister wore, with big box pleats (though the heat has melted their sharpness), and low loose waists, and although some of these girls look as though they're almost 20, they wear ankle socks, like much younger children, and their shaven heads make them look like babies. And the desks: small, ancient, stained black with ink, they are desks he remembers from infant school. And that scrape of chairs as they all stand up.

But the faces: no. Nor the expressions. They are curious, yes, but they are not deferential. There are stony eyes, there are mutinous mouths. And there are so many of them, staring at him, all jam-packed into this dreamlike school which he himself grew out of so long ago. And he thinks of the schooling of his own son, the clubs, the courses, the extra classes, the gyms and swimming pools and treats and outings that went into the making of Justin ... Education coming out of his ears. Yet he's sometimes thought the boy is a bit of a drip. He's wondered if Vanessa spoiled him.

In the first classroom, which holds the older children, Trevor puts his foot in it. There are three Macmillan textbooks on the teacher's table, so he holds one up, and asks, 'Do you like reading? And books?' There is a chorus of 'Yes', though to Trevor, the books look a bit uninspiring. Trying to be matey, he follows up with, 'I bet you like television better, though!' At the word 'television', these tall, thin children look at each other, blank, unsmiling. He can't read the reaction. It's as if they are ashamed.

It is left to Mary to educate him. 'Trevor, these children never saw a television.'

After that, he says nothing during several introductions. Then in the last classroom, he resolves to do better.

'Good afternoon, children!' thunders Jacob again.

'Good afternoon, Master,' they reply as usual.

'Good afternoon,' interpolates Trevor. He has to make an effort. His country is painted on the side of their school. But what's he got to say to them? These aren't like any kids he knows.

'This is Mr Patcher, a famous engineer. You will say to him what?'

The eyes look back at him, and then there is a ragged chorus of 'Good afternoon, Mr Patch.'

'I am from London,' Trevor announces. 'Who can tell me what country London is in?' And seizing the stub of chalk on the table, he writes 'LONDON' in capitals on the blackboard. Then Jacob threatens the class in Luganda, inciting them to rise to the challenge. Several eager boys shoot up their hands, but most of them are quashed by a look from Jacob, who evidently knows this class well. One favoured boy remains, and Trevor says 'Yes?'

'*Bungereza*,' the tall boy says, triumphant.

Trevor can't make head nor tail of it, so he says 'Write it', and mimes writing, proffering the chalk; the boy looks to Jacob for permission, and then writes '*BUNGeReZA*' on the blackboard.

Trevor looks at it blankly. 'I'm afraid not,' and the class laughs as the boy goes back to his seat, his face puzzled and indignant, but

Mary is pulling Trevor's arm, urgently, as he writes 'ENGLAND' next to *BUNGeReZA*, and she's hissing something in his ear.

'Oh, I see, sorry,' Trevor tells the boy, who sits there, taut, his eyes holding Trevor's. 'So *Bungereza* is your word for England. It's not an English word, that's the problem.'

'It is the right Luganda word,' Mary says loudly, and then repeats it in Luganda. '*Wama ori mutufu. Bungereza kitufu muluganda.*' The boy nods and smiles, vindicated.

But Trevor thinks to himself, why don't they teach them English? Otherwise they can't communicate.

The headmistress has something to communicate, in a moment alone as he signs the Visitors' Book in her 'office', a corridor whose bare brick walls are decorated with a neat handwritten list of the School Rules, also in English, so the children won't know them.

'I am a headmistress,' she says to him, suddenly, pressing his hand and looking hard into his eyes. 'I am a headmistress. Do not forget me. I should have a proper office, and a car.'

It's the children, in fact, that he finds hard to forget. However you look at it, it doesn't seem right.

21

It's early evening at the Sheraton. Vanessa will soon be doing her reading. As usual, she is a little on edge, and not entirely able to pay attention to the tide of political debate that ebbs and flows between the delegates, who are drinking complimentary glasses of wine.

'Museveni is finished!' a Ugandan declares, a bright young poet and lecturer just back from two years at the University of Iowa. His presentation about the marginalisation of local languages was misted with French deconstructionist words, but now he is crisp and vigorous. 'He has become old and greedy, like the others. The westerners have eaten too well. Ugandans are tired of it. We will not re-elect him.'

'That's what people said before the last elections,' says a white South African. 'When he'd sworn he wouldn't stand another time. Then he changed his mind, and they voted for him. Africa basically has kings, *ja*? Like Moi and Mugabe. They're in for a lifetime.'

'Well, you've got to admit he's made things better here,' says Geoffrey Truman, who feels almost Ugandan, with his thrice-a-year visits to Sanyu Namamonde, where he has a comfortable berth, nourishing food, and cold beers beside the Speke Hotel's sunlit swimming pool while Sanyu gives him gentle massages, in return for which, he helps her out – there are school fees for the elder boy, and the younger one, too, will soon be boarding-school age, which is causing him to make a few calculations, and yet ... *The good life. So much sweeter than London.* He could never get a woman like Sanyu in London, young, healthy, affectionate to him. 'You've seen Kampala. Lots of new business, hotels going up, prosperous. You feel safe on the street. The police are on top of things. Otherwise CHOGM would not be coming here. It's a different country from what it was twenty years ago. You just can't compare Amin and Museveni.'

'But you should *not* compare them,' says a writer from Femrite, the organisation of Ugandan women writers. 'It is like comparing the German leader, Angela Merkel, to Hitler. Of course, the new person will look better.'

Then another Ugandan takes up the discussion. 'In fact, under Museveni, there has always been war. For the Acholi in the north, as you are aware, there is genocide. In the east, there have been massacres of Museveni's enemies, things that in the west you do not hear about ...' (As he looks, briefly, at the foreign delegates, his voice drops slightly, for you never know who's listening: in the deepening sky outside the window, there are storks, as ever, small as mosquitoes, casually planing on the early evening thermals: friend or enemy? How can you be sure?) 'And in Democratic Republic of Congo – Ugandan army has been very busy there. There was a four-year war, in which millions died. And now our wonderful Museveni might go to war again. Perhaps State House needs more gold, and diamonds. Perhaps there will be another war, in Congo.'

Unconsciously, Vanessa is recording these words, for attention later, after her reading, but now she cannot bear to take them in; she is marshalling her thoughts; her palms are sweating. She checks she has numbered all her pages. Five minutes later, Heather calls them to attention.

And Vanessa reads, at sunset, from her autobiography, the only chapter of it she has finished, a passage about her father and the chickens, and the audience grows quiet, leans forward, listens, and the warm, squawking things seem to flutter round the room, and the listeners' sharp bright eyes make her think of the chickens, and she even dares to imitate the birds' contented clucking, and at once the room explodes into laughter and approval, and *they like me*, she thinks: *yes, they actually like me.* She is suddenly herself; herself, completely. After she has finished, the questions keep coming. They are fascinated by her move from the village, the transition to the city that so many of them have made, unless their parents, or more rarely, grandparents, did it for them. It's true, she thinks, we all have to come here. Many people volunteer their own story. A Nigerian poet quotes himself, and now they are all nodding, all united:

'... "Writing is the dark breath of the city."'

And somehow she finds herself thinking of Mary: Mary Tendo, too, made this epic voyage.

Mary, Mary. Where are you now?

Later Vanessa lies in the warm hotel night and lets the warm glow of approval linger. All of them had shared her childhood memories, and when the writers told stories from their own childhood, they saw the lost children in these clever adults. She thinks, that was the closest our group has come; for once no-one was excluded ...

Then she starts to think about the week that lies ahead, with a little ebbing of happiness as the words of the Ugandan writer come back to her, perhaps there will be war in Congo. And she has her plans to drive to Congo. Her huge white bed starts to soak up darkness.

The boy lies in the swamp, which is rotting his feet. He dragged himself here in a search for water. He drank and drank, but then he vomited. The sun is setting. Will he live through the night? He thinks, this ditch will become my tomb. Something's sucking at his leg   he blacks out, briefly

Once he was a child   he had two parents

he made the wrong choice   he went the wrong way
Now he will have to be punished for ever
God's eye is in the tomb with me
It looks at me like a sun staring   it is red as a wound and hot as
fire
His throat closes as the sun bores down. The All-seeing One.
Vengeance has found him.

'Animal book, Daddy,' Abdul Trevor yells. 'I need the ANIMAL
BOOK, not the silly BIRDS.'

'But the bird book has got some nice animals,' says Justin, who
is trying to read Hans Andersen to his son, a really very attractive
copy that Vanessa had bought Abdy for his third birthday – too
young, of course, but that was typical of her. Justin likes the rhythmic
language, and the stories. Perhaps it reminds him of the good side
of his mother, who read to him at bedtime when Mary had gone
home. Now he's reading to himself as much as Abdy. 'There's a nice
froggy, isn't there –'

'TOAD!' Abdul Trevor corrects him. 'Not a nice toad. It's a
hobble smelly toad.'

'There's a reindeer you can ride on, in *The Snow Queen*.'

'I like a reindeer,' Abdul Trevor more peaceably agrees, and then
veering back unpredictably, 'Daddy, get my ANIMAL BOOK from
the garden.'

This was half the trouble, the fact it's in the garden, and requires
an arduous trip downstairs. For Justin is sleepy, as he so often is by
Abdul Trevor's bedtime – young children *are* tiring – and once he
lies down on the bed beside his son, with the Babydreams Pillow
tucked under his shoulders, he often falls asleep in the middle of a
sentence, to Abdul Trevor's outrage: 'Daddy NOT to sleep.'

'There are funny storks in this book,' Justin persuades him. 'Don't you like the storks? They can talk like us. And a nightingale. That's a bird that sings. And mermaids. They're, sort of, animals.'

But Abdul Trevor begins crying, softly, a whining, fretful noise untypical of him. The rash is worse. It can't be the eggs: he hasn't eaten any eggs. But Zakira also suspects avocado, which Justin likes to feed him because it's nutritious. Alas, they had avocado for lunch.

'It's all right, baby boy, I'm going,' says Justin, yielding to forestall the storm.

'NOT a baby,' says Abdul Trevor, and cries harder, and pushes all his covers off. 'Not go, Daddy.' And then, unreasonably, 'Daddy go!' Justin puts a cool hand on his forehead, and frowns: the little boy's temperature seems to be back, and this afternoon he was coughing again, and when Zakira rang up (she couldn't come home because she had to do an unexpected presentation) he had suddenly told her that his throat hurt.

'He hasn't mentioned it to me, darling,' Justin had to reassure Zakira. 'Don't worry, I expect he was winding you up. I think he's fine. Maybe a little cold. Just forget about it and do your presentation.' There's some talk of her having to go to Brussels. He doesn't like it when she goes away.

And he wishes she didn't have to work late as he treads the small damp garden in his bare feet, looking for the missing Animal Book, and hears his son starting to wail from the bedroom, and a small sharp thorn sticks into his foot, and there is a low-key rumble of sound that might be a tube train, or might be thunder. Thank God, there's the book, under the hollyhocks, and he scoops it up and pads back upstairs. It's close, in the house. Yes, it was thunder.

'Want a drink,' says Abdul Trevor, as soon as Justin gets there. But he's stopped crying, and is playing with his toes. His long dark lashes are bright with tears, and he smiles an angelic smile at Justin.

He knows that parents get cross about drinks, especially when it's long after bedtime.

'I wish you had asked me before,' says Justin.

'Was Ganma in the garden?' Abdul asks, conversationally. 'Was the gorilla in the garden? That's funny, isn't it, Daddy?' And he chuckles, a little stagily, at his own joke.

Yet he does want to know. It's a concern. Both grandma and gorilla are hiding somewhere. She hasn't been to see him for ages.

'Grandma is still in Uganda,' says Justin. 'There wasn't a gorilla in the garden. But soon, Grandma will go and see the gorillas.'

Abdy doesn't like to be reminded.

'Where's my drink? I got a thirst in my throat.'

'Can it wait until we have read the book? Look, clever Daddy found it, out in the garden.'

'Want THIS book,' says Abdul Trevor, cunningly, pointing to the formerly despised Hans Andersen. 'Daddy, read "Mary had a little lamb".'

'But that's in *neither* of the books,' says Justin, floored. 'Never mind, Abdy, I know it by heart. "Mary had a little lamb, Its fleece was white as snow, And everywhere that Mary went, That little lamb would go ..."'

And he thinks about Mary: Mary Tendo. When she'd come to the house, he was the same age as Abdul. He can just remember her: round, funny. She let him have chocolate. She made him laugh. And she'd taught him all sorts of things his mother didn't know, in her own language, and his mother didn't like it. *I suppose Mum was jealous*, he realises now. Sometimes Zakira is jealous of me, because Abdy and me have our little secrets.

'Wanta lamb,' says Abdy, sleepily.

'Read it again?' Justin asks, incredulous. He can never get over the child's capacity for wanting the most boring things again and again.

'No, wanta LAMB!' says Abdy, pointing.

'Oh, you want your fleece, sorry. Silly Daddy.' And Justin fetches his son his lambskin, on whose soft wool he used to lie as a baby, but which, Justin reflects, as he scoops it up, must have come from a very young dead lamb. 'Isn't it a bit hot for the fleece?'

'Lamb,' says Abdy happily, clutching it. 'I love you Daddy'. And he curls up his knees. 'Too hot,' he mutters, but Justin can't hear him.

Abdy's coughing, again, but half asleep, and Justin decides to tuck him down. 'Do you still want that water?' he asks, softly, too softly to wake him, because he'd rather not go, and the boy turns over with a little grunt, his thumb in his mouth, dead to the world. Justin almost lifts him gently on to his back, just for reassurance, to feel his small forehead one more time, to check it isn't really hotter than usual, but he's tired too. He wants a cold beer. No point in worrying; he turns down the child light, pulls up the blanket over fleece and baby, closes the door, and almost stumbles and falls as he slops downstairs, his loose heavy sleepy body crashing into the banisters. The noise is so loud that he fails to hear the deep operatic rumble of the storm, coming closer.

22

I am in the village, thinks Trevor. I've got here. This is me, on my own, with nothing else.

He has just become a lot lonelier, having tried to switch on his phone in the dark, the fragile filament of electronic life that links him to the city, and got less than nothing, the 'phone crossed out' icon. A definitive X. No reception. Oh bugger. He has really arrived.

But where is he exactly? It feels like nowhere.

He is lying on a mattress on the floor. It is very hot. There are crickets singing, and other insects, somewhere, rustling and whining, not very far off, but apart from that, he's in a great, deep pit of silence, torn across briefly, from time to time, by hoots and shrieks that must be birds or monkeys. He didn't really wash, at bedtime (except down there, where his mother taught him to wash every day), because his bowl of tepid water wouldn't go very far, and besides, he didn't want to wash his face and arms because then he'd have to reapply his insect repellent. He's brushed his teeth, but he couldn't find his toothpaste – he hasn't had to go to bed in the half-dark since a power cut in London ten years ago, and then what a fuss all the neighbours made! Though he, Trevor, thought nothing of it. For the village, of course, this darkness is normal.

Is he getting a toothache? He hopes he isn't. Too far from home. He thinks, *root canal*, and the dodgy nerve winds down into the dark, and he dozes, worrying, then jerks himself awake: he isn't going to get a bloody toothache. He's Trevor Patchett. He's perfectly all right.

(Will he be bitten, though? By mosquitoes? By snakes? He's never been a coward, but this is the unknown. OK, Mary's nearby, in the next-door building, but she's not the same woman he remembers from England, easy-going, sensible, admiring him. Once her family was there, she had practically ignored him, talking solidly to brothers and uncles and nieces in the language he naturally could not understand, though he sometimes knew they were talking about him by the way they turned and stared, half-smiling. What the hell was Mary Tendo telling them?)

Bloody hell, I'm on the other side of the world. No, I've fallen off the edge of the world.

No lights, no electricity, no gas, no phone. No anything. Just people, goats, chickens. Not much farming, and I was a chump to think that they were resting the land. Mary soon put me straight on that. 'It is because so many have died of AIDS. Those who remain cannot work the land.' Hardly any adults, but so many children. An army of children compared to back home. I couldn't believe there were so many of them, and so few of us, so few adults. Back home it's the opposite; like Justin and Zakira, two adults fussing over every little kiddie.

(And then it strikes him: *or like Ness and me*. We never managed to have any more children. Didn't hold it together. Too young and daft. So Justin had to hack it on his own, with two great grownups dancing around him.)

Plus the nannies and minders and carers and what-not. Not that Justin and Zakira have got a nanny.

But those village schools I saw today ... they were like *factories* of children. Sort of mass-produced. Learning everything by heart, in identical uniforms. A few knackered teachers and hundreds of children. And those buildings. In England, they'd do for farm animals. No lights, no glass, no floor, no loos.

And they're going to grow up. One day they'll grow up. What if they found out how rich our lot were? They might grow up and come looking for us.

Trevor Patchett tosses and turns on his itchy mattress. He's never gone in for insomnia, but he's never slept in an African village. In the middle of nowhere. The back of beyond.

Is he anyone, really, if no-one here knows him? He hopes he can be some use to them.

Then suddenly it starts, on the roof above him. A stuttering, a tapping – then the skies fall down. Trevor's stunned into sleep by Ugandan rain.

In London, Justin is half-woken by crying. The digital horror: 3.30 AM. Rain blows against their windowpane.

'I'll go,' says Zakira. 'It must be my turn. I expect Abdy's kicked off his covers.' Then she lies there. If you give it a minute, he sometimes stops crying.

(Alternatively, Justin goes instead, but she does not consciously count on this.)

In fact, Justin is snoring again. Zakira hauls herself up from the beautiful depths of adult slumber, and tries not to think about work tomorrow, and needing her sleep to be on top of things. There is still a possibility she'll have to go to Brussels, but they didn't ring, so she's praying it's off. She loves her son more than life itself. Is it possible she loves him more than Justin? She reminds herself there's no need to decide.

Justin wakes up to find her gone. Her side of the bed feels cold; she's been away some time. He can hear Abdul Trevor snuffling and whimpering, and the soft intermittent voice of his mother. Zakira is there; he can go back to sleep.

She is back. 'Hallo Mummy,' he says, dozily. 'Is he OK?'

'I think he was cold. He had kicked off his covers. It feels like winter to me,' says Zakira. 'I covered him up, but he was very restless. And that rash ... you didn't give him eggs again?'

'Course not. Or avocado. Don't ask. It's not always my fault when he gets a rash.' (It's a white lie about the avocado.)

They lie in the dark. Nearly a quarrel. But they don't want to quarrel. They love each other.

'Maybe you should take him to the doctor,' says Zakira. 'I know it's a drag.'

'No,' says Justin, 'it isn't a drag.' (But it is, it is. You have to wait for ever. And he plans to drop in on Davey, in the morning. They don't need the doctor. Abdy will be fine.) 'I think he's just hot,' Justin continues. 'You're Moroccan, you think our autumn is winter. Anyway, well done, he went to sleep.'

'Well I gave him some, you know,' Zakira sighs. 'It always works.' Baby paracetamol.

'You don't think we give him too much?' asks Justin.

'Well, it's meant for children,' says Zakira. 'Baby paracetamol, the gift of the gods.'

'The gift of sleep,' says Justin, kissing her. They cuddle like children, they make spoons, warm spoons, he curves soothingly against her, till the spoons start melting, become meltingly tender, and some parts soften as other parts harden, and although they need sleep, the sweet chance is there, they're awake and not busy, they're soon moving together, and their cries of contentment merge with rain and autumn, the first birds singing, a late awakening.

7.30 AM. They have missed the alarm. Zakira's annoyed to have overslept. The problem is Justin, who rarely hears it. The day ahead looms, full of challenges: she's new in her post, she must prove herself, and if the markets keep falling, she won't be there long. She pulls on her clothes, grabs coffee, leaves.

Abdul comes in, coughing, and strokes Justin's face.

'We're going to play with Dubois, today.'

'Yey!' shouts Abdy, then coughs again.

The morning, actually, goes well for Justin. Davey thinks he has work for him.

23

Breakfast and goodbyes. It's the last morning of the International Conference of African Writing.

(Last night's session on *The Heart of Darkness* became a little edgy as the delegates argued for and against Joseph Conrad. Was he an imperialist? Was his narrator, Marlow? Or were they both outsiders, in London and the Congo? It's complicated. Voices were raised. Everyone was sure of their point of view. A woman used the 'r'-word: racist. It was racist not to call Conrad racist; it was racist, in fact, to disagree with her. 'We're just storytellers,' Vanessa said, finally, and found she was listened to with respect in the afterglow of her successful reading. 'And so was Conrad. And so was Marlow. We're all just trying to make sense of the world. Maybe Conrad was struggling, too?' To her surprise, it stopped the argument. Then the writers danced, and got a little drunk, and some shy bodies befriended others. Geoffrey had had an argument with Sanyu, so was there on his own, and he waltzed with Vanessa, his hand vaguely speculative on her spine. 'Weren't bad, what yer read,' he said at the end, when he'd tried to kiss her, and she turned her head away. He took the refusal good-temperedly. 'Keep at it, lass, yer might get somewhere.' But this was high praise, from Geoffrey Truman. Yes, she would definitely write this memoir, she thought, finishing someone else's rosé. And she found herself remembering Mary Tendo's journal.

The parts Vanessa read were really quite striking. And publishers all got very excited, even if in the end it came to nothing. Perhaps she could take some tips from Mary Tendo ...? But she's definitely had a little too much wine.)

Much activity today in Reception as the staff try to convince the departing writers of the number of drinks they have not yet paid for. 'The British Council is paying the bill,' some writers suggest, but the Sheraton staff are familiar with the ways of the British Council, and know they do not pay for gin or whisky (which are all imported, and fantastically expensive, especially with the extra Sheraton markup): or the Room Service orders of steak sandwich and chips that Geoffrey Truman's been wolfing down after midnight: or Deirdre Mullins's facial and massage. Reluctantly, the writers fork out, though as they've spent all their Ugandan money, they are forced to go to the hotel's Bureau de Change, which changes their dollars at extortionate rates, and they all hang around in the lobby, complaining in a genial, hungover, accepting way, because arguing the bill is part of the fun, though for the receptionists, it is stressful: they don't want missing money to be taken from their wages.

Nobody tips. They are poor: they're writers, and writers are the outsiders of the world: why should they tip the receptionists? In any case, this is the Sheraton. 'It's bloody American capitalism!' says Geoffrey Truman to Deirdre Mullins, which makes them both feel better, though in fact, the hotel is a mere franchise that Sheraton US sold off long ago. Now it's owned, some say, by an Ethiopian, and others say, by a North African Arab, and the staff are not sure what is happening, if they'll be sold again, if their pay will go down, if the Sheraton will survive at all now there are other, more modern hotels in town.

But 'After all, they're on salaries, unlike us writers,' laughs Deirdre to Geoffrey, as they quietly discuss (though just within earshot of the staff) the etiquette of tipping in the third world, how hard it is, actually, to get it right, and conclude, as usual, that it's best not to do it.

Vanessa's listening, and learns something, and congratulates herself on her acuteness. They're fooling themselves. She will tip, in future. Her pale cheeks flush with good intentions. It all adds to her happiness. The conference has gone well, she was a triumph. (She had texted Fifi to this effect, this morning, but somehow the text felt a little empty: *Was a great success, darling. How are u and Mimi? xx*) But she knows that something real has happened. People liked her work; it spoke to them. So her difficult childhood, which has caused her such shame, was all along one of her greatest assets! Sometimes, she reflects, I am a little obtuse. Though mostly, of course, I am very perceptive.

She has swapped emails and invitations to visit with at least a dozen of the better writers, and she fully intends to visit them, though she'll have to point out, if it comes to it, that her house is actually on the small side ...

But then she remembers a conversation she had with a writer from Sierra Leone, to whom she had made this very point, partly because the woman was admiring her laptop, and Vanessa felt guilty about being too rich. 'My house is tiny, really,' she had told the woman. 'It's a shoebox.' Then the other writer smiled with new warmth and revealed that her house, too, was small, that she shared a room with three sisters, that they're all still living in their parents' home, which is a fifth-floor two-bed flat. Vanessa had to change the subject quickly before any questioning could reveal that she herself lives entirely alone in a semi-detached house with four bedrooms.

No, she corrects herself, of course I'll put them up. I mustn't be mean. I am not too busy. So long as they don't bring their boyfriends, like Mary. Vanessa had never actually met Charles, because he came for Christmas when she was away in the country, but the pair of them drank her best champagne, Dom Perignon 1990, and Mary just said, 'We thought it was old', so Vanessa has a prejudice against boyfriends.

Much hugging and laughing in the foyer as the British writers drift away to the Sheraton minibus that will take them off to Entebbe airport, then the BA jet that will take them back to London. And as Geoffrey Truman's grey crest disappears through the door, his round shoulders, his stooped writer's spine, followed by the porter with a mountain of luggage and gifts for the children of his three marriages, Vanessa suddenly feels a twinge of disquiet. In some ways, she would like to be leaving with the others. She misses home. She misses Justin, and darling Abdy, and normal shops, and coffee chains. And even Fifi, though she doesn't listen.

But then she thinks, no, the best lies ahead. She has always wanted to see the gorillas, she hasn't entirely given up on finding Mary, and she needs to unwind, to simply – be – in Africa. She has a week left, and the conference is over, so now she has a chance to get to know Uganda. It's time to relax: she has worked hard. The safari is planned, confirmed, paid for. She is leaving the day after tomorrow.

But Vanessa is Vanessa. She can't relax. She is always restlessly thinking and planning, always trying to control the future. As soon as she sits down in the Piano Bar, and orders a coffee, and reads the *Daily Monitor*, she finds there are floods in rural Uganda. Where is Bwindi? She's not quite sure. Somewhere in the west ... near DRC Congo. If the roads are bad ... Will the jeep be OK? Will she be safe? Will she get a decent driver?

She starts a conversation with the charming young Ugandan who manages the Piano Bar. Does he think there will be floods? 'No, Madam. It is rare that we get floods in Kampala.'

But Vanessa is going to western Uganda. His face falls slightly, but then it brightens. 'The road is very good. You will stay on the road.'

'Actually I'm hoping to go in the jungle. To Bwindi Impenetrable

Forest, in fact.' She feels proud as she says it. Now he will admire her. He winces slightly at the word 'jungle'.

'You will have a good driver?' the young man asks. 'If you have a good driver, there will be no problems.'

'I am going with Great Gorilla Safaris.'

'Oh yes, they are fine,' the young man says. 'You are going with the other writers?'

'I am going alone,' Vanessa says. His face falls again. They are strange, these *bazungu*, travelling alone. Even living alone! For he has read that the new houses they are building in England are all for single people, mostly homosexuals. Why does England encourage them? But Vanessa's wearing a wedding ring.

'You should ask them to send a nice driver,' he suggests. He is losing interest now, passing on, to another *muzungu* who will tell him his problems. He himself has never been to Bwindi, but the guests are always crazy to go there. Why drive on bad roads to see wild beasts? But the doings of the *bazungu* are a mystery.

'That's a very good idea. I will go to see them.' And Vanessa tips him rather generously.

At 10 AM Vanessa is ringing on the door of Great Gorilla Safaris, the company who will be taking her to Bwindi. She has marched through the streets feeling brave and cheerful, dodging through the traffic, she thinks, like a Ugandan, managing not to trip over sudden shelves of red earth where the paving-stones have cracked and crumbled, negotiating the sullen groups of workmen sweating in the sun in their hot navy overalls, counting the storks gangling haughtily along the roof-ridges of government buildings like a line of lawyers proceeding to their chambers (she stops at thirty: it's enough for one day), smiling at the sellers setting up on the pavements, though it's notable that most of them don't smile back. Probably they're angry about CHOGM, which is giving the government an excuse to clear the streets. The skies are milky: milky white heat. Her money is hidden in a money belt that she wears under a long-sleeved shirt and trousers (because you shouldn't tempt them, though Ugandans are honest), and the flesh of her stomach streams perspiration and chafes a little where the wad of cash presses. The sky is so white, so hot, so bright. Out here, she thinks, the world is more vivid.

Great Gorilla Safaris has a basement office. She blinks, blindly, as she peers through the glass. But as soon as she enters, more Ugandan sunshine. Five different employees come and shake her hand, and smile at her as if they really like her (they are ready to like her: she did not bargain, she has paid up front, she was not too afraid to come and meet them). Every question she asks receives a comforting answer.

There aren't really any floods: it is 'too early'. The road to Bwindi is 'very good'. The trouble in Congo is 'in another part'. There are no problems with security. They 'update themselves every day on this aspect' (which she briefly thinks shows a degree of concern, but their smiles continue jaunty, untroubled). Her driver? Ah, David! Her driver is a paragon. They all join in to praise him. 'An excellent driver.' He 'speaks eight languages'. 'He is a graduate of Makerere.' The hotel where she'll be staying, the Gorilla Forest Camp, is 'the best in the area. Comfortable.' 'Has it been there long?' she asks, and seems to see them look briefly across at Mr Ronald, the Manager, as if they are uneasy. 'Long,' says Mr Ronald, his brow slightly furrowed. Then his smile returns: 'Very comfortable.'

They give her an itinerary to take away. First stop 'The Equator': she feels excited, though the treats promised sound prosaic: 'Comfort Break, Coffee, Certificate, Visit to Traditional Shop'. But the equator ... the equator. The middle of the earth. She is piercing, now, to the heart of things, having bobbed all her life in the urban shallows. 'Where is the equator, exactly?' she asks. 'You don't have a map I could borrow, do you?'

But maps are rare, and expensive, in Africa. 'Ah no, sorry. Try Aristoc bookshop.'

'So Bwindi ... Bwindi is beyond the equator?' That makes it sound quite a long way away.

Now Mr Ronald, the Manager, gives her the full benefit of his knowledge. 'It is half-a-day's drive beyond the equator, beyond Masaka, beyond Mbarara, near the borders with DRC Congo and Rwanda.'

So very far away. But he's smiling at her. Rwanda. Hang on, that's not good news. 'I didn't realise we were going near Rwanda. Isn't that where, you know, there was civil war? Between –' she searches. On the tip of her tongue. 'Between the Tutus and the Hotsis?'

His smile broadens, then represses itself. 'Between the Hutus and the Tutsis, Madam. It is over now. The country is peaceful.'

And yet, as she walks back to the Sheraton Hotel, her mind is still full of nightmarish phrases: war without end, child soldiers, massacres.

Is it a boy or a man? So thin, so a-quiver. Wet African morning. He comes on, drenched and shining, and the people waiting by the track watch him, not one of their own, not acknowledging them. The big boots make his legs look like twigs of black bone, until you look, and see they are corded with muscle, but drawn too tight, with no flesh on them. And the boots look new, but the boy-man walks strangely, in a limping, crab-wise half-shuffle, half-run. Is he running from something, or running to something? He's alone in Congo: it's best to run.

The villagers draw backwards from the dark, intense figure, limping, loping, leaning on a stick and hop-scurrying along. Yet one whispers '*Muzungu*'. The darkness they shrink from is not the colour of his skin, which, under the baked layers of dust and dirt is definitely lighter than theirs, it's a cone of darkness which spins from his eyes, his taut mouth, his bones, from the stick he is leaning on, which is a gun.

Or from things he has seen, things he has done. They avert their faces. Best not to see him. They shiver, glad this one travels alone.

24

Trevor wakes to pleasure: he's survived the night. Sun on his face, though his hut has no window: sun pours in between the door's crude hinges, a band of glorious golden light. The space looks small now, and holds no secrets, though at 4 AM it had seemed endless and formless. Good, there's his tool-kit: and there are his trousers. Relief floods through him. He has his essentials.

He focuses on the wall beside him. It's made of a brownish kind of plaster, uneven, probably covering wood, he guesses. Then he looks again. My God, it's dried mud. I am really in a mud hut. That's something! He chuckles. How Nessie would laugh about that.

True, the brick-built, tin-roofed structure next door where at first he had been meant to sleep with Mary had neat check curtains and a proper bedstead. And a paraffin lamp, two stools, a table. The bed would just about have held them both, if they had really been a couple, as Mary's less-sensible sister Martha had presumed: this house belongs to the other sister, who is taking her daughters to boarding school. Mary's face when she realised they had put them together! There was a lot of shouting in Luganda. 'I am telling them you are not my husband!' she briefly explained to him, without dipping her volume. 'They have confused you with my first husband, just because poor Omar was also a *muzungu*.'

'I thought he was Libyan?'

'Yes, a *muzungu*.'

He'd agreed to his billet in the hut alongside (which was usually the home of an aunt-by-marriage who looks after the sensible sister's children) to calm things down, though Mary did a lot of tutting. 'Their level of culture is low,' she said. 'I myself could not live at this level.'

In the middle of the night when the rain had poured down he had wondered if the straw roof could take it. It seemed impossible: that black roar of rain. Waking up, though, this morning, he feels quite happy. Maybe a mud hut is all a man needs.

Lists! Maths! Vanessa's standbys. When life presents obstacles, Vanessa will surmount them, with the aid of new ropes, axes, crampons. Adrenalin starts to spurt through her veins. Bwindi is simply an emergency for which due preparations must be made.

Some of them are harder to do in Kampala. Phone: her mobile is useless here. The Femrite writer has explained that it's simple, she just has to change the chip inside, get a new chip and a new Ugandan number. Right, that's obvious, she'll do that first (but she doesn't do it: too busy making lists). Now she rules two columns in her notebook, 'To Do' and 'To Buy'. At once she feels better.

Her socks and pants must be washed: that's easy. She washes them with soap in her hand-basin, and spreads them on the balcony.

(Later the wind will blow them away, flying like clumsy birds, spiralling downwards, ending up on the Sheraton's wide green lawns, from which the gardener removes them, tutting, for every weekend there are weddings here, they will come in their dozens, the snowy-white brides, English-style, who have never seen snow, with their glowing dark faces and small matched bridesmaids in pinks or blues or sunflower-yellows, and everything must be perfect for them, and the trains will be spread like dazzling pale paths for the photographers to capture, and sometimes the bridesmaids sit on the trains; so the gardener's always having to scare off the storks, great ribald things dropping shit and mocking him, and hardly stirring till he actually attacks them: or else removing objects that fall from the skies, the wrappers of expensive foreign chocolates, a selection of odd socks and knickers and vests, even shirts and blouses, which his wife appreciates – they're quality goods, and they have five children – or distasteful things like used condoms, which would soil the snowy-white thoughts of the brides.)

When Vanessa returns from Great Gorilla Safaris and finds her underwear is gone, she knows the maid has stolen it: at first she is furious, but then she considers. The girl must be poor, so she will say nothing. She adds 'Socks and pants' to her To Buy list.

To Do: break in her new walking boots again: (since she's been here she has only worn them once. But £100 boots! They will keep her safe ...) Soon her list has two neat complete columns that will surely translate her straight to Bwindi.

But no sooner has she finished, than she starts again, propelled by electric shocks of dismay. Her digital camera needs new batteries! She ought to have another waterproof notebook! Her insect repellent is running out! There will be millions of insects in Bwindi! True, used sparingly, her cream might last a week, but the thought of not-thoroughly repelled insects swarming all over her sensitive flesh, which has always been preternaturally attractive to insects, makes her shudder and return to her list. (She remembers Rome, long ago, with Trevor, when the two of them lay awake most of the night, Trevor because he was passionate, she because she was tormented by mosquitoes, and in the morning, with him smugly untouched and her a dotted canvas of bites, he'd said, 'Vanessa, you're the perfect woman: you're a fabulous lay and you keep off insects!')

The memory sends her scurrying off by private taxi to Garden City for insect repellent, underwear, socks, batteries, and she ticks off each item with a sense of achievement, a tiny bright victory over chaos (why is she going off into nothingness, a place without shops, lights, artefacts?).

The Garden City pharmacist's a disappointment. His insect repellents do not contain DEET, the only thing that works against malarial mosquitoes, and so she buys, randomly, what he has: coils of incense to burn like tiny spiral turds and strange plug-in things which hold repellent tablets (and too late, she wonders: are there sockets, in the jungle? Is there actually any electricity, at Bwindi?) Her plastic bag bulges with useless acquisitions, and the man doesn't even want to give her a bag, for suddenly the government is banning *kaveera*. 'I'm sorry, Madam, but it is Museveni. He wants to clean up the city for CHOGM.'

Buying things briefly makes her less anxious. But not for long. Then it starts again: did you buy enough? Did you buy too much? Or perhaps the wrong thing? Back to the shops for more buying. But she's going far beyond the reach of shops.

Back in her room, Vanessa decides to spread out everything she's going to pack on her bed. That enormous bed, so white and blank. It stretches out before her, strange, lonely, bare as the canvas of her life, for Justin is married and Trevor is gone ...

The room is silent, but outside the glass a low wind is moaning, a skyscraper wind, the breath the earth blows at high buildings, saying *Why are you here*? Testing its strength. *Why, why? You won't be here for ever.*

Is it Death, she thinks? Is it back again?

Why am I here? Vanessa wonders. How has my life brought me to this? If I'm going to die, why is no-one with me?

The day slips past, the light slips away, as she checks, discards, rethinks, amasses. Till the whole white duvet is a grid of possessions. A city in miniature: her fortifications. Seen from above, it's a labyrinthine puzzle, a piecemeal shell for some small white snail. Where does she fit in, in this chaos of detail?

By the time she's had supper, her notebook by her plate, Vanessa has ticked off everything she needs to take, and has crammed it, with an effort, into her rucksack. She can lift it, yes, but not carry it far. Never mind, her driver will carry it. That's why he's there: to look after her.

She thinks, I've cracked it. Well done, Vanessa. Only 9 PM: it has gone well. Now she can relax, look at the map, read the papers. And yes, of course, she should ring home.

And then she remembers, with a little shock of fear, she hasn't done the most important thing. Her phone: too obvious to put on the list. She can't possibly go to Bwindi without it. With a phone, she can summon an air ambulance, or alert British police and politicians. Thank God, there's an MTN shop in the foyer, where a listless employee sits every night till 10, fluorescent-lit as blind guests troop past her.

I must speak to Justin: I must, I must. I must know how little Abdul Trevor is …

And Trevor. He won't mind me having a word. After all, he might never see me again. I ought to say something nice to him.

And she's knocked off her feet by a flood of regret. It washes across her, the lonely thought of her maddening ex-husband, so far away in England, going about his business as normal, perfectly content on his own, without her – talking to Soraya, or watching TV – maybe (it hurts) in bed with Soraya – with no idea what Vanessa is facing. Not admiring her courage or rooting for her. *He would have wished me luck. Yes, he would have worried.* He might have told me not to go, and then allowed himself to be persuaded.

But by the time she's gone down and fixed up the phone, it's already 10.30. 12.30 in London: too late to call him.

There's a lump in her throat, a globus of terror. To calm herself, she starts to read the paper.

M7 DENIES TROOPS MASSING ON BORDER

25

Trevor, in bed without Soraya, a mere 100 miles away from Vanessa, has decided Uganda's a brilliant country.

The day has gone so much better than expected. For a start, Mary Tendo had managed to get the whole well situation arse over tip. The village already has a well: it is basic, a pipe in a basin of concrete, but whoever put it in, knew what they were doing, which is more than he would, starting from scratch. More of a protected spring, really. What he sees straight away, though, is why it's hardly working, just a dribble of fresh water in a sea of brown. The concrete is cracked, and the area is filthy: mud, twigs, pebbles. The ground around the basin is sodden and smelly. Mosquitoes hover. (He has taken his pills, but he suddenly thinks about Vanessa: if she were here, he would be all right: all insects make a bee-line for Vanessa.)

This is going to be a mucky old job. But he's a plumber: he can deal with mess. It's what he enjoys: making things right. (Like the time he went round to sort out Zakira, which was how she and Justin got together! And his little grandkid – that smashing little boy – if it weren't for Trevor's plumbing, he might never have existed.)

'Ask them if anyone taught them to look after the well,' he says to Mary.

She fires a succession of rapid questions at the men who have come with them, and nods her head, slowly, as they reply. 'Of course the engineer taught a woman to do it, and she taught another woman, and so on. But the first woman got sick, and then the second woman did it, but she didn't remember everything. Then the second woman's daughter became ill, at school in Kampala, so the second woman had to go to the city, and she taught another woman, before she left, who was clever, but the woman after her was not clever. There is a Water Committee in the village, but they are too busy, and so they do not meet.'

'Didn't anyone write down the engineer's instructions?'

'Trevor, some of these women cannot read,' says Mary. They look at each other, with their shared possession of so many things the villagers can't take for granted.

'Never mind,' says Trevor. 'I can sort this out. And I'll write down the instructions, and we'll give them to the head teacher. She can bloody read, I hope,' he says *sotto voce*, and Mary giggles.

'She will charge a lot of money.'

'I could have it up and running by lunch-time, Mary,' he says, getting down into a plumber's crouch. 'But really, the whole system needs disinfection. It needs something called a chlorine shock. So I'll give it one, with that bleach we bought. The water won't be usable for a few days. And then they're going to have to see to the apron. It's cracked, see, here, and there. That's why there's hardly any flow. But any decent local builder could see to that. And maintenance – they're going to have to do that. If there's a Water Committee, I need to meet them. I'm going to have to explain to our friends that it will need a look-over, every single day. Looks to me as if cattle have been around here.'

Mary fires orders at the villagers, who look impressed, and smile at him.

'Maybe not *every* day,' he concedes. 'But when you get really heavy rain, like last night.'

'Oh no,' says Mary, decidedly, 'that rain was not at all heavy,

Trevor. You do not understand Ugandan rain.' And she turns and repeats what he has said to the men, who laugh at Trevor, heartily, and look at Mary Tendo with their own shared knowledge of so many things these *bazungu* only guess at.

By one o'clock, he is stunned with heat, and surrounded by children from another school, the Catholic one, in yellow uniforms, this time, who watch him delving in the bowels of the concrete, the ones at the front reporting his progress to the ones behind, with much pushing and shoving.

'Lunch-time' turns out to be a bit optimistic. A teacher joins the children, to shoo them back to school. He speaks to Trevor in English. They are very pleased the well will soon be working.

'So where do you get your water at the moment?' Trevor asks him.

'There is a well in the next-door village. But that well is four or five miles away. Of course, my school is very lucky. We also have a tank.'

'Oh yes?' says Trevor, frowning up at the sunlight. He has never worked in heat like this: it's a hammer, knocking, knocking at his brain. Nothing will stop him finishing this job. Yet he's swimming across a great coma of heat. His neck, back, biceps are drenched in sweat. He knows his head is getting burned, because he can't stop his silly bloody hat falling off, and his hair is not quite so thick as it was. 'Tell me about it.' He's thought of something.

By teatime – he glances at his watch, and its sharp little numerals swell in the heat, swell and retreat, he is falling asleep ... by English teatime, such a long way away, *egg and chips*, he is happy, dreaming, *a nice Swiss Roll or a couple of biscuits, Vanessa fussing with her flipping Earl Grey: it was cucumber, yes, cool cucumber sandwiches, she liked to make those, and I didn't turn my nose up: cucumber sandwiches, both of us young, long wet grass because I hadn't mown the lawn, but she didn't object, she let me in, the grass was shining and I heard her moan, sort of soft and low like a wood pigeon: were either of us ever so happy again?* – 'Trevor! Trevor? Are you finishing?' – he's almost ready to pack up his tools and get the chlorine into the system. But the well, on its own, won't solve the problem. He has another idea about that.

The Catholic school is near the well, and also has a collection system for rainwater. The Protestant one has zilch: nothing. When the well is working, the Protestant children come in their lunch-hour to get a drink of water, if they have the energy, which most of them don't. It takes them twenty minutes there and back. If they don't come, they don't drink all day.

'You mean there's no water at all at the Protestant school?' Trevor had said to the teacher, incredulous. Our little tykes wouldn't put up with it, he thinks. Nothing to drink all day, in this sort of heat. They don't know they're born, British young people.

Mary has boiled up water for African tea in the beautiful new teapot. (And in two days' time, Trevor has promised, there will be water from the well again, clean sweet water! A miracle!) It is strong and sweet, with milk and ginger. She is very happy. The news is spreading. The *muzungu* has come and worked his magic. Her brother's wife is killing a chicken for dinner! Trevor has proved his worth. She smiles upon him.

And she thinks of the prayer she first heard in London in the cold English church near Vanessa's house, where the vicar was kind, the Reverend Andy, though she did not like his sermon about television, since she did not watch TV in Vanessa's house. The second time she went, the Reverend Andy's sermon was about a nun who lived sealed in a wall, in the east of England, many centuries ago, and who wrote the first book by a woman in English. Mary liked her strange name, Julian of Orange, and wrote it in her notebook, when she got home. Julian's wonderful words have come true today, and Mary imagines them in golden orange, glowing in the sunlight of late afternoon: 'All shall be well, and all shall be well, and all manner of things shall be well. Amen.' 'Amen,' Mary now says aloud, and Trevor is startled, but she pours him some tea, and smiles and smiles. Trevor has done it!

(But after the service, in cold distant London, there was coffee and hard biscuits in the hall at the back and she told the Reverend Andy about Jamil, because she saw that he understood sadness, and he promised he would pray for her. *His prayers were not answered.* Do not think about that. Of course, he has many people to pray for. *Perhaps Jesus has forgotten her.* Do not think about this, do not think about this. Today is a time for happiness. Mary leaves her sorrow in the sealed chamber where Julian prayed for years and years.)

Mary has other business to sort out in the village, people to see she has not seen for decades, stories to learn, hurts to soften, the quarrel over her sisters' children, the sadness over their parents' death. But first, most important, the story of the water.

Mary has invited the reproachful uncle to come and listen to Trevor's conclusions. The uncle and Mary are friends again: she has tried to explain her life in Bungereza, the efforts she made, the sorrow she suffered; besides, he is very pleased with his jacket. At the end, he called her 'Daughter', and stroked her hair, and although Mary Tendo is no-one's daughter, this uncle is very important to her. Not just because he is a councillor: he is the oldest man in the family.

'So Mary, it's simple,' Trevor says. 'What your brother's school needs is another collection tank, as big as possible. With a filtration system. Depending on how much rain you get, that ought to keep them going all year.'

The uncle is listening. He says nothing.

'I've been working it out. You need a 10,000-litre tank. That should supply 300-odd children, with maybe a bit over for other people. I mean, it's a long walk, to the well.'

The uncle nods, but still says nothing. 'What do you think, Uncle? It is a good idea.'

But the uncle says something to her in Luganda. Mary's face falls. They talk for a while.

'He does not want to say this to you, but the school has no money to buy this tank. The school has no money for salaries, because the government sends everything late. Jacob has been waiting two months for his pay. The school has no money, for doors, or windows, as you have seen yourself, Trevor. But my uncle thanks you for mending the well.'

'Thank you for the well,' says the uncle, in English. 'Jacob's wife will prepare a chicken.' He smiles at Trevor: his smile is forgiving. How can this white man understand the village? They already know about collection tanks, it is an old idea, *okulembeka*, though this Patcher thinks it is his own invention. And it has its drawbacks, with irregular rainfall.

'They aren't expensive,' says Trevor, embarrassed. 'The other teacher said the small-size tank was less than a million Ugandan shillings. That's three hundred quid, isn't it, Mary?'

The uncle speaks to Mary in Luganda. They look at each other, excluding Trevor.

'They cannot afford it,' Mary says, briefly.

And at that point, something speaks through Trevor.

Surely not his own voice, for back in London, he always holds out for his call-out fee on top of his charges, he always gets VAT, he isn't a mug (except for the very occasional old lady he doesn't like to see in a state, so naturally he has to sort her out): 'I can afford it. It's not a lot of money. Mary, you tell them not to worry about it. I'll see to it all. Patchett will pay. The 10,000-litre size, while I'm about it.' He likes the sound of it; Patchett will pay.

He goes to bed blissfully smug and drunk. The local beer (at least, he thinks it is beer, though it tastes like no beer he has ever drunk, and someone tells him it's made from bananas: 'Banana beer?' he asks, and everyone laughs) is red-hot stuff, the chicken is accompanied by freshly slaughtered goat, chewy but tasty, roasted on the fire, and there is rice, and *matooke*, and sweet potatoes, and twenty-odd villagers show up. He's eaten everything except the special delicacy, *enswa*, en-sway, it sounded like: giant fried ants. (Bloody insects, I ask you! He's open-minded, but he has his limits.)

There are speeches, in both English and Luganda, and most of them, he thinks, are addressed to him. 'Patcher! We have written a song for you. It can be translated, "The Bringer of Water" ...' Just once in a while, it is good to be feasted. In England, plumbers aren't exactly princes (no wonder: no-one goes thirsty for hours, or pants for water in boiling heat). Course, they're keen to get hold of him in their hour of need, when the tank has just burst or the radiator's leaking. They might offer a backhander to jump the queue, which Trevor has to explain is offside, because even plumbers have their sense of honour. But this is different. They make him feel special. The skills he takes for granted really mean something, here. He's never felt proud to say he is a plumber (and Nessie, he thinks briefly, was ashamed of him; she always thought he should have bettered himself; always thought he had no ambition). But today Trevor Patchett is 'the Bringer of Water'. He wishes his ex-wife could hear them sing his praises.

Mary is translating the councillor's speech. 'Now he's saying *omugga gwamagala*, you are the Fountain of Life, Trevor –'

'Fair enough,' says Trevor, drinking deep of the beer.

'– and referring to the fountains you built in London, the ones by the lions in Trafalgar Square –'

'Bloody hell, Mary, that was over-egging it –'

'And now he is saying that *you* are a lion.'

'Bloody good!' says Trevor, and raises his glass in the direction of the councillor, who is winding down. 'I'm with Winston on that one. The old British lion.' He sinks the last of it, and burps gently. It's all slightly crooked: the faces, the fire. But he is a man: this is his moment.

'Trevor,' says Mary. She is staring down on him, which means he must be on the floor, and although they are all laughing, she speaks quite strictly. 'How much have you had to drink, Trevor?'

He is disconcerted. It's a funny angle to be looking at Mary Tendo from. 'Itsh the heat,' he explains, but it comes out wrong. 'Didn' wear m' hat. Only had two pintsh.'

'Two pints of *waragi*? Poor Trevor.'

But they are all helping him to bed in the hut, although he would like to drink more, hear more praise, stay longer.

26

That night, the floods come to Uganda. Torrential rains hit in the east and the west: thirty inches of rain fall in an hour. Roads wash away. Bridges collapse. Only a few drops of rain fall in Kampala. But the rain pours down: the rain pours down; the rain pours down over most of Uganda. Museveni receives bad news, in the morning. The floodwaters are rising in many regions. In only two days, the UN will declare Uganda, yet again, a disaster zone.

Trevor sleeps like the dead until 4 AM. He wakes up to hear the rain thundering down like an endless landslide upon the roof: like the end of the world: like the end of this hut, for somewhere a soft pat-pat-pat is starting. Then a loud hissing voice is saying his name.

'Trevor, let me in, it is me, Mary.'

In fact, she is in, she is tapping his leg, it is Mary, as well as the rain, pat-pat-patting.

'Mary? What's the matter? What's going on?'

Wind whistles and screams through the straw of the thatch, and the rain pounds on, inexorable. It sounds like the headache he will have in the morning, although at the moment Trevor still feels drunk, blood roaring in his ears as he lurches upright. He can only see her in silhouette, blurred by his mosquito net. He wishes, deeply, he were still asleep.

'I have come to see that you are all right.' Her answer comes after a curious pause.

'Why shouldn't I be? What's happening?'

'I am very glad you are all right.'

There is another pause. Mary isn't moving. 'Mary, what is going on?'

'There is nothing in your hut?'

'Like what, Mary? Stop talking in riddles.'

'Trevor, I will sleep on the floor of your hut.'

For one dim moment Trevor thinks, *she likes me*, but then common sense reasserts itself. 'What will the village have to say about that?'

'It is not a question of the village.'

Now she's settled on the floor, with much sighing and wriggling as she wangles her way under his mosquito net. He hopes no mosquitoes will come in with her: he hopes the net is big enough for two. Mary Tendo is not a small woman. She's very near him. She smells sweetly of sweat. She wriggles so much he starts wondering again. If she *does* like him, he'd better not ignore it. Maybe the feast in his honour has turned her head.

'So what is it, Mary? Were you, uh, lonely?' He gives her shoulder the lightest of squeezes.

She sits upright with furious energy, imperilling the net, but she doesn't care. 'Trevor, there must not be a misunderstanding!'

'All right, Mary, relax, no problem.'

'You remember that Vanessa used to keep frogs?'

'I remember, Mary. You hated them.'

'You remember when I saw them I chased them with a broom.'

'Yes, and Vanessa was not very happy.'

'In fact, I chased them because I did not like them.' There is a pause, then she starts again. 'Perhaps I was afraid of them, although in general, I fear nothing, Trevor.'

'I believe you, Mary. Um, go on.'

'Now the house where I was sleeping is full of big frogs. I woke up to find them chirruping like birds round my bed. I did not have anything to chase them with. They have come with the floods; *Bibi nyo*! They are filthy, disgusting ... Trevor, please save me from the frogs.'

She has never asked him to save her from anything since she was young and a stranger to London, nearly twenty years ago when she cared for Justin, and Vanessa couldn't seem to stop criticising her. Poor kid. He had tried to stand up for her. The new Mary always seemed so strong, so confident ... In fact, in the past week he'd slightly gone off her. But now she needs him. Trevor is touched. Mary is a woman, and he is a man.

'You have this mattress. I'll get down on the floor.' His brain knocks hard against his skull as he moves, but it still feels good to make a manly sacrifice while Mary compliantly takes the mattress.

'Thank you, Trevor. You have excellent manners.'

They lie side by side while the storm rocks above them. Outside, a plague of fat bullfrogs passes by, chirruping loudly and insolently, a coarse, fat, farty, squelching sound. Mary prays quietly. They do not enter.

The roof starts collapsing twenty minutes later.

By 6 AM, when the sun comes up, Mary and Trevor are half-sitting, half-crouching in a corner where the mud and thatch still hold together. He has taken his possessions to the brick-built house, but Mary Tendo refused to go back, and he could not leave her there all on her own. They have their arms around each other. They fell asleep talking about lost sons. Before that, there were other, more intimate discussions, and a resolution in the tender dark. As they wake up to a riot of birdsong, first Mary and then Trevor smiles.

PART 4

Do-si-do

27

Vanessa wakes up with a shock of terror. 5 AM on the dreaded morning. It's here: the day she must go to Bwindi. Switch on the light, switch off her phone alarm. She lies for a second, stomach clenching. Should she call it off? Is she going to die?

But she can't call it off. She would look silly. She has told so many people she's going to Bwindi. She shoots out of bed, and starts checking the essentials, which involves unpacking most of her rucksack. Money, camera, notebook, good. Malaria pills, sunhat, pen. Glasses, contact lenses, sunglasses. Phone! It's been on all night for the alarm, so she must recharge it! She plugs it in. She's just standing up again when the lights go out. Shit! But it's fine, she tells herself, the electricity always comes straight back on, at the Sheraton. A beat, then another. Dark. Silence. Nothing happens. She starts sweating. Why hasn't the generator come on? Why else do people stay at the Sheraton? And why does it have to happen *this morning*?

In the dark, on her own, she feels totally helpless. How can she assemble her possessions? Without her possessions, she cannot go. If she could find her torch, that would be something. She starts feeling with her fingertips, but things slip away, twist out of her reach, are not where she thought, elude her, betray her, crash down into chaos. They're suddenly useless, all her possessions.

Shaking in the dark, she's an unshelled crustacean.

The boy-man is happy. The rains have come! He is soaked and filthy, but his lips are moist. He could have drunk it for ever, the sweet clear rain, sucking it from leaves, from twigs, from his hands, but he remembers you must not have too much. He learned many things, while he was in the army. Were they an army? They were all that was real. They had taken his life, and consumed it all. Now all that remains to him is water. He has no possessions but shirt, shorts, boots. Each item was stolen from someone else. But now he has water. He laughs. He drinks. For the first time, he dares to think he might live. Is it possible he is near the border? The water sinks through him, cool, thrilling.

Not until later does the hunger begin.

He stays low in the bushes. It's mid-morning. He sees the woman clearly, through his mask of leaves. She is slender and tall. Perhaps Rwandan? Perhaps a Munyankore. He listens: he could be anywhere, still in DRC, already in Uganda, or even Rwanda, there is no way of knowing. She is talking to her child as she does her washing. The child is naked: playing in the mud. She has some blue soap: a rich woman. Three dresses (he counts), two pairs of men's shorts. He needs those trousers, civilian trousers, but even more, he needs what she's eating, he can't see clearly, some kind of grain cakes, maybe baked millet. And she has sugarcane for the baby. How old is the baby? He's forgotten such things. All he knows is, the child is too young for the army. He knows he should strike, take what he needs and move on, quick, before other people come to the river and all of them turn on him and kill him.

For what he has done he can never be forgiven. It is the one thing he knows without question.

But what is she doing? She slips down her robe. A breast appears, round and beautiful and terrible, not long starved sticks like the breasts he has been seeing. He is stirred and afraid. He must not see this. He does not know what it will make him do. But she casually picks up the plump, calm child and suckles him, talking to him softly and sweetly, while she squeezes out the washing, the drops of water falling like gold in the sunlight. He pinches himself, hard. Why is he paralysed? The sun moves an ingot of heat on to his head. He will have to make his move. The cover is pitiful.

What happens comes so quickly that he is left gasping. She puts down the child, and it runs straight up to him. Stares through the leaves, bright-eyed, unafraid. The child is smiling and pointing at him. He cannot understand what the child is saying. Everything is over. He clutches his gun. But the child is smiling. The child is smiling. Split-second decision: his grip loosens. He pushes the gun away behind him. He gets up, slowly, in the full dazzling sunlight, and the woman is startled, and hides her breast quickly as she calls the child to her. She stares at him.

He points to her food. His mouth is watering. He points to his lips, he rubs his belly. Her eyes run over him like water, his thin corded legs, his knobbed shoulder blades, his ribcage protruding like an empty basket, his whipcord muscles, his eyes, imploring, his eyes which are those of a boy and a man.

She says something he cannot understand, but he knows at once it is full of pity. She strokes her own boy as she offers him food, the starving creature who came from the forest. As he gnaws and gulps, she looks more closely. Where did he get those wounds, those scars, those ridges and valleys by his eyes, his nose?

'He's still very clingy,' says Zakira to Justin, her voice sharp with anxiety.

Justin and Zakira are up too early: the markets are jittery, and Zakira has got to go to Brussels after all: that's stressful enough without Abdy being ill. Zakira tries not to think, *it's bad timing.* But it's cold, so cold. Soon the clocks are going back. 'You should have taken him to the doctor yesterday.'

'It's OK for you to say that *now*, Zakira –'

'I said it yesterday. I did.'

'In any case, he had a playdate.'

'YOU had a playdate with your mate Davey. Take him today, for goodness sake.'

'Fridays everyone goes to the doctor.'

She stares at him, furious, his sulky face, that look of premature defeat. Why did she marry him? He's hopeless. 'Take him to the doctor or I'll never forgive you.'

'Don't threaten me!' He is suddenly shouting, and Abdul Trevor starts to cry in earnest, instead of just grizzling in his mother's arms.

'Don't shout. You're a bully. You've made Abdy cry. You're a dreadful father.'

'You're a hopeless mother. I do everything! You're never fucking here!'

She shoves the child at him, like a stone or a weapon, eyes flashing with fury. 'I hate you! That's IT!'

She is grabbing her coat, her laptop, her blackberry, her chic little chocolate Chanel suitcase. She's going. Justin is gripped by panic. Abdul Trevor is sobbing, 'Don't go, don't go, don't go, Mummy don't go,' in a hiccupy, snotty stream of sorrow.

'I didn't mean it, sorry, Zakira,' Justin pleads. It's their worst-ever row. He has never called her a hopeless mother. *But I do do everything. It's true*, he thinks.

She returns, briefly, to kiss the boy, who has wandered away to the television, but she stares at her husband, disliking him. The mortgage on the flat is huge: the jeep isn't paid for: she's the only one earning. She feels afraid of everything. 'You fucking get a job,' she says. 'You do something, then I *can* be a mother. And in the meantime, fucking keep him warm. Can't you even do that? Can't you do anything?'

'Is that what you think? I should kill myself.'

'How dare you say that in front of Abdy! I'm not going to listen to this shit.'

The unthinkable happens: she slams the door. She's gone, without them making up, without kissing him, without taking back the cruel words he heard her say. She doesn't love him, or care about him. What's the point of his life? No-one loves him.

It's not as if Abdy appreciates him either, for now his son has started to cry. 'Where's Mummy?,' he calls from the other room. 'I want MUMMY!'

So do I, thinks Justin. But we can't have her. I'm all you've got, so be nice to me. He is tempted to put out his tongue at Abdy. He does, and feels better. Then he feels guilty, goes through to find him, picks him up, sighing. Abdy's almost too big to pick up: not a baby any more, a big heavy boy who will be starting school in less than two years; yet today he feels limp, and damp, and hot, suddenly like a much younger child. Is he shivering? Yes, he is. But he can't be cold: he is wearing a jumper. 'Mummy,' he whimpers, in a heartbroken voice, then just as affectingly, 'Daddy'.

Justin suddenly thinks about his own mother. He wishes she wasn't so far away. She can be a terrible pain, of course, but she's also a useful source of advice. After all, she had raised him without killing him, whereas he and Zakira are both amateurs. She's not been in touch. She's abandoned him. Because he's a fuck-up. All women leave him.

28

Vanessa has seen her driver before!

Their greetings, in the half-dark, were perfunctory. He's smallish, youngish, and he smiles. 'Great Gorilla Safaris, Madam,' he says.

'Vanessa Henman. *Dr* Henman,' she answers. She peers at him. A suspicion strikes her.

But she's kept him waiting, so explains about the power-cut: 'It was, frankly, impossible. The power only came back ten minutes ago.'

He looks at her blankly, eyes half-veiled. His room does not have electricity. One day, he thinks, I shall have it too.

As they bump through two blocks of early morning Kampala, Vanessa stares fixedly at the driver. Yes, she knows where she's seen him before.

'You're the man who drove me from the airport,' she says. 'When I missed the bus, so I had to use you. You said you had no money for breakfast.' So I paid for it, she thinks. Too generously.

The man looks vague. 'It is possible.'

'Your name's Isaac, isn't it?'

He denies it. 'My name is Mutesa Isaac.'

'I was told I would be driven by a man called David. A graduate of Makerere. Their top driver. That's not you, is it?'

But it's all too late. They are leaving the centre. They have joined the endless caterpillar of white Toyota taxis, each segment jostling independently from one side of the city to the other. She is stuck on a conveyor belt with the wrong driver.

'I am a top driver,' Isaac explains. 'But David cannot come. His friend is sick.'

'That's really not a very good excuse,' says Vanessa. 'You can't just not do things, because your friends have problems.'

The man shoots a look at her, surprised, but he does not want her to be angry. She has a thin, spiteful face, this *muzungu*. How is he to know that she is just frightened?

'I think he has broken his arm, and legs,' he says, eventually, to calm her. As they leave the city, the mist is lifting. Isaac is happy to be going to the country. He has business to do along the way. Besides, he has never been to Bwindi. There are deals to be done, money to be made. The rich *muzungu* will probably tip well. 'David is my cousin, I am doing him a favour.'

'Are you insured to drive this car?'

Isaac doesn't answer. He smiles at her. 'I will start to explain all places of interest,' he says, keenly, as the buildings thin away and the early sunlight falls on bright green vegetation stretching out to the horizon, heavy-headed plants, taller than a man, papyrus plants, but he doesn't know the name. 'Now we are entering the swamp land. The swamp land is very interesting.'

Justin sinks into paralysis. It is pulling him down, sapping his will. It seems he can't get Abdy to the doctor. At 8.29, he is on the phone to the Health Centre: the maddening voice of the answering machine, which asks him to wait to be put through, so he waits, and pays, for their phone bill's enormous, until they cut him off, without warning, and the cycle repeats, he keeps ringing and ringing (thank God Abdul Trevor is watching TV), it's 8.45, it's 8.47, then suddenly there are only five minutes left, his fingers hit the 'repeat call' button faster, more angrily, God help me, why is this happening to me, it's 8.58, there's no time left – it's 8.59 when he gets through, and a real voice answers, thank God a human, but she says, 'Oh no, you're too late for today.' All appointments have gone. He's failed. That's that. He's a hopeless father. He can't do anything. All Zakira's words come back to him. He sits there, paralysed, cursing himself. Then he slouches through to the sitting-room. Ah, that's why Abdul Trevor was quiet. Curiously, he has gone to sleep, which is quite unusual when he's watching television. But at least it gives Justin a little respite.

He plonks himself down by his son on the sofa, and although he knows there's a lot to be done, the breakfast dishes, the rubbish, the washing, Justin watches the Tellytubbies; lost to time, he joins all the babies in La-la land, swaying to the music, chewing his fingers, sucking the comforting pad of his thumb. Yes, she's abandoned him, just like his mother. And Mary, too. And where is his father? Usually he rings up every few days. They've all gone gallivanting off, like Zakira.

29

'Trevor, you deserve a holiday,' says Mary, sounding very loud and cheerful, to Trevor, whose eyes and ears seem too sensitive, today, as if the whole world is shouting at him. They are driving down a long straight road, but the slightest bump makes his head lurch horribly. Here, only thirty minutes from the village, you would think last night's rains had never happened. Lorries and coaches thunder past. She is driving him away, away ...

'So is this a holiday?' he asks. All Mary has said is that they're going on an outing. His tools, his possessions are in the boot.

'I am driving you to the equator, Trevor. This will be very interesting for you. And then I think you should go to Queen Elizabeth Park. There is a nice hotel, it is called Mweya. I saw you have brought your American Express card. *It was lying on the mattress beside your shoe.*' (This she says quietly: there are people in the back, and you never know who is listening.) 'The *bazungu* always go to Mweya. Lions, hyenas, crocodiles,' she continues brightly, but Trevor's not encouraged.

'I thought we might just go back to Kampala,' he says. 'You know, a bit of the old civilisation.' He thinks, Charles and Mary's place is not the Ritz, but at least there are cold bottled beers in the fridge, there are newspapers, I've got my own bed. Whereas in the country ... it's all so different. I'm a city boy, I can't get my head around it.

When that hut fell down, the village people just laughed. *Che sara, sara*, kind of thing, I suppose. (Being that laid-back didn't help with the well ...)

But now he is infected with the same spirit. When Mary announced they were going on a trip, he didn't argue, he just packed his things.

'Charles expects us to be in the village for a week, but you have finished the job already. Now I think you deserve to see Uganda. There is more to Uganda than a hut which falls down. It is very beautiful, western Uganda.'

And the road leads west: straight to the west. Charles's red Toyota bowls along at speed. Mercy and the child have been left behind, so Dora can get to know her cousins in the village. They will travel back to Kampala by bus. Mary's aunt is in the back, and the neighbour, for both of them have errands on the way to Mbarara, the other side of the equator, and the neighbour's brother is going also, a skinny, smiling man called James. 'You will pay him, Trevor. He will drive you to Mweya.'

Out here, Trevor thinks, a car is a business. It's a business opportunity, a car journey. Whereas at home, a car is just another car. Every bugger's got one. We don't think about it. Travel's easy, for us. We just set off and go wherever we want to.

'I hate to leave the country when he's poorly,' says Zakira, ringing from the Eurostar platform. 'I'm so sorry I shouted at you, Justin, it's just ... you know ... it makes me so uptight ... I said terrible things. Awful things. Can you ever forgive me?'

'It's OK,' says Justin, but his voice is dead. He can't forgive her at this moment. He's pulled himself together, and left an urgent message with one of the Health Centre's Indian receptionists. She seemed to understand him. Now it's up to fate. But they're going to call back; he can't talk now. Half of him longs to leave like Zakira, walk out of the door, take a plane or train. Half of him is terrified, and wants Zakira here. A little voice inside him is crying, pleading: 'Help me, someone. I'm only the father.'

'You *are* taking him to the doctor?'

'No, but the doctor's going to ring. I've done my best. Don't criticise me.'

'Do you know I love you?'

'Uhn,' grunts Justin, and then he relents, just a second too late, and tries to mumble 'I love you too,' but she's getting on the train, they are cut off.

Do something, Justin. Instead, he just sits there, slumped on the sofa, and thinks of his mother, who told him the sofa was bad for his spine.

Vanessa sits in a hot, metal box (where she cannot do so much as an ankle circle, though she desperately needs to do Salute to the Sun, and her back's crying out for some Pilates), chained to a monomaniac who is bouncing them both through the dust of Uganda.

'It is the fault of the First Family,' says Isaac, for the umpteenth time. He is pointing out the lack of trees on the hilltops, whose clear, rounded outlines Vanessa had admired. 'They cut down the trees to make charcoal.'

'What, personally?' asks Vanessa, sarcastically. 'Museveni's wife comes and cuts down the trees?' She's kept silent for hours, in the face of his obsession, but it's hot, in the car, and the dust blows through the window, and her blood sugar is low, because she didn't eat breakfast, and Isaac is certainly not the man she wanted. Everything's the fault of the First Family. Malaria, AIDS, deforestation. There must be other things to say about Uganda.

He does not respond. He has not understood her.

'I was told my driver would speak eight languages,' Vanessa

remarks to the air, indignant. 'I was told he was a fully-fledged professional driver.'

'I am fledged,' Isaac remarks, after a little pause. 'Of course, I am professional. I am a good driver.'

'I was told I would have a driver-*guide*,' Vanessa says, with heavy emphasis. 'Someone who knew about the country.'

'I know about it,' the man insists. 'For example, I know about the equator. It is the middle of the earth. We will be there, soon.'

'We have made too many stops already,' says Vanessa. 'Or else we would have been there sooner.' In fact, she is anxious about time. They must get to Bwindi before it is dark. She explains to him that the British Foreign Office advises its nationals not to drive after dark. In Bwindi, after dark, she thinks, anything might happen.

But the British Foreign Office does not impress Isaac. He simply says, 'Do not worry, we will get there ... And you asked me to stop, so you could photograph tomatoes,' he adds, indignant, taking his eyes from the road so at the last moment he has to wrench at the wheel to stop their jeep hitting a stationary taxi. The passengers, some getting off, some climbing in, crowd at the roadside, black in the sunlight, and gaze up at them, surly, as they go past: one goes on staring as they zoom into the distance. *Bazungu* go too fast: for them everything is easy. No waiting at bus stops by the dirty road.

'You actually only stopped once for me. Mostly you refused to stop for photographs. You pretended that I asked too late. You have stopped to see your friends, and do deals,' she says. 'You stopped to get fuel, because you had forgotten, because you were not organised.' She's aware she sounds miserable, and petty, but she feels dreadful: she's got prickly heat; her eyes are watering; this man is a chancer. Why did the proper driver's friend have to break his arm? Why didn't the safari firm cancel the trip? Or at least delay it until after the floods, and after the war, and after the Ebola – for today's *Monitor*, which Vanessa bought through the car window as they rocked through the streets of early-morning Kampala, was almost comically full of bad news. Each story she read made her heart sink further. The floods are getting worse. The war is imminent. An outbreak of Ebola is reported in Congo. Of course, Congo is a big country. But Vanessa feels fate is picking on her, as surely as she was once picked on at school. Her luck has turned, or she's pushed it too far. Now she's being driven, unstoppably, towards a constellation of disasters near Bwindi. The world beyond the window looks bright and heartless, flashing past too fast, as if she's saying goodbye.

'My phone,' she says suddenly, to no-one. 'My phone. I have to ring my son.'

And as soon as she has said it, she remembers. She has left it charging, in her room. It was the fault of the power-cut, the rush, the panic, this stupid driver, the Sheraton ...

'I've forgotten my phone!'

Is Isaac smiling? 'I am sorry,' he says, but she can see his mouth twitch. He's definitely smiling! She is furious.

'I am upset,' she says, childishly. 'I don't feel safe without my phone. And I have to ring my son. My family.' There is a pause. She stares at his profile, impassive now, a mask of wood outlined black against the sun. 'It would help if you were sympathetic, honestly. I'm sure you drivers are supposed to be helpful.'

'I am sympathetic,' he argues, self-righteously. 'For example, you can use my phone. You must give me some money, so I can get credit. I am sorry that you have forgotten your phone.' Now his mouth seems to be twitching again. 'I am sorry you were not organised.'

Trevor thinks: this road is pretty bloody good. Straight to the horizon, like a Roman road, like a road made by people who are heading for the future. Most of it is tarmacked. It's in much better shape than the rutted, pockmarked roads of Kampala. Last night's water has run off and lies in dark strips along the edges. His hangover is loosening, lessening. The *matooke* plants stretch away in neat rows. He's starting to change his mind about Ugandans. Maybe they are quite organised. Every so often, by the road, there is a group of trestle tables selling fruit and vegetables. 'Look like altars, don't they?' says Trevor. 'I like that. Looks like they're taking trouble over things.'

'What you do not know, Trevor, is that these stalls are alive. They are bark-cloth trees. You plant a stick in the ground, and it grows, and then you put another, and so on.'

'I've got just one thing to say to you, Mary,' says Trevor. 'Uganda is a bloody fantastic country.'

The fruit are beautifully arranged in neat little pyramids, tomatoes and potatoes rising up like offerings, as if each thing people have grown is precious: which it is, he reflects. But they're lucky, here. Ugandans haven't built over all their land. What would we do, back in England, without imports? We've grown fat and lazy. We can't feed ourselves.

The bright reds and yellows look glorious to him, beside the dust of the road, like displays of jewels, as they zoom past yet another row of stalls. Food was precious to us, after the war, in the fifties, he reflects, when I was tiny, and everything was rationed. We knew what was what, in England, in those days. My grandpa got a pineapple, down at the pub, and my mum said I mustn't tell my teacher. It was a great day when we had two bananas. Here there's so much, but they still show it to advantage. Yams and breadfruit and bananas and marrows, and those great rough greeny-golden numbers Mary despises –

'What were those big green things, Mary?'

'Those? They are just jackfruit – for poor people and children. You would not like them.'

But as they pass a new stall, she spots something different on offer, and screams to a halt at the last moment, causing shrieks of laughter and protest in the back seat. 'It is a special kind of passion fruit,' she says. 'I will take some back for my family and Mercy. And perhaps you would like to try some also, Trevor. You must have the best that Uganda has to offer.' She is smiling at him with tender humour.

'Hold your horses, Mary. I'd like to get a picture.' He gets out of the car and takes a photograph of Mary as she bargains for a neat mound of small yellow fruit. She comes back a couple of minutes later with a satisfied smile and her hands full of fruit, yellow, delicately wrinkled, scented things which she distributes with an order to 'Suck'. 'They are passion fruit,' she says, 'but not the usual ones. This is something very special, of Uganda, Trevor.'

Everybody gets sucking as she starts the engine. 'Ooh,' says Trevor. It's stronger than the hangover. He is transported. 'That's paradise.' And he looks at the photo in his digital camera. 'Very nice, Mary. You look very nice.'

'Stop,' says Vanessa, spotting a fruit stall, one of the amazing ones with pyramids of fruit, and they've got something yellow that she's not seen before. She has asked Isaac to stop each time they've passed a fruit stall, and each time he has pretended not to hear. 'No, I mean it. I'm paying for this vehicle! Stop when I ask you!' She is suddenly shouting. It's true, she is paying. She will make him listen.

He brakes, sulkily, and swerves to a halt. They are already a quarter of a mile past the fruit stall where she has seen other foreigners parked, and a man taking a photograph. 'OK, we stop,' he says, shrugging. 'You get out here, and take your photograph.'

'This isn't the right place,' says Vanessa, furious. 'The fruit stall is absolutely miles away.'

'You want me to turn round?' He doesn't mean it, and she doesn't trust him to turn across the traffic. There is nothing for it except to drive on.

'Why didn't you stop when I asked you to?'

He doesn't answer, but revs back on to the road so fast that the little red saloon from the fruit stall has to swerve to miss them, and sounds its horn. 'Those people were taking photographs. I saw them.' The little red car is ahead of them.

Now Vanessa's desire for local information overcomes her wish to chastise her driver. 'Why is it always the women selling fruit and vegetables? And often it is women working in the fields. Do the women do all the work, in Uganda?'

He adopts the infuriating, patronising tone she has quickly grown used to when he tells her things. 'Ugandan women cannot ride bicycles, because they are different in their lower bodies, so they cannot take their produce to Kampala. Ugandan women cannot drive cars. There are many things Ugandan women cannot do, and so they do this easy job, and sit by the roadside. And also, they work in the fields, sometimes.'

'But I think it was a woman driving that red car.'

'She was not a woman,' Isaac says briefly, 'or else, she is not a normal Ugandan.'

'It *was* a woman.' But she mustn't be childish. She reminds herself about cultural difference.

'We shall see,' says Isaac, and accelerates, grimly, until they are sitting on the tail of the saloon, but the dust is so thick they can only make out the black heads of the passengers in the back seat. The saloon, in turn, accelerates. They scream up to the straggle of huts and billboards that marks the line of the equator in Uganda in a hugger-mugger, undignified race.

Pretending nothing's happened, they park well apart, in the raw expanse of dust surrounding the buildings, but Vanessa is ecstatic when the driver gets out, and stares across defiantly from 100 metres' distance, a big-hipped, erect, African woman.

'See, it's a woman.'

'She cannot be Ugandan. In any case, she was a bad driver.'

'She certainly drove faster than you.'

Isaac stares at her. She is a *muzungu*. He must be respectful. If he angers her, his friend David will be in trouble. But she is the most irritating of all the *bazungu* he has had to drive, in his life as a driver. And they have to spend three more days together. He does not like her skin, which is like a plucked chicken, her long thin nose, like the mission teacher's, her hair like a layer of thin flat straw, her strange expensive flowery smell that is not like any flower he knows, the way she has spread white dust on her face, the way she argues about everything, as if she was a man and an expert, the way she cannot stop asking questions, but does not listen when he tells her the answers. He wants to instruct her, to shut her up. Even better, to leave her here, by the roadside. But he has no choice. It is she who has the money.

'It is true, Madam,' he says, and smiles. 'Over there you will buy presents,' he indicates a shop. 'And there is the Equator Experience. And there you can buy coffee. Which will you do first?'

Vanessa has never seen such a smile. Though the muscles move, they move over a void, like bright water over a crocodile. She sees terrible depths of humiliation where things with teeth are hiding, waiting. His eyes are dog-like, but the pupils are stones. The effort of it all leaves him heavily sweating. She can smell him, suddenly. Does he smell her?

She is swept with fear. They are alone together. She is thousands of miles away from home. They have to get on. 'May I buy you a coffee?'

She sits outside the café at a plastic table, drinking milky coffee in solitary state and eating a packet of chocolate biscuits. Isaac has accepted a Coca-Cola and gone off to drink it with 'my friends over there' – he has 'good friends' in the souvenir shop; she has strict instructions to come and buy gifts when she has finished her coffee. She watches, from a distance, the people from the red saloon having their Equator Experience. She sees, with mild interest, it's a mixed couple. The black woman's with a middle-aged white man; they are bending over something on a table. It's some tourist thing, but Vanessa thinks, I'll do it, whatever tourists do in this invented spot. But not with other tourists; I'll do it on my own. She has given Isaac money to get credit for his phone. She will text Justin to say she's at the equator.

Soon she's in the shop, to be greeted by Isaac as if they had never had a quarrel. He is clearly in cahoots with the woman by the till, and herds Vanessa anxiously from corner to corner, penning her in next to the most expensive items.

It's mostly tourist tat, she thinks. Terrible souvenirs 'From the equator', thermometers or eggtimers or paperknives, things that nobody uses, and nobody needs. There are soapstone statues and crude wooden carvings. She enjoys not buying them, discriminating, not loading herself up with useless objects. Travel light is my motto, she thinks, proudly (though somehow she always has a lot to carry). But Isaac is hovering. She takes pity.

'I want something for my grandchild.' She feels pride as she says it. It's like a statement that she is a good person, the fact she has a grandchild, and cares for him.

'Yes, there are toys for children,' he says eagerly, driving her towards a stand of wooden animals. 'These are very cheap. You can buy many. How many grandchildren do you have?'

'Oh, one,' she says, and is slightly ashamed. 'I expect I will have more, I am still quite young.' He looks at her, amazed at this. After a pause, he says, 'Yes, Madam, you are still young.'

In the end she buys a small wooden lion. Isaac's disappointed, but time is getting on. 'For my little grandson,' she says to the woman, who smiles at her.

'The last customer also has bought one for his grandson,' she says as she wraps it. 'They are popular. But he bought a male one, you bought – Madam, I do not know the word for this.'

'Lioness,' says Vanessa, pleased with her knowledge.

'Yes, thank you, a lioness. You do not have lions in the USA?'

'Oh no, I'm from England,' Vanessa says proudly. 'How funny that we both bought one for our grandsons.'

'And now, the Equator Experience,' says Isaac. As she comes out of the shop, Vanessa sees in the distance the American man getting back into the red car, and the black woman's still in the driver's seat; they are talking and laughing: then the driver gets out and beckons three Ugandans in country clothes, walking back from the café at a stately pace, who must be the other passengers: then the whole group poses for photographs. They're a long way away, but she can hear their laughter. Vanessa thinks, they are having fun.

But I am having fun as well, she reminds herself. And suddenly, she *is* having fun. War and flood have receded in the distance. Ugandan life is going on as normal. The sun is shining. Her blood sugar's back up. She pays ten dollars and receives a certificate to say she has been to the equator. She watches the wonder of water being poured into a yellow tin basin on one side of the equator, running down counter-clockwise, a swift rope of water twisting down into the dark, and then walks three feet to the other side and watches the water unravel, twist clockwise: it must be a trick: she pays another ten dollars. But it's fascinating. She stands and stares.

Does she understand anything? No, not much. Is there time to learn?

Oh *try*, Vanessa. But there's not much shelter here: a deaf wind blows.

The white-bearded, dignified Ugandan in charge of the Equator Experience urges her to sign the big leather book she had seen the couple in the red car sign earlier. She thinks, I suppose they want our addresses so they can ask us for money. Oh well ... There's a new page: she puts some of her details: not her email, not her phone. But she enjoys writing '*Dr Vanessa Henman*'. It still means something, at the centre of the world. When she feels very small, that 'Dr' makes her larger. She's just about to flick idly back through the pages, to see who has been to the equator before her, when her driver calls her, pointing to the sky. 'We should leave, Madam. It will rain, later.' A surge of anxiety. She comes at once.

In the car, she borrows Isaac's phone. She sees with surprise it is more up-to-date than hers. 'Am at Eqtor! Very exciting! Driving to Gorilla Fst Cmp tonight! How r u and Abdy and Z?' (She hates text language, but it's quicker.) 'Bought A a present. Did u put out my bins? Be well! Mummy'. She presses 'Send'. The sun disappears as the message goes.

30

In London, Justin realises that Abdy's been asleep for nearly two hours. It's been blissful, actually, just watching television, his son sweetly comatose on the sofa, and sleep, after all, is nature's medicine, but why has the doctor not rung back?

He goes over to the sofa and strokes Abdy's head, gently. He's lying face down on the sofa cushion. It's hot, but as usual, Zakira's overdressed him. Justin remembers the row with shame, as he lifts the child back to vertical. He will ring her in Brussels and apologise. Abdy is bound to be better by then.

But he seems to be surfacing from very far down. His lids lift and fall, and his eyes aren't focused. One hand gropes vaguely at the back of his neck. Then Justin sees that the sofa cushion has left red marks all over his face. Indeed, the white is so rare that it's almost as if the pattern is reversed: it's white on red. Then he sees the rash stretches down both sides of Abdul Trevor's neck. He's had nothing to eat, so it can't be an allergy.

Then Justin remembers what Davey had said, about an outbreak of meningitis. What were the symptoms? He has forgotten. It's Zakira who is expert at diagnosis, hunting down diseases on the internet, consulting her friends in the Health Food shop. What's happening? Suddenly he's choked with panic. And Abdul Trevor is asleep again.

He rings the surgery. They're just closing. When he describes the symptoms to the doctor on call, he is told to go straight to hospital. Calling an ambulance would take longer. He enters a dream world of haste and terror. The jeep, which was serviced last week, will not start, but Abdy's already belted in in the back, awake, crying quietly, hopelessly. Justin leaves him sitting there and runs into the house, to phone his father, who he knows will come, wherever he is, whatever he's doing, who would come from the ends of the earth to help him. He calls his father: there is no answer. Only Trevor's usual, cheerful message, designed to reassure people facing flooded bathrooms or collapsing ceilings. But to Justin it sounds cruel, maddening. By now Zakira's on the Eurostar: being carried away from him, into the tunnel, beyond contact, beyond helping. His mother's text arrives, from Uganda. He reads it, sobbing. Now they've all left him.

But his son is still here. Justin must save him. There's a ring on the door. It's Davey Lucas. 'Why's Abdy out there in the jeep, crying?' He takes in Justin's wet terrified face.

Soon they're driving to Central Middlesex Hospital in Davey's ecologically-friendly car, his horribly slow and cute little car, which could park on a sixpence, but can go no faster.

In Mbarara, the place of cooked meat, where the smell of charred pork is sweet on the air, where the sellers surround the queues of cars with trays of succulent cheeks and knuckles, as red as plums, things fly apart. Vanessa and her driver, having eaten, uncompanionably, silently gnawing on the stubborn bone, take the left road towards Kisoro and the Congo: while the red Toyota with the white man in the front is borne away from her, right, towards Mweya.

Goodbye, Trevor; goodbye, Vanessa.

In fact, he says a fond goodbye to Mary, who has to be back at the Sheraton tomorrow. Via her friends in Sheraton Travel, she's made all the arrangements for him at Mweya. She is taking the bus back to Kampala, and spends the last half hour that they drive together rattling off a list of instructions about Charles's car, for the benefit of the man from the village who has been selected to be Trevor's driver. 'The engine is good, but you must not rev it. If someone tries to pass you, let him go.' (Trevor thinks, Mary has not taught this by example.) 'Do not put fish or chickens on the seats. Or other live animals,' she says sternly.

But her tone to Trevor is affectionate. 'Thank you, Trevor,' she says, simply. 'I will not forget what you did in the village. And what you have promised to do, also' (just a hint of a reminder: *don't let us down*. But she knows that Trevor will not let her down.) 'I am sorry there was a small problem with the hut ...' (and now her voice is bubbling with laughter, and he interrrupts her: 'If you ever see Vanessa, for heaven's sake don't say a word, Mary. You know she would go clean round the bend.') '... And now you will be happy, things are fine at Mweya.'

'No frogs at Mweya, then, Mary?' he asks.

'If there are, they will chase them. But look out for lions.'

The skies are darkening, filling up, getting heavier. In Juba, the peace talks between the LRA and the Ugandan Government are going nowhere. A message of no comfort has been sent to the Congo, where Kony and his henchmen are hiding out. 'No deal on the International Criminal Court indictments for war-crimes, but if Kony gives himself up, there will be amnesties for others.' But the LRA are still in thrall to Kony, who kills his lieutenants when they step out of line. Kony says he is full of the Holy Spirit, which he inherited from Alice Lakwena.

What Spirit is it? Hard to tell. At first Kony said his rule was based on the Ten Commandments. But in fact, he commanded his men to kill all who got in their way, all who stole the ancestral rights of the Acholi: they would take Kampala, and drive out Museveni.

Actually the LRA stayed in the north, in charge of an army of abducted children, and many of the children are Acholi, the same people whose rights Kony claims to be protecting, though Acholi parents are left despairing. Then Kony announced he had become a Muslim. Kony's Spirit, whatever it is, Christian or Islamic, or perhaps Satanic (for he fears no-one) remains horribly strong, despite the ceasefire. Perhaps if they kill him ... But his henchmen do not dare to do it. He has such eyes. He has killed so many.

Besides, how can the LRA trust the Ugandan Government? The LRA are all northerners, while President Museveni comes from the west. They believe he means to drain all power from the north, which supported his predecessor, Obote. The war with the LRA has been useful: Kampala has grown richer, the north poorer. For the ordinary Acholi, the north is now hell. Thousands of people have been forced to live in camps – miles of identical small metal huts – where the Ugandan Government promised to protect them from rape, kidnap, torture, murder. In fact, they were prisoners, with nowhere to go. The camps were protected by Ugandan soldiers, but rape, kidnap, torture have continued. It's the usual pastime of men without women, even when they are meant to give protection. Children have been born who do not know their home. Old people have died without seeing home again. How can the International Criminal Court help with this?

The LRA take part in the peace talks, they agree to each stage except the final signature. But why should they trust the peace process, why should they yield to the ICC? If they lay down their arms, Kony will be arrested.

The people of Uganda have a different story about how the long war can be brought to an end. Funded by international donors, soft-spoken delegates have been touring rural parts of the country. Local leaders are being asked, what is more important, justice or forgiveness? How can these two essential things be combined?

But the people of the north are very tired. Their sense of what is essential has dwindled. It has no glory now, no magnitude. The questions seem too pompous, too abstract. Their answer is simply, we want an end to the war. We do not mind if there is punishment or not. We want an end to war, and we want to go home. Perhaps if there is punishment, the war will continue. And so most of the people vote for forgiveness. Maybe there could be traditional justice: ceremonies, reparations. It's a good idea, but no-one listens.

The Prime Minister of Belgium gives an interview: what Kony has done is 'a stain on the soul of humanity' (though the Belgians themselves have never been punished for what they did for decades in the Congo: the rape, kidnap, torture, murder). And another ICC signatory state, America, joins in. 'Make peace quickly or we'll be coming after you, US tells Kony,' is this week's headline in the Kenyan paper, *The East African*, which also claims they will send in the marines (yet the Americans have not been punished for their own war-crimes, which they are still busily committing in Iraq). They all feel better for holding the line. They puff up their chests and mouth their mantras, the war against terror, the rule of law; the ICC indictments must go ahead.

Oddly, Kony and his henchmen do not agree. When this message of no comfort arrives, they send out feelers for more supplies, more grenades, more ammunition. Weapons can be found in DRC: everything is there, if they slip away westward. Business as usual, then. Peace falls apart.

31

'Soon we will be at the Rift Valley,' Isaac tells Vanessa. 'This is very important. It is historic. You may take a photo.'

She thinks, he talks as though he owns this country, and then she realises, he does, in a way. 'I know about the Rift Valley,' she says. 'In fact, we all come from the Rift Valley.'

He casts a sideways glance, unbelieving.

'Yes, even *bazungu*,' she pushes the point. 'We all came from Africa, originally.'

He stares, briefly, at her tense pale face. This madwoman believes she is African.

Then the car bumps and lurches. They have left the tarmac. The road from now onwards will be unmade. It has been cut, with great effort, into the hillside. They roar uphill, but the motor is straining. It starts to rain: slow, getting faster.

She looks out of the window, very quickly, then back again. The land has gone. There is nothing but air. She watches a tiny group of bright birds, hanging on nothing, for a second, a scintilla, the last bit of sunlight catches their heads, then they drift slightly leftwards, swoop, soar – and fall into the valley, plunge over the edge, disappear like a cloud of pollen into darkness. She dare not watch to see if they come back up. She can't breathe, for a moment. Something has happened.

The talks between Uganda and DRC are ending in failure, in bad temper, tired people, the smell of stale air in exhausted rooms. The DRC delegation gets ready to fly home. M7 asked for everything and offered nothing. Why should DRC offer to do Uganda's dirty work by expelling the renegade LRA from its borders? Who wants to take on the LRA? Museveni's been trying to crush them for years. But the men from DRC do not actually say this. They talk like statesmen, at the conference table, about respecting the peace talks in Juba, about respecting international law, about the rights of Congolese fishermen who live on the islands of Lake Albert; as if that was what mattered about Lake Albert, and not the billion barrels of oil beneath it. The Ugandan delegation knows they are liars. It is all about territory and power and money. It is all about gold, all about oil. And because they don't talk completely frankly, the two countries press on towards war.

Trevor gets on fine with James, the man from Mary's village who is happy to be driving him to Mweya. Has James ever been to Mweya Lodge before? The man explains, no Ugandans go there, but he has a friend in a nearby fishing village. Trevor finds this information reassuring. The trip is more relaxing now Mary is not driving, refusing to let any other car overtake. The two men mostly keep a companionable silence. It's a bloke thing, Trevor thinks, it's international. With Soraya, there was always, well, nattering. And she complained I didn't communicate. Funny, because Vanessa talked more than her, and I didn't mind it. It's weird how I miss her.

They have to drive through an epic rainstorm. The tarmac road ends abruptly as it starts to rain, giving way to a long straight swathe of red dust which is soon a ribbon of splashing mud. Trevor stares through the opaque boil of rain on the windscreen and contemplates Mary's instructions for the car: 'Do not rev the engine. Do not dirty it.' In the end, James has to go more and more slowly; they can see nothing: there is only blind rain, grey gallons and gallons of thick sliding water. They can't see the trees, the sky, the road. It all goes on for a very long time. But then, just as suddenly, the windscreen lightens, the sun comes out, and a vast rainbow leaps across the horizon, from side to side, as bright and clear as if painted on a window. It hangs there, amazing, on the blue darkness, above which the African sun pours down. 'It's quite something, your country,' says Trevor. And then they leave even the red mud behind, turning off on to a narrow dirt track through scrubland.

Now James rocks the little car through two hours of scrubland, of long yellow grasses darkened with rain, thorntrees that remind Trevor of ones he's seen on television, shaped like low flat-topped thunderclouds. At last the track climbs with a new sense of purpose. 'We are nearly there,' says James with a smile. There's a lake on their left, but they go on climbing, and at last turn a corner to imposing double gates. Then an elephant! Huge, glossy, brown, its trunk upcurled, catching the sun. A brief double-take, but it is made of resin. Yet all around them, the cricket-trilling bush, the howls of animals, snorts and gibbers. The clouds have retreated; late golden light. Suddenly Trevor sees lawns and flowers.

They arrive to the offer of a warm wet scented flannel on a china plate in the huge shining foyer. James is carrying his bags, despite Trevor's protest, and one of them, of course, is the heavy toolbag, but the porter takes them away from him, silently, then grunts with surprise as he feels the weight. Then James fades away: there is only one flannel. Bit rich, thinks Trevor, when James did the driving. His hands need a warm flannel more than mine. But I suppose, to them, he is just my driver – same as how, in London, I was only the plumber. We aren't really people. We aren't really there.

So he's glad, for a while, not to be seen as a plumber. He is paying: he's Sir: he's a gentleman. The flannel soothes his hands, then there's an ice-cold fruit juice. Trevor yields to it all. Yes, he's in bliss.

That night, the restaurant repels the dark with 'International Cuisine' and piped music. The waiters wear white jackets as spotless and stiff as the snowy napkins, and Trevor chooses chicken, Coronation Chicken with Duchesse Potatoes that are whorled and curled like a duchess's hairdo, and taste dry, like paper, but he's glad enough to eat them, and down two large whiskies on the trot.

'Your Queen is coming to Uganda,' says the waiter. 'She first came here after her coronation. She is welcome.' Trevor's just heard him say the same thing to the man at the next table, who also ordered Coronation Chicken. 'Glad Her Maj is welcome,' Trevor smiles. The whisky burns beautifully, like life, like the rich strong flavour of his week in Uganda. He is dozing at his table when the waiter comes and asks him if he's putting the meal on his tab. 'I'll pay,' says Trevor. He always pays up-front. His parents were too poor to dare to do different. It was something he and Nessie both understood. In many ways they were quite alike, though people often said they were an odd couple.

'So are you going on the game drive tomorrow?' asks the waiter. 'Service is not included, Sir.'

'Oh, right,' says Trevor, and adds on a thousand, then another when he sees the man's slight disappointment. 'They tell me I am,' he says. '6 AM start.'

'That is interesting, Sir,' says the waiter.

Back in his room, Trevor is too tired to switch his phone on. Early wakeup: he's going on a game drive. He likes the sound of it: a game drive. Whoever would have thought Trevor Patchett would do that?

32

Far in the west, the green west of Uganda, Vanessa has quarrelled with her driver. How badly, she is not quite sure. Or whether he'll be there in the morning. And yet they have made it to their destination, at the very end of the journey of horror!

The rains had eroded one side of the road so badly that they had to inch their way forward, hugging the side of the steep mountains that form the upper rim of the Rift Valley. OK, Isaac was not such a bad driver (despite his negligent attitude) but she could not help blaming him for her terror. And perhaps it annoyed him when she winced and gasped and clutched her seatbelt, or grabbed at the dashboard, but the terror was so visceral: when they nosed up, she feared slipping backwards: when they went down, they might fall for ever. Isaac offered, several times, to stop for a photograph, but she almost wept as she begged him to drive on. The idea of stopping on that hideous road ...

And then came the rain. A black wall of rain. The windscreen wipers could do nothing against it. And Vanessa closed her eyes and prayed. She clung to her notebook, herself, her camera. She bargained with Death, for she was not ready. She had things to write, Justin needed her ... suddenly she thought, I have nothing to offer. Perhaps she doesn't understand how Death chooses, for the rain lessened and the sun came out; like grace, like beauty, her prayer was answered, and the road eased, and they were out of the Rift Valley. But they had lost time. Was the light already going?

Isaac drove through the narrow central street of Butogota, the last big village before Bwindi, at five, and the streets were thronged with tall people, women with long necks and high noble cheekbones, men wearing suit-jackets over cloth wraps, walking home from work or just standing and staring. She felt they were driving through a field of wheat, like an ugly machine with a single purpose, but she needed him to hurry, she was still afraid.

Buhoma, when they got there, was just a small huddle of shacks, a few hotels. Then at last they are on to the track to Bwindi; banana thickets, then increasingly tall trees, then the forest cover thickened and darkened, darkened and thickened. There was no more light. Vanessa thought, have we left it too late? But her eyes adjusted. It was not quite nightfall.

And then the argument began.

After the silence of terror, she had started talking. Most recently she had been speaking, not quite honestly, about her 'husband', an 'engineer', in a last-ditch effort to impress on Isaac, before journey's end, that she was married, a person of substance (for an ex-husband is almost a husband, and a plumber is practically an engineer). She became a little strident: she insisted. She was talking to an impassive profile. And then the vehicle bumped to a halt. 'You will get out now,' said Isaac, tersely.

Is he going to murder me?, thought Vanessa. But she could not sit in the jeep on her own. They were standing at the bottom of a flight of steps that led up, and up, through the tall trees. Isaac pointed to them, unsmiling. 'It is up there,' he said, and shrugged. She spotted a small notice: GORILLA FOREST CAMP.

'The Gorilla Forest Camp?' she asked. 'I have to walk to it? Up through the forest?' He nodded, stern-browed.

'Then you will have to help me.'

'Of course I will help you! Or you could not do it.'

Did he have to remind her?

He struggled up the steps ahead of her, loaded up like a pushbike carrying a bedstead, precariously balancing all her bags. Sometimes he slipped backwards, sometimes forwards. But it seemed to her that he was going too slowly. The trees to either side blurred away into blue darkness. Some of the shadows looked like men, watching. A harsh bird cackled overhead, and it mizzled, drizzled, down the back of her neck.

'Are we late?' she asks. 'It is nearly dark. Perhaps you could hurry –' (he grunted, furious, and tripped on a tree-root, and nearly dropped a bag) 'or no-one will be there to welcome me.'

Suddenly Isaac began talking again, loudly, aggressively, though panting with effort. Isaac was determined to inform her about the etiquette of welcome in Ugandan houses. 'In Uganda, wives welcome their husbands by kneeling,' he says, shooting a malicious look over his shoulder.

'I don't believe you,' she says, annoyed. 'I believe it is just one particular tribe. One people, I mean. Is it the *Banda* people? Some name like that. A rather backward people.'

He was actually snickering. Yes, she could hear him. 'Banda is a word for house,' he said.

'In any case I think it's ridiculous,' Vanessa snapped, lobbing cultural tolerance away into the trees. She was tired, it was steep, she wanted her tea. '*My husband* would not want women to kneel. *My husband* would laugh at that idea.' And she tried to laugh, but it came out wrong, like the humourless, jarring cry of a peacock.

At this Isaac stopped, put the bags down, looked round. He stood above her in the blue-green light, furiously male, utterly different. They stared at each other, didn't like what they saw. 'But even in UK, I think,' he asked her, earnestly, 'surely you do not believe men and women are equal?'

She was speechless for a moment. He hauled up her bags again, ready to go on, but paused there a second, his back to the slope, and held her gaze, demanding an answer.

'You Ugandans are living in the last century.'

'You British people have gone crazy.' He was haring up the slope again, a lopsided Christmas tree.

'You are backward! Very backward!' She screamed it after him. It seemed he neither saw her nor heard her. She was paying him, yet he did not respect her. Vanessa can't bear being called crazy; she feels like a hated child again, the girl in the village who no-one liked, with the sullen father and insane mother. 'NOBODY WANTS A BACKWARD DRIVER!'

Isaac dumped her luggage three metres away from the wooden verandah of the Gorilla Forest Camp, without saying goodbye, and disappeared into the gloom. An engine roared. Her driver was gone. (She will never know that he wept with anger. He is bitterly hurt. He is twenty-one. He is not backward, he's intelligent, he knows he is, he has thoughts and opinions, but until he has saved a million shillings he cannot afford to be a student. It lasts a few minutes, and then he stops, and the hurt contracts into a tight ball of hatred which will stay with him for over a decade, long after Vanessa has forgotten him.)

For an hour she feels utterly justified, and then small doubts start creeping in. Perhaps she should have shown more understanding. Although very annoying, he was still quite young. Is it possible she has let herself down?

Vanessa does not sleep all night. No-one had explained to her in advance that Bwindi is literally a rainforest: that most of the time, they will be in cloud. No-one had explained that the Gorilla Forest Camp is not so much a single, luxury hotel as a series of isolated, upmarket tents, separated by dense, dripping jungle and reached by long narrow paths through the leaves, which is perfect if you've come with a lover or husband, but if you are on your own, pure terror. Leaves crash against the window: things shoulder through the bushes, maybe monkeys or bush-pigs, but maybe humans: soldiers, rebels, murderers.

Every time she begins to drift off to sleep, there are dizzy flashbacks of the journey here; as her blood pressure drops, she keeps tripping, falling, waking herself up in a plunging panic. And Isaac has probably gone for good.

She starts the night warm: the staff have left two hot-water bottles waiting in the neatly turned bed. Soon she finds out why: all the sheets are damp. Then she realises, everything is damp. Everything is damp because they are in cloud. And when things are damp, their natural state is cold. Within an hour, she is clutching the lukewarm rubber of the rapidly cooling hot-water bottle.

And tomorrow is the test, the ultimate test, when she, Vanessa, goes to look for the gorillas. She has wanted to do this for half her life, but is she fit enough? Can she do it? The website says you need 'above average fitness'. Of course she is fit, superbly fit, she is always doing sit-ups or yoga or Pilates, but when she first saw the forest, her heart failed her. It seemed to go straight upwards, so the top of one tree was waving against the bottom of the tree behind. At supper, the staff had explained about tomorrow. There are four groups of habituated gorillas, but some of them are a day's hike away, whereas some of them are relatively close.

Which group will Vanessa be assigned to? Will she be unlucky? She is often unlucky. She stretches, anxiously, against the damp duvet, and flexes her muscles: above average fitness. Then her knee starts hurting: savage little prickles that she associates with arthritis. Of course, she was cooped up in the car all day. But what if her body lets her down? At 5.30, with half an hour to go before her phone alarm shocks her awake, she falls asleep, thinking, 'Health is all that matters.' Light is filtering through the curtains.

33

Wincing, limping, he keeps on walking. Where is the border? He has no idea. He knows where is east, because the sun is rising, red sky leaking through the gaps in the leaves. Once red sky did not make him think of blood. Once he was a child like any other. He must keep heading east, but where is he going? If you lose your past, can you ever go back? How can he ever explain to his father: his mother? (Once his mother used to hold him close. She loved to talk to him in funny voices. He cannot bear to remember his mother.) He has become a shame to them, a curse, worse than nothing. And yet, he gets up, and he forces his feet to accept the cruel yoke of his ill-fitting boots, and he ignores the hunger, and the sores on his back, which he has not been able to resist scratching, and his eye, which is infected, and half-closed. Through crooked lids, he sees leaves, sunlight, as the sun strains up above the horizon. He is sick of leaves. He is sick of sunlight. He is sick of it all. But somehow he keeps going.

Davey Lucas sits with Justin in the waiting area at the big North London hospital, which is undergoing modernisation, which has been undergoing it for over a decade. The waiting area and foyer are splendid, but the wards and corridors are crowded and narrow. The local paper says infection rates are high: MRSA, Clostridium difficile. Old people go in and never come out. But it's still a hospital, with modern medicine, and highly trained doctors hurrying about. The two men sitting here have to be hopeful.

They're not talking much: there's not much to say; but they're thinking, hard, in their own separate worlds. Davey Lucas is ashamed of the direction of his thoughts, and keeps trying to swing them back to kindness, but he's swept by tides of anxious self-interest: 'If poor little Abdy has meningitis, will Dubois get it, and Harry? Will I? *Please don't let my children catch it.* What about the new car? Is that infected?'

He looks across at Justin, and pats him on the arm. 'All right, old son?' he asks.

'Yeah,' says Justin. 'Thanks, mate. It's just, you know, the waiting.' But really Justin's thinking, 'It's all my fault. Why didn't I take Abdy to the doctor earlier?' But perhaps it is Zakira's fault, as well. Why was she so sure the rash was eczema?

Now Davey is wishing he could wash the hand that just patted Justin on the arm. 'I know he'll be fine,' he says. 'Just fine. But I'll have to get home to the kids, in a bit. My mother's gone round to baby-sit, and Delorice doesn't really trust her with them.'

Home to the kids. Justin's swept with envy. Those three words sound like heaven to him. But he has to relax. It will be all right. 'Can't see your mum as a baby-sitter. Amazing woman,' he responds, vaguely. He has met Lottie Lucas: an art collector, still blonde and beautiful in her sixties. But rather self-centred. Not exactly motherly ... *Why is the doctor taking so long?*

'Women,' says Davey, 'They're not what they were,' and the two men smile at each other, wryly, but at the same time, some part of them means it. What happened to comfortable, stay-at-home mothers? Why is it *them* at the hospital?

A white-coated doctor appears in the doorway.

34

Mary Tendo is back in Kampala. Mary Tendo is back at her post. The Sheraton liner churns on through the water, high on its hill, on the crest of its wave.

But to Mary, as ever, it's theatre.

Mary is at the back of house, with the huge rattling washers and steaming dryers, the ironing machines and polishing machines, the unpainted corridors, the rickety doors, making sure the scenery is all in order.

At the front of the house, when the guests aren't looking, the Floor Supervisors are walking round checking; the Shoe-shiner is scraping red mud from guests' shoes or bringing them back in his neat cane baskets (he smiles slightly too much as he knocks at their door and they offer him a small yellow coin, or nothing); insects are being sprayed against, plastic bottles of water, two per day, are being left by basins, so the *muzungu* can clean their teeth in bottled water, the Director of Procurement is driving a hard bargain, the Food and Beverage Manager is frowning at the lamb which is more like mutton than ever, today, the Ken Fixit are packed into the tiny service lifts in their navy blue boiler suits, burrowing up or down to the floor which has sprung the latest leak or breakage ...

But none of this happens in front of the guests. The essential illusion: here is ease, and calm. Life is a cruise: it's the Sheraton.

Mary's happy to be back, with her uniform on, in her own office with the mirror on the wall so she can see what's going on in the Desk Clerk's room. She goes and wipes a smear off the glass of the door, and smiles through the panel at Pretty, the Desk Clerk. But why is Rachel, the Assistant Housekeeper, with her? Why is she talking earnestly to Pretty? While Mary was away, Rachel has done her job, but now Mary is back, she has her eye on her, though she does not dislike her: she is just young. Perhaps she is too ambitious, also. 'Watch and learn,' Mary has told her, rather often. Now Mary is back in the driver's seat.

She checks occupancy rates on her computer. 77 per cent: that is not bad. There are more guests than usual, because of CHOGM: building contractors, diplomats, business people. Once CHOGM actually begins, they will be full. She looks back at the statistics for the week she was away. 'Rachel,' she calls, and Rachel comes in, looking smart and keen in her gold jacket.

'Were the International Writers happy with their conference?'

'I believe so, Miss. In fact, mostly they were African, but there were some *bazungu*, and of course the British Council.'

'We see a lot of the British Council.'

'Yes, they are running seminars on Leadership, Miss. They have booked the ballroom for the next eight weeks.' Mary does not react, because she does not want Rachel to think she has told her something she doesn't know, though in fact, she didn't. Knowledge is power.

Rachel hesitates. 'Perhaps I could go? I would be interested in Leadership.'

Mary looks at her sharply. 'Why is that? This department does not need more leadership. You need education, not leadership. Your maths is still poor, and your English.' She glowers, and Rachel looks away. 'Whereas Pretty's English is excellent.'

The Linen Room Supervisor knocks and enters. 'Welcome back,

Miss Mary. I have a little problem. Two pairs of sheets will not respond to stain removal.'

'And the reason for this is?' Mary asks, eyebrows astonished. Her staff have grown to dread this astonishment, which comes whenever everything is not running smoothly, and seems to suggest, 'It must be your fault.'

'The reason is, the International Writers. They were drinking too much wine in their bedrooms. In fact, they were drinking too much in the foyer, also. I am glad they have gone,' says the girl, indignant. (She is twenty-five years old, and a born again Christian. She has never drunk wine. She is a virgin.)

Rachel risks a smile, though Mary is cross. 'But they were funny,' says Rachel. 'I thought they were amusing. One night they were dancing in the Rhino Pub.'

'And how did you have time to go in the Pub?' asks Mary strictly. The Pub is not a pub, though you might think so if you had never lived in London. It has just been renovated, and reopened, but it's just another bar at the Sheraton, a noisier, rougher one than the Piano Bar. It makes Mary feel strange to hear these girls talking as if writers were a certain kind of human being. She, Mary Tendo, is also a writer.

'I went to take a message to the new barman.' Mary knows that Rachel likes the new barman. Normally she would tease her about it, and tell her she must concentrate on education. But her thoughts are on the International Writers. Will she ever be an international writer? She would like to write at length about the visit to the village. It filled her with so many complicated feelings. The mango tree where she sat with her cousins and told stories, gone. And her mother dead, and her brother grown old, and her uncle the head of the family, in place of her own father, who is lying in his grave, and her sister unable to discipline her daughters. But the women of the village were a comfort to her. Her brother's wife, and the remaining cousins, these women she had known since they were children together, and when she told them about Jamil, their sorrow was real, they were all weeping. She could write how their grief made her less alone, whereas Charles will not accept that Jamil might be dead. Perhaps because Death is always in the village. They accepted it as something life brings. She will think about all these things in her journal. Yet how can she bear to write Jamil's story? It is lost to her, he is lost to her, the flesh of her flesh, bone of her bone. For a moment, the edge of her desk blurs with tears.

'People say many writers are too fond of beer,' the Linen Room Supervisor dares to say, pertly. 'And some of them did not pay their bills. I heard about it from Rebecca in Reception.'

Mary stares at her. She knows nothing, nothing. 'I think you are too young to give your opinions.' (If the British publisher had published me, I could have already been an international writer. And then, would they say I was an alcoholic?) 'Please put the sheets through stain removal again. I cannot authorise a new purchase.'

The Linen Room Supervisor sighs and goes, but tries to regain lost ground by giving a piece of special knowledge over her shoulder. 'When I passed by Reception, a man was asking for the writers. He did not understand the conference was over. I think his name was Julius Something. He had a nice voice. He was a handsome man.'

'That must be Julius Ocwinyo,' says Mary Tendo, hiding her excitement by speaking coldly. 'It does not matter if he is handsome. He is a famous Ugandan publisher. I must go to Reception now, to check my figures.'

She must not run in the Sheraton, and indeed Mary Tendo hardly ever runs, but she cannot wait for the lift to arrive, and she goes down the backstairs as swiftly and smoothly as a panther who has just smelled a deer on the air.

He is turning to leave when Mary confronts him. 'You are Mr

Julius Ocwinyo,' she says. 'I have many of the books published by Fountain.'

'So people are still buying our books?' he asks, his eyes smiling behind small glasses.

'I am buying your books. And I am a writer,' Mary says. His face falls at once, and she is not surprised, for Mary had discovered, when she was in UK, that publishers fear and dislike writers. If they could publish books without writers, they would. And Julius happens to write well himself.

'That is interesting,' he says, but perhaps insincerely, his eyes on her Sheraton uniform. 'Did you catch any of the international writers' events?'

'In fact, I was away.'

'Oh, here's a list. Come and visit us sometime in our bookshop.'

She takes the piece of paper for attention later. She must make this man see her for what she is. An unusual person, who can think and write, who has traveled widely, a person of talent, not just a Ugandan in a uniform. We Ugandans, she thinks, do not respect one another. He cannot believe I am really a writer. Or perhaps Julius is just busy. He has already switched off, he is on his way.

'My book was to be published by Harpic, in England.'

And then he looks up. 'Harpic? It's a well-known name.'

'I did not let them publish me.' Which was a simplification, but not a lie. 'My editor there was clean round the bend.' It's a very nice phrase she has picked up from Trevor. 'But other publishers wanted to publish me.'

This time she really has his attention. She leads him to the empty Piano Bar, where one of the maids is vacuuming, and lays the list of writers carefully on the table, and commands her friend Joshua to bring them coffee. When Joshua arrives with two glasses of pale latte, sweet milky urban coffee-soup which makes her want to laugh (for she has just returned from the village in the country where the red fat berries of the coffee are grown, yet no-one ever thinks of drinking coffee), Joshua is so busy smiling, to show her respect in front of the bespectacled, distinguished young man, that he spills a little coffee as he puts the cups down, a leak of mild fluid on the International Writers' Programme. Mary tuts, forgivingly, and picks the paper up, and finds she is looking at a name she knows well.

In a little stain of darkness, Vanessa Henman. In the list of International Delegates. For a second, she cannot make sense of it. *Vanessa Henman, here in Uganda.*

The world is very big, as she knows very well, for Mary Tendo is a woman of the world, and has made the biggest journey of all, the journey that so many people dream of making, the great journey from the village to the city. But the world is also very small, she sees, as she stares at the paper, and feels dizzy: the world of the educated, rich, lucky. Vanessa Henman has got there, somehow. Can Mary join it? She's touching it, suddenly; she's nearly in; she's on the edge.

By the end of coffee, she is over the frontier. This is her chance, and Mary takes it. Julius Ocwinyo will read her manuscript. Mary is quietly confident.

35

Vanessa's little group of trekkers has nearly made it to the top. They've gone almost vertical for over an hour, single-file, dogged, left-foot-right-foot in the toe-holds, which are growing muddier as each one passes, the rain-slicked head of each sweating pilgrim bent earnestly over the back foot of the one before, stopping at first every ten minutes, then every five, then almost every minute, and ahead of her, Vanessa sees another woman her age in trouble, being hauled up bodily by two porters, and she hardly has time to feel superior before, as she rests, blood thudding in her ears (and the caravan below her has to halt as well as she pants, gulps, gasps at damp air), her porter Barnabas climbs lithely up beside her, overtakes her, magically not slipping in the mud, smiles down at her kindly, seizes her hand; she's too relieved to protest, and they go up in tandem. By the time they crest the first slope, her heart is racing, her face streams sweat, and there's a hard band of heat where her sunhat's pulled down over her forehead, serving as a rain-hat as they climb through the drizzle; her thighs feel as if a giant has squashed them. But her feet, in their leather boots, are standing up well, and Vanessa thinks, 'I've always had good feet. I'm lucky that way. I'm an excellent walker.'

Once they've made the top, her energy returns, though now that they are really in the forest, the vegetation's thicker, catching at her knees, whacking at her thighs, scratching one cheek, and tree-roots and creepers tangle with her ankles, and the rain sounds heavier, battering the canopy hundreds of feet above her head. The guide reminds them to beware of ants; she looks down, and with a gasp, she sees them, great columns of them seething through the undergrowth like treacle; but alas, her feet still have to go down somewhere. Vanessa's having problems with her combat trousers, which wouldn't be useful in a real war. Every time she stops to tuck them back inside her socks, they descend to her hips, leaving a swathe of bare belly, which gets bitten, instantly, by small stinging midges, so with alternate hands she is hauling up her trousers and clutching at her camera and binoculars; but she doesn't care, she feels young and free: war has stayed away: she has made it to Bwindi! 'They are near,' says their guide, at the head of the column, and then the most magical words they could hear, as he turns round to face them, smiling, triumphant, and lays his finger on his lips: *'They are here.'* They pass it down the line, his whispered message: *'They are here.'* Yes, they have found the gorillas! And the rain, with perfect timing, eases off. No (she looks upwards), the rain has stopped. Just a curtain of raindrops released by the branches.

I am lucky, lucky. Thank you, God, thinks Vanessa, the proud and vocal agnostic.

There's a juggling of bags, a fluster of cameras, whispered swearwords as people fix settings or swap batteries or remove their raingear, and then crowd onwards, jubilant. Vanessa is peering where the guide has gone. She sees nothing, then briefly, blackness, moving, two patches of something, and then they are gone. Was that it? Their guide holds up his hand: *Stop*: then goes forward on his own. Then beckons.

As she comes through into a small clearing, the sun breaks through, the sun floods down, they are in a paradise of greenness, brightness – she sees them, suddenly, so long desired, the black beating heart at the centre of the sunlight, and where she had imagined a scattered troupe, there is one living organism, a family, a nest of interwining, yawning gorillas, sprawled on their backs, drying out in the sunshine, stretching, luxurious, languorous, dreamy, a cloud of golden midges dancing above them. The humans fan out, hardly daring to breathe, individual, intent, competing for places, determined to get the best camera angle, but the apes can hardly bear to move apart. As one passes another, the second reaches out, gently, casually, and catches a limb, and the passer-by pauses, patient, to be groomed, or they lie stroking and cuddling, face to face, or a smaller one pulls burrs and ticks off a larger one, or a young one, half-enfolded by an older sibling, begins to roll and sprawl and play and slowly kick up one small, horny grey foot in the air, and wriggle and extend each toe, sensuous. *Their faces.* But they are so like us. Wrinkled yet childlike, wise and passive. Their eyes are shiny, dark and still.

Happy, thinks Vanessa. It is almost not a thought. Her muscles register the pleasure of their muscles. She forgets, for a minute, to use her camera, but all around her they are busy and intent, the humans determined to freeze the moment, two rows of them, fingers flickering with effort.

An hour. It is all the regulations allow. Time passes fast, time passes slowly, for nothing happens, nothing at all, as a group of eight gorillas recover from a storm, eat myenopsis leaves, rest in the moment, watched at close quarters by a group of eight humans, who dare not look at them directly, but protect themselves from that long, opaque gaze with cameras, zoom lenses, sunglasses, layers of glass and metal and plastic, and the humans are both frozen and restless, their bodies immobilised with fear and excitement, with once-in-a-lifetime gorilla decorum, but their deft little digits are constantly twitching, their necks poke out, thrilled, anxious; whereas the older group of primates move slowly, unbothered, or make little rocking runs at an insect, a baby, a delicious leaf, each other. The adult gorillas ignore the humans: the silverback, Ruhondeza, takes one dismissive look under massive bone brow-ridges, and turns his great back: he still has a baby to decide about – will it live, or die? Is it his, or not? He has killed several of the recent infants, for he has to keep control of things; it isn't easy, being a leader. But he picks up the tiny, spider-small baby with its comical quiff and liquid eyes and stares, longingly, into his pupils. Something like him. He likes this baby. Its boldness, little pink paws, round belly. *If only the stink-apes would go away* – two adolescents, though, stop and gaze: what creatures are these, so pale and foul-smelling, staring, immobile, neither feeding nor playing, each in its prison of stone-things, twig-things? A young female lies on her back, stretching; she farts, gently, prrr-prrr-prr-prr, and eases her back on the bed of squashed leaves: she has eaten enough; hot sun on her fur; her long leathery feet are curled in the air; no insect is biting; this is ... she is ...

and her eyes meet Vanessa's, who's laid aside her camera: shadows pass over them, sun and shadows; *part of it all*; they look at each other;

alive like me; alive like her –

After the hour, which is over in a second, the guide makes a signal, the humans get up, bones creaking and groaning from the unaccustomed crouch, for they need to be supported with chairs, stools, sofas; and in the other team the silverback rears up, grey, mountainous, and heaves himself away, square shoulders swaying, but look, look, the skinny baby clings on to his back, and the others follow Ruhondeza with one accord, grey ships on the greenness, riding low in the waters.

At once, the humans break into a torrent of noise. The guide leads them back to the place where they left their porters. He tells the tourists how lucky they were. 'You have had a good experience. You have seen them from close! Close!' He thinks, and I hope you will tip us well. The pay for a porter is only 10 dollars, and without porters, you would never reach the top: you are fat, or old, or weak; you are soft and overloaded. He knows what tourists pay at the Gorilla Forest Camp: 200 dollars a day, plus extras. And yet they only pay the porters 10 dollars. He has discussed it many times with the other guides and porters, and one man said, 'But of course they cannot pay us, they must give all their money for accommodation,' and another man said, 'But that is unjust, since the Gorilla Forest Camp is not owned by Ugandans. So you can understand what happened before.'

Because something very bad had happened before. When tourists from the GFC were rounded up and killed, not by the local people, who would never do such things (indeed a local guide was killed as well, though his name was not in the English newspapers that somebody's uncle read in Kasese). The manner of their killing was terrible, and so the hotel had to change its name, and none of the new tourists know about it, though local people have not forgotten, and indeed it was only a few years ago. But they do not like to think about what happened before, though sometimes, when the tourists are ill-mannered, it is tempting, or when they are mean, and forget to leave tips.

Lunch-time! The hotels provide huge packed lunches, doorstep white sandwiches, English-style, cake and yogurt and fizzy sodas. The male tourists swap raucous stories, as soon as they have exhausted the gorillas, which happens quite quickly: 'There wasn't much narrative to it, was there?' quips Cyrus, the talkative young American medic, a film buff, who has the biggest camera, and a cotton balaclava to protect him from insects, and a GPS, which he consults at too regular intervals – 'You're tired? We're only at 7,000 feet' – and elaborate gaiters, all straps and buckles.

Before they have lunch, he offers all the tourists medicated wipes. ('You don't know what's out there.') Vanessa refuses them, to make a point. She thinks, 'He's what Americans call a smart-arse.' Then she realises they have to eat with their fingers, and regrets saying 'No'. By then Cyrus's talking about simian immuno-viruses, or SIVs, which are 'prevalent here', and are 'precursors of HIV'. 'At least you can't get that through your fingers,' she quips, but he says, with a humorous popping sound of his lips and knowingly lifted eyebrows, '*Nope*, if you haven't broken the skin, that is.'

Has she broken the skin? She won't think about it.

But the women – there are only two of them – sit there agreeing how wonderful it was. 'It was spiritual,' says the American woman, who had had to be hauled up bodily, but her eyes are earnest, and Vanessa agrees, and surely, in fact, that's why the men, embarrassed, are swapping jock-stories about sex and hospitals, discussing *Top Gun* and *Mission Impossible*. The release of nervous tension is palpable. Hard to find words to describe their feelings. And so they fall back on claims of achievement. They've done it; they saw them; it's in the bag.

But Vanessa thinks, I believe she saw me. That young female. And I saw her. I think we wondered about each other.

She chews her way through her second huge sandwich. And then she looks upward: flying buttresses of trees, the distant blue sky, a fine golden maze of insects; so much, so much, and I understand nothing, I saw the gorillas but there's so much else ... A patch of brilliant colour, emerald, ruby, floats quivering and scintillating under the canopy, a butterfly, a tiny bright distant world, and is followed by others, glittering in the sun or glistening dark as they dip into shadow, weaving in and out of the sunlight, dizzying, so many self-willed microcosms ... And at night, Vanessa thinks, if I looked up through these trees ... And she dozes, briefly, nods and dreams of kinds of life she has never known, planets where humans have never been, stars shining like a million dancing midges.

There is a gap of ten feet between the guests and the porters. The guide calls across, 'I think there are mosquitoes. Perhaps someone has got some insect cream?' The porters are uneasy; something is biting them. A tiny shiver of unease, as well as the hunger they are used to feeling. There have been too many bad stories recently. Troops are arriving not far away. And in their brother park, just across the border, in the National Park in the Virunga Mountains, six gorillas were butchered a month ago. There is madness brewing in DRC. The guide tries again, correcting his English. 'Has anyone got some insect cream?'

Vanessa and the other tourists hear, but they are not sure where they've put their repellent, it's probably at the bottom of their bags, and the bags are probably over with the porters, and their legs are tired, and they're eating their lunch, so they pretend the question was addressed to someone else. In any case, a guide should have his own insect protection. 'This is perfect,' says the American woman, chomping her way through all the courses. 'Have you found your piece of pineapple yet?'

He is near, near: he is almost here. He is happy, because he must be in Uganda. He has crossed the border. And now he hears English, real English English, and American English, the first time he has heard it for over three years, except for voices crackling from the radio, and he heard the mad woman yesterday evening, screaming in the forest like an evil spirit when the driver was carrying her bags up the steps. He presses himself low into the bushes and watches, ignoring the pain from the sore on his knee. He sees two groups of human beings. The white people are eating as if they are starving, yet many of them are fat (and he sees the thin spiteful one from last night!). Bread, fruit, cakes, sodas, things he has forgotten, so bright, so sweet that his mouth waters as he has to watch it all disappearing. The black people are thin, and do not eat. Some of the porters have bananas, but they have no bread, no cakes, no sodas. He wonders why they don't take the food from the tourists. The white people are old, and greedy, and weak. He will follow these people, at a safe distance. Wherever they go, there will be plenty. For now, he lies down in the sun, and sleeps.

Now Vanessa is too full to eat, and looking across, she sees the dark group of porters sitting quietly, their hands not in constant motion like the tourists. But every so often one glances across, and she catches something in Barnabas's eyes. Oh God, it's hunger. Of course, she thinks, and blushes with shame. 'Excuse me,' she calls, across the gulf. 'Could you help me out? I have too much cake.'

Her porter comes across straight away. 'You want help?' he asks, uncomprehending. But she gives him the cake, and her heart lightens.

36

It's the Peaceable Kingdom, thinks Trevor, as he sails on the Kazinga Channel, which runs between Lake Edward and Lake Albert, about half a mile away from Mweya Lodge, and his eyes unexpectedly fill up with tears. The Peaceable Kingdom was a colour plate in his mother's battered Bible. A picture of heaven, or the Garden of Eden. They all came down to the water to drink.

Trevor and a group of camera-hung guests are in a little steamer with a painted tin roof, chugging slowly, peacefully through the water past things he has never seen before, things he has never dreamed of seeing; great groups of hippos half-submerged in the water, fitting tightly together like a shiny hippo jigsaw-puzzle, patches of pink round their wrinkly eyes, patches of pink at the backs of their ears. The guide is excellent, a woman. She shows them white-headed black fish-eagles perched on treetops, surveying it all; yellow weaver-birds; pied woodpeckers; mats of floating papyrus grass; a yellow Nile crocodile sprawled snake-like on the shore, suddenly baring a long serrated smile; the flash of a tiny blue Malachite kingfisher; enormous conker-brown African buffalos with great top-heavy yokes of yellow horn, pushed down low over their faces; a wide net of swallows dipping and dancing as they skim the water for the clouds of pale lake-flies. And then there are the storks; so many storks; tall ones, probably the country cousins of the ones who paraded about in Kampala, gentler-looking somehow, with pinkish-cream wings and slender yellow beaks.

Trevor passes it all in slow dreamlike motion; he is dozing in the heat, and everything pauses; the fish-eating eagle never plunges, the stork does not stab with its long yellow beak, the lake-flies are suspended just beyond the swallows; it's heaven, he thinks; I am in bliss, though when he jerks awake, a little later, the guide is pointing out hippo bones, great arching things along the edge of the water. 'The male hippos often fight. Sometimes hippo males kill their babies.' But he hardly hears. This is paradise. A hippo's ears suddenly twizzle in circles, like tiny helicopter blades, and he laughs, so funny, those swift tiny ears on the sides of the massive hippopotamus head.

Later, at dinner, he tries to tell the waiter. 'You've got so much here. I mean, they live all together, all the different animals coming to the water. Back home there isn't very much left.'

'That is interesting,' the waiter says, but Trevor feels he has explained it badly, and later he hears the waiter listening to the tales of the next-door table: 'That is interesting,' the man says, automatically. 'You saw a hippo? That is interesting.'

It doesn't matter. Trevor's very happy. He knows he has done a good thing, in the village, and today he has been wonderfully rewarded. He drinks his whisky. Life is sweet.

After dinner, he goes into the bar. Silver-haired couples with carefully-coiffed hair and neatly pressed, brand-new safari suits are sitting docilely sipping their spirits, dwarfed by enormous furniture. But it's different from most international hotels, because there is an atmosphere of communal excitement, they're all eager to enjoy a great adventure, and conversation blows back and forth between the islands as people take it in turn to boast, or share their narrow escapes from destruction. Mostly it's lions, hyenas, elephants.

But one man, older, in a neat black suit that looks out of place among the beiges and khakis, speaks more graphically, sibilantly, emphatic, the low light glinting on the steel of his spectacles. He tells a story that hushes the circle. He breaks when a smiling waiter appears, but then resumes, and all of them listen, the hairs standing up on the backs of their arms, 90 per cent horrified, 10 per cent thrilled. 'There's a darker side to this country,' he says. He has marked cheekbones and cavernous eye-sockets. The glass of his spectacles hides his eyes; you could almost think they were an absence. He could be American; he could be British, or a foreigner who has learned perfect English.

'Ja, the LRA,' says a portly German. 'We know about zis. But zey are not here. I am more worried about ze Congo situation. It is not looking good. There could be a war.'

'The LRA is one thing, this is worse.' says the man. He goes on to tell the story of what happened in 1999, in western Uganda. 'You all heard about the massacres in Rwanda, in 1994, how the Hutus tried to exterminate the Tutsis, and they made a film about it, *Hotel Rwanda*?'

A woman asks her husband, 'Wasn't that fiction?'

'You wish,' smiles the dark-suited man, and continues. 'Well, although they were driven out of Rwanda, some of the Hutu fighters fled into DRC. And in 1999 they came over the border to Bwindi, and went to the smartest camps in the place, where the rich people went, and you know they still do, though they had to change the names after all this happened – do you know the Gorilla Forest Camp? I expect some of you have been there – and they abducted seventeen tourists, you know, white people, Europeans, Americans, Australians, and marched them off into the jungle ...' Now he tells how eight tourists were cut up with machetes. As he describes the massacre, his hands chop the air. They are long, and bony, and catch the light. Trevor starts to hate him. He looks like a death's head.

I mean, bloody hell, we're on holiday. No good frightening the horses, or upsetting the ladies. 'No-one went to Bwindi for a long time after that. So you see, you good people should have a care!' And he laughs, a light, mirthless laugh, a repellent sound which no-one echoes.

'Well, that's very cheerful,' says Trevor, breaking into the silence, which is full of fear. 'That may be so, but it's a long time ago, and I can tell you, today, out on that little boat, I felt as though I was in heaven. I thought, this place is paradise. The way all the animals were there together.'

There's a rustle of relief, a murmur of assent, and soon they are sharing their stories again. Instead of waving to a waiter, Trevor strolls to the bar. When he looks round again, the dark-suited one has vanished. There's a price-list on the counter, and spirits cost the earth. The barman is the tired waiter, the one who said, 'That's interesting' to everyone. 'One more of these, and I'm for my bed ... may I buy one for you?' Trevor asks, on impulse.

With a flash of pleasure and a look over his shoulder, the man accepts, and they chat for a bit. Yes, he has a wife and child; the staff live in 'huts', in *busisira* at the back of the hotel. '*Tikwo kiri*. It is not like this.' He indicates the ambience here with his hands. He has a degree, in Tourism, from Makerere. 'That's more than I have, mate,' says Trevor. Then the waiter asks Trevor about Manchester United.

And just before he goes, Trevor asks him if it's true, the story of the murders at Bwindi. By then, the man has finished his drink. 'It is not true,' the waiter says, quietly. 'It is not true, what it sayed on television. My friend saw the news on CNN in Kasese. They sayed that eight *bazungu* were killed. But they did not talk about our people. There was a ranger from Ugandan Wildlife Authority. And other people earlier, in the same year. They come over the border, these Hutu Interahamwe. They cut people in two, with machetes, like this' (he slices sideways, and Trevor lifts up his drink, anxious).

'Or they cut them with axes, like this' (and he chops his hand down hard on the counter. The salted peanuts jump in their bowl.) 'But CNN only talks about the tourists.'

Trevor looks at him appalled. 'Blimey!'

Nothing for it, really, but to go to bed.

But Trevor's lucky; he's an optimist. The images of murder and mayhem fall away. As he walks upstairs, in his mind's eye he sees hippos and weaverbirds and narrow blue fishing-boats darting like kingfishers across the wide lake with James aboard, his genial driver who had gone off to stay with his friend in the fishing village. Trevor walks himself back into the Peaceable Kingdom.

Back in his room, though, he's still restless. He's not quite ready to go to sleep. He wants to tell his story to somebody he loves; someone who might really be interested. Pride and happiness have to be shared. Vanessa's phone's been on answer all day, so Trevor has left her three messages. No-one at all has contacted him. Now he switches his phone on: 'You have one new message'. Perfect, he thinks, that will probably be Ness.

But it's a message from Justin. His voice is all wrong.

'Where are you, Dad? The jeep's fucked. I have to get Abdy to hospital. If you get this in the next twenty minutes, ring me back.' Trevor looks at the arrival time: it came this morning. And it's already 11 PM, 1 AM in England, too late to ring, to talk to his son.

In a single second, everything changes.

In Bwindi, the heavens have opened again, but the trekkers are happy as they eat their dinner, and afterwards Vanessa, under one of the GFC's huge rainbow golf umbrellas, does not shiver with foreboding and look over her shoulder as she walks down the long narrow path to her tent. She is insulated by wine and achievement. How quickly the strange becomes familiar: and surely what is familiar is safe: nothing bad can happen to Vanessa here, because nothing bad has happened so far. She's seen the gorillas. Now nothing can touch her.

She sits on the bed and looks at her photographs. Some of them are beautiful, others are a meaningless mosaic of gorilla parts, dark among excessively bright vegetation, and none of them manages to catch the wholeness she saw in the forest, the net of life; the camera's too small; a blind little aperture. She looks again, more slowly, enjoying it, but still the sequence doesn't come together. But in her head, behind her eyes, it is there. She doesn't want to put out the light, and so, out of habit, her traveller's habit, the anxious habit she cannot forget, she checks for her phone (but of course she hasn't got it: oh tragedy, she would love to tell Justin, or boast to Trevor, but it's back in Kampala), then goes to the money belt she's hidden in the bed and counts her money: the rustle of notes. When she was a child, when things were very bleak, when her mother had one of her periods of blankness and her father was unable to talk about it, Vanessa used to lie in bed and count sweets. Something of her own, against the night.

My money (which I earned) has brought me to Bwindi, she tells herself, and feels proud, for a minute. Neither of her parents had ever left England after her father was invalided out of the army, from Burma (which he only mentioned once, in her hearing, as 'that shithole', before her mother shushed him), and limped back to the village, back to the farm. But she, their daughter, is here, she has made it; she has plenty of money, as they did not. She hides it again, with a squirrelling motion, then takes it out and counts it one more time. Tomorrow, she's gorilla trekking again. Another gorilla group, perhaps more distant. She starts checking, again, checking, counting: torch, camera, malaria pills … Twenty minutes later, she puts out the light.

But the boy-man is watching. Close: coming closer. The thickness of glass, a gap in her curtains. He has crept out of the bushes and under the sheltering overhang of the rich woman's tent, just a miserable arm's-length of semi-shelter, but the rain is phenomenal, inhuman, and why should he alone in all the world have no comfort? And there she is, tiny, framed by the dark, the old white woman with the miserable face, the one he saw quarrelling with her driver, then sitting with the tourists who did not share their lunch, and she's hunched there, stroking her wealth like a miser, old, ugly, understanding nothing, and he feels his power, for he knows, he sees her, and she's showing him everything that she has. All she takes for granted. All that he wants.

37

'It is 8 AM, Sir.' The soft, polite African voice on his bedside telephone soothes Trevor as he wakes to Mweya. A flood of white light behind the veil of mosquito net. His first thought: pleasure, as he stretches down the sheet, a glorious lie-in, an enormous bed. They had offered him another game drive this morning, but what plumber on holiday gets up at 5.30? – it's bad enough doing it every day for work.

Then he wakes properly. Horrible. The boy. Abdul Trevor. Justin's message. He shoots upright and reaches out for his phone.

'Justin lad. It's Dad. How's Abdy? I only just picked up your message.'

'I'm at the hospital at the moment. It was awful last night. He might be stabilising now. Whatever stabilising means. I only just got hold of Zakira. She was in Brussels. They'd switched the hotel. There was no-one in the office. Total cockup.'

It's a flood of misery. He sounds exhausted. 'The boy's all right?' Trevor shouts, anxiously, aware they are half the world away, and Justin moves the phone six inches from his ear. He's out in the hospital car park, smoking, though he gave up smoking a year ago. The smoke is bitter, but also a relief, like the air on his face after the warm soupy ward. At least Abdy's alive, and Zakira's on the train, speeding back towards the Channel. But he's still on his own, still very worried.

'You don't have to shout. Where are you?' he says. 'The thing is, he's apparently got measles, which sounds like nothing, but they say it's dangerous, cos it went to his brain and made him sleepy. Encephalitis. We thought it was meningitis, at first. Well, first of all Zakira decided it was eczema. We never got him vaccinated. But at least his temperature's down this morning. It looks as though he'll be OK. It's the first time I've come out and got some air. Can you come over, or have you got jobs all day?'

'Thing is, boy – I'm in Uganda.'

A long beat of silence, across lands and oceans.

'You can't be!' Justin says, trying to understand.

'Mary Tendo asked me to keep it a secret.'

'What do you mean, Mary asked you to keep it a secret? Mum's in Uganda as well. For a conference. And I know Mum was going to see Mary.'

'Your mother's in Uganda?'

They both take it in. Trevor feels dizzy. Vanessa in Uganda! Not possible.

'We'd better come back, if Abdy's ill. Where is she, in any case?'

'Kampala. No, actually, she must have left. She's on a gorilla trek. Some posh safari place. I can't remember ... The Gorilla Forest Camp.'

'The Gorilla Forest Camp,' repeats Trevor, dazed. 'The Gorilla Forest Camp. It can't be.'

PART 5

Heart of Darkness

38

In the border towns of Kisoro and Katwe, and in the villages along the edge of Lake Albert, where there was the recent unfortunate incident between Congolese and Ugandan forces, the atmosphere is tense and subdued. Lorries of smartly dressed UPDF soldiers are rumbling down the flood-softened roads, going west, west, always westward. The men get out and hastily pile rocks and uprooted trees under flood-destroyed bridges. Nothing must stop their grim progress towards DRC and the designated war zone. Young women walking to work in the country look up, sideways, at straining lorries and the lean muscled arms and black-booted ankles of very young men, who want to be heroes. In fact they are just excited, afraid, in uniforms too big for them. An old woman's sprayed from head to foot with muddy water as the lorry gathers speed, and she shakes her wrinkled fist after them. Soldiers: they never bring good news. The skies are dark. The eagles gather. In Kampala, Mr Museveni is shouting down the telephone, his small, impish face made heavy with blood.

But Trevor – Trevor is on a mission. Trevor has bought the best map he can find in the Mweya Lodge gift shop, which is run by an improbably beautiful, six-foot tall Ugandan woman, with tiny features, languidly graceful, not interested in him. 'Will this show me how to get to Bwindi?' he asks her, trying to open up the map on the counter.

She looks at it, regally, not focusing. 'I do not like maps,' she says, 'I do not use them. You really want to go to Bwindi?'

'Yes,' says Trevor. 'I need to go today.'

'Maybe now is not a good time to go to Bwindi,' she says, eyes lowered, re-folding the map.

'If you have to go, you have to go,' says Trevor.

He tries to explain this to the man from Mary's village, but Bwindi is a step too far for James. 'I have to go back to my village,' he insists. 'You can find another driver. There are many.' Trevor gives him money for the bus trip back to his village, and money for driving him to Mweya, then offers him double to come on with him. 'I'd feel happier, see. You've got the language.'

'I do not know the language of the Bakiga. In Uganda we have over fifty languages.'

Trevor digests this information, impressed. 'Oh well then, you're no better off than me. I'll be OK. I am not a bad driver.' But he feels a little lonely as he watches James's back, thin, slightly lopsided, in a bright pink shirt, getting smaller in the distance. He'd been a friend. Two blokes together were better than one. James is walking fast, as if he knows where he's headed, as if he is keen to get away, as if western Uganda, where Trevor's going, is the last place on earth he would want to go.

Trevor's on his own. But there isn't any choice. Trevor must go and find Vanessa.

Soon he is driving through sheeting rain. Charles's little Toyota handles quite well, but it was never meant for unmade roads. The windscreen wipers flap gallantly, forlornly at the oceanic slurry of water, blurring and hazing every outline, hissing and whispering *you are nothing*. Life is a detail, a mere detail in the sweep of this rain. In the north of Uganda, schoolchildren are drowning as their playing-field crumbles into a river that has suddenly turned into a roaring torrent, a hungry mouth that will suck them down. Trevor thinks, I must stop, or I'll drive off the road, and that won't bloody help anyone, will it.

He stops, and eats some chocolate he finds in his pocket, melted and re-set again in strange new shapes. It tastes delicious once he prises it off the paper. He thinks about his life. It's so unexpected, him, Trevor Patchett, out here on his own, in the middle of a game park on the edge of Uganda, driving to find the woman who divorced him over thirty years ago when they were both children.

We were both children. We knew nothing. It's true. Maybe we'd have made a fist of it, if we'd met later, but as it was ... She was very pretty, and very clever, and perfectly mad, as well. I couldn't put up with any of it. It was feminism all day long. And yet in bed, she was this gorgeous soft thing ... as if all the angles melted away. We were all right there, and all wrong everywhere else. But she broke my heart when she chucked me out. Since then I've never really had a heart to break. Losing her and the boy. How do blokes get over it? So I just stuck around, and took the shit, and had the odd lady friend, of course. Who all deserved better than what they got, which was half a man, if that.

The rattle of the rain on the roof of the car is suddenly so loud that he looks up, worried, to make sure the roof is holding up. He wishes he still smoked, and had those fags that Mary Tendo had pretended to buy him (and Mary was puffing away, in the village! Although she gave most of them to the men.) It's all so fragile. We are bloody small. What if the road gets washed away? There wasn't much of it to start with. And Abdul Trevor ... He can't bear to think about it. *No-one in the world knows where I am.* He flicks his phone on, but there's no reception.

Perhaps he's set off on a fool's errand. There's not been a lot of time to think about it. As soon as he put the phone down on Justin, he was ringing Vanessa, and getting nothing. Her phone was still on answer. That maddening message. So he'd found the GFC number, and tried to phone there. Everything seemed to be a muddle. At first someone told him she had gone home. Then there was an argument in Reception, and another voice came on, speaking better English. 'Good morning, Sir. Mrs Henman has not gone home. Mrs Henman is chasing the gorillas.' (He sees her little white head, butting through the jungle, begging the gorillas to come back.)

'Why did they tell me she had gone home?'

A pause, then a slightly awkward answer. 'Sorry, Sir, it was an error. Mrs Henman's driver has gone home.'

'Why on earth has her driver gone home?'

'Perhaps there was an argument.'

Oh dear, oh lord, that sounded like Vanessa. And in a split second, Trevor had decided. There was war, and machetes, and she'd lost her driver, and he has to tell her about Abdul Trevor. And now he's halfway, and it's all clear as mud.

By the time the rain, with a sigh, grows lighter, the windows of the car are completely misted up. He sits there in a cocoon of steam, blind to the world, not sure about the future, and it comes to his rescue, the old cheerful Trevor. He'll just get on with it, whatever comes. He'll take whatever life throws at him. The last patter on the roof dies away. Of course the boy will be OK. He opens a window to let out some steam, and it's staring at him, huge as the sun, dark-haloed, the strangely familiar face of a lion. And then its breath, bitter, meaty.

'Fuck!' He winds the window up, hasty, clumsy, and as he does it, the lion makes a move, and the car rocks, *oh fuck, fuck*, the fucking great animal has jumped on top, vibration of its feet as it treads the metal, then an extraordinary sound like showers of coins, going on, on – what's the bloody thing doing? – then the roof twangs like tin as it launches itself off.

Nothing on earth smells like lion's urine.

Zakira is fretting on the Eurostar. There is 'a short delay', as the announcer puts it, a short delay deep under the sea, where she sits imprisoned with hundreds of others in a tube of steel thousands of feet below the sand. What trust they show, to travel Eurostar, that there'll be no earthquakes, that the world won't tremble! A short delay! To her it is a lifetime. She's been calling Justin every twenty minutes or so for bulletins, but now there's no reception. She sits on her hands, pulls at her hair, stares at her glamorous, senseless reflection on the infinite night outside the glass.

All that matters is Abdy and Justin. She hungers to hold the small body of her son. She wonders how she can ever have left him. *But you have to leave them. You have no choice. You have to earn money to live in London.*

The other voice says, Never leave him again. Never, never. Hold him for ever.

39

Vanessa thinks, this is absolute hell. Why am I putting myself through this? They have been trekking through the trees since breakfast, but this time there has been no magical resolution. They have glimpsed the gorillas, always fleeing onwards, grey anxious shadows in the dense dripping forest. Once the actual rain started, it took only thirty minutes before the trekkers were drenched to the skin, despite their layers of hi-tech rainwear, their boots and gaiters and gloves and balaclavas. This rain is different. This rain is the ocean. They float about, helpless, inconsequential, marshalled by their chief guide, who fears to lose them, and fears to give up the trek without a sighting. (He has his instructions. FIND THE GORILLAS. If not, the tourists can ask for a refund.)

So the only way to go is on and upwards, but the *bazungu* are cold and weary, and some of them are taking it out on their porters, who are miserable: today's going wrong, there'll be no tips and no 'thank yous', and what if some of the old ones die in the jungle? One day it will happen, they have always known this, and then, because no *muzungu* must die, because no *muzungu* expects to die (unlike Ugandans, with death all around them) there will be police, and inquiries, and unfair law-courts, and some of their people will die in prison.

The little group of tourists is ragged, depleted. One of the old women has twisted her ankle; one of the men has an agonising knee; a young woman has developed a migraine, and is walking along with a hand over her eye; two fat Americans have heat exhaustion and are each being swung along by two porters. They ate all their lunch a long time ago. Too long ago. Now they're running out of water.

'Can't we go back?' Vanessa asks at last, making a furious effort to catch up with the guide and panting so much he can hardly understand her. He looks at her: white hair, wild and wet, small triangular face, gleaming with effort, pinched grey lips, too many layers of clothing, little pale eyes with a fierce, blind look. He doesn't want to argue with this *muzungu*. But why do these old women flock into the jungle?

'The gorillas!' he says, and points ahead.

One by one, they have all asked him if they can turn back, but he has his instructions, and they press onwards.

She remembers yesterday, so magically complete, and wishes, fervently, she'd left it at that.

They plough on upwards through the undergrowth. Ahead of them, a nervous group of gorillas scatters and flees, always higher, unable to settle, becoming increasingly irascible as their attempts to rest and eat are frustrated. At the end of the equally wretched human column, one of the fat American women is weeping, soundlessly, and the other one is cussing slowly and rhythmically every time her boot cuts into her bruised Achilles tendon. 'I need the bathroom,' the weeper says, but her voice is lost in the hiss of the rain, the squelch of the boots, the rustle of rain-clothes. '*I need the bathroom*!' She is suddenly screaming.

'You will frighten the gorillas,' the guide admonishes.

'Screw your gorillas! I need the john!'

In Kisoro, not far south of Bwindi, the lorries of soaked troops are arriving. The peaceful border town is awash with rain, adrenalin, hungry men. Once down from the lorries, they swarm in a chaotic, angry way, like half-drowned bees. But ten miles away, beween Kisoro and Bwindi, a peaceful meeting of eighty people is going on. They are small people, only four feet tall, and the British used to call them pygmies, but now they use a Bantu name, the Twa or Batwa. In these borderlands between feuding countries, many people have lost their parents, many people have lost their children, some of them in wars, some of them in crimes, as when the raiding parties of Interahamwe came over the frontier, not so very long ago. But these small, brave people have lost their forest, the forest that was father and mother to the Batwa for hundreds and thousands of generations; they have been driven off the mother's body, the beautiful home that gave them food and medicine, shelter and stories, and now they have nothing, and are despised, and work as slaves for the tall people. (Though in fact, the Batwa are clever and resourceful, and know things that everyone else has forgotten, and one day, perhaps, when the world is different, this secret knowledge will become golden, of trees, and plants, and herbs, and medicine, this knowledge, too, of what to do without. For now, though, they have to survive in the present.)

The Batwa are having their third Annual General Meeting, observed by two American lawyers. At the first AGM, someone had asked the Batwa what they wanted most. 'Office,' one said and they all chimed in: 'Yes, office, office, then they cannot ignore us.' Now the Batwa have got their office, but it isn't large enough for this meeting, which they hold in a church with a corrugated iron roof. It has been going very well: they have all spoken in turn, without much overlapping. It's not bad to be inside when there's such heavy rain. But when the rain suddenly gets heavier, the noise on the roof is deafening, infernal, and the Batwa all look round at each other, and a ripple of laughter runs around the room, and then with one accord, they get up, they leave their places at the conference table, they free their papers to blow in the wind, and the Batwa dance; the

Batwa dance. They become their history, and nothing is lost; they become eternal, they become the forest.

If you had nothing. But if you had no-one. If you were something you could not bear. If you were forced outside yourself, to become the worst that is in anyone. If you were no longer, to yourself, even human. If you could never forgive yourself. If you could never be forgiven. You would feel something like the boy-man.

When the scarred body wakes, late, cramped and bitten, where it slept in the bushes at the back of the hotel, his hatred for himself is like a cleft in his brain. He has failed, he failed. He failed again. It was there for the taking, and he had the right, he was justified, no-one could stop him, but something in him was weak as milk, was the feeble thing he had been, before ...

She was there in the light, the ugly little woman, the shrivelled whiteness, counting its money, the thing he needed and must have. Only glass protected her. Only glass stopped him. The moment when his hand veered away, the hand that should be turned against every-one, that was wrapped in rags ready to break through the pane.

The transparent skin between doing and not doing.

A glistening film, and now he is crying, sobbing like a child with rage and frustration, and the water on his cheeks stills and stops him. He is still very near. The chance hasn't gone. What he needs most is shoes that fit him (he needs to remove those torturing boots which have left his heels raw and bloody). These tourists have endless pairs of shoes and trousers, shirts and jackets, money and spectacles, books and drinks and tickets and cameras. They draw all the good things in the world to them like magnets. In his life, everything has fallen away.

Now he circles, carefully, watching the camp. He is ravenous, but he has learned to wait. He watches the servants take things away to wash them, so many clothes from every tent. He shins up a tree, every muscle complaining, and stretches along a branch like a panther. Below him, two girls not much more than children are doing the laundry outside in the drizzle, squeezing and twisting till their arms must ache to get out the mud-stains from the forest. But their laughter as they work affronts him. They have something he lost so long ago. He sees an old man, who should be respected, carrying pairs of polished boots back to each tent in turn, humbly, and lifting one leather pair to his face so he can see his own reflection. He writhes with anger. So many boots.

And all these people, both guests and servants, are lucky, because they take their lives for granted, because they are part of the world of men. He slipped through the net, was dragged through one day, on that hellish morning in the blinding desert when the driver of the baking bus he was on saw children spread across the road ahead, and the passengers were shouting at him to drive on, but the driver could not make himself drive over children, and soon he found out what kind of children they were as they clambered on the bus, screaming like monkeys, and one held a choking stick up under his jaw while another jagged a dirty blade up into his entrails.

The boy himself was lucky: too young to kill. The boy was unlucky, he was cursed, he was doomed, for soon he was so thirsty he was drinking his own urine, soon (how long? was it days, weeks, hours?), soon he was so desperate he was helping other children to kill a girl sergeant who tried to escape. If you wanted to live, you obeyed orders. One blow each, hammering with great bloodied stones, grunting as they struck, just wanting it over, battering her face so her lids would close. She was looking at them, and her lips were moving. Ten of them surrounded her, hating her. Then another great blow made a smashed red rose in which two small white teeth were slowly sinking. Turn by turn until the thing was not human. Turn by turn, until just a dark bladder of blood was lying in the heat, quivering. Two of the older girls held each other, laughing, and then he saw that one was sobbing, but they had hit her as hard as the rest, and then it was over, they all marched on. And all of them knew they could never be forgiven. And all of them knew they would do it again.

He beats at his scalp, which has something eating it. Soon it is quiet. He slips down from his tree and pads as lightly and carefully as his pained toes allow down the path towards the old woman's tent. First he'll pick up her money and her mobile phone, then he'll take someone's boots, and then he'll move on.

Now fate favours him. He turns the handle, gently: the door is not locked, he slips inside. But his stomach distracts him. There are packets of nuts on her bedside table and two whole bananas, though a third she has started is covered with ants, shimmering and heaving, glistening, quivering, because the stupid old woman knows nothing. He stuffs the rest in the pockets of his trousers. Now he feels in the bed for the place where she hid the money. His arm is deep under the cold, wet duvet and his fingers have just touched the edge of something when he hears footsteps approach down the path, and he dives through the door behind him to crouch, shivering, in the bathroom.

When Gregory, the room servant, switches off the vacuum he hears a strange noise the other side of the wall. A red-tailed monkey has got in again! He picks up a broom and goes in to do battle, but what he sees is two skinny human legs in boots disappearing through the open roof of the bathroom, and someone is pulling himself up into the tree, and he shouts and beats at the intruder's boots, then runs round through the door and calls for help. It is gone midday when they give up the pursuit. 'One of those thieving Batwa,' says Gregory. 'I am sure it was. His legs were small.'

Now giant wheels are being put into motion to ratchet Uganda back from the edge of war. How can gold and oil be extracted from a war-zone? Many powerful nations have an interest in this. America,

Canada, Britain, for a start. What can the donors offer to prevent a war? Money. 'Aid.' Oh, and weapons. You need new weapons to prevent new wars. The soldiers sit at the border, bored. The rich countries wrangle about money.

But in an isolated stretch of forest near Kisoro, two opposing border patrols spot each other. They pause. One Ugandan soldier lifts his rifle to his shoulder. A man from the Congo raped his sister, or that is what she told their mother. Through his rifle sight, the enemy's impossibly tiny.

40

Mary Tendo is in church. It was not easy to return, after half a year of not showing her face.

She had nearly gone to the morning service. Charles looked at her dressed in her best at breakfast and smiled. 'I will escort you, my sweet,' he said. He has never been a churchgoer, for which she forgives him, since she says he is a Christian man in his heart, and a better man than many churchgoers; but not going to church has not made her happy. Yet when he offered to escort her, she only said, 'As yet, I have not decided.' The hour of the morning service came and went, and Charles looked at her with his head on one side and said nothing. At last, at 5 PM, when the heat had lessened, when far-flung families of storks began drifting down from their high thermals, circling each other, now coming closer, something shifted and melted in Mary's heart, and she put on her hat, and took his arm.

Mary walked in swiftly, with her head held high, in her best blue dress which matched the hat. She has stayed away for nearly six months, partly because her prayers were not answered, partly because they ask for too much money. But when she was in the village, she had gone to church with her brother, her uncle, her aunt. They walked two miles to church and back, and when her brother said how lucky Mary was to have churches in Kampala on every street corner, she thought, I have not been using this luck.

But as she came in, there was Sarah Tindyebwa, the last person in the world she wanted to see, who used to be Mary's superior, the Assistant Housekeeper, long ago, at the Nile Imperial Hotel, when Mary ran the Linen Room. Sarah Tindyebwa has never accepted the fact that Mary has done better in life than her, with her splendid job at the Sheraton. When she saw Mary, her eyes sharpened.

'Is it really you, Mary Tendo? Have you been ill? We were worried about you. We have not seen you for so long.'

It was easy for Mary to translate this. 'Where have you been? You have not paid your tithes. I expect you were busy with satanism, or have you become a prostitute?'

Mary certainly got the better of her. 'Sarah, it is nice to see you. Is that a new hat, or is it your mother's? I have been with my family in the village.'

Yet none of this was very Christian.

Now she kneels on the hassock on the hard cold floor and prays, looking between her fingers at the wood of the pew, the red of her Bible. She no longer knows where to look for God. Once she thought that God was everywhere, but now she is no longer sure, because he did not find Jamil for her. Perhaps she has driven Him away. And she asks Him, humbly, to come back. *What I have lost, may I find again. Help me believe in You again.*

But the red, real, cover of the Bible distracts her.

She is grateful, at least, to be here, to be still, despite the singing, despite the people, as they wait for the minister to arrive. She is here alone. She is not working, or caring for the baby, the daughter she cannot bear to talk to, or giving orders to the maid. She can think about her life, and the visit to the village. And the thing like a stone, the loss of her son.

I have not been grateful for what He has given. I am too angry with everyone. Perhaps I have been trying to punish God by not coming to church, because of what happened. But He gave the village water. The water of life. He made Trevor able to mend the well. And yet I tried to punish Trevor, also, for being an ignorant *muzungu* in Uganda ... I could not stop being angry with him.

Still it was good for Trevor to feel like me, when I was in my twenties, and first came to London, and cleaned their toilets and their offices. The English made me feel like an ignorant Ugandan. They thought I knew nothing, and understood nothing. No-one saw me, or valued me. *The English did not value me*, just because I was not born in their country. But I cannot blame Trevor. He is a good man.

When we used to go out and smoke in the garden (which Vanessa did not know, or she would have been angry, and when she discovered it, she screamed like a mad thing), Trevor listened to me when I talked about Jamil. He did not say very much, but he listened. He made me feel my sorrow was something. And then, for a while, I could be happy again. And often, the sorrow almost disappears, like a cloud no bigger than a tiny bush sparrow, hopping in the yard towards Theodora ...

And as she thinks that, it comes back again. So sharp, so heavy, the loss of a son.

'Are you OK?' Her reverie is broken by her neighbour in the pew, who pats her shoulder, and she realises everyone else is standing and singing: they are nearly in the middle of the first hymn, while she is still on her knees in pain, still thinking of Jamil, and she pulls herself upright, but the hymn is ending, and she sinks back down. 'I am well, thank you.'

Soon the priest, a new one she has never seen, which shows how long she has been away, is doing the first reading.

'There was a man who had two sons. The younger one said to his father, "Father, give me my share of the estate." So he divided his property between them. Not long after that, the younger son got together all he had, set off for a distant country and there squandered his wealth in wild living. After he had spent everything, there was a severe famine in that whole country, and he began to be in need ...'

She thinks, Jamil set off for a far distant country. If he still lives, is he in need? Is he cold, or hungry? Does he think of me? The sunlight behind the stained glass windows makes the green panes glow like grass and leaves, and the reds like the blood that Jesus shed, the blood that taught his children forgiveness. Now its brightness fades with the end of day. Maybe one day her pain will lessen. She closes her eyes and listens, listens, drinks in the psalm as she sits and rests.

'It is good to make music to the Lord, to proclaim his love in the evening. A new heart have I given you, and a new spirit have I put within you. I will take from your breast the heart of stone and give you a heart of flesh ...'

In Bwindi Impenetrable Rainforest, the trekkers have finally turned back, and at last the gorillas can have some rest. Their cortisol levels start to settle, their heartbeats under their thick pelts steady. But identical chemicals still flood through the humans, driving their bruised, strained tendons onward, for they know they are in danger: night is coming. They are in the wrong place, at the wrong time. Vanessa thinks, I never should have come to Bwindi. Or even Uganda. I should have stayed at home. It's all been a failure: I haven't met Mary. What if I never see Justin again? Abdy, Abdy. My darling boy. And I didn't say goodbye to Trevor ...

How will her loved ones manage without her?

The rain has stopped, but they are sliding through mud, and the branches they clutch at drench them with water. The guides and porters have changed their nature. They are dark, focused, muscled, efficient, they no longer chat or laugh or take breaks, they have become a wave or a river, combining with each other and the land they know in one sole intent, to get the *bazungu* out of Bwindi. They have gone too far, stayed too late.

The dark comes up suddenly like a tsunami, overwhelming each tree, from the roots to the tip, as the sun slips precipitously down behind the hilltops. Two of them happen to have torches: too few, and now the *bazungu* deliver a judgement. 'Why didn't you guys come equipped with torches?' The porters look grim. They have no money for torches. Now they slow to a halt, for at every step, they stumble.

'We aren't going to make it,' smart Cyrus says. 'Without any light, we'll never make it.'

'Put a lid on that,' says the fattest woman, her voice all of a sudden surprisingly sturdy. 'None of that kind of talk. I got grandkids.'

And they shuffle onwards, cursing the darkness, dreading sharp branches coming at their faces, the sudden fall, the sharp edge of bone. And each of them starts to think someone is behind them; dogging their heels, a quiet, dark figure. The fat women's hearts are beating too fast. Step by step they go, like old, blind people. They are being hunted; they are being harrowed.

It leaves them, the last of the afterglow. Now they have found it, the heart of darkness. Now their feet will no longer carry them. Whatever follows them, overtakes them.

Kabila's envoy has come to Kampala. He has been received in Museveni's home. He felt he was entering a dream, or a film, a Hollywood film with a wedding cake: there are rows of white pillars along the front, white as icing in the blaze of lights; the steps are wide and slippy as glass; gallons of white water spring out from a fountain like the skirt of a European wedding-dress. There is marble everywhere, like hardened clouds, clouds that are trapped under more glass, more polish. The Congolese feels ill-at-ease in State House; every inch of every room shows his adversary's power, the blood-red carpets on the floor, the blood-red curtains in the windows, the plasma televisions in great dark cabinets, the strange gold and cream chairs which must be European, with legs like severed haunches of cattle. Museveni sits in the biggest chair, but this, reflects the man from DRC, is perhaps a mistake, for its size makes the President look smaller and older.

The room is full of people, assiduous, muttering, bringing statistics, making interventions: Museveni's people, Kabila's people. They are ready to sit far into the night. They are trying to make this 'an African solution': which means American, Canadian, British, Chinese. They are thinking numbers: enormous numbers. They are thinking economic co-operation. They are thinking, principally, of joint exploitation of the oil reserves under Lake Albert, whose shores are divided between the two countries. It's where war will break out, unless they can contain it. They are thinking, too, about the National Parks, how some of them are sitting on a gold mine, literally, and others are blocking the path to oil. Bwindi, Virunga, Queen Elizabeth Park, the syllables are uttered with greed and anger, and irritation about the 'donors' who are sentimental about gorillas, these stupid *bazungu* who like trees and animals and don't want Africans to have electricity.

'And yet there is money in gorillas,' says the Minister of Tourism, softly, smiling. He has to defend his own department.

They nod, slowly, these opposing statesmen.

But the trouble is, there is not enough money. Too much of it has to be divided with the people, these greedy local people who clamour for it, whining and complaining they have lost their livelihood. And now even the Batwa dare to ask for some! Those tiny people who are less than nothing!

The Minister of Tourism makes suggestions. He links his suggestions to Museveni's ideas. Museveni smiles: he approves of enterprise, particularly when he gets the credit. A new Eco-tourism initiative? He likes the sound of it. Yes, why not. He will launch a new Eco-tourism initiative. Divide the money in a new way! It will be all good news: he has learned from the British. Nothing will be lost, and much will be gained. And some things will remain as they have always been, since laws were passed 'protecting' the forest. The Batwa, the children of the forest, who lack addresses, and bank accounts, will get what they have always got: they are too small, too light, too mobile: no-one can see them; they will get nothing; they are light as midges or stars, dancing upwards, though sometimes they irritate, like a mosquito. In the end, where can the Batwa go?

And as for the gold, and the oil reserves: for now there is plenty outside the Parks. There must be joint exploitation, co-operation, and the international donors must help them to co-operate. And then, of course, they will take their cut. It will all work out, except when it doesn't. But the LRA (and M7 bangs the table) – the LRA must be brought to its knees. And for this, they need DRC's co-operation, to flush out the LRA from their borders; and more encouragement; and more donors.

A minion sees, and swats, a mosquito, about to alight on the presidential arm. The President must be protected. Even great men can be vulnerable. Museveni smiles and speaks again. Perhaps this will last for several hours. Kabila's envoy must stay awake. But he grasps the essential before he dozes: there will be new peace talks, in Tanzania. Kabila and Museveni will meet in person. An African solution. A global solution. Unseen, a mosquito, moving fast and low, a tiny creature with arcane knowledge, lands lightly on Museveni's foot.

'I'm being crucified by mosquitoes,' says Cyrus. Vanessa is too, but she won't complain. Exhaustion has turned her into a stoic. They huddle together, most of them silent, saving their torches. They can't find their insect cream. All of them are bitten. They accept it.

And then light appears, bobbing in the distance, one light, then another, then a spread net of lights, moving up through the forest, coming dancing towards them, little stars of orange and gold on the darkness, and the guides and the porters start talking excitedly and giving little yelps and shouts of glee.

'What's going on, feller?' An American voice, rough with hope, from the rear of the column.

'Now we will wait. We will all wait here, because help is coming. The people of Buhoma are bringing lanterns. The people of Buhoma are coming to save us. The people of Buhoma will take us back home.'

41

The restaurant of the Gorilla Forest Camp is kindly lit, with candles and oil-lamps, but the older faces who look at each other across the long table at 10 PM are haggard, exhausted, ten years more ancient than when they set off on the trek this morning. Several of them were too tired to wash, so they've come in to dinner just as they are. In the flickering flames, the younger ones carry it off like a festival, a wild, sylvan style, rather charming, mud dappling and stippling fine urban features, fragments of bark and leaf in their hair. When you look more carefully, though, they are just exhausted: their eyes have a blank, thousand-mile stare. But yes, the forest has played with them. It has picked them up, and shaken them, and printed them all over with its feral footsteps; it has stolen their hats, one shoe (as its owner was carried, helpless, one leg swinging free, dangling laces), two pairs of sunglasses, a teeny-weeny camera which was '*so costly*', its owner laments, a mobile phone, a GPS – young Cyrus moans, '*See, I don't know where I am*!' It has taken their things away from them.

'I started to think, I had stayed too long,' says Vanessa, gazing at the menu for tonight. 'If I'd left yesterday, I'd have got away with it.' One or two people nod at her. In their present state, they can't make sense of what's on offer. Potted Shrimps, *Choice of* Plaice with Lemon Butter or Grilled Lamb Cutlets with Mint Sauce, *Choice of* Apple Crumble or Treacle Pudding with Custard. Pure 1950s England: in the middle of the night, in the middle of a rainforest, in the middle of sub-Saharan Africa. They eat, tonight, hastily and quietly, as if they are afraid they have been caught out, as if the illusion won't hold much longer, as if '50s England is falling apart. The two enormously fat women who had to be carried by the porters sit stolidly, mutely drinking whisky. In the end, one of them looks up, and speaks: 'I thought we were stuck in the forest for the night.'

'But those wonderful folks came out and helped us.'

And their faces soften: they smile at each other. They like to think about human goodness. Too often, there isn't any evidence. They love to remember the folks with the lanterns.

The boy-man has crept back, under cover of darkness. While they were eating dinner, he has stolen some boots, a beautiful leather pair, freshly cleaned and polished. They are his size, but even so, they chafe on flesh that is purpled, half-shredded. The shining orange leather looks strange on his feet. Now the boy-man limps swiftly to the old woman's tent to get her money before she returns. The windows are dark; so far, so good. He can hear faint sounds of laughter from the restaurant. He turns her door handle: but this time she has locked it. He swears, swiftly, fiercely. He will climb in through the bathroom.

But just as he decides this, he hears her coming, and sees her torchlight wavering towards him, a beam of bright fear bobbing down the long path, snagging on trees, leaves, creepers. His heart pounds. He draws back into the shadows, and crouches, strong hands ready to pounce. He will take her by the neck, he will shake her like a rat and strangle her before she makes a sound. He has done it before, has been forced to do it, and now he will have to do it again. Every muscle and sinew is tensed and ready when she comes round the corner, silhouetted from behind – but stop, because a waiter is carrying her lamp, is seeing her safely back to her quarters, and he pulls himself back, panting, amazed, almost laughing at the thwarting of his expectations. 'I hope you are fine, Madam,' the man says, obsequious, begging the *muzungu* like a dog for a tip, but she is too stupid or too mean to notice. 'Thanks very much, I'm fine now,' she says, and before either man can take what they want, she is gone, and the light comes on inside, and both of them are left outside with nothing, the waiter wringing his hands with disappointment. *Mugende mufwe*! What a waste of time.

He walks away down the path, quietly cursing. But the boy-man is different. The boy-man stays on. As he stands irresolute, her light goes out. And then he and Vanessa are in the dark together, the terrified, terrifying boy and the woman, the two of them again, with just a flimsy door between them – a door Vanessa has forgotten about, as she hurries to pull off her muddy boots, her torn jacket, her soaked socks, and finds her pocket is full of small spiders. Shuddering, she forgets to lock up.

He hunkers down, tense, to listen and wait. In half an hour or so she should be asleep. He can enter unchallenged, and then, when she wakes, he can easily force her to give him her money. And if she resists, he will have no doubts, because everything he's seen of her has been hateful. She is proud, and angry, and she has no pity.

And yet he cannot quite imagine it this time, the moment that has closed on him so often, during his endless days as a devil, when he cut, because he had to, and cut, and cut, at living flesh, at hair and skin, cut at the terror of a human face screaming, cut at his enemies to cut himself free. For days, weeks now, no-one has hurt him. It is as if his strength is going. It is getting cooler. He starts to shiver. He will have to do it before very long. He clutches the handle of the knife in his pocket. In the distance, he hears the sound of a car.

Trevor's nosing Charles's tired Toyota up the track in a mixture of hope and desperation. He knows Buhoma is near Bwindi, but the roads have been impossible to drive at speed so he got there two hours later than expected, leaving him with the last stretch to do after dark. The few people still on the streets of Buhoma could have been robbers or murderers; could have been the very murdering thugs he has come here to save Vanessa from. But stopping to ask them has to be better than driving blind into the forest. 'Speak English?' he asks, and they repeat it, parrot-style, 'English,' but smiling, apparently friendly. They try to point him towards a hotel. The Buhoma Forest Lodge, the Gorilla Refuge. He keeps saying, patiently, over and over, 'Gorilla Forest Camp,' and the men he is talking to repeat, respectively, 'Gorilla' and 'Forest', nodding and pointing in different directions. And then he tries one more time: 'GFC?' and their faces in the headlights suddenly clear, 'GFC! GFC!', and delighted, they show him the road he is now driving, slowly, carefully, a foot at a time.

'I must be mad,' he is muttering. 'In fact, I am. Oh, fuck it.' Of course he won't find her. Of course he won't. And if he does, she won't want him, and won't thank him. She won't – need him. And that was the nub of it, always had been. Vanessa coped all right on her own.

Besides, an hour ago Justin had phoned to say Abdy is definitely out of danger. It's the miracle of penicillin. 'Amazingly, he seems right as rain. You'd almost think he hadn't been ill. The rash is still there, and they're keeping him in, but they say we can take him home tomorrow ... Yeah, in an hour Zakira should be here.'

At first, Trevor had felt elated: but a few minutes later, as he drove onwards, he also noticed a slight disappointment, which he's ashamed of feeling, but still. So there wasn't really an emergency. So he hadn't got such a good excuse. OK, Vanessa might still need a driver, OK, there was the question of the war, but he wasn't driving to save the family.

I suppose I wanted her to think me a hero. Same old story: she won't need me. *Don't forget, matey, she chucked you out.*

But his gloomy thoughts are interrupted by the sight of something by the road ahead, something in the veering beam of his headlights, going up, now down, but they've caught it again, and it swims into sharpness, the most beautiful sign, the most beautiful thing he's seen in ages, and it's easy to miss but his lights steady, yes, there, there: GORILLA FOREST CAMP. A small clear sign. He stops and gets out, puzzled, seeing nothing, for there's no building, only more forest. Then he swings his torch round and spots an even smaller white-painted arrow, pointing clearly up some steep steps into the trees. Sighing, smiling, he heaves out a bag, locks up Charles's car and starts to stride up the steps, but his pace soon flags as his ankle, sore from driving, complains at the unexpected exercise, and by the time he finds the lit-up reception, he is limping.

Mary Tendo lies in bed beside Charles. He is starting to snore, just a small gentle trumpet, but tonight, Mary does not mind it. She curls towards him, tucks her toes under his feet. She is thinking about church. How good to go back. She is happier than she has felt for weeks.

They had welcomed her without too much comment. Even Sarah had been silenced by the mention of the village. Because every Kampalan understood about the village. The village is where people really live. In the city, they were only making their way, looking for a future for their children. And even when they have never been to the village, it stays in their heart like a lost garden, because their parents have told them about it.

I came here like so many others, Mary thinks. And then I went further, away to London ... but today, in the church, they welcomed me back. It did feel like a homecoming. There were smiles from the heart, and glad embraces, as if they had all been waiting for me. And perhaps God meant me to return today, because the gospel reading was the story of the Prodigal Son.

'"I will set out and go back to my father and say to him: *Father, I have sinned against heaven and against you. I am no longer worthy to be called your son ...*" So he got up and went to his father.'

And what does he feel, the crouching boy-man, as the engine gets louder, and then cuts out, as he hears someone climbing up from the road, someone grunting, panting, it must be an old man, and then there is a clamour in Reception, and finally, the boy melts away into the dark, because two or three people, all with torches, are coming through the trees to the old woman's tent, and one of them's an old man talking in English. English English, that sound from the past.

As he lopes, limps through the loud dark of the forest, as the lights and the voices fade away in the distance, he realises with shock that he is not disappointed. He did not turn the handle. He did not go in. He did not touch her. He did not hurt her. He has not added to his terrible burden, to all the things that can never be forgiven. What he feels, as the damp air fills his lungs, as the cool wet leaves brush against his face, as he drinks from a pool in the bole of a tree, is relief, yes, a great flood of relief, and something he almost does not recognise, something he has not felt for years, a strange little surge of feeling that he hardly knows is happiness.

42

'Trevor. *Trevor.* Oh Tigger ...'

She had shot up in the bed, terrified, when she heard the feet coming down the path and the flickering lights playing on her curtains. Hutu Interahamwe. Robbers. Murderers. War has broken out; the soldiers are here. She pulls the chilly sheets up around her, then changes her mind, jumps out of bed, fumbles for her shoes, clutches her glasses, for she must be ready for whatever comes. She is many things, but she will not be a coward. Her heart is beating like a drum in her chest. Something in her shoe briefly tickles. The light switch seems to have moved from the wall. She pats at the stiff canvas in desperation.

'Madam, Madam ... Very sorry ... Madam, Mrs Henman, someone is here.' The bark of the male voice makes her shudder, but it's speaking English, it's deferential.

Is it a trick? she wonders, to make her unlock. Then her stomach sinks. Did she even lock it? But the next voice floods her with incredulous emotion.

'Ness. Nessie. It's me. It's Trevor.'

'Trevor? Trevor?' She runs to the door. The voice, unmistakable, infinitely dear. She opens. The warm Ugandan night.

Trevor: Vanessa. They stare at each other.

It takes some time and dispensation of money to convince the

GFC staff that Trevor can stay here, that he isn't an intruder, that she's safe with him. Mustapha speaks with passionate sincerity about 'the security of our guests'; Trevor says, 'Exactly, mate, you don't want any more murders here.' Vanessa squeaks, alarmed, 'What murders?' and Mustapha accepts a small wodge of notes.

Once the men have gone, they are suddenly shy. She stands, wild-haired, in pyjamas and glasses, with insect cream all over her face, shivering a little with shock and emotion. 'How on earth did you get here?' she asks him. 'Am I dreaming,' Tigger? Are you really here?'

She has taken his hands, both his hands in hers. They stand like children, waiting to dance.

'You aren't dreaming. Well, I drove.'

'You drove? Yourself? You can't have done.'

'I did, Nessie. There was nothing else for it. There's a lot to explain. But ... I was worried.'

'You came all the way to Uganda for me?' Her little pale face is wreathed in smiles: the torch he had carried glints softly on her lenses.

It's too soon to explain, to wreck the moment. 'May I say one thing? You look beautiful, Ness.' She's old; she's frail; she is his Vanessa. Torchlight streaks her hair with white gold; years of affection; so many lost summers. Her long pale neck is printed with lines. She is here, and alive. She is his love. And look, she is wearing their wedding ring, the thin gold band that was all he could afford. They have passed ten minutes without quarrelling.

'I can't do, darling. I'm covered in *Doom* or whatever they call this insect cream. You must be exhausted. I should offer you something. But I've only got some nuts. Oh, and some bananas.' But she can't find them. Her foot still tickles.

'How did you find me .... *AAAAAARGH*!' She is suddenly scream-ing, at full volume, and in fifteen seconds there are running feet, and the men are back, knocking hard on her door, and it isn't easy to convince them, this time, that the only trouble is a half-squashed gecko, a poor little shape in the tomb of her shoe.

Within half an hour, they're in bed together, and this time Vanessa isn't shivering. They are not young. They know this is precious. Each fragile inch of flesh must be loved. The thing they have always been able to do that loosens the weight of time and space, that turns everything into a single moment, the wave of the present reaching for the sunlight, the swell of the instant that floats them away ... It was lost for so long, and they're old enough to know that one day it will be lost for ever. The wordless miracle of the body, the living body of the person who loves you.

And then it passes, and they are still here. And Trevor's ankle doesn't feel quite right, and Vanessa scratches some of her bites. But they stroke each other, and it all hurts less, as they tell stories, remember each other. And he is still there as she falls asleep. He's falling too, still holding her. As the damp cold air creeps in all around them, Trevor and Vanessa cling to each other, warm and dry on their shrinking island.

43

By morning, many things have been resolved. Large things and small things: though all of them are small things, looked at in the life of the planet, where human wars ebb and flow like seas, many times a day, the names forgotten, where species come and go like mayflies, thousands of lives in a day's fast flicker.

Uganda and DRC announce a new agreement that will 'allow us to go forward together'. There will be talks, in Tanzania. Kabila and Museveni are both 'hopeful'. (And besides, Kabila has trouble at home. Laurent Nkunda's on the move again.)

Troops are to be pulled back from the border, though it takes for ever, on flooded roads. The soldiers are dissatisfied; they didn't want to die, but they earn more money when they are on active service. Their girlfriends will hardly be impressed. Why can't their leaders make up their minds? Ebola breaks out once more; this time it is in north-west Uganda. Many people die: Death creeping closer. Museveni frowns, in the capital, and consults his ministers, and issues statements. The floods destroy schools, churches, hospitals. The rich countries begin to think about aid, but they are already paying so much money to prevent the war that it hardly seems fair. The people in the flooded districts agree with them; it is slightly awkward to lose your home, your school, your clinic. But this is Uganda. Life goes on. The peace talks in Juba, too, stagger onwards, though no-one really expects Kony to surrender until he knows he might be forgiven, and only Ugandans are prepared to forgive him, the people who have so much to forgive, yet somehow they manage to start again.

PART 6

The Long Road Home

44

They set out for Kampala full of talk and laughter. Trevor has become Vanessa's hero.

Why didn't she know that he was coming to Uganda? This question is easy to gloss over. The well was 'an emergency'; 'I sent you a postcard.' If she knew he'd kept it secret, she would be hurt. In any case, Trevor's in the clear: why didn't *he* know *she* was here? 'I did ring Soraya but she wasn't very friendly ...'

They agree how much they have missed each other. They daren't quite confess they would like to be together, but it's early days. And the night was such fun! All the things that they know how to do to each other better than anyone else ever could. 'You were always a cracker in that department,' Trevor tells Vanessa, fondly.

Trevor (who feels a little tired, this morning) has phoned Mary Tendo, to fill her in about his miraculous rescue of Vanessa, and had a long consultation with the GFC manager about the best way to drive back to Kampala. He warns Trevor there are big troop movements on the road from the DRC frontier to Masindi, and there may be soldiers elsewhere, too. He doesn't know which way the troops are going.

'Vanessa is not too keen on heights,' Trevor tells the man, who is frowning, distracted, waiting for news about the war. 'So, it doesn't have to be, you know, scenic.'

'Scenic,' says the man, jumping on the word. 'Yes, this way the country is beautiful.' He innocently directs Trevor to the road along the side of the Rift Valley along which Vanessa came two days ago, hardly daring to look down, white-knuckled, trembling. 'Of course, you will drive carefully. But tourists like very much this road.'

Since then, two days of heavy rain have fallen. But they start in hope; they drive off laughing. Many of the staff come and wave them goodbye, for they sense this is a romantic story, a comedy with a happy ending, and too much of life does not end well. And perhaps it has something to do with the fact that Trevor has tipped them royally, and so, not knowing that, has Vanessa! And they laugh behind their hands, but then run forward, genuinely caring and distressed, when Trevor slips on the last step down as his ankle turns under him, making him shout and landing him firmly on the road on his bottom.

'Don't worry, my rear is big enough,' he tells them, slapping it. 'Good padding!'

And they laugh again. 'Ah, sorry.' Mr Patcher is a nice *muzungu*.

(The nice *bazungu* get smaller in the distance; the GFC staff are left with their worries, their threatened green world, and a little more money. But the soldiers have not come. It is a very good day.)

Trevor's driven about a mile down the track through the forest when they round a corner into radiance, as the tall trees yield to banana plantation. The road ahead is a ribbon of sunlight. They cannot be very far from Buhoma. But strange human figures are spread across the road forty metres ahead, in a loose shifting pattern, shambling, ambling figures lurching through the bananas.

'Gorillas,' says Trevor, 'Bloody hell.' He slows to a crawl. The gorillas watch them coming. They have a benign, faintly raffish air, as if they have been sitting around and drinking. Some of their paws clutch yellow fruit. And look, there's the baby, tiny on the brightness, trying to run headlong, his quiff bouncing, then boff, he's down, and a big hand catches him, the broad black wrinkled hand of the leader. (*He won't kill this baby. He is the father.*) Just for a second, he looks straight at Trevor, a single, dry, assessing stare.

'What's his name, that feller? Didn't you tell me?'

'The silverback? They call him Ruhondeza. Mind you, I don't know what the gorillas call him.'

The red Toyota crawls through the animals. They're almost too relaxed, drunk with bananas. An adolescent playfully thumps on the bonnet.

'Oh dear,' says Vanessa, 'Mary won't be pleased.' Trevor has told her the car is Charles's.

'She won't think much of the lion piss, either.'

They are through them, now. They are passing beyond, but the apes turn to watch them, curiously. Vanessa gazes over her shoulder. They look so at ease, like happy campers, on the margin between the farm and the forest. But they're very exposed, out there in the sunlight. The forest looks smaller, retreating in the distance.

'Trevor – do you think they will be all right? I thought they had to stay away from human beings?'

'I'm more bothered about us at the moment. I don't think this drive will be a picnic.'

Quite soon the little car is lurching over potholes where the rain has sucked the surface of the road away. A tiny tremor of apprehension. He is her hero, but can Trevor do this? 'Are you all right, darling?' Vanessa asks him. 'In a while, if you like, I'll drive for a bit. As long as there aren't any precipices.'

'No, don't worry, I asked the manager. I told him you did not like heights.'

'Oh thank you, darling.' There is a pause. 'Mind you, on the map, we were surrounded by mountains.' Another pause. 'Actually this looks familiar. It looks like the road I came before.'

'What was that like?'

'Oh, you know, horrific. One long precipice. Don't worry. I just think all forests look alike. Are you wincing? Are you OK?'

'Fine, Ness. Just a twinge in that hip.'

And then the road sinks into a shallow gully, which hems them in. No turning back. And then, imperceptibly, it starts to climb, and now she definitely recognises it, she knows they are driving towards the Rift Valley, and as that recognition settles, like a sudden dark liquid sinking through her veins, the land shears away, this time to her right, the solid land is no longer there, and this time she has no Ugandan driver, this time she has no four-wheel drive, this time she's in a small, rackety saloon, and she and Trevor are on their own. She closes her eyes. 'It's the Rift Valley. Oh God. Oh God.'

'We'll be all right. We're fine,' says Trevor. 'Look, you're going to have to trust me, Vanessa. Say you trust me. Or we're going nowhere.'

But he doesn't tell her about the pain in his foot, which has been steadily increasing, a dull throbbing that sharpens every time he uses the clutch. She's a highly-strung woman. Best say nothing.

'I trust you,' says Vanessa, her eyes tight shut.

By morning, the boy-man's on the Rift Valley road. He has walked most of the night; he is exhausted, but something in his mind has clarified. Like everyone else, he must make for home. Even though nobody will want him. And even if she. The name he can't say. Even if she will not take him in. Because he has been away so long. Because of all that he has done. He will go home, even if he has to go to prison. He listens to the word. Home. Home.

He is high on the road, overlooking the drop of thousands of feet to tiny fields, the silver river, when he sees three boys fifty metres ahead, on a short section where the road widens, a viewing-place, a turning space, and they are holding out tin bowls of something yellow. As he nears them, he sees it is fruit. They draw closer to each other. He must look frightening.

He points to the fruit. 'Give,' he says. They look at each other, silent. Then the biggest one says, his lip trembling, '*Shillingi bishatu*. Three hundred shillings!' The boy-man raises his hand to strike him, and the seller steps backwards, then senses the cliff and instantly steps forward again. 'Two hundred shillings,' he says, very quiet. 'Give,' says the boy-man, then changes his mind. He points to himself. 'No money! Give.' The three boys look at each other, wordless, then the smallest one takes a fruit from his bowl and hands it over, with some small soft word. The oldest one says something angry under his breath, but a look at the boy-man's face decides him. He is so thin: so wired with hunger: and something desperate in his eyes. Each of them gives him one fruit from his bowl. He eats, greedily, and spits out the stones. Both acid and sweet. But the sweetness lingers. It is like honey: bees and lemons. He remembers the woman, before, in the Congo, who gave him of her food to eat. Then a strange word comes from his mouth: '*Webale*. Thank you. *Webale. Urakoze cyane*!' His mouth wobbles.

By the time Trevor sees the three boys on the corner, waving and holding out their merchandise, the pain in his ankle is changing colour, from a dullish ache to a red alert. How long, he thinks, will this road go on? Because until we're off it, I can't hand over to Vanessa.

'Boys selling fruit', he says to her. Her face is white, her forehead is clenched, her eyes are crimped shut like the cowrie shells they were selling in the shop at Mweya Lodge. 'Don't stop,' she says. 'Please. Please. Let's get this over.'

'I need a break. Tiny twinge in my ankle from when I fell. There's a stopping place.'

She moans with fear as he stops and gets out. What if it rolls back down the hill? He buys three bowls at a thousand shillings each. The boys wave after them, noisily grateful, but his foot feels worse after the interruption.

'I'm glad you did that,' she says, suddenly, not opening her eyes, but reaching out her hand and patting his thigh, which puts pressure on his ankle and makes him gasp.

'What's the matter?'

'Nothing. That twinge again.'

'Buying things. That's what we should be doing, here.'

'It is one thing.'

She wants him to admire her, as she admires him. She says, 'I'm so proud about you and the well. And I'll pay half, for the collection systems. Or more than half, if you want me to.'

'No,' he says. 'That's my thing, Nessie. I mean, I can afford it, thank you. There's bound to be something else you can do.'

He glances sideways at her pale, intense face, the light blue veining of her closed lids, the almost colourless lashes, trembling. 'I'm glad you said it, though, Vanessa.'

It is starting to rain again, slow and deliberate, the noise on the roof a sharp little knock, saying *don't-relax, don't-look-back*, and it somehow connects to the pain in his ankle; *come on, Trevor, you're not done yet.* The rain quickly intensifies, redoubles, veils the windscreen, becomes Ugandan.

Something living, brown, perhaps furry, suddenly shoots across the road, and he brakes, without thinking, and serious pain transfixes him, just for a second, and he gasps so loudly that she opens her eyes, which is why it is Vanessa who sees it first, just a troubling blur in the watery future, but it suddenly resolves into the boy-man, drenched, skinny, half-naked, pitiable, hobbling up the road, very close to the mountain.

'Look,' she says. 'Poor child. Look.'

'That's not a child,' says Trevor.

'We should give him a lift,' says Vanessa, suddenly. Yes: she knows this is what they must do. Now it is she who is the good person. Her cheeks flush with the effort of virtue.

'No. We don't know who he is,' says Trevor.

But Vanessa, hyperventilating from her fear of heights, electrified with unused adrenalin, has turned all these chemicals into elation: she is now suffused with the desire to give. 'Stop when there's a safe place,' she says.

'Vanessa –'

'Please, Trevor. You know we ought to.'

They pass the dark figure, press him into the bank, and stop fifty metres ahead of him. She watches him coming, in her mirror.

Trevor tries one more time. 'I don't like the look of him. Remember, this is not my car.'

'Too late. He can't hurt us, he looks like a cripple.'

Trevor winds down the window and bows to her will. 'Get in.' The boy stares, stares, stares at him: and very slowly, dripping, panting, hating them, suspecting, unbelieving, gets in.

As he opens the door, the rain comes in with him, a great wild gulp of everything they're fleeing, wind, water, the unpredictable. Of course she should have expected the smell. Sour and dark, with an undertow of sweetness. She hopes he won't leave dirt on the seat. She tries to talk to him. 'Hallo,' and in a minute, 'Terrible rain.' But of course he sits there saying nothing, just out of their sight, rustling, breathing.

Time limps, crawls, now the boy is inside. Each minute in his presence seems a danger survived. They crawl on upwards, effortful, cautious. Vanessa babbles to Trevor, for reassurance, asserting a bond which might save her skin.

'So Zakira is getting back this morning, did you say? And Abdy's definitely off the danger list?'

But Trevor seems curiously unresponsive. He is peering forward, through the veils of rain. 'I think we've got a problem,' he says.

He stops the car, on an incline so steep that Vanessa moans lightly and clutches her seatbelt, sure they will run back down the hill, will roll for ever; she is sick with fear. 'Don't worry, girl,' he says to her, 'I've just got to do a little reccy,' and he tries to jump lightly out of the car, partly to impress his youth and strength on his passenger, to show who's boss, but as his weight lands on the dodgy ankle, something definitively goes; something yields, tears, and the pain is so great he has to cling to the bonnet.

But Trevor was not in the Territorial Army for nothing. He takes the pain, and limps forward, and sees that what he was afraid of is true: a third of the road has fallen away along a section of about thirty metres. It looks as if a giant has taken a bite. What is left is surely not quite wide enough, and great cracks like tree roots run across it. There is nothing for it but to reverse, but if they back down this road, Ness will have a breakdown. And then he looks down, down into the valley where the road they have come along winds and climbs, and he sees that lorries of soldiers are following, still small, still tiny, maybe half an hour away, but gaining on them: growing. Mud-coloured, grinding. And who the hell knows whose soldiers they are? He tries to limp back, and now he cries out. It can't be born. His only way back to the car is to hop.

'I think I've sprained my ankle,' he says to her. 'Ness, we're in trouble. The road has gone. And I can't manage the brakes with this foot. I'm very sorry. You'll have to drive. I think we're going to have to go back down.'

'I can't,' she says. 'I can't. I'm sorry.' Her face is white, her pupils are pinpricks. 'We'll have to sit here until help comes.' They stare at each other: terrifying knowledge.

Both of them jump and clutch each other when a voice suddenly comes from the back. It sounds rusty, more of a croak than a voice, something harsh and powerful, a caw, a crow sound, but what's more surprising is, the voice is English. 'I,' he tries. Then, more clearly, 'I will drive. I can see the road. I know I can do it.'

'No,' says Vanessa. Then: 'You speak English?' He sounds English. It is surreal. But no stranger than everything else that has happened.

'Can you drive?' asks Trevor. 'Have you passed a test?'

'Yes.'

'Right then. There's nothing else for it.'

'No,' says Vanessa. 'No, please.' But Trevor is already opening the door, and then the smell of death is getting in beside Vanessa.

'Come on, Ness. We've got to trust him.'

She shrinks inside herself. Death is so near. They will fall and be crushed. She knows it is over. But some tiny part of herself sees something different. They want to live. This might be a way.

'All right,' she says. Her voice is almost a whisper. Then once again, she thinks no, this is madness, but before she can get out, the boy is gunning the motor, and she closes her eyes and hides her head in her hands, because this will be like flying, and she cannot fly the plane, and Trevor, behind her, takes her neck between his fingers, her thin bony neck under her nest of pale hair, and pats it, strokes it, kneads her shaking shoulder as the engine catches, roars, takes off, and she screams as the boy revs madly on forwards up the stretch of road where she has seen the long cracks crawl out black as night across the sun-bleached surface, spread towards disaster like great forking tree-roots, drawing on nothing, sucking in blank air, breaking up like dust on a cracked cusp of nothingness, spilling down the thousand-metre drop into the Rift Valley

how strange, they will die where life began

and they tilt, right themselves, tear on

and Trevor in the back is letting loose a great chain of expletives, one after the other   and the sickening, yawing, jolt of their motion makes Vanessa drive her nails into her forehead for comfort   yet she also feels Trevor's fingertips, pulsing   and they have been doing this for a lifetime   until, desperate, she half-opens her eyes   and she sees to her horror they are only half-way   but she also notices the ultimate madness: as they jerk wildly forwards, both men are laughing

45

In Kampala, it's hardly rained all week. In the flooded parts of Uganda, some mutter that the President has done a pact with the devil and sent all the rain to them instead. The storks chatter and stretch their wings in the sunshine, and eat the rubbish, as they always do, and listen in on the doings of the humans.

Mary Tendo is on Kololo hill, buying mangoes and spinach for Trevor and Vanessa, who should be back from Bwindi today. Trevor's phone call has galvanised her. Poor Trevor, having to save Vanessa! And the Henman will have spread her messy things in Charles's car. Still, she's glad nothing bad has happened to her. Ah, Vanessa. But Mary's smile is gentle. She enjoys shopping at the end of the day, still wearing her Sheraton uniform so the stallholders treat her with proper respect. In this market, many of the customers are house servants from the embassies, girls and young women that Mary Tendo pities, for their job is nameless, their prospects non-existent. She would never slave like that for the *bazungu*. At the Sheraton, she has power, and status. She smooths the golden sleeve of her jacket, and smiles at a young girl buying cassava. She is looking forward to seeing Trevor, and even the supposed 'international writer'. The light on the trees of Kololo is golden, and children play football on the green of the airstrip.

She stops, for a moment, and watches them, and the familiar

sadness catches her heart, the sadness she will have to live with for ever. And yet, she is glad to have read in the paper that war has just moved further away, so there will not be sorrow for thousands of mothers. Life is sad: yet Mary Tendo will be happy, she tells herself that she must be happy, because she has a job, and a child, Theodora, and a husband she loves, even though he is small, and because they will have a feast today. A boy scores a goal: cries of jubilation.

She is in her kitchen, making sure that Charles has put enough beer in the fridge for Trevor, when she hears a car slow up outside. She straightens her hair, removes her apron. 'Charles,' she calls. 'I think it must be Trevor. At last you will have your car again! And it smells as though the chicken is nearly ready.'

'I have forgiven you for lending my car. I am sure your Trevor has looked after it. And tomorrow, I have a surprise for you. It is no good asking, I will not tell you. Truly, your chicken smells delicious ... but why isn't Mercy doing the cooking?'

'I said she could have some time for her lesson. In fact, she can have some time each day, to improve her low level of education. And in any case, she is not so bad. *Simubi nnyo. Ndabye abamusinga.* I have had worse maids, as you know, my love.'

He thinks, Mary is strangely sweet today, and then he remembers how she used to be: how he had once loved her for her cheerful sweetness. Perhaps there is something in this church business.

He peers through the window: a little down the road, there is the red of his Toyota. Thank heavens, the *bazungu* have returned it. 'I will go out, my love.' He picks up Theodora, and sighs as he does so: his beautiful, mute, un-mothered daughter.

But Mary smiles. '*Tujja kugenda ffena.* Charles, we will go out together.'

Inside the car, Vanessa's weak with relief as the strange, stinking boy, at Trevor's instructions, passes one of many small brick bungalows, then stops. 'You're sure that was the house?' she asks Trevor.

'I'm sure, Vanessa.' He adds, 'My darling.'

'You got us here. Thank you,' she says to the boy. 'Thank you. You drove so well. You seemed to know Kampala.'

'Now I must go,' says the boy, shrugging, but she thinks she glimpses the hint of a smile. She has learned the hard way to praise the young, for Justin complains that she rarely praised him.

'Hang on a sec,' says Trevor, patting the boy's arm, and as he bends closer, the sweat is overwhelming, there is dirt but also the sharp sweat of terror. 'We owe you a lot. Don't you need a feed?'

But the boy is fighting his way out of the car, fumbling and tripping in his panic. Trevor catches his sleeve, and he snatches it away. 'Get off me, fuck off,' he shouts, desperate, and limps blindly away from them, back down the road.

And walks head on into a smart woman, their foreheads banging, bone on bone, head to head, making her stagger back, winded.

Mary Tendo shouts at him, furiously, this rough dirty boy who has no manners – 'Obadde okolaki mumotoka y'omwami wange! What were you doing in my husband's car?' – Have Vanessa and Trevor gone mad? she thinks.

The boy looks back at the shouting woman, briefly: looks back, gapes, crumples in an instant. Now he's on his knees; he begins to cry, like a hurt crow keening, harsh, painful, his voicebox breaking, barking with sorrow, and she clutches her breast, she screams like a banshee, tears at her heart as she falls like him, they are both kneeling in the dusty road, crawling towards each other like children, open-mouthed, gasping, the tears spurting, scrambling over the dust and stones until Mary can seize him in her arms, and Charles, not understanding, scared, says, 'Leave her alone!' and thrusts the boy away, but his wife encircles her wounded son, her strong arms enfold his thin shaking body, his cheeks are scarred, his neck is scarred, one eye is reddened and half-closed, he smells of excrement, earth, decay, but the curve of his mouth she knows so well – she looks up at her husband, face streaming with tears, and gasps, sobs, 'It is Jamil. It is my Jamie. My Jamil.' And to Vanessa: 'You found my son. God be praised, you have found my son.' And then she turns to Theodora. Her tongue loosens, she speaks to her. '*Laba, Dora mwana wange.* See, my Dora, my darling girl. *Mwana wange omwagalwa*! It is your brother. It is Jamie! *Wuuyo mwanyoko* Jamie!' And after a while, she embraces Vanessa. Through their thin clothes, they feel the hearts thudding. Through tears and tiredness and the limits of skin.

Mary: Vanessa.

Vanessa: Mary.

Then she hugs Charles. And then Trevor.

People stare and linger as they pass by. It is some time before the little group of people in strange, dramatic attitudes out in the road are composed enough to go inside. They keep shouting and sobbing, laughing and hugging. It must be the new American evangelism, a Muslim in a flat round embroidered hat decides, nearly falling off his bicycle, staring. But at least they look happy. He does not want trouble. And trouble, it seems, has backed away from Uganda: war has not broken out with Congo. They have a miracle: the ordinary. To look forward to the next ordinary day. A day of peace, with its ordinary struggles, and for this little group of actors, happiness. He keeps on riding down the sunset road.

46

After the feast, there is a long reckoning.

Jamil has done things that can never be forgiven. We have all done things that might never be forgiven: but people forgive us, or fail to forgive us, and everyone grows older, and we stumble on. But when soldiers steal children (for Jamil was a child: a boy of nineteen is still half a child) they are forced to do things so horrible that those who love them might never forgive them. So the stolen ones are marked with sin. But Jamil, by a miracle, has come home. The prodigal son is home, is home.

And Mary makes Jamil sit in the kitchen, though he finds it hard to sit down for long, while she reads him the end of the story from the Bible.

'While he was still a long way off, his father saw him and was filled with compassion; he ran to his son, threw his arms around him and kissed him. The son said to him, "Father, I have sinned against heaven and against you. I am no longer worthy to be called your son." But the father said to his servants, "Quick! Bring the best robe and put it on him. Put a ring on his finger and sandals on his feet. Bring the fattened calf and kill it. Let's have a feast and celebrate. For this son of mine was dead and is alive again; he was lost and is found." So they began to celebrate.'

And yet, it is painful to be celebrated; and Jamil feels he has lost his father.

There are things he will have to confess to his mother, things he can only confess to his father, when finally he manages to go and see him, and Omar will go pale under his tan. There are things Jamil can never confess to anyone, things he is doomed to relive for ever in bloody dreams in the middle of the night, anxious, endless fleeing and killing. But Mary will be forced to receive it all: she will hear him shouting at 3 AM, will come out half-dressed to find him bolt upright, sitting rigid on the mattress with his eyes closed; sweat-drenched, muttering, moaning, dribbling, thin limbs twitching as he stabs or is stabbed, sleep talking all the terrible detail she hoped never to discover.

There are times when she will wish that he had never come home. Times when she will say, though only to Charles, that it might have been easier to go on without him, to have kept the absence, her old lost son, the kind, loving, innocent one she could grieve. Not the new, real man, scarred and muscled, this man who she cannot approach without warning or else he will grab her by the throat and half-strangle her before he remembers, the one who makes her shudder with horror and snatch up her daughter, his sister, in fear.

And then love creeps back. Like air, like water. Little Theodora has started to talk, a few words here, a few words there: she is awed but impressed by her new brother. And her mother, her mother who had silently loved her, secretly afraid of losing her – Mary Tendo is talking to Dora, singing and chatting as she gets ready for the office, just as long ago she talked to Jamil, when he was a baby, helpless, tender.

Mary finds Jamil out in the yard one Saturday, and Charles is letting him play with his sister, and the terrible one is a child again. For the first time he sits and eats with the family, instead of standing in the kitchen, ravenously gnawing, tearing at the flesh, always ready to go on the run. One day, Jamil will pick up a kitten and say to his mother, who is watching him closely, 'I have been looking on the internet. There is a Faculty of Veterinary Medicine, at Makerere University. Do you think it is too late? Could I, could I ... Could I go back to what I wanted to be?' And she will embrace him, but take away the kitten. Start softly; start slowly.

Somehow they will learn to live with the past. The people of Uganda must live with their past, like the people of every flawed, sinful nation. They are tired but still hopeful. They will try for forgiveness.

But the day after the feast, nothing is simple. Their cat has had kittens: four, two grey-and-white, one grey, one white; they're tiny, and sweet, and pee on the floor. 'I cannot have Vanessa staying here,' says Mary to Charles, in a loud stage whisper. Last night they had given the *bazungu* their bedroom, and stayed up most of the night with Jamil. 'I will always be grateful to them, it is true. In a way, from now on she will be like my sister –'

'Yes, like a sister,' enthuses Charles. 'And it is nice that she admires your husband, also, because she remembers how bravely I saved her, when the thief attacked her near the bakery.' (In fact, though he recognised Vanessa, she had not remembered him without his striped suit, but once she was reminded, she was very grateful, and Charles had repeated the story several times.) Charles sees something less friendly in Mary's eyes, also.

'– And I will like her more than my sister in the village, whose daughters behave like prostitutes. And I forgive her for how she was in London, when I was her cleaner. But she cannot stay here. She asked me this morning if I have a space she can exercise in. Then she said, "If not, it does not matter, I can do my sit-ups in the kitchen."

How can I cope with her and the kittens, and persuade Jamil that the shower will not kill him?' Mary is indignant, but Charles is laughing. Mary tuts at him, and carries on. 'I will arrange a special bargain at the Sheraton, for my friend the General Manager owes me a favour, and Vanessa can use the Sheraton gym, and exhaust herself and Trevor with endless yoga.'

'It is a good idea, my love,' says Charles. 'But I think I heard a little something last night, and it was not yoga she and Trevor were doing. Though he did look a little exhausted this morning.'

And he sees something pass over Mary's face, a hint of an expression he cannot fathom, but perhaps it is jealousy, which makes him, in turn, jealous, and he turns away, but she puts her arms around him, two round strong arms, and smiles into his eyes, and says, as she strokes him, 'Charles, my *kabite*, you are never tired.'

Trevor and Vanessa are together again. Too late for the storks to bring them babies. But young Abdul Trevor is out of hospital: they get bulletins about him every day. He and Dubois, his friend, Davey Lucas's son, are both in love with the same little girl, whose name is Taleisha, a bright spark with red lips and a sweet shiny head of ribboned braids. She has explained she can only have one boyfriend, and at this stage, Abdul Trevor is ahead, because she likes it when he pulls up his shirt so she can look at the measles scabs on his tummy. Delorice and Davey Lucas are pregnant once more, so Dubois will soon have a little brother, which will make Abdul Trevor demand one too. It sounds good to Justin, though Zakira will take some persuading: there's cause for even more persuasion later, when the baby is a girl, and they have to choose a name, and Justin loves his mother, so they compromise on Amina Vanessa, which means 'Peaceful butterfly' ('*Not* like your mother'). And the Bwindi gorillas have produced three babies, for this planet is not only for humans ...

'So many of them,' says Vanessa to Trevor, pointing to a line of storks along the rooftops. They are wandering together through the streets around the Sheraton, as night sinks down, as the stars come up. 'What do you think they think about us, darling?'

'Fair point,' says Trevor, and he stares at the storks, their long tapering beaks piercing the blue sky, elegantly dark as warm night sinks down. 'They're like chorus girls, getting ready to dance. I saw some once, at the Lido, in Paris. Weren't there storks on the cover of that book you gave Dora?'

'Not that Dora seemed interested.'

'She might have been a bit young for it.'

'Never mind, the maid loved it. I showed her the pictures of the Little Mermaid.'

He kisses her, lightly. She'd been sweet with Mercy, making an effort in sign language and sending Mercy into peals of giggles, but both of them seemed happy enough.

'What do you think the gorillas thought of us?' Vanessa asks Trevor, stroking his hand, his dear old hand, strong, familiar. 'The leader of the troupe, out in the road, the last morning. He seemed to be staring straight at you.'

'I felt the old bugger liked me,' says Trevor. 'I think we liked each other, yes. I wanted to think they all liked us.'

'But then, they didn't know us for long,' says Vanessa thoughtfully, staring at the hills, the seven low green hills of Kampala. 'I think they liked you more than me. Everyone likes you more than me.'

'It *is* pretty universal, to be fair,' says Trevor, and laughs, and Vanessa does too, though she knows it is true, and it hurts, a little, and then, above them, a magnificent colony of black and white crested crows start to echo their laughter in a harsh cackle which rings round the roof-tops, and they both feel small.

The birds look down on the tiny humans. Something's going to happen. A beginning, or an ending. Maybe love, maybe war.

Something that has happened many times before. But the humans always think they are unique, the one-and-only. Fixed on the shining edge of the moment, already regretting they must slip into the past –

and in that millisecond, they slipped into the past.

'We're not – very much, in the end, are we?' said Vanessa. The night felt cooler, suddenly, the sun sliding gently behind one of the hills and the clouds in an instant turning grey, then black. They stood like actors on a darkening stage.

'It doesn't matter, Vanessa, love. We won't be here for ever. And I'm here for you.'

'You always were.'

'I always was.'

They were silent for a moment, but the birds were not: they seemed to be laughing more than ever.

'And you don't like Mary more than me?'

'Ah, *like*', said Trevor, stroking her hair.

'You do like Mary more than me.' In Vanessa's voice was proud despair.

'Mary is a cracker. A force of nature. Though she seemed a lot crosser than she was in England. But it's you I love. Now shut up for a moment. I want to kiss you.'

'But –'

'We're here, now. It's got to be enough.'

'Will we always be here?'

He didn't let her finish, cramming his lips over her thin, hungry mouth. 'I'll be with you for ever. For ever, Vanessa.'

And the birds laughed louder, and the city honked and roared, and the storks clapped their bills together like a rattle, and Mary got into her nearly-new car which Charles had bought her when she was in the village, because she should not have to wait until her birthday, and drove home contentedly to Charles and her children, the rush-hour over, driving fast and well, past the half-completed buildings hung with visions of glory, all ready to welcome the Queen to Uganda even though she'll only be with them for a day, a day of flags and promises and dancing: tooting on her horn as she sped into her future, because nothing mattered now the lost was found; and the sun slipped away from the green-red-yellow of the forest and farmland around Kampala, and in the far west, in the wild body of Congo, the light burned the golden silt in the river and darkened back into the safety of water; and Death did his swift, impartial collections, creeping closer, now, to Vanessa and Trevor, then turning away, they had a little time yet, and in England, thousands of miles distant, Abdul Trevor woke up with a start as Zakira was tiptoeing out of the room at the end of the story she was reading to him, in which all the animals slept, and dreamed, clutching her fairy-tale wedding ring for comfort because she is tired, they are all tired now ...

He waves his toy lions, a boy and a girl, and says, 'Do you think Taleisha loves me?', and the stars wheel up, and the galaxies shift – and all over Africa, all over the world, millions of animals sleep and dream, and Vanessa and Trevor lie down together. Lie down together. A night, a morning. Nights, mornings. Getting older, smaller. Neither wants to leave without the other ... Vanessa and Trevor are saying goodbye, for no-one can live on this earth for ever.

And finally even Abdul Trevor – little Abdul Trevor, which can't be borne – finally even Abdul Trevor is silent. And the stars shine on. The stars shine on.

Acknowledgements

I am grateful to Cheltenham Festival for sending me to Kampala on the 'Across Continents' exchange with Ugandan writer Ayeta Anne Wangusa in 2003; and to Hannah Henderson at the British Council for inviting me to the 2005 International Writers' Conference in Kampala, whose programme and personnel were not the same as the ones imagined in *My Driver*. Thanks above all to Nick McDowell and Arts Council England for the bursary that enabled me to spend a longer time in Uganda in 2007, where I wrote much of this book. Thanks to Sophie Kandaouroff and the Committee of the beautiful Chateau de Lavigny writers' retreat near Lausanne (www. chateaudelavigny.ch) for their generous hospitality, which allowed me to finish my second draft three feet away from the room where my literary hero Vladimir Nabokov used to sleep.

In Kampala, grateful thanks to three friends, Sandra Hook, formerly at the British Council, and writers Jackee Budesta Batanda and Hilda Twongyeirwe, whose combination of editorial judgement and local knowledge helped me to fine-tune *My Driver* and to avoid certain errors. Jackee Batanda is the author of *The Blue Marble* (Sub-Saharan Publishers, 2006) and many prize-winning short stories, Hilda Twongyeirwe has published, inter alia, *Fina the Dancer*, (Longhorn Publishers, 2006, PO Box 18033-00500, Nairobi, Kenya). Julius

Ocwinyo, who makes a brief imaginary walk-on appearance in *My Driver*, is the author of *inter alia* the impressive novel *Footprints of the Outsider* (Fountain Books, 2002). Other gripping, readable fiction by Ugandan writers including Jackee Batanda and Ayeta Anne Wangusa can be viewed on Femrite's website (www.femriteug. org/publications.php/, info@femriteug.org) and ordered from the African Books Collective (www.africanbookscollective.com) or directly from the Femrite Offices, Plot 147 Kira Road, Kamwokya, Kampala, Uganda.

In London, thanks to my friend and editor Anna Wilson for initiating my first visit to Uganda, and for her insights into this book. I am grateful to John Ryle, Chair of the Rift Valley Institute (www.riftvalley.net). Thanks always to Mai Ghoussoub and André Gaspard; to Lynn Gaspard for her design, and to Ana Mendes. Lastly, thanks to beloved Barbara Goodwin, Nicholas Rankin and Rosa Rankin-Gee for being my first readers as well as my family.